JUSTINA IRELAND

Dread Nation

BALZER + BRAY

An Imprint of HarperCollins*Publishers*

Library of Congress Control Number: 2017943393

ISBN 978-0-06-257060-4

Typography by David Curtis

18 19 20 21 22   PC/LSCH   10 9 8 7 6 5 4 3 2 1

❖ First Edition

For all the colored girls. I see you. <3

In Which I Am Born and Someone Tries to Murder Me

The day I came squealing and squalling into the world was the first time someone tried to kill me. I guess it should have been obvious to everyone right then that I wasn't going to have a normal life.

It was the midwife that tried to do me in. Truth be told, it wasn't really her fault. What else is a good Christian woman going to do when a Negro comes flying out from between the legs of the richest white woman in Haller County, Kentucky?

"Is it a girl or boy, Aggie?" When my mother tells the story, this is the point where she pushed herself up on her elbows, giving the midwife's pale, sweaty face some powerful evil eye. And then, depending what kind of mood she's in when she's telling it, my momma either demanded to hold me, her cooing baby, or she swooned and the villainous midwife gave me over to Auntie Aggie, who cleaned me up and put me into an ivory bassinet until one of the mammies could suckle me.

But if you ask Auntie Aggie, the woman who mostly raised me up, she would say that my mother was thrashing around on the bed, still in quite a bit of pain on account of the whole birthing thing. Aunt Aggie would say that Momma had no idea what the midwife was about, and that the realization of my near demise came much later. She was the one who, when she saw how the midwife was about to put a blanket over my face and declare me stillborn, stepped forward and held out her hands.

"Wasn't that lady's fault," Aunt Aggie said as she told me the story. "Ain't no white woman going to claim a Negro bastard, and I'm sure it wasn't the first time the midwife seen it." Aunt Aggie shook her head sadly, like she was thinking of all the poor little babies that didn't make it just because they happened to come out the wrong color.

"What happened then?" I asked, because there's nothing better than the memories of others when you're little and have no stories of your own.

"Well, I turned right to that midwife and said, 'I'll take the girl and get her cleaned up right.'" That's what Aunt Aggie says she said, and I believe her. If I close my eyes, I can imagine it, my momma's big bedroom on the east side of the main house: the windows open to let in the evening breeze and the sounds of crickets and workers singing in the fields, the coppery stink of blood heavy in the humid summer air. The bed linens, no longer crisp and white, a crime punishable by a whipping if the mess had been caused by anyone but Momma. She would never tolerate a stain anywhere, especially not on the bedsheets of her big four-poster. I can see Aunt Aggie there, her voice calm, her dark hands outstretched, her spine straight, her gaze unwavering and stern, an island of calm amid the chaos of house girls running to and fro, bringing the midwife hot water to clean and towels to sop and a cool glass of iced tea because it's hotter than the dickens out.

Yes, I can imagine Aunt Aggie saving me from the clutches of that well-meaning midwife. Aunt Aggie was the one that done raised me up right, despite what Momma says when she gets in one of her fits. Aunt Aggie was more my momma than my real momma, in the end.

And I suppose I might have grown up better, might have become a proper house girl or even taken Aunt Aggie's place as House Negro. I might have been a good girl if it had been in the cards. But all of that was dashed to hell two days after I was born, when the dead rose up and started to walk on a battlefield in a small town in Pennsylvania called Gettysburg.

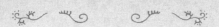

PART ONE

The Civilized East

Dearest Momma,

I hope this letter finds you well. It is coming up on my third anniversary here at Miss Preston's, and although I have not received a letter from you in quite some time, I felt that I would be remiss in letting such an important anniversary pass without acknowledgment. I only hope the fortunes and future of Rose Hill are as bright as my own. Why, I think it is more than fair to say that the teachers treat us as warmly as they would their own children, had they any. I don't think there is a single teacher here at Miss Preston's who isn't completely devoted to our prospects for advancement....

Chapter 1
In Which I Am Found Lacking

"All right, ladies. We shall try it again. Scythes up, and on my count. One, two, three—SLASH! One, two, three, SLASH!"

We lift the weapons up into the ready position, adjust our grips, take a breath, and slash them across the space before us in time with Miss Duncan's count. Up, adjust, breathe, cut through an imaginary line of the undead.

Sweat pours down between my bosoms, and my arms ache

from the weight of the scythe. In all of my seventeen years I ain't never been so tired. When Miss Duncan said we'd be doing close-combat training I'd been expecting to work through some drills with the sickles, which everyone in Miss Preston's School of Combat for Negro Girls knows is my best weapon. But instead we work with the twice-damned scythe, which is a two-handed weapon and not at all good for close combat, in my opinion.

"Jane, your grip is faltering," Miss Duncan says, those eagle eyes locking on me. "Raise it up . . . up . . ." Her voice climbs in pitch, as if she could use it to lend strength to my overtaxed arms.

I swallow a groan and raise the scythe a few inches higher. It ain't like my weapon is lower than anyone else's. Miss Duncan must have just heard my dark thoughts. She's punishing me.

My arms tremble as I hold the scythe up in the ready position: vicious curved blade pointing down, body-length handle at an angle across my chest. Miss Duncan waits until I'm about to scream from the holding before she gives me a small nod and turns back to the class.

"Aaaaaaaaaand, relax."

The scythes drop and the group of us let out audible gasps of relief. I shake my arms out, one after another, willing the burn to go away. Next to me, Big Sue catches my eye.

"She ain't human," she mutters, talking about Miss

Duncan. I nod. No, Miss Duncan ain't human. Because there ain't no way a normal woman, and a white woman at that, could survive ten years in the Army hunting down shamblers. I can just imagine how that went, the other soldiers falling all over themselves to lay down their jackets every time Miss Duncan needed to cross a puddle. No, I cannot believe a woman could maintain her virtue and serve honorably with the troops out west. So while I do believe Miss Duncan is a fine instructor, I do not believe that she is human. Perhaps she's a revenant, like the creature in Mr. Alexander Westing's latest weekly serial "The Ghost Knocks Thrice." Miss Duncan is pretty enough; I tend to think she would make a fine revenant, possessing the bodies of young women and using them to avenge crimes of passion. Of course, that raises the question as to why Miss Duncan is here at Miss Preston's instead of out seeking her vengeance. Perhaps even revenants need steady employment.

"All right, again. Scythes up."

I lift my weapon, focusing on Miss Duncan and trying to decide if she is indeed a revenant instead of thinking about the deep burning in my poor scrawny arms.

"And, on my count. One, two, three, SLASH!"

As we go through the movements for what has got to be the hundredth time—God's honest truth—I watch Miss Duncan walking carefully around us, just out of range of our one-two-three-slashing. Today her brown hair is pulled into what my momma would call a messy knot at the back of her head. She wears a prim, high-collared dress of moss-green cotton, perfect for the warm weather we're having. Her skirts are a little higher than a real lady would wear, midcalf just like the rest of us, modesty leggings underneath. The shorter length of the skirts is supposed to let us kick shamblers easy-like and not trip us up if we need to run. I think we'd have to get all scandalous like the working girls down in the city, hems barely brushing our knees with nothing but bare leg beneath, if we wanted to really be able to run comfortably. But that's a whole other conversation.

I slash the scythe across the empty air until my arms feel like overcooked green beans, limp and wobbly. A glance toward the observation pavilion at the edge of the practice ground reveals why we're being worked like rented girls.

A couple of white women in fashionable day dresses stand under the awning of the pavilion, a white wooden structure covered in wisteria erected specifically for the comfort of the fine ladies that sometimes visit Miss Preston's looking to engage an Attendant. An Attendant's job is simple: keep her charge from being killed by the dead, and her virtue from being compromised by potential suitors. It is a task easier said than done.

"Sue," I whisper.

"Yeah?"

"Who're those white ladies?"

She glances over toward the pavilion and grunts. "Don't know. But those dresses are from this season, so they must be somebody important."

"Well, at least now I know why Miss Duncan is determined to make our arms fall off. We ain't seen finery like that around here in a fair while."

Sue grunts again, which this time I take as agreement.

Finally the evening bell rings, and Miss Duncan turns toward the main building.

"That's all for today, ladies. Before you go, I have a treat! Mrs. Spencer has brought lemonade for you, with ice."

On the edge of the green is Mrs. Spencer, a white woman whose farm borders the school. She waves at us, and everyone starts to chatter excitedly about the prospect of lemonade. Miss Duncan ain't finished, though. "I will see most of you later this evening for the lecture at the university. Please make sure you wear your Sunday best for this fine event." Miss Duncan watches as we heft our scythes and head over to the table Mrs. Spencer has set up.

"Hello, girls, hello. There are cookies as well!" Mrs. Spencer grins at us. The Spencers are the nicest white people I've ever met, and at least once a week Mrs. Spencer brings us a treat to enjoy after we're done with our training. Next to her stands a smaller girl with pale skin and a smattering of freckles, her hair in pigtails. I smile at her.

"Hey there, Lily," I say as she hands me a cup of lemonade.

She gives me a tight smile but doesn't say a word. Once upon a time I used to keep an eye on Lily for her brother, but that's our secret.

I drink the lemonade too quickly, sweet and tangy and cold, and watch as Miss Duncan invites a few girls over to talk to the fine ladies. I ain't in the mood to play show pony, so I file into the building with the other girls, heading back to the armory to secure our weapons. Big Sue falls into step next to me.

"You going to that lecture?" Her voice is deep, and she sings a fine baritone in church. She's the tallest of us here, big and dark and imposing, with arms like John Henry. But she's also ace-high at braiding, and my own perfectly straight braids are thanks to her nimble fingers. She's the closest thing to a friend I got here, just all around a nice person, and that's something Aunt Aggie taught me you don't find too often in this world. So even though Big Sue might be a little dense sometimes, she's my friend, and that's that.

"Me, go to that university lecture?" I snort and shake my head. "I ain't about that. What do I care what some trumped-up rich white man thinks about how the dead rose up? He probably ain't never even seen them out there shambling about. You know how it works. He lives his life sheltered away behind the walls of the city while us poor Negroes go out and kill the dead."

"Jane McKeene!"

Katherine (*never* Kate) Deveraux stands before us, blocking the way to the armory, arms crossed over her generous chest. She is one of those girls that makes you question the school's admissions criteria. With her light skin, golden curls, and blue eyes I wonder how it was she ended up in a Negro school in the first place. Katherine is passing light; a body likely wouldn't even know that she was colored unless someone told them. She's the prettiest girl at Miss Preston's, and I figure that's as good a reason as any to hate her.

Not that she ain't good with a weapon. She is a crack shot with a rifle, invaluable in a long-range capacity. But she is also from Virginia, and I ain't had much cause to like Virginians. Partly because most of them are Baptists and Momma ain't too keen on Baptists, being a staunch Presbyterian and all. But mainly it's the way they're so damned self-important, like they'd single-handedly stopped the dead at the Mason-Dixon Line or some nonsense. It is downright ridiculous.

Katherine and I have been butting heads since I showed up at Miss Preston's School of Combat, and not just on account of her being so offensively pretty. She is one of those girls that doesn't know when to mind her own business, and she's a know-it-all that could try the patience of Jesus Christ himself. I ain't a very good Christian, so you know where that leaves me.

"How dare you slander Professor Ghering!" Katherine continues, now that she has my attention. "He is an expert on all scientific matters pertaining to the deathless. Why, the man even traveled to Europe and Asia researching the undead. What would you know of the realm of academics?"

"First off, they ain't deathless—they're dead. That's it. Just because they happen to run around terrorizing the countryside doesn't make them anything but the walking corpses they are. Anyone who says otherwise is a fool and wouldn't know a shambler if it held him down and bit him, including this professor character. Second, I'd be much obliged if you would keep my name out your mouth. The last thing I want is you sullying it with your silliness." I make to push past her, my scythe still an awkward weight in my hands, but she blocks me once again.

Big Sue frowns down at me and Katherine, her dark brow furrowing. "What's it matter? If he's wrong, then he's wrong. All this arguing is a waste of time, especially since you're gonna make me late for supper." She shoulders past Katherine, who puts her hands on her hips and huffs a little.

"Professor Ghering is a brilliant man. Miss Anderson says the papers say he's going to cure the undead plague! The two of you should attend his lecture. Homespun wisdom can only get you so far."

I snort. Ever since Baltimore and a handful of the other major cities were certified shambler-free more than a year ago, the government has turned its attention to finding a cure. You ask me, that's a luxury we ain't earned yet. I've tangled with enough shamblers to know there ain't no such thing as "shambler-free" while just one of those drooling corpses is still walking about.

But according to the "experts" there haven't been any major attacks within the city limits—or even in the county at large—since before the last Rising Day, and I've heard enough political speeches to know that letting rich white city folk think that we've made even a small part of America safe again is a better stump speech than telling them that we're still in trouble five years after the Army stopped fighting the dead. Especially when the current political party has been in charge that whole time.

But I don't say another word to Katherine, just walk past her into the armory. All the girls at Miss Preston's have their own weapons locker, and I am no exception. I place my scythe into the bracket set into the wall specifically for it. Next to it are my sickles, the blades as curved and sharp as Miss Anderson's tongue. Beside them are my batons, short wooden clubs with a metal spike in the weighted end and a leather thong at the bottom, a last resort in the case of a melee. The crown jewel of my collection is the well-oiled Remington single-action, the close-range gun of choice for Miss Preston's girls. I love that six-shooter. According to the newspapers, the Remington single-action is the gunslinger's pistol of choice, which makes it even more ace.

There is also a rifle near the bottom that's seen better days, a relic from the War of Northern Aggression and damn near useless. I hate that rifle with a passion, all because it is hands down my worst weapon.

When I come out of the armory, Big Sue and Katherine are gone but Miss Preston's girl, Ruthie, is waiting for me. "Jane! Miss Preston says you need to come and see her right away."

I take a deep breath and let it out, praying to Jesus for patience. Ruthie is just a little thing, with big eyes, dark, velvety skin, and braids that are more fluff than braid. I don't want to take my frustration out on her. Ain't her fault that it's pork chop night and I missed lunch because I was taking remedial etiquette training with Miss Anderson. And the remedial training is probably why Miss Preston wants to see me, anyway, so it ain't like I'm in any hurry to get to the firing line.

"Tell Miss Preston I'll come see her after supper, okay? I'm so hungry I could eat a whole hog."

Ruthie shakes her head and latches her tiny hand on my skirt, pulling me in the direction of Miss Preston's office. "She says you gotta see her now, Jane. So come on. She's already in a fine fit. You ain't gonna want to make her mad."

I reluctantly nod and let Ruthie pull me down the hallway to the main office. The school was once a fancy university, but after the dead rose up, most of the students fled. The building still looks like a school: fine wallpaper, maps of far-off places, writing slates in most of the rooms. The floor is a pale wood polished to a high gloss, and there are carpets so that you hardly even notice the bloodstains here and there.

During the Great Discord, right after the dead began to walk and before the Army finally got the shambler plague under control, the building was empty. Back then people weren't so much worried about education as they were not having their faces eaten by the undead. But then as the cities were cleared out and recaptured, folks got civilized once again. Shortly thereafter, Congress funded the Negro and Native Reeducation Act and dozens of schools like Miss Preston's were created in cities as large as Baltimore and as small as Trenton.

The minority party in Congress was against the combat schools from the start, saying that Negroes shouldn't be the ones to fight the dead—either because we're too stupid or because it's inhumane. But once the act was passed and the schools were established, there wasn't anything they could do, even if they'd wanted to. The federal government is the law of the land, but it doesn't have much say in how things are truly run within the walls—most cities are small nations unto themselves, with the mayors and their councils in control. And anyway, I don't much mind the schooling. Those congressmen probably ain't seen the dead shambling through the fields for years, going after folks, trying to eat them. But I have. If I can get training on how to keep everyone back home at Rose Hill Plantation safe, then why shouldn't I?

Ruthie pulls me through the main foyer and down into the left wing of the building, to the big office at the end. I get a whiff of meat frying, the smell most likely coming in through the few open windows. The big summer kitchen is out behind the left wing of the house, and I can already imagine the crisp fried deliciousness of Cook's pork chops, my stomach giving its own noisy approval.

I have half a mind to slip out of Ruthie's little-girl grip and sprint back down toward the dining room, but she's already rapping on Miss Preston's door. A creaky voice calls for us to come in, and Ruthie lets go of my skirt to open the door.

"I brought Jane McKeene, ma'am."

"Thank you, Ruth. You may run along now and get supper."

"Yes'm." Ruthie gives me a pitying look before taking off back down the hall, to a meal that I am beginning to fear I may never get to enjoy.

"Jane McKeene, stop loitering in the doorway like a vagrant and come in."

I straighten and enter the room, closing the door behind me. Miss Preston's office looks like the master's study back at Rose Hill. A massive desk—covered with documents, an inkpot and pen neatly placed in one corner—takes up most of the room. Bookshelves of leather-bound volumes fill the walls with the exception of the one directly next to the door.

That wall is covered with the same set of weaponry as my locker: twin sickles, a Remington single-action revolver, a rifle, a pair of spiked batons. Instead of the scythe there are a pair of Mollies. They're named after Molly Hartraft, the woman who led the defense of Philadelphia after the undead first rose. Only the most elite of Miss Preston's girls get to train with the short swords, no longer than a woman's forearm, and my hands itch to pick them up and test their weight. I've gotten to use the swords twice, and I'm passable with them, though I need a lot more practice.

On a table behind Miss Preston is a beaded buckskin bag that she says was a gift to her family from a Sioux chief. From what I know about folks I think it's more likely one of her ancestors stole it. Rumor is that Miss Preston's people had gone west to the Minnesota Territory before the war but came back when the undead got the better of them. There were whispers that Miss Preston had taken a Sioux lover while out west and that she kept a single eagle feather in his memory, but I don't believe any of that. Seems a little too much like the "True Tales of the West" stories printed every week in the paper. Plus, there ain't a feather to be found on her desk anywhere. I would know; I spend a lot of time in the headmistress's office.

Miss Preston occupies the chair behind the desk while Miss Anderson sits in the chair in front of the desk. My instructor wears her lemon-eating face, so I know this ain't going to be a pleasant chat.

I inhale deeply and drop down into a curtsy. "Miss Anderson, Miss Preston, good evening."

"Save the pretty manners, Jane McKeene. You know why you're here." Miss Anderson is a widow, and even though her husband died in the War between the States—fighting for the Confederacy, no doubt—she still wears her widow's weeds. Personally I think all black suits her. With her pale skin, hatchet-sharp nose, and constantly down-turned mouth, I can't imagine her in any other color.

"Miss Anderson, I'm afraid I am ignorant as to the reason of this visit. Honest Abe," I add when she opens her mouth to call me a liar. Momma used to tell me, "Deny it until they've got you dead to rights, sugar. If they can't prove it, it never happened." It's good advice, and it's served me well.

Miss Preston clears her throat, distracting Miss Anderson from whatever she is about to say. "You're here because your progress in your etiquette training is inadequate. In addition, Miss Anderson tells me she found you sneaking in newspapers yet again. As you are already on probation for previous infractions, these latest shenanigans don't bode well for your continued enrollment here."

I nod and clench my hands in my skirts. I should have known that Miss Anderson would run to Miss Preston as soon as she found that newspaper under my bed. Most of the girls here can't read, so sometimes I read out loud to them.

But reading isn't something an Attendant needs to learn, so it's frowned upon. Newspapers and novels are considered unnecessary distractions. From the way Miss Anderson acted about us girls reading, you'd think it was something dangerous.

But the contraband was peanuts compared to my test. I wasn't all that surprised that I'd failed my most recent etiquette examination. Seemed like a bunch of tomfoolery to me. Who could care what spoon was used for what or the proper address for a European noble? Still, I thought I might've had a bit of respite before I was going to be marched into Miss Preston's office. I was already on academic probation on account of not caring enough about the importance of gravy boats. Now it looks like I'm about to get the boot.

And then where would I go? I don't even know if Rose Hill still stands. I haven't gotten a letter from my momma in nearly a year, though I still write faithfully. And Rose Hill and Miss Preston's are the only two homes I have ever known.

I take a deep breath and let it out. "Miss Preston, I've been trying. You have to believe me when I say that I've been working my fingers to the bone trying to get better at drawing place settings. Why, I went through an entire box of chalk just last week." I actually went through the chalk because a few of us girls were drawing unflattering pictures of Miss Anderson on our slates, but that is beside the point. "I daresay my efforts have been derailed not because of my difficulties with etiquette but because of Miss Anderson's treachery."

The smile that had been ghosting across Miss Anderson's face while Miss Preston admonished me drops off real quick, and Miss Anderson's usual sourpuss face reappears.

"Treachery? What treachery?"

I sniff, indignant. "Why, that last test wasn't even fair. Questions on the proper address of European nobles? And European-style place settings? We ain't even talked about that stuff in our lessons."

Miss Anderson jumps to her feet, her face redder than boiled beets. "A ploy? Treachery? It was important etiquette, you ungrateful little brat! I'm preparing you for the noble endeavor of serving as an Attendant to polite society, but it's like trying to teach manners to an animal. You think I don't know what you say about me behind my back? That mother of yours—"

"Sarah, that is enough!" Miss Preston surges to her feet, a mountain of calicos and lace. "You will excuse yourself from this meeting. Now." I've never heard Miss Preston yell before, never really even seen her mad. It is awe-inspiring, a woman of the headmistress's considerable girth moving so quickly.

Miss Anderson stands, gathers her skirts (no small feat, she has to be wearing at least four petticoats), and saunters out, slamming the door behind her. Once she's gone, Miss Preston takes a deep breath and lets it out on a sigh.

"Sit," she commands, and I fall gracelessly into the chair Miss Anderson just vacated. Miss Preston lowers herself back into her own chair, her lips tight with dismay.

"Your sardonic nature has worn through Miss Anderson's tolerance, Jane. I spoke to a few of the other girls about their most recent examination, and I fear you are correct in your estimation of Miss Anderson's faithlessness. The questions she submitted for you were far more difficult than those of your peers."

I school my face to blankness, but, inside, my emotions are raging like a creek after a spring storm. The truth and I ain't very close—uneasy acquaintances at best—so imagine my shock to discover that Miss Anderson really did go harder on me than the others. When I'd said all that nonsense about perfidy, I'd been telling a yarn, hoping that I could distract everyone from my questionable manners. But to know that Miss Anderson has been intentionally sabotaging me . . .

Well, that ain't such a good feeling at all.

"Jane, I know that etiquette isn't your strongest area. Many of you girls have trouble with it, which is why we wait until your last year here to introduce it. But providing the ladies of the better families with well-heeled and well-trained girls is central to our goal here. You're a bright girl, and so I'm going to be frank with you. There isn't the same demand for Attendants as there used to be. With the cities being declared free of undead, people are beginning to feel there isn't much of a practical requirement any longer. An Attendant is becoming more a luxury, a mark of social standing. An ornament. Something to demonstrate one's wealth, at dances and dinner parties. Not a life-and-death necessity. And in this context, etiquette and fashion are more important than ever." She leans back and takes a deep breath. "I care deeply for you girls. Truly, I do. I want you all to find good homes, to get the right start in this brave new America. And that means training you properly to be a part of it. So while you might feel that finishing classes are a waste of your time, I assure you that your lack of proficiency places you in very real danger of expulsion from this academy."

A lump blocks my throat, and I swallow it down right hard. I ain't going to cry, but it's a near thing. Because failing out of Miss Preston's means going to one of the other Negro combat schools, and none of them are half as good as Miss Preston's. Not only that, but I probably won't be there long before I'm sent to work a patrol. Only fancy schools like Miss Preston's are longer than a year, and I've heard tell of schools that ain't more than six months. Six months! That ain't enough time to learn to kill the dead proper-like. Half the Negroes from those programs end up a shambler their first month on the job.

I have no interest in working as a show pony for some coddled white lady, but an Attendant Certificate from Miss Preston's means I can go wherever I want. It means I can make my own way in the world. And even though I want nothing more than to go back to Rose Hill and the life I left, I need to have options if Rose Hill no longer exists. As much as I'd like to quit Miss Preston's and make a dash for home, I'm a smart girl, and running across the country half-cocked is definitely not my style.

I need that diploma.

The headmistress continues. "All of that having been said, you have some of the highest competency scores in the combat modalities. So I'm going to reassign your etiquette instruction to Miss Duncan, since she has some free time in her schedule. As for this most recent failure . . . I think it would behoove you to attend the lecture at the university tonight with Miss Duncan's group. Get some real-world experience as to how a Miss Preston's girl conducts herself."

I squirm a bit in the chair, because there ain't no way listening to some old white man drone on for the better part of the evening was in my plans. "Miss Preston, by 'behoove' did you mean—"

"I meant that you had best get some supper and wash up. The carriages leave after dinner. And if you aren't on one of them, you can consider your enrollment to be terminated."

I give Miss Preston a tight smile and stand. "Yes'm. That's what I thought you meant." I drop into a quick curtsy before leaving.

I head down to the dining room, though my appetite is

gone. Even the golden stack of pork chops on my plate can't erase the sick feeling in my middle.

I need to start taking my studies here seriously or I'm going to be out on the street, a vagrant for real.

That just ain't happening.

One of the tenets of our instruction here at Miss Preston's is to attain enrichment beyond the schoolhouse walls, an endeavor that often takes us into nearby Baltimore. I daresay I have learned almost as much in the streets of the city as I have in the classroom and on the practice field.

Chapter 2
In Which I Look the Fool

Half past five finds me running down the main corridor, hastily tying my bonnet. After a hurried dinner and a swift face-washing there was just enough time to change into the only nice dress I have before the carriage came. At least that's what I thought, until Big Sue saw me in the dormitory.

"Aren't you going to that lecture thing?"

"I am," I said. I was trying to get my hair to do this front frizz thing that I saw in a fashion magazine I pinched from

Miss Anderson. But my stubborn curls kept going up instead of down, and I was cursing the good Lord above for giving me hair that would've been better suited to sheep.

"Shouldn't you be out there waiting on the carriage? It's leaving at half past."

I stopped my fiddling and turned to Big Sue. "Miss Preston told me the lecture was after dinner."

"The lecture is at six, but the carriage is leaving at half past five. Haven't you been paying attention? Miss Anderson and Miss Duncan've been talking about it all week."

So that is how I end up running a full sprint through the school, sliding to a stop in the front yard just as Miss Duncan is closing the armored carriage door.

"Jane, how nice of you to join us. Come, you can ride along in the other carriage with Katherine and me. I'm going to head inside and see if we have any other stragglers." Miss Duncan wears a fashionable riding ensemble, her hair curled and her creases knife sharp even in the humidity. I am now more conscious of my disastrous hair and ugly blue-flower dress.

I climb into the cab while Miss Duncan goes back into the school. Katherine sits inside, fiddling with a pair of the whitest gloves I've ever seen. She doesn't say anything as I sit in the seat opposite, and that suits me just fine. I ain't got nothing to say to her, anyway.

The pony is a newer model. It's sort of like a train but

without tracks, and the driver sits in his own protected car up front with the stove that heats the steam engine. The passenger compartment is made of steel, with bars over what would be glass windows in the wintertime. The glass has been removed on account of the heat, and although it is still powerful hot out, the beginnings of a breeze makes its lazy way through the compartment, providing a bit of relief.

I lean back in the wooden seat and try to relax. I don't much care for the ponies; the noise they make, all that clanking and wheezing, tends to attract the dead. But it's a long way through forested hills to get to Baltimore, and we'll be returning after the sun goes down. Trying to travel by foot at night is a death sentence. It's amazing how quickly the dead can creep up on you in the dark.

In the old days, carriages were pulled by horses, and that's why we call them ponies now. Horses were big, stinky beasts that snorted steam and had eyes of fire. At least, that's what Lloyd, the older boy that used to cobble shoes back at Rose Hill, told me they looked like. I ain't never seen a horse. The dead are hungry, and the thing they're hungry for is flesh. Most horses met a sad fate at the hands of the shamblers back in the early days, eaten by the very same people who'd once cared for them. Momma said that's why you had to be wary. "Janie, you mark my words, you be careful who you trust. You never know when the man you married is going to turn around and try to take a nibble out of your neck."

That actually happened to Momma when her husband, Major McKeene, returned from the War between the States, which inevitably turned into a war against the dead. Of course, I ain't ever planning on getting married, much less to a war hero that got changed to one of those restless dead, but you never really knew what was in store for you. I'm sure nobody ever expected the dead to get up in the middle of a pitched battle and start eating people, which is what they did at the Battle of Little Round Top. And no one expected those dead boys to bite their buddies and turn them as well. But that's the way life goes most of the time: the thing you least count on comes along and ruins everything else you got planned. I figure it's much better to just be all-around pre-pared, since the best defense is a good offense.

That's why I'm smuggling my six-shooter under my skirts. We ain't supposed to carry firearms when traveling into town, but I'm always ready for someone to try and take a bite out of me. Especially at the university. Everyone knows that academics are the most ruthless cutthroats around.

What I ain't prepared for is the look that Katherine gives me from the other side of the carriage. My dress ain't all that nice compared to hers. She is tucked into a pretty blue frock with a big flounce in the back. It's not a bustle, on account of the fact that Miss Preston finds them hideous and banned them from the school, but the cut of the gown makes it look like she's wearing one. It's a lovely dress, especially with the way the corset cinches her waist to nearly nothing.

I fiddle with the curly mass of my bangs and slouch down, feeling like the plainest girl ever next to the fashion plate that is Katherine Deveraux. If I didn't hate her before, I am absolutely positive I despise her now.

"What happened to your hair?" Katherine asks, breaking the not-so-companionable silence. My face heats as she stares at it, her light eyes taking in every flaw and faux pas. I try to sit up a little straighter, but that just causes the bodice of my dress to strain against my rib cage. Katherine's eyes narrow. "And why aren't you wearing your modesty corset?"

I take a deep breath and muster up all my bravado. I am not going to let spoiled Katherine Deveraux get the better of me. "Why, Kate, don't you know? This is the way the ladies are wearing their hair these days. It's called the Fritzi Fall. Very popular in New York City, and no one would be caught without a bit of frizz in Paris."

Katherine grits her teeth. "Katherine. Not Kate. I'll thank you to use my given name."

I swallow a smile and shift, settling back against the seat. "As for a corset, well, every woman knows that wearing one of those things is pretty much suicide if you want to be able to fight effectively. A punctured lung if a stay goes awry, lost flexibility . . . I mean, how are you going to be able to do a reverse torso kick if you can't even breathe?"

That wasn't so much a lie as a half-truth. I had no idea what most women did outside the confines of Miss Preston's. We didn't wear true corsets. Instead, we bound our breasts with a fitted undersmock called a modesty corset. It was supposed to mimic the support of a corset without yielding too much in the way of flexibility. But wearing the thing is blazes hot in the summer, so I spend most days forgetting mine. I can perform our daily drills better without it on, improper or not. It's not like the Lord saw fit to endow me with huge bosoms like he did Katherine. Plus, I like being able to breathe when I want.

"Jane McKeene, only you would think that we'd run into any shamblers in the heart of Baltimore—" Katherine stops short and studies me with a narrow-eyed gaze, her eyes settling back on my head. "Is that my bonnet? The one I lost last month?"

"Kate, the day I go around pinching your scrap bonnets is the day I dance a jig naked in the dining room. No, this ain't your bonnet."

That is a bald-faced lie. It is most definitely her bonnet. I nicked it from her during our school picnic last month out of nothing but pure pettiness. But I ain't about to give it back to her right now, not with my hair acting the way it is. This bonnet is the only thing keeping me from looking like a startled chicken.

Katherine purses her lips in a perfect imitation of Miss Anderson's lemon-eating face, but she doesn't say anything else, and that's when Miss Duncan climbs in with a smile. "Well, it looks like we are ready." She rings the bell in the carriage, and the thing lurches forward like it's drunk on rotgut. We settle back into our seats and begin the slow trek to the university.

While Miss Preston's is housed in an old university, it ain't the same university as where we're going. I don't know how many universities there were before the dead walked, but there must have been a few. The one we're headed to is the kind where doctors learn to cut people open. I guess back in the day, when the dead first rose up, all of those future surgeons were pretty quick to figure out that cutting off the head of a shambler was the way to keep them from rising yet again. Either way, most of the students in that university survived, while the one where we go to school became a bit of a slaughterhouse. Most of those fancy folks were studying philosophy and such, and from what I can tell they made fine shambler chow.

That was lucky for us, I guess. Not many girls get to go to school in such a nice building. A lot of the Negro girls' combat schools are in old plantation houses, while the boys' combat schools are in abandoned military barracks. I heard that in Indian Territory they tried to send Natives from the Five Civilized Tribes to combat schools, but they quickly figured out what was what and all ran off. The Army was too busy fighting the dead to chase them, so the government gave up and just focused on us Negroes.

I guess that's another thing Miss Preston's has going for it. No one runs off, because we have nowhere to go, and we have very nice accommodations, bloodstains notwithstanding.

While we travel, Katherine and Miss Duncan chatter on about the professor's theories on why the dead rise and whatnot. I ignore them and stare out through the bars, watching the forest roll past. The trees have been cut along the road, felled and burned. That's to give travelers a fighting chance out here on the byways. The dead ain't like bandits. They ain't going to come jumping out of the underbrush. Instead, they'll come lumbering out of the woods like drunken farmhands. That ten or twenty feet of clear-cut land on either side of the road gives travelers enough warning to shake a leg or make a stand. Here in the great state of Maryland that usually means making a stand, since it ain't no picnic running up and down them hills.

The rate of survival when a mob of dead set in on a settlement ain't good, according to the headline I saw in the paper. But Maryland has been declared one of the safest states, on account of our work patrols and the very active militia, with Washington, DC, being nearby. I've heard in places like Pennsylvania it's a lot harder to get around, except for in the winter, when the dead lie down and become dormant. That's why great former cities in states like Georgia are pretty much ghost towns these days. It's always shambler season in Dixie. General Sherman's March to the Sea, where he and his men marched across the South, burning and putting down the dead, wasn't much more than a temporary setback for the shamblers. The waves of dead are like dandelions. Just when you think you've beaten the weed, it pops up somewhere new. The Lost States of the South are called that for a reason.

We move along the road, the engine chugging and wheezing up the hills, the carriage rocking back and forth. Outside, near the wood line, there's movement.

"Shambler," I say, interrupting Katherine and Miss Duncan's conversation.

"Where?" Katherine leans forward to see out the window.

I point past the bars, to where a little white girl with blond pigtails stands on the side of the road. She wears a flowered dress with a pinafore and her mouth gapes, a toothless black hole. The ponies are too loud for us to hear her raspy moans, but as we pass she jogs after us a bit, her yellow eyes locked on mine.

We're quickly past the shambler, and Katherine sits back in her seat. Miss Duncan frowns. "I'll let the patrolmen know when we get into town. Rare to see shamblers this close to the city. I do hope the Edgars made it home safely."

"The Edgars?" I ask.

"The women who observed your training earlier today. Grace and Patience Edgar and their mother, Wilhelmina

Edgar. They're newly arrived from the Charleston Compound and were interested in engaging a couple of Attendants."

"Yes, Mrs. Edgar said they've seen a few undead around their property of late," Katherine interjects. "I imagine they're likely being spooked by a couple of shadows, but if it finds them looking for a few girls from Miss Preston's, I'm certainly not going to tell them otherwise."

I roll my eyes. She's obviously showing off for Miss Duncan. Of course Little Miss Perfect stayed to talk to the fine ladies. She's practically the image of the Attendants they're always advertising in the paper, the Negro girl holding short swords and smiling prettily: LADIES! DON'T GO IT ALONE! KEEP YOUR SELF SAFE WITH A MISS PRESTON'S GIRL!

"Mrs. Edgar told me the same thing." Miss Duncan looks back down the road, her lips pursed in thought.

"But she can't be right, can she?" Katherine asks. "Mayor Carr has declared Baltimore County safe for months now."

I turn my head around. "The Survivalists would have you believe they saved Baltimore, Philadelphia, and Boston single-handedly if you listen to them long enough. It's all that 'America will be safe again' nonsense—"

"Please, Jane, how many times must I tell you, there will be no talk of politics," Miss Duncan admonishes gently. "That is entirely too coarse a subject for young ladies to discuss, even ladies of color."

I sit back and cross my arms, biting my tongue on the

hundred things I want to say in response. As Miss Duncan and Katherine resume their conversation, I reach into my shirt and touch my penny. It's a luck charm Auntie Aggie gave to me before I left Rose Hill, and it hangs on a string between my bosoms. It's warm at the moment, as it usually is; but there's a small bit of magic in it, and when it goes cold, I know I'm in danger. I flick at the penny and eye the other two women in the carriage before I go back to staring out of the window.

I know you probably worry about the number of undead out here in the East, but Baltimore County is the safest in all the country. They say so in the newspaper, and you know the paper would never lie.

Chapter 3
In Which I Relate My First Encounter with a Shambler

When I was little, back at Rose Hill, I used to sneak out of the kitchen, away from Auntie Aggie while she and the other aunties worked to feed all of the hungry mouths on the plantation. Once they were distracted I'd tiptoe out past the ovens and slip away to freedom in the fields.

Rose Hill mostly grew tobacco, which Momma and a couple of the bigger field hands would ride into town to trade for cloth and other essentials. Early on, back before I can remember, Momma had tried growing tomatoes and other vegetables; when it became obvious that her small bundle of tobacco was worth more than all the food combined, she switched. Momma is savvy like that. The dead may have risen and we might have been living in the end times of Revelation, but folks still wanted their tobacco.

The tobacco plants grew tall, and the leaves were broad and green. In the summer I could duck down and run through the rows undetected, which is what I did on this particular day. My goal was always the same: find the other kids, the ones that got to run the fields because their mommas weren't ladies who owned the plantation. The kids I liked best would be near the barrier fence at the far side of the tobacco fields, so I made a beeline for that patch of trouble.

A barrier fence is the line of security between shamblers and the rest of us, and Rose Hill had three such fences: white-painted fence rails that had been our original property line and weren't more than pretty decoration, a dense forest of wooden poles with sharpened ends implanted in the ground at an angle that worked like stakes to impale any shambler enterprising enough to get to it, and, at the outer edge, a wall of five-strand bobbed wire that was our primary defense against the dead.

Once or twice a day the stronger men would go out to the bobbed wire and end any shamblers tangled up in it. Momma would have them bring the corpses in and burn them for the compost pile. If there were any valuables on the bodies, Momma and a couple of the men would sell them in town, bringing back something fine. One time there was a shambler that musta been a fine lady, since she was decked out in gold and jewels. Momma used the baubles to buy several hogs, and that was how Rose Hill came to have pork chops every Sunday after the Scripture was read.

But I didn't much care for that business. I was more interested in the children who hung out playing games in between the fences. I scrambled over the white split rail fence and carefully picked my way past the sharpened stakes of the interior fence. And there, between the safety of Rose Hill and the danger of the outside world, were the plantation kids.

Everyone on the plantation but Momma was a Negro, all excepting for Mr. Isaac. There had been other white men, once upon a time, but after the dead rose they'd either ran off or turned shambler. Mr. Isaac was different; he came to Rose Hill after the war. He lived on the plantation because he was married to Auntie Evelyn and relations between Negroes and whites were frowned upon. Momma didn't much care for, as she called it, "the spiteful leanings of biddies with too much time on their hands," and welcomed folks into the house staff as long as they didn't make too much trouble and were happy to work hard. So Mr. Isaac and Auntie Evelyn lived on Rose Hill with a passel of boys, the worst of which were the twins.

Auntie Aggie said twins were an ill omen, and anyone

who knew the Isaac twins would agree. The boys were light-skinned, lighter than me, sandy-hued with unnervingly blue eyes. They always had a scam running, like the time they'd stolen a watermelon from the garden and climbed up a tree to share it, or the time they'd let loose all the dogs as a distraction so they could run off to fish in the creek on the north side of Rose Hill.

The Isaac twins were always up to no good.

They were my favorite people in the whole damn world.

"Hey there, Jane!" called Ezekiel, Zeke for short.

"Aww, Jane's here, now we're gonna get the strap for sure," said his brother Joseph, who was saltier than Lot's wife.

"I snuck off!" I said, as the other kids began to give me dirty looks. "Ain't no one know I'm gone. What're you doing?"

Each of the kids held a stick, the end sharpened, and had the look of someone with a secret.

"None of your business. Go back to the kitchens," Joe said, picking up a rock from the dusty ground and throwing it at me.

The rock missed by a mile, but the one I picked up and flipped back at Joe didn't. It hit him right in the middle of his forehead, and as he cried out I picked up another rock.

"Next person throws a rock at me is getting what for right in their eye," I said, shaking with anger.

"No one's going to throw any rocks, Jane. You should come with us. We're going to kill the dead." Zeke smiled wide and handed me a sharpened stick. While Joseph was prickly and hostile, Zeke was all smiles and warmth, the kind of person people liked to be around. And he had the best ideas. It was no wonder Joe was so tetchy. Who would want to share such a wonderful brother with everyone?

I took the stick. "What do you mean, kill the dead?"

"There's a shambler stuck in the bobbed wire. We're going to kill it."

"That ain't a good idea." As soon as the words were out of my mouth I knew it was the wrong thing to say. But I couldn't help it. I liked trouble as much as the next kid, but this seemed different. Dangerous.

"We're gonna kill it so that we can go on patrols with the rest of the grown-ups," Zeke said with a grin. "No more chores for us!"

"You can stay here, Jane. No one wants you tagging along, anyway," Joe said.

I set my jaw. Whatever Joe said, I was going to do the opposite, just to spite him. "I'm coming. You probably ain't found a shambler, anyhow."

"Oh, it's a shambler all right," Zeke said. "You'll see."

We marched in silence, along the line of the fence rails. A few of the kids began to whisper excitedly, but a single glance back from Joe shut them up real quick. My stomach surged and gurgled, roiling with hot dread. I'd heard Momma and the other farm hands talk about how the dead worked, how they came out of the brush, overwhelming the unwary and wary alike. That was what made shamblers so scary: even when they were predictable, they could still surprise you.

As we rounded the corner a loud moan split the air. There, twisted up in the bobbed wire, was a shambler.

We stopped, and all the celebration and shouting died down real quick. I'd always imagined the dead as some kind of monster: mouth gaping as they came to eat you. But the shambler caught in the bobbed wire looked almost normal: a white woman with long brown hair pinned up on her head, wearing a day dress of green linen. The skirt was torn, and her petticoats showed through. Her eyes were the yellow of crookneck squash, and the nails of her grasping hands had been broken down, her fingers covered with dirt. Still, I recognized her.

"That's Miss Farmer. Her family owns Apple Hill Plantation," I said. Miss Farmer hadn't cared for me—she thought Negroes shouldn't be allowed in the house, since we were dirty—but she loved Momma's blackberry jam enough that she came to call every so often, when it was safe to travel.

"She ain't nobody no more," Joe said, poking her with a stick.

The shambler growled and reached for him. Joe danced out of the way, much to the delight of everyone.

Even me.

I ain't sure why we thought poking the shambler with our

sharpened sticks was a good idea, but everyone started doing it, creeping in close enough to stab the creature and then dancing out of the way before her hands could reach us. The game might have gone on longer if the dead Miss Farmer hadn't managed to pull herself free.

Bobbed wire ain't a long-term fix for a shambler wanting in to the plantation. Since they don't have any kind of survival instinct it's no big deal for them to eventually pull themselves free of such an entanglement, ripping off great big swatches of themselves to do so. And this is exactly what the undead Miss Farmer did. One moment she was jammed up in the bobbed wire, the next she was stumbling toward us, half her dress and a good bit of arm skin left behind on the fence, which now listed to one side.

Most of the kids, myself included, screamed and ran. I took off for the field of sharpened sticks, knowing that would slow the undead woman down. But when I looked over my shoulder I realized that not everyone was with us.

Joe was standing right where he'd been, not moving, frozen in the path of the dead woman and her gaping maw. The boy had always been a bully, and the thing about bullies is they never learn how to run like the rest of us do. So Joe stood his ground, sharpened stick at the ready, convinced he was going to kill that shambler.

At some point in the woman's lunge toward Joe he realized that a stick wasn't much of a weapon against the dead, but it was too late. Joe was about to be shambler chow.

If it hadn't been for Zeke.

It was Zeke that slammed into Joe, pushing him out of the way of the woman. It was Zeke the woman bit, sinking her teeth deep into his throat. It was Zeke that cried out like a wounded animal, trying for a few precious moments to push the much heavier woman off him as she tore away a great chunk of flesh. And it was Zeke that let out one soft, anguished cry as his life bled out into the dirt of Rose Hill, the sound almost indistinguishable over the noise of the dead Miss Farmer feeding.

"Joe!" I yelled, and the boy looked at me, expression distant and caught somewhere between grief and horror. I ran back to where he'd landed, pulled him to his feet, and dragged him by the hand through the field of sharpened sticks, to the safety of Rose Hill.

As we ran back we passed the patrol coming to put down the dead. I didn't stay to watch; I'd seen enough carnage for one day. They say when they got there Miss Farmer had started on Zeke's face, and that two of the men vomited before they even got to putting her down and driving a nail into Zeke's head so he wouldn't come back.

Momma gave Zeke a proper burning, and gave Mr. Isaac and Auntie Evelyn his ashes. Joe ran off a few years later, presumably to one of the combat schools, and so their heart-break was complete, Auntie Aggie clucking her tongue and saying, "Told you them twins was an ill omen."

It took me a long time before I left the safety of the main house, and I never ventured to the borders of Rose Hill again, not until I came to Miss Preston's years later. I learned two valuable lessons that day.

One: the dead will take everything you love. You have to end them before they can end you. That's exactly what I aim to do.

And two: the person poking the dead ain't always the one paying for it. In fact, most times, it's the ones minding their own business who suffer.

That's a problem I still don't have an answer for yet.

One of the finest parts of attending Miss Preston's is all the friends I've made. Momma, you would not believe the camaraderie and esprit de corps in these hallowed halls.

Chapter 4
In Which I Dodge Unwanted Advances and Engage in a Bit of Blackmail

I'm staring at the scenery outside the window of the pony, brain tangled in bloody memories and a few regrets, when Miss Duncan asks me, "So, Jane, what do you think?"

I blink and sit up, suddenly quite conscious of the two pairs of eyes on me. "I'm sorry, Miss Duncan, I wasn't listening. What are my thoughts on what exactly?"

Miss Duncan gives me a polite smile. "On the reason behind the dead rising. Of course, we've all heard preachers insisting that it's our sins, of one sort or another, that have caused this plague upon our soil. But the country's best minds have been trying to ascertain a scientific basis, and they are quite divided on the cause and the reasoning behind it. I'm curious as to what you think."

I clear my throat and nod. I'm wondering why science is a better discussion topic than politics, but I don't say anything because that would be entirely too cheeky. Miss Duncan is a strange one, always talking to Negroes like she cares what they have to say. But I like her well enough, so I indulge her question.

"Well, I have been read—hearing some folks talk on the subject, and I think it's a tiny little critter that causes the infection. You know, like the same thing that makes milk sour."

If Miss Duncan noticed my near-admission to having gotten my hands on a medical journal, she doesn't show it. Meanwhile, Katherine stares at me with her mouth slightly agape. "A tiny creature, inside of the dead. What, like a mouse?"

I shake my head, feeling agitated and frustrated. "No, not like a mouse. Smaller. Like, too small to be seen with your eye. Microscopic. I read an article in the evening post a few weeks ago about a man named Joseph Lister over in England. See, he had a whole bunch of patients dying from infections, so he started sterilizing his surgical equipment with alcohol—"

Katherine frowns. "So now you're saying that we should all drink ourselves stupid to avoid being turned into one of the restless dead?"

"No, not like that. The alcohol kills the tiny critters, like cleaning a mess up with soap." Both Miss Duncan and Katherine are staring at me like I'm speaking in tongues. I let out a breath and fall back onto the unyielding seat. "Never mind," I mutter.

This always happens when I start talking about complicated stuff with people. In my head the ideas are so clear and make perfect sense, but when the words come out they're a mess. They might be looking at me like I'm insane, but the stuff I'm saying is true. That's the thing with me. Once I read something, I know it forever. Whether I'm supposed to be reading it or not.

Miss Duncan gives me another small, pitying smile. "Well, Jane, that certainly is an interesting theory."

We bump along in a decidedly uncomfortable silence. I can almost feel Katherine's self-righteousness swelling up and filling the carriage. I bet she can't wait to get back to her know-it-all friends and tell them how Jane McKeene is a mad half-wit that believes in invisible creatures swimming around in our blood. The rest of the trip passes in uneasy silence. There ain't even any more shamblers outside the carriage window to break up the monotony of dirt and trees and the occasional farmstead.

Finally we approach the high stone walls of Baltimore. On this side, it's covered in scaffolding, and men at the top appear to be adding more stones and bobbed wire. That thing's tall enough if you ask me, but I suppose you can't be too careful. We wait as the massive main gates of the west entrance are opened for us, and then pass into the city, the carriage letting us off at a central stop. The cobblestones are a nice change from the hard-packed dirt roads of the country. There are dirt roads in other parts of Baltimore, but this part of the city nearest to city hall has nicer streets.

I climb down, and while the rest of the girls disembark I study the gates. They are monstrously huge; I heard tell that each one takes three strong men to open and close. The wrought iron is painted black. Red, white, and blue ribbons are woven though the bars. Nearby a sign proclaims:

Come celebrate the five-year anniversary
of the construction of Central Gate
on Rising Day, July 2nd, 1880
A project funded by Mayor Abraham Carr and the Survivalist Party
Dancing, food, and fireworks!

It would be nice to go dancing, but that celebration ain't for me. No way colored folks would be allowed at a Survivalist shindig. Not unless we were serving the punch, that is.

Right before Katherine gets off the pony, she pokes me in

the side. "I want my bonnet back right after the lecture, you lying thief," she says, low enough that Miss Duncan can't hear. She goes off to join her friends, a couple of younger girls who are just as well-dressed as she is.

I scratch at the frizzy mass of my hair and watch her walk away. I'm feeling mighty out of sorts, and I ain't sure this day could get any worse.

"Hey there, Janey-Jane. What you doing in town?"

I turn around and coming down the walk toward me is Jackson Keats.

I was wrong. It just got worse.

Jackson swaggers up, his derby pulled low over his eyes. His light brown skin is more red than tan, which is how he got his nickname, Red Jack. Jack's a true redbone, fair enough that you know at least a few of his people come from Europe, not Africa. His close-cropped curls even bear a hint of auburn. I once met an Irishman with hair the same color. He weren't long for this world, seeing as how he got put down by a shambler, but I think of that poor fool every time I see Jackson.

"Can't help but notice you ain't been around lately," he says. Jackson runs the roadways between Miss Preston's and the city, and there ain't much in Baltimore County that goes on without Red Jack being involved, legal or otherwise. His blue-green eyes gleam. "We missed you last Saturday, Janey-Jane."

I shrug and glance around. Miss Duncan is still occupied with the pony drivers, most likely arguing about the fee. Drivers always like to up the price of a ride after the fact. Everyone knows they're as crooked as they come. Most likely Jackson is here to collect his piece of the action.

"Well, I ain't miss you or your hoodlum friends. And I told you to stop calling me that. My name is Jane, not Janey."

He grins at me, revealing a flash of gold tooth. "Aw, now, that ain't no way to talk to a beau. You keep it up with that sassy little mouth, I'm going to start to questioning your manners."

I cross my arms. "You. Ain't. My. Beau." And he ain't. What we have together is business, not personal. Not anymore, at least. I dart a quick glance toward Miss Duncan, who is still dickering with the carriage driver. "Scram before you get me in trouble."

Jackson puts his hands in his pockets, rocking back and forth on his heels. His gold watch chain catches the light at the waist of the brand-new green paisley waistcoat he's wearing. It's fancy and eye-catching. Silk maybe, and nicer than anything I've ever owned.

He notices me noticing and gives a wide smile. "You like it? I remember you saying green was your favorite color."

It is my favorite color, and it does look very dashing on him. No doubt about it, he is a fine-looking man. But he's also a mountain of trouble, and there are lots of other good-looking boys that ain't running around on the wrong side of the law.

"You did not wear that for me, so don't try to talk sweet. I know you, Jackson. You were probably on your way to see some poor farm girl that you tricked into believing you were the deputy mayor of Baltimore. Don't try to rope me into your shenanigans."

Jackson flashes me that wicked grin of his again before his eyes shift to something over my shoulder. I turn my head to follow his gaze. Katherine watches the two of us with narrowed eyes. One of the girls says something to her and pulls her attention back to the group's conversation, and I swear under my breath. "Lookit that. Now Miss Bigmouth is going to tell on me for sure. I've got to get back."

He grabs my arm, that devilish smile playing around his lips. "Come down to the barrelhouse after you get back to your school. I got a surprise for you."

"I don't want any surprises you might have, Jackson."

That is a lie. He's the one who smuggles me my news stories, even a book every now and again, in exchange for helping him with this dark deed or that one. So I do want whatever he has. But I ain't about to tell him that.

He tilts his head, his smile fading and a serious look taking its place. "Oh, this you do. Trust me."

I blink, because I ain't used to such solemnity from

Jackson. I once saw him beat a man near to death, all while wearing a smile.

I spy Miss Duncan heading back our way and I nod. "Not tonight. Tomorrow."

The smile reappears, and he gives me a low bow. "I'll count the minutes."

I snort. "I doubt you can count that high."

He gives me a wink, and just as quickly as he appeared, he fades back into the crowd of respectable folk moving down the sidewalks, anxious to finish their business and get inside before dark.

I move back to the knot of girls just as Miss Duncan rejoins our group. Her cheeks are flushed, and she wears an expression that says she'd like nothing more than to smack someone. That's what trying to deal with one of them carriage drivers will do to you. They're as frustrating as Jackson, but without the charm.

"All right, ladies, let's make our way down to the university. We don't want to be late for the lecture." Miss Duncan sets off at a trot, and we all follow her. Running might be undignified for well-bred ladies, but for a passel of Negro girls destined to work cleanup, it's just fine.

Katherine falls back next to me, her face reddening after only a few steps. I glance at her out of the corner of my eyes and can't help but shake my head. She sees me and her already sour expression turns stormy.

"What, Jane?"

"You shouldn't have worn that corset. That thing is going to get you killed."

"This thing happens to be the height of fashion. But I'm not surprised you don't know that."

"Kate, I like pretty clothes as much as the next girl, but I ain't about to let them kill me."

She sniffs and adjusts her gloves. "It's Katherine, Jane McKeene, and you know that. Never you mind about me, who was that ruffian you were speaking with?"

"Ruffian? What ruffian? I'm afraid I don't know who you're talking about."

She stumbles on a cobblestone and I reach out to catch her, steadying her with a light touch to her elbow. She shakes off my hand and picks up the pace.

"That guy. With the . . . natty . . . waistcoat." Already Katherine is out of breath, and we've only gone a short ways. If we keep on like this, she's going to faint and end up splayed out on the road like a well-dressed corpse.

I hop-skip a little, falling back from the group. "Miss Duncan," I call, doing my hop-skip-limp. "I think I got a rock in my shoe!"

Miss Duncan half turns but doesn't break stride. "Katherine, wait for Jane. You two catch up to us at the university."

I wave at Miss Duncan in acknowledgment and hop over to a nearby stoop. Katherine is panting at this point, her hair half fallen down after our impromptu trot.

"Stand up straight," I tell her. "You bend over like that and you're gonna be kissing the road."

She does, still gasping for breath, and gestures at my shoe. "Well, get your rock."

I snort. "I ain't got no rock in my shoe, I did that so you could catch a breath. You get found out wearing that corset you're gonna be on kitchen duty for a month."

Katherine takes a handkerchief and dabs at the sweat on her lip, her eyes meeting mine with a grimace. "And why do you care?"

I smile. "No reason at all. I'm just being a good Christian." At her look of disbelief I shrug. "Should we start walking?"

Katherine watches me for another long moment before nodding. I climb to my feet and we make our way the few remaining blocks to the university in silence.

Outside the imposing columned entryway of the school the steps are already clear. I make to walk inside, but Katherine stops me with a firm hand. "You never told me who it was you were talking to, Jane. That coarse-looking fellow. You know courting isn't allowed."

I smile, showing all my teeth, and tilt my head to the side. The things Jackson and I used to do can't really be called "courting," but Katherine doesn't need to know that. And now our connection is purely business, no matter what my heart might say every now and again.

"Why, that was no one, Katherine. Just like you ain't wearing a corset. Right?"

Katherine opens and closes her mouth a few times, but she's caught in a snare. So she says nothing and settles for storming up the steps in a fine flounce. I follow her a little more leisurely. Blackmail ain't really my thing; I prefer more direct kinds of sneakery, like lying and stealing. But I can't have Miss Duncan or any of the other instructors finding out about what I do with Jackson on the side, so this is what I'm reduced to.

We live in a terribly ruthless world.

I wish I could explain to you how fascinating and stimulating are the lectures that we receive here at Miss Preston's, but I'm afraid my descriptions will never do them justice. . . .

Chapter 5
In Which I Attend a Very Educational Lecture

The Baltimore University of Surgery, Medicine, and Thanatology is located in a fine building, meticulously restored in the years since Baltimore was reclaimed. The entry doors are made of wrought iron and glass, and just past them, marble columns and impressive oil paintings of bearded white men line the hallways. Like Miss Preston's, the building gives off the feeling that important learning is happening somewhere, somehow, someway. Unlike Miss Preston's, there is no lively chatter or the tantalizing smells of supper. Instead, a faint, foul chemical smell and a cool, humid emptiness waft out from the main doors of the building. The tainted air is reminiscent of a tomb. It is not at all pleasant.

Maybe that's why only men get to attend the university. What woman would want to spend time in such an awful, damp, smelly place? No learning is worth having to endure such melancholy.

Katherine is at the large entryway, her progress blocked by a couple of rough-looking white fellows. They lean against the door, their expressions amused. As I get closer I can see they wear the felted hats and long coats of the city police. Their mustaches are patchy, and even though they look stern they're probably only a few years older than Katherine and me.

"Miss, I'm afraid we can't let you in without checking you for weapons," says the shorter one. He's got a sly look to him, like a fox promising to be good around the hens. "The mayor's inside, and we're tasked with keeping him safe. So, are you gonna let us pat you down or not?"

As polite as they're being they must not realize Katherine is really a Negro. No surprise there. She's haughty and well-dressed enough to pass as the daughter of a man of middling political success.

Katherine must have decided the same thing, because she crosses her arms and gives the guard that narrow-eyed look of hers. "I have already told you I have no weapons, and I will most definitely not let you touch me. Now, will you please let me by? The rest of my class is already inside, and I do not want to miss a moment of the esteemed professor's lesson."

The short one smiles, revealing a gap where his front tooth should be. "Well, how about that. The pretty little lady here doesn't want to miss the professor's lecture." He gives the other copper, who has a big gap between his front teeth, a bit of side-eye before looking her up and down like a sweet in a display case. "Sweetheart, what are you really here for? You a working girl? If you're looking for a bit of coin, you ain't gonna find anything but disappointment in there with those grandpas." The two of them chortle a little, and Katherine flushes.

An ugly feeling rises up in me. I may be a liar and a cheat, but I absolutely despise bullies.

"Ay, hey there! Hoo-wee, I bet dis a humdinger of a lecture if it can get old Jelly Belly out of city hall. Dey ain't serving food, is dey?" I chuckle a little, then shuffle my feet in a little dance, and the cops stop laughing. They forget all about Katherine and push off of the doorframe and move over to me.

"What you doing here, girl? This ain't no place for your kind."

"That's right." The taller, leaner cop looms over me, and I duck my head in a pose of mock humility. Behind them,

Katherine draws herself up, a huffy look coming over her, and I shake my head just a little.

"Why, I jes looking for m'lady. She's come here for dis lecture, and shore enuff I done lost her." I shake my head like I am the dumbest Negro to ever walk the earth. For a moment I'm afraid it's too much. But there's no danger of that with these two.

"Oh yeah, and who's this lady you're looking for?" Gap Tooth moves close enough that I can smell his foul breath and I'm wishing I had a pocket full of mint to offer him.

"Why, the mayor's missus, of course. I brought her broach, 'cause she don't like to go out without it. She got it from the Belle of Baltimore herself! That fool Attendant of hers forgot it, and the house girls sent me out with it." I paw at my skirts, like I'm looking for something. "Now where did I put that fool thing?"

I keep feeling around like I'm searching for something small. There's movement out of the corner of my eye and I look up and scream, giving it all I got. The cops stumble back a little, reaching for their billy clubs.

"It's the dead! I just saw one, oh Jesus, oh Lordy, oh good God above, please help me. Where's the patrol when you need them? This is why it ain't safe in the city, no matter what those politicians would tell you. It ain't safe!" I fall to my knees on the steps of the entryway and begin to pray, like I'm absolutely terrified. A few passersby on the street look at me and then hurry in the opposite direction of where I point. I sob and even manage to squeeze a few tears out. It's overkill, but ain't no sense in doing something if you ain't going to go for broke. "Shamblers in the city! Oh what is this world coming to when even the city ain't safe? Ain't nothing but dead walking around in Baltimore, and we're all gonna end up joining them." I shake my head in denial, like this is the worst thing that's ever happened to me.

Here's a thing about me: I have always considered pursuing a life on the stage if this whole killing-the-dead thing doesn't work out.

The police officers don't know what to do, looking between me and the street where I pointed, their confusion clear. I look up from my praying and give them a look of complete alarm, widening my eyes till they near water from the effort. "What—what are you still doing here? Ain't you gonna go catch that shambler?"

They look at each other and take off down the avenue in the direction I point. I jump to my feet and approach Katherine, who watches me with a scowl.

"What was that?"

"Now don't go giving me that sour look. That was just a bit of acting. My momma always said the best way to get what *you* want from people is to give them what they think *they* want. They expected me to be stupid, so I used that to our advantage."

I move to enter the university, but Katherine doesn't budge. "You just lied to officers of the law," she says. "And why were you talking like that? You never talk like that."

I shrug. "Sometimes you have to live down to people's expectations, Kate. If you can do that, you'll get much further in life. Now quit dallying and get inside before they come back."

I push Katherine ahead of me through the fine double doors, anxious to escape before what passes for lawmen return.

The lecture hall is inside and to the right of the main entryway and we easily find our classmates. They sit in the last two rows of the room, the space reserved for Negroes. If the hall had a balcony we'd be up there, but it doesn't. Directly in front of us are a few of Baltimore's educated colored men, who teach at the city college for Negroes. I recognize a few of them from their visits to Miss Preston's. Most of them are Survivalists, and I don't much care for their message of knowing one's place and following along with the *natural order*. "Grow where you're planted," they say, while telling us what great futures we'll have bowing and scraping for our white betters. Seems to me those "enlightened men" worry more about keeping the mayor happy than the plight of colored folks.

It's surprising our class was even able to get seats. The lecture hall is packed to the rafters. Toward the middle of the audience is a group of well-dressed ladies, their pale skin glistening in the heat. Their dark-skinned Attendants are stationed along the wall, looking bored. Katherine eyes the white ladies, with their fine clothes and decorative fans. There is hunger in her gaze before her usual expression of disdain returns. I understand that look, though. Those ladies are the crème de la crème of Baltimore society, and their brightly colored dresses are the height of fashion. Who wouldn't want to be one of them?

But that ain't our future. Ours is leaning against that wall, ready to give our lives for a few coins, should it come to that.

In front of the ladies, closest to the podium, are the men. Most of them are large, their width an indication of their wealth, and Mayor Carr is largest of all. He's a big bull of a man, dominating the second row, wearing the red-and-white-striped ascot of the Survivalist Party. Survivalists believe that the continued existence of humanity depends on securing the safety of white Christian men and women—whites being superior and closest to God—so that they might "set about rebuilding the country in the image of its former glory," the way it was before the War Against the Dead. I don't particularly hold no truck with the notion, since being a Negro pretty much puts me in the inferior column. But people really seem taken with the mayor, especially those that are just as pale as he is.

The only reason I recognize Mayor Carr is because his

picture is in the newspaper nearly every week, the headlines proclaiming this victory or that accomplishment, usually in relation to containing the shambler threat and securing the Baltimore city limits. It's the Survivalists that lobbied to retake the cities nearly a decade ago, the idea being that if the cities were safe they could provide an anchor to regain the continent. But I don't know about all that. Momma used to say that a politician was a man that had perfected the art of lying, so I always read those articles with a certain amount of skepticism before turning over to the serials. The serials are the best part of the paper, anyhow. Reading about adventures out west or the tragedy of fine ladies with lecherous husbands always makes my day.

I don't recognize any of the other men around Mayor Carr. They look a lot like him, with their chin whiskers and pale skin and bold ascots. There are a few members of the Egalitarian Party in the rows as well, with their yellow-and-blue-striped ties, but they are far outnumbered by the Survivalists.

I settle into a chair, perching on the edge, careful not to bump the gun strapped to my thigh. Up front, the professor, a bald white man with small spectacles and a florid face, has already started delivering his remarks. He stands at a lectern in the front of the room, wearing a suit that is several years out of fashion, rambling on about organisms and spoiled milk. When he starts talking about things like pathogens and disease transmission I look sharply at Katherine, who is staring at me like I just grew an extra head. I give her a smug grin. Her sainted professor is talking about the same science-y facts I did in the carriage.

That gets me to pay attention.

"So these pathogens, or very small creatures, are transmitted from one victim to another through the bite of an infected corpse. Over the years these pathogens have evolved, which explains the shift from the Gettysburg strain—which would turn the victim only after he expired—to today's dominant strain, which initiates the transformation in the victim only a short time after they've been bitten. We've taken to calling this the Custer strain." He chuckles a little at his own joke, but when no one in the audience joins him he clears his throat and continues. "It's named after Custer's stunning defeat in Cleveland at the hands of his own infected men, of course. Now, overseas in Scotland, at the behest of a doctor there, Mr. Joseph Lister, they have had great success with burning their dead, which prevents the corpse from rising after burial. In addition, a few of our own local academics, including Mr. Irvington, have just returned from a sojourn to British India. There, the raj has ordered the beheading of their dead regardless of whether they've been bitten. This has kept the rates of infection from both the Gettysburg strain and the Custer strain very, very low.

"In addition—and more relevant to our discussion

today—there is comparably less of the infection west of the Mississippi River, especially amongst the Indians. It's similar to what we've seen in the South with the Negro, where the plague often fails to spread widely within populations of colored peoples."

There is considerable murmuring at this, and Professor Ghering smiles, his full-moon face glistening. I lean forward and frown. Fewer cases of the shambler plague amongst Negroes? That is a bald-faced lie if ever I've heard one.

The professor wipes at his brow with a pocket square before continuing. "I personally believe that the low rate of infection amongst the red man and the Negro is a direct consequence of the fact that neither the Indian nor the Negro is as highly developed as their European cousins, and thus show some of the resistance to the pathogen that we see in animals. Many argue this is an indication that, as polygenesis proponents have speculated in centuries past, the Negro is descended from a species entirely separate from the European *Homo sapiens*—one more closely related to the wild apes of the African jungle."

The crowd stirs again, while a few of the girls from my school look at one another in shock. I've learned a bit about evolution thanks to the books and newspapers Jackson smuggles me, and the comparison doesn't sit well. I cross my arms, as next to me Katherine mutters, "He did not just compare Negroes to apes."

I grimace. "Oh yes, he did. I told you this man was a crackpot."

At the front of the hall, Professor Ghering holds his hands up for attention, a benevolent smile on his face. His eyes scan the room, not even bothering to land on our group in the far back. I guess he pretty much figures where we stand on the whole nonsense, being beastly Negroes and all.

"Now, I believe this divergent ancestry indeed gives the Negro and the Indian a natural resistance to the undead plague. Not only that, but I am going to prove that a simple vaccination can increase this resistance, much the same way Louis Pasteur has vaccinated livestock against various diseases in France."

Katherine sniffs. "Livestock."

I know what she means. The more this man talks, the less I like him.

The professor is feeling his oats now, and he struts across the stage confidently. "And in order to validate this theory, I have prepared a demonstration that I am certain you shall all find fascinating." At that he gestures to the side, offstage. There's a creaking sound, and then a chorus of moans echo through the auditorium.

It's the dead.

They say once you hear the shambler's call you never forget the sound, and I don't know who "they" are, but they're right. It ain't a moan, and it ain't a groan; it's a sound somewhere in between, mixed with the keening whine of a starving animal. I'd been hearing that noise in the distance, past the walls of Rose Hill, since before I can remember, but the first time I heard it up close was the day Zeke was devoured. The second was when I was a little girl sleeping with my momma in her big four-poster bed, the major standing over us with a look in his bright yellow eyes like he was about to enjoy a whole pan of cobbler. Neither memory is one I want to revisit, so when that sound fills the lecture hall it takes everything I got not to jump up, whip out my revolver, and start plugging away at anyone that ain't looking right. But I don't. Instead, I dig my fingers into my thighs, biding my time so I can see what kind of foolishness this professor is playing at.

The rest of the room ain't so patient, and several of the men in the front are already drawing their guns and aiming up at the stage, not waiting to see where the sound is coming from. But the professor holds his hands out in a placating gesture. "Gentlemen, please. The situation is completely under control. You may retake your seats and put away your firearms."

The *creak-creak-moan* sound resolves itself into a colored man pushing a sheet-covered contraption. I can tell from the size and shape that it's a shambler's cage. They use them during roundups, which are usually in the spring after the first thaw. The risen dead will lie down during the winter, since, like most folks, they don't much care for the cold. The first few warm days of the year, the patrols will put out cages and tie a chicken or turkey or hog to the metal bars inside. Since shamblers can't resist living meat as they wake, they'll come out of the woods, jamming into the cage. Once it's full, the patrols will close the steel door and set the whole mess on fire. It ain't fancy, but it keeps the undead from attacking settlements and multiplying like rabbits come the spring.

This cage is on the smaller size, like the sort a farmer might use in his field, and once the man has pushed it into the middle of the stage the professor pulls the sheet off with a flourish. Inside are three shamblers: two men and one woman, all white folks. Sympathy for them twinges through me—I ain't seen a sight like this in a while. They ain't decayed much, so they must be new turns, and it makes me feel a little maudlin to think that a few weeks ago they probably had lives, families that loved them, jobs they didn't care for, petty grievances they nursed grudges over. Now they're nothing but yellow-eyed creatures out of a nightmare.

"Ladies and gentlemen, here we have three specimens, all recently infected. I would like to thank our fine Mayor Carr for allowing me to utilize these poor souls, gathered from the outskirts of Baltimore County, for our demonstration before their disposal." A smattering of uncertain applause breaks out around us, and a sick feeling sits heavy in my belly, like I just ate a peck of too-green apples. But the professor ain't finished. "I'd also like to introduce you to my assistant, Othello, who will be helping me with my demonstration."

The colored man next to the professor waves at the crowd uncertainly. A murmuring intensifies, the room buzzing like a beehive poked with a stick. Under it all, the calls keep coming from the cage, and my sick feeling gets near to crippling. Katherine grabs my arm, horror widening her eyes. "He is not about to do what I think he is. Is he?"

Nothing that is about to take place on that stage is going to be good. I can feel it in my gut. I reach under my shirt for my penny. It's cool to the touch despite being nestled against my skin, and I know that danger is near.

A lady's Attendant is always supposed to have a pleasant expression, but I can't seem to keep a grimace from my face. I shift in my seat, rearranging my skirts so I can more easily reach my sidearm. "You need to be ready to get the littler girls out. I'm pretty sure this ain't going to end up well for poor Othello, and this time Iago ain't going to have anything to do with it."

Katherine gives me a confused look before nodding as she gets the gist of what I mean, even if she doesn't get the reference. Now that most of the chatter has died down, the professor has moved across to the cage.

"Now, Othello here is going to willingly submit to a shambler's bite in order to demonstrate the increased resistance of a vaccinated Negro. Earlier this week Othello received a series of shots, which were painless." The professor takes out his handkerchief and mops his brow once more before tucking it back into his pocket. I'm certain he ain't told the truth the whole time he's been up there, since he's sweating like a murderer in church. What is this man playing at?

The professor continues. "This experiment is intended to ratify the prudence of our mayor's Negro patrols, which, under the close guidance of our excellent keepers of the peace, fulfill their role of service that God intended, keeping our city safe. Just as the undead plague is born of God's will, so also is the Negroes' resistance—vaccinated Negro squads make sense from both a moral and a scientific standpoint. I am confident that this experiment will also demonstrate that the Negro and Native Reeducation Act is entirely unnecessary. The cities are safe, the controlled territories are largely secure . . . Why should our citizens pay to educate colored boys and girls to do a job they're already biologically equipped to do? And when our esteemed mayor finds himself in the District after being elected senator"—the professor pauses for applause from the Survivalists up front—"I'm sure he will make every Baltimorean proud by helping to repeal the NNRA."

The professor smiles a little and inclines his head in the direction of the mayor and the man sitting next to him. Old Blunderbuss, as the newspapers call Mayor Carr, was the one that established Baltimore's Negro patrol squads a few years ago, right after I arrived at Miss Preston's. Before he was elected, the squads had been integrated, but now few whites serve in anything but command roles. I suppose it might have been a controversial move if it hadn't been so successful. As Momma once said, "Keeping the peace in this country isn't that hard, as long as nobody important dies."

I don't like this blowhard professor very much. I get the feeling his research is less about science and more about the mayor's impending run for Senate.

The man gestures to poor, dumb Othello who hasn't left his spot near the cage, and I can't hold my tongue any longer. The Negro scholars ahead of us don't seem inclined to say anything, and I cannot just let a man commit suicide, even if it is in the name of science.

I jump to my feet and clear my throat. "Excuse me, Professor Ghering?"

Everyone turns in their seats, and a few of the ladies nearer the front gasp, though whether because of my terrible hairdo or because I dared to interrupt, I ain't certain. Either way, I have everyone's attention.

Here's a thing about me: I ain't all that good at knowing when to keep my fool mouth shut.

The professor turns to me, adjusting his spectacles. "Yes, um, miss?"

I wave and smile large. "Hi there, Professor. My name is Jane McKeene, and I'm a student at Miss Preston's School of Combat. Before we get to all the biting, I just wanted to say thank you for having us here at your esteemed lecture. It is an honor."

The professor's guarded expression fades, and he gives me a benevolent smile. "Well, yes, of course. You colored girls are part of the future of our great nation, and it is vital for all Negroes to understand how important they are to the fight to save humanity. This is also why we have invited your Negro scholars and leaders here to witness such a momentous experiment."

"Oh, of course, Professor. Most definitely." I nearly choke on the words, because the men in the row in front of me are looking very uncomfortable. They know this lecture is a sham just as much as I do, but none of them are willing to stand up and lose what little standing they have with the mayor. Leaders they are not.

I swallow hard, my heart pounding in my throat. "Now, I just have one question, and I was hoping you would answer it before you get to your demonstration."

Next to me, Katherine grabs my arm and tries to pull me down, hissing at me under her breath. The Negro scholars in front of me are also muttering, saying some not-so-nice things about me. I ignore them.

The professor laughs. "Why, go right ahead."

"Well, see, in the event—however unlikely—that your vaccine does not have the desired effect, and Othello there turns, I was wondering what your contingency plan is. Have you taken the vaccine yourself?"

"Oh, most certainly not," the professor says, his already

ruddy face going positively crimson.

"Oh. Well, sir, that is a problem. See, shamblers are pretty strong when they first turn, and I can't help but notice that you don't have anyone at the ready to put the big man down. You do understand he's going to go after you first, don't you?"

The crowd shifts uncomfortably, and the professor forces out a dry laugh. Next to me Katherine whispers, "Sit down, Jane!" while a few of the ladies in the gallery exclaim over the rudeness of this new crop of Negroes.

This was a bad idea. This is the worst idea in the long and storied history of terrible ideas, right on up there with Julius Caesar marching up to the Roman Senate when he knew everyone wanted him dead. Why did I open my mouth? Why don't I just learn to mind my place, like Miss Anderson is always harping on about? For a moment my bravado falters. Maybe I should just sit down and leave Othello to his fate.

But, along the wall, one of the girls catches my eye and gives a slight nod. I know her. Her name is Maisie Carpenter. She was in her last year of Miss Preston's my first year there. Her silent approval warms me.

"Miss McKeene—" the professor begins, but he's interrupted by Mayor Carr himself climbing to his feet.

"Girl," he begins, in his condescending politician's voice, "your concern for your betters is a credit to the fine training you've received out there by Miss Preston's. But you can rest assured that this demonstration is going to go quite as expected. That is to say, our good man Othello here will only experience but a little discomfort from the shambler's bite. There is nothing that I value more than the safety of the good citizens of this fine city, and Professor Ghering's work is a testament to the vision of the Survivalist Party and the future of these American states. It is men of science like him, and brave patriots like Othello, who will restore this nation to its former glory." The mayor grins wide, and there is a smattering of applause in reaction to his speechifying. Then he makes a shooing motion in my direction. "Now, why don't you take your seat. With due respect to Miss Preston, this ain't your place."

His words are mild; his tone is not. And what he says unlocks some long buried memory. Just like that, I'm no longer in the lecture hall but back at Rose Hill Plantation, watching as the major slowly uncoils the horse whip from its hook.

This ain't your place, girl. You run back on inside 'fore you're next.

I blink. This is where I cash in my chips. No way I can outtalk Old Blunderbuss, especially now that my moment has passed. After all, he's a professional liar. I might be good, but I ain't no politician.

"Well, Mr. Mayor, that is a relief." I force a shaky smile and bob a curtsy before sinking back into my chair.

"You are most unseemly sometimes," Katherine whispers

next to me. "Honestly, Jane, I don't know why you even bother with Miss Preston's. It's obvious from anyone paying attention that you'll never make it as a lady's Attendant. Why, can you just imagine—"

"That big, dumb fool up there is about to turn into a shambler, and everyone is just going to let it happen," I whisper curtly. "Do you really think I could sit back and say nothing?"

"If Professor Ghering says—"

"Professor Ghering just said you ain't much more than livestock. You really gonna put faith in that man's words?"

That shuts her up, and I turn my attention back to the stage.

The professor marches over to where Othello stands next to the cage, a matter-of-fact smile on the academic's face. Othello ain't smiling. He looks terrified. Second thoughts and all that. "Now, go ahead and stick your hand in the cage," the professor says. In the audience someone coughs, and the crowd is so quiet that it echoes like a gunshot.

Othello just stands there, shifting his weight from foot to foot. He looks at the shamblers, and then back at the professor, who clears his throat and gestures toward the cage. The shamblers are reaching through the bars, their faces pressed into the spaces between, their mouths agape. "Go on, Othello. There's nothing to fear." His voice is kind and confident. Othello turns to the crowd, and for a moment I think that maybe he's finally going to put a stop to this, walk away and live out whatever time he has left in this world.

That's when his shoulders slump, and he sticks his arm out.

They're on him before he gets more than his fingers into the cage. One of them gets a hold of his hand and pulls him closer, biting down on his arm like it's a drumstick. Othello's shout of pain echoes through the auditorium, and in the rows ahead of us a few of the ladies get the vapors. Their girls are on them immediately, passing smelling salts under their noses and escorting them out, half carrying them. I'm sad to see that Maisie Carpenter is one of them. She was a solid marksman. It would be nice to have her here when it all goes to hell.

Up on stage, the professor and another man are pulling Othello back from the cage and settling him into the stage's lone chair. The shamblers are frantic now that they got the taste of fresh meat. They sniff the air, their yellow eyes scanning the crowd as they look for their next meal. Someone should walk up onstage and put them down, but no one is paying any attention to the caged dead. Instead, everyone is focused on Othello, leaning back in his chair, panting like a man that just ran a footrace.

"Kate . . . ," I begin.

"Jane, I am not sure why you insist on calling me by that horrid nickname, but if I've told you once I've told you a million times—"

"Look at the stage, Kate. Look at Othello."

Her gaze meets mine. "He's going to turn."

Professor Ghering addresses the crowd. His benign smile is less sure now, and people in the audience are beginning to speak amongst themselves, concern rising like the tide. "Please, calm yourselves. Othello is quite unaffected, but even if something should go wrong, research has shown that a living person bitten by a shambler will take at minimum a half hour to turn. If we all check our pocket watches—"

"I'm afraid that estimate is incorrect, Professor." Miss Duncan stands, her voice ringing out loud and clear over the rest of the crowd. It's the same voice that has led us in countless drills, and everyone stops talking. "I know it's likely been a while since you city folk have witnessed a turning, but those that have been bitten can and do change immediately. The thirty-minute rule is outdated and has been summarily disproven by Mr. Pasteur over in France. I recommend we evacuate now, before we have a catastrophe on our hands."

The professor opens his mouth, but before he can speak, a low growl comes from the rear of the stage. Othello stands behind the good professor. His eyes are yellow. Saliva drips from his mouth and his lips are turned up in a feral snarl.

He leaps.

Shouts of alarm echo throughout the auditorium. In the cage, the other shamblers are going wild, throwing themselves against the bars in an attempt get a bite of their own.

People panic like a herd of spooked cattle, men and women pushing against one another to get out of the lecture hall. No one ever keeps a cool head when shamblers are about.

"Ladies." We're on our feet at Miss Duncan's gentle summons. "Katherine, go out and see if you can get a rifle from one of the men who were supposed to be guarding the door. Jane, take the sidearm under your skirts and put those shamblers down."

I open my mouth to deny it, but Miss Duncan gives me a stern look. "Not now, Jane. We shall discuss your concealed weapon later, in addition to your highly improper outburst. Girls," she says, turning to the younger ones, some of whom are crying. They've probably never seen a shambler go after a man like Othello is going after the professor. Or if they have, the sight is probably waking some very unpleasant memories. "We need to stay calm and escort these nice people out of the building before they trample one another. Jane, if you could get their attention?"

I nod, reaching up under my skirts and pulling out my revolver. I fire a shot into the air, and the sound is enough to startle folks out of their terror for just a moment.

"Ladies and gentlemen," I say, "if you would be so good as to follow Miss Preston's girls out of the lecture hall, we have the situation under control."

That last bit is a lie, but the easiest lie to tell is the one people want to believe. Even though a man is being devoured onstage, they're still more worried about their own hides. They begin to file out quickly but much more calmly, the professor all but forgotten.

It's a cruel, cruel world. And the people are the worst part.

And I daresay you would be incredibly impressed with my marksmanship skills. I am a crack shot, far beyond any of the other girls, and that is not boastfulness. I often wonder if part of that might be due to your tutelage at Rose Hill.

Chapter 6
In Which All Hell Breaks Loose

I push my way through the crowd to the front of the room, where Othello has just about had his fill of the professor. Ghering is still mostly alive, but before I put him out of his misery I have to put down Othello.

While at Miss Preston's I've ended enough dead to give myself a lifetime of nightmares. The trick is not to think of them as regular folks. When you do that, your emotions get all tangled up. You start to wonder whether it's right or wrong and what kind of person that makes you for taking their life, whatever kind of existence it may be. Your brain starts doubting, and those second thoughts can get you killed.

But when you think of shamblers as things, as mindless creatures who have to be put down so that we might live, ending them gets to be a lot easier. The farmer doesn't cry over slaughtering a hog.

So that's what I think about when I slay shamblers. Not who they might have once been and what kind of life there is after death, but how them being gone makes the people I care about safer, and how each body gets me closer to getting back home to my momma and Rose Hill Plantation.

For Othello, his end puts me one step closer to my beginning. I don't even flinch when I put the bullet in his head. This close to the stage, it's an easy shot.

Suffice it to say, the result is untidy.

I climb the stairs to the stage and look down at Professor Ghering. He's a mess. His throat is missing and his fancy waistcoat is soaked with blood. He ain't breathing, and most folks would usually assume that means he's not getting up again. But I know better. My time at Miss Preston's has taught me a few things. In all my killing the dead, this is the first time I've stood over a man I thought deserved it.

"I ain't sorry this happened to you. With a fool's pride comes disgrace. Or something like that." I don't know what good it is to say I told you so to a dead man, but it makes me feel a little bit better, especially after being humiliated for speaking out. I shoot Professor Ghering right between the eyes, just as I did Othello, then once more, because seeing a man so casually turned for some blowhard's cause has put me in a fine temper. I'm about to holster my revolver when there's a low growl behind me.

The thing about a shambler's cage is that it ain't designed to hold anything long-term. When you set those traps up you're supposed to hide somewhere nearby, so you can put the dead down real quick. Unfortunately Professor Ghering and his Survivalist cronies thought they were smarter than the average foot patrol.

So I shouldn't be surprised when the iron lock finally breaks loose, releasing three blood-crazed shamblers.

What is left of the departing crowd goes frantic. People nearest the stage shout in alarm and begin shoving. Their fear draws the attention of the shamblers, and one of them jumps off the raised platform, right down into the seats.

I'm quicker on the draw, and once I get a bead on the shambler, I put him down with a head shot. But the crowd's already spooked. I ain't got time to worry about a bunch of dandies running for their lives.

Shamblers ain't like normal people, but they do have an eerie ability to recognize a threat when they see it. Putting down their hunting buddy effectively made me a target, and when the two remaining shamblers turn toward me, slack mouths open in a hungry growl, I know I'm in for it.

They stalk toward me across the stage. Inside, my heart is pounding, my blood thrumming in my ears as the fear response urges me to *run run run*. But I ain't no coward. I've got two shots left. I just need to make them count.

I line up my sights on the bigger shambler and squeeze the trigger. The revolver recoils, smoke filling the air. He drops and I take aim at the last one. She opens her mouth wide, growling low in her throat. She's fresh dead, so she doesn't have the blackened saliva that so many of the older ones do. Still, drool runs down her chin and the front of her calico dress. I feel bad for her. She wasn't rich in life, her clothing belying her poverty, and even her death has been insulting. Changed into a shambler, locked up in a cage, paraded onstage. That ain't a fitting end for anyone.

I think through all of this in the few heartbeats between lining up my shot and pulling the trigger.

Click. Empty.

Quickly I count through my shots. One in Othello. Two in the professor. One in the jumper, and another in the other male. That's only five.

And one in the air to get everyone's attention, Jane, you damn fool.

The shambler ain't waiting for me to figure out what happened to my last bullet. She vaults toward me, a murderous blur set on a collision course with disaster. I swear—under my breath because a lady's Attendant never curses aloud—and brace myself for impact.

A shot rings out, and I turn to see an Attendant in the middle of the aisle, her hands shaking. Behind her is a crumpled heap of crinolines and lace. The Attendant's charge has passed out, and the woman's serving girl is trying to alternately drag her or revive her with smelling salts while the Attendant provides a distraction.

Unfortunately the Attendant is providing the wrong kind of spectacle, because the shambler lurches off the stage and after the trio in the aisle. I launch myself off after her.

The shambler runs up the aisle toward the prone woman, who I can see now is the mayor's wife. The serving girl looks up, her eyes round as saucers as the shambler bears down on her.

"Shoot it!" I shout to the Attendant in the aisle, but she drops her sidearm and runs, the girl with the smelling salts close behind. Needless to say, neither of them were ever Miss Preston's girls.

"Damn it to hell," I yell, this time not quite able to keep the language to myself. The shambler is close enough to Mrs. Carr to get a good bite out of her, and I decide to do the stupidest thing ever.

Eeny, meeny, miny, mo, catch a shambler by the toe.

I dive at the dead woman, grabbing her one-handed by the ankle. She goes down, flat on her belly, only a few inches away from the unconscious woman. The shambler kicks out, her heel catching me in the mouth and splitting my lip. I grunt and my grip slips. She tries to drag herself toward Mrs. Carr, and I grab the shambler's ankle again with both hands and haul her back, groaning as I climb to my feet.

The dead woman lets loose a sound somewhere between frustration and fury. She twists around in my grip, lunging for me. The woman is faster than I expect, and I take a stumbling step back. My feet tangle in my skirts and I fall, the shambler following.

I throw up my hands, using my forearms to block the weight of her torso before she can take a bite out of my face. She claws at me as I hold her back, my hands locked around her throat. I push her up and away, locking my elbows and hiding my face in my shoulder, trying to avoid her scrabbling hands. She pulls at the brim of Katherine's bonnet, more interested in yanking my face to her teeth than in freeing herself. I'm trying to figure out how to get her off of me when there's a loud report and something cold and wet splashes on my face.

The shambler goes limp and I push her to the side, climbing to my feet as I wipe blood and the shambler's brains off of my cheek. I look around to see who just saved my bacon, and I meet the eyes of the most remarkable man I've ever seen.

He stands at the back of the room, a rifle in his hand. His straight dark hair is chin-length, his jaw square, his skin the same deep brown as mine. He wears a strange outfit, some kind of canvas pants that I've never seen before with a checkered shirt. My mouth falls open, part shock and part plain old rudeness. I ain't too proud to admit that I stare at him as he watches me. But it ain't entirely my fault. I never saw an Indian before.

Of course I've read the newspaper weeklies about them: "The Chieftain's Son," "Plains Bride," and my favorite, "Two Braves of Yellow Rock," which is a story about two Cherokee brothers, one that chooses the white man's way and the other who becomes the chief of his tribe. Momma loved those stories, and when the paper would come we'd read them together, marveling over tales of a frontier untouched by the blight of the restless dead.

Momma used to say the Indian was even worse off than the Negro, because instead of being taken from his land he'd had his land taken from him. The man looks across the rapidly thinning audience at me, just as I'm staring at the fellow that saved my life. But then the Indian gives me a scowl, as though I am the most repugnant thing he's ever seen, and turns and leaves the lecture hall.

Well.

Katherine comes running up, a revolver in her hand, huffing and puffing as she tries to get a full breath.

I glare at her. "Where've you been?"

"I had to run all the way down the street to find those

dimwits. They were still searching for the shambler you sent them chasing after." Katherine looks at me and frowns. "What happened to my bonnet?"

I don't answer her. I just take it off, hand it to her, and walk out to find Miss Duncan.

I've had enough higher education to last me a lifetime.

A few of the girls here seem to find all sorts of mischief, constantly in trouble with the headmistress. You'll be happy to hear that I am not one of them.

Chapter 7
In Which I Receive Invitations Both Expected and Unexpected

Someone shakes me awake. I crack one eye open, notice the pale gray light filtering through the bars on the windows, and grunt. "You better be shaking me for a good reason."

"Come on," a voice says from the dark. It's Katherine. She stalks off, and I reluctantly rise for our fourth straight day of house duty.

After we'd put down all of the shamblers, Mayor Carr had been kind enough to let us use his personal carriage to get back to the school. I'm guessing this generosity came on account of me saving his wife and all. The engine chugged through the twilight, moving down the road much more quickly than the rented carriages we'd taken to Baltimore. The steam engine had been nearly whisper-quiet, the hiss low enough that we didn't attract a single shambler from the surrounding woods. The seats had also been more comfortable, and the interior large enough to fit all of us in one pony. I didn't think the tax-payers would be too keen on hearing that their elected official traveled in unrivaled luxury while they were forced to ride in barrels pushed along by clanking old engines.

When we got back, Miss Duncan had marched us right into Miss Preston's office. At first I thought maybe we were going to get a ribbon or something for our valorous conduct. What we got was another lecture.

"I'm surprised at you girls." Miss Preston yawned wide, likely on account of the late hour. "You know better than to gallivant around wearing corsets and carrying firearms. You're in your last year! I expect better from students about to graduate."

"Miss Preston," I said, raising my hand. "Can I just say that I am truly remorseful for my conduct? I understand that it is dismaying to know that a girl might be wont to strap a revolver to her thigh before attending an educational event. However, without my revolver those shamblers could've easily turned half that room. Wearing a corset is far more egregious a transgression. After all, the stays of the corset limit movement, and not being able to draw a proper breath could be the difference between life and death for the wearer."

I could feel Katherine glare at me as I offered her up in the hopes of saving my own hide, and I'm certain that by the end she fairly had steam coming from her ears. Small price to pay to avoid getting the switch. But Miss Preston was having none of it.

"Jane, your point is well taken, but heroism means little when it rests on lawlessness. And don't think Miss Duncan didn't inform me of your outburst during the lecture. There are rules in this world, rules that are the only thing separating us from the restless dead. This isn't the wild days of the Years of Discord, when anarchy reigned. We expect you to hold yourselves to a higher standard in civilized society. No, your choices were just as poor as Katherine's. Both of you can look forward to getting the strap tomorrow after breakfast."

Miss Duncan cleared her throat, and Miss Preston let out a sigh. "Yes, Amelia?"

"Headmistress, if it isn't too much to ask, perhaps the girls could be given house detail instead of the strap? I know their behavior was appalling, but I'd hate for them to have to miss any of the upcoming drills this week because they're laid up. The first-year girls are learning the sickle this week, and I need Katherine and Jane to help instruct. Also, I believe it should be recognized that, without them, this evening could surely have ended in tragedy. I know Mayor Carr is a close personal friend of yours, and even he was quite insistent that the girls had done a remarkable job."

That last bit was a little fabrication on Miss Duncan's part. What the mayor had actually said was, "It's nice that we can depend on the Negro to do their part." His tone had been almost insulting.

If you ask me, neither the mayor nor any of these other folks were taking things seriously enough. For all the mayor knows, there's some other professor bringing the dead into city limits to work experiments on them—who knows how long it will be until we're back in the dark days of the War Against the Dead?

Regardless, it fell out that Katherine and I were saved the corporal punishment and instead assigned house duty for two weeks. Housework ain't too bad, and I ain't ashamed to say this ain't my first time doing it. It was a standard punishment whenever a girl did wrong. Poor marks, laziness, a general bad attitude? Miss Preston was convinced that the best way to correct minor misconduct was a little drudgery, and housework was the pinnacle of drudge.

So Katherine and I spent our free time polishing silver, dusting bannisters, beating carpets, and a dozen other randomly assigned tasks. We got up early in the morning and dragged ourselves to the kitchen, eating cold porridge that the cook gave us with a scowl. Then we started our chores two hours before class, returning after dinner to help Cook scrub the day's pots and pans before heading off to bed.

For three straight days, Katherine refused to speak a lick. Now, on the fourth day, though, she talks.

"Your friend is here."

I don't even look up. We're on our hands and knees, scrubbing the marble floor in the rear of the main building. It's one of Miss Preston's favorite chores. Sometime before the school was taken over by Miss Preston's, some poor soul was killed here, his lifeblood seeping into the stone. It would've been easier to take up the stained tiles, but marble is expensive and hard to come by. So instead we scrub, trying to erase the signs of some bastard's last few breaths.

This is the fiftieth time I've been made to scrub this same patch of floor over the three or so years I've been at Miss Preston's, so I know it well. The rust-colored stain ain't coming out, but scrubbing ain't the worst way to pass an afternoon. The foyer is cool thanks to the marble and the sounds of girls outside practicing their remedial drills drifts in through the open windows.

"Jane!"

"Hmm?"

Katherine nods toward one of the big windows. "Your friend, the ruffian, is here. And you know that's against the rules."

I look over, and climbing in through one of the open

windows is Red Jack, looking fresh as a daisy in a yellow waistcoat. His bowler is new as well, and he presents a dapper image.

I straighten but don't stand, kneeling with my hands on my hips. "What are you doing here?"

"You didn't come by the barrelhouse on Sunday. You said you'd bring me some of that sugar." He says it with a wink that makes it abundantly clear that he's being unseemly.

"I forgot, Jackson. And I wasn't bringing you anything but my blade."

"Anyway, I heard about your escapade through the grapevine, so I figured that, as per the usual, Jane McKeene had found herself in a spot of trouble with her headmistress. Hello there," Jackson says, tipping his hat to Katherine.

She scowls and climbs to her feet. "I'm going to go fetch Miss Anderson."

I grab her skirts. "Not if you want to keep those pretty curls, you ain't."

Katherine's eyes narrow. "Are you threatening me, Jane?"

"Naw. I don't make threats."

She looks from me to Jackson one last time before stomping out into the hallway.

I drop the scrub brush into my bucket and climb to my feet. "Now is not a good time, Jackson. Give me whatever it is you mentioned in Baltimore and get going."

He shrugs. "Don't much care. And I ain't here about that.

You owe me one, and I aim to collect."

"Owe you? Since when am I owing you anything?"

"River Bend. Two months ago. I saved your life."

"You nearly got me killed!" I shriek.

The echo of voices in the hallway filter toward us. At least two women, probably Katherine and Miss Anderson. Of course that high yellow Jezebel told on me. Girl would rat out Jesus to the Romans.

I sigh, grabbing Red Jack by his arm and dragging him back toward the window. "Listen here, Redbone, and listen well. This is not a good time. I don't know what you think I owe you, or why, but we'll settle it up later. You need to go. I get in trouble again and I'm either going to get the strap or expelled. I'm already on probation, and getting caught with you ain't going to help my case."

Red Jack pulls his arm from my grip and adjusts his hat. "Lily is missing," he says, his voice low and choked.

That stoppers my rage. Lily is Jackson's younger sister, sweet as sugar and as pretty as a summer day. There is no one Jackson cares about more than her.

"Well, she can't have been gone long. I saw her the same day I saw you in Baltimore. She and Mrs. Spencer brought us lemonade."

"Yep, they're still letting her stay with them, God bless them. But they've all disappeared."

"Maybe they went on a trip? Mrs. Spencer's people are

from Delaware. Mayhap they traveled up that way?"

"Can't be. Laverne just had a babe two months past."

Folks rarely just up and vanish like that. Unless . . . "Shamblers?" I ask, trying to be as delicate as I have the wherewithal to be.

He shakes his head. "No. There hasn't been an attack reported in months. And I didn't notice any blood when I went by there. I would've found some sign of them if it had been the dead. There's just . . . nothing."

I take a deep breath and let it out slowly. "So you want me to look and see if I can find something you missed?"

"You're smarter than anyone I know, Jane, and I'm not just saying that so you'll help me. If I've missed something, some sign of what happened to them, I know you're the person to find it."

A year ago, I would have chalked this up to shamblers and been done with it. But if what Red Jack says is true, it does sound like a bit of a mystery. I reach under my shirt and run my thumb over my lucky penny. There's no chill and no flash of brilliance, so my luck charm isn't any kind of help this time.

Red Jack watches me but says nothing, his face a pleasant half smile that could easily mean he's enjoying a fine tale or he's planning on stealing someone's watch. That's his worried face, which makes me even more concerned.

"Fine, I'll help you."

He breaks out into a wide grin. "Thatta girl. You got a letter for me to send?"

I dig the envelope out from the hidden pocket I've sewn into the hem of my day dress. We're not supposed to send letters home, because Miss Preston thinks that it's a distraction from our studies. But I can always count on Jackson to smuggle something to the post for me.

"You got any letters for me?"

Jackson shakes his head. "Nope. But don't worry. I'm sure your ma's just been busy."

"For a whole year? Not likely." I hold the letter out and he tucks it into his breast pocket.

Jackson's expression goes soft. "Thanks for agreeing to help me."

I nod. "Just, enough of this 'owing you' nonsense. We're either friends or we're not, Jackson. And friends don't keep score."

"Ah, Jane. Obviously you haven't had many friends." Before I can snarl a reply Red Jack tips his bowler, flips something at me that I catch in midair, and slips out the window, quick as he came.

I look down at what he tossed me. It's a new book: *Tom Sawyer*, by a fellow named Mark Twain. I tuck it into my hidden pocket and then button the thing shut for safekeeping.

"I'm going with you."

I turn around. Katherine's hands are on her hips and she

looks to be spoiling for a fight. Surprisingly, Miss Anderson is nowhere to be found. Maybe she didn't tell on me.

Doesn't mean I'm about to take her with me on my late-night escapades.

"I ain't going anywhere, Kate. You about done with this floor? I'm going to see if Miss Preston has anything else for us before I wash up."

"Stop calling me Kate. I detest that nickname. And don't lie to me. You're going to sneak out tonight with that boy to visit the Spencers' farm, and I'm going with you."

What a sneaky little eavesdropper. "Why?"

"My reasons are my own business." She sniffs, just as haughty as ever.

"You're going to have to do better than that."

"Fine," she huffs. "The Spencers are good people. If something happened to them, I want to find out what. Besides, you could use my help if you get into trouble. That Jackson boy doesn't seem like the most reliable in a fight."

I open my mouth to protest, but she ain't done. "Anyway, it's the least you can do after destroying my bonnet."

Right on cue a pounding sensation begins behind my eyes. "I didn't destroy your bonnet. Like I told you, it was that Indian man with the damned rifle." That intriguing man with a rifle who had looked at me with disdain. I'm still wondering how he happened to be there ready to put down a shambler just when I needed him.

"Really, Jane. You shouldn't swear. Either way, you still owe me. For the bonnet, and for sullying my relationship with Miss Preston. Besides, I didn't tell Miss Anderson about your beau. Or the book he brought you. And I still could."

She's right. Trying to give Katherine over to save my own hide hadn't been my finest moment, and if I really think about it I do feel the tiniest bit guilty. Plus, now she's got a whole load of dirt on me. It's in my best interest to keep on her good side. If she wants to tag along, then that is on her.

"Fine, but you need to listen to me and listen well. We get caught and the punishment is going to be far worse than housework. We will get the strap. Or worse, expelled. So make sure you know what you're asking for. We leave two hours after lights-out. Now, can we please dump this dirty water and get on with our lives?"

Katherine nods, and we each grab a bucket, hefting them back to the kitchen. We're halfway down the hall when Katherine murmurs, "So, about your beau—"

"He ain't my beau."

"Really? Because he seems like your beau, bringing you gifts and all."

I turn to look at her, but she's serious. Does she really think that's what courting looks like? Red Jack inspires feelings of murder in me, not love. It wasn't always like that, but Katherine ain't asking about ancient history. "No, he's a mistake I have no intention of repeating."

"Oh. I was just wondering."

I watch her as we haul our buckets down the hall. Does Katherine fancy Jackson? She's pretty enough, and Jackson's type is anything he thinks he can tumble. Still, the thought of them together is enough to make me more than a little stabby. Jealousy is a terrible thing, and I swallow the emotion down hard as I can.

I consider warning her that taking a turn with Jackson is beyond a terrible idea, but I decide to save my breath. If anyone had tried to tell me a year ago that blue-green-eyed Jack would break my heart, I wouldn't have believed them. That's the way it is when you fancy someone. Your heart starts doing the thinking, and your brain? Well, it gets left out of the equation until too late.

Either way, Katherine can discover what kind of scoundrel Jackson is on her own.

My one regret about leaving Rose Hill in such haste all those years ago is that I feel like I never got to give you a proper good-bye, Momma. I know how you sometimes see fit to hold a grudge. I hope your lack of letters isn't tied to you being in a fine temper. It's hard to apologize when the miles steal every last bit of affection.

Chapter 8
In Which I Relate the Circumstances Surrounding My Departure from Rose Hill Plantation

The day the truancy officers came for the children of Rose Hill Plantation, I hid in the summer kitchen with Auntie Aggie. That wasn't the first time the white men with their long beards and narrowed eyes had come to Rose Hill, taking every Negro boy and girl away to be educated. But it was the first time it was obvious to the naked eye that I was of an age to get carted off along with the rest.

So Momma had grabbed me by the arm and dragged

me around the back of the house when she heard the chug and wheeze of the government ponies coming into the front yard, the federal seal painted on the side of the steam-powered metal carriages. "Keep her away from those bureaucratic bastards. Keep her safe," she said to Auntie Aggie before sweeping out to greet the truancy officers. She was, after all, the lady of the estate, and it fell to her to pay for one of the better combat schools for her charges, should she be so inclined.

The government called it an investment. Momma called it extortion.

Either way, Momma had entrusted Auntie Aggie to hide me, to keep me at Rose Hill Plantation. I'd been hiding every year since I'd been eleven, and now at fourteen I was more than old enough to get carted off to one of the government schools. Momma wasn't about to let that happen.

Auntie Aggie had other ideas.

"Jane, come here." I walked over, and she held me out at arm's length, an expression equal parts sadness and acceptance working across her dark features. "You got to go with the officers, girl."

"Momma doesn't want me to go." I didn't much want to go, either. There was a big scary world beyond the boundaries of Rose Hill. I was bold, but not so foolhardy as to think there was something worthwhile on the other side of the barrier fence that kept the dead out.

Auntie Aggie nodded, as though she'd heard my unspoken thoughts. "Yes, but your momma don't always do what's best for you. Sometimes your momma can be powerful selfish, and this is one of those times."

I knew that what Auntie Aggie said was the truth. I'd witnessed Momma's fits firsthand.

"But if I go, I'll die," I said, my voice half a whine.

"No, you won't, Jane. Don't you know that you're special? Ain't your momma told you as much?"

I shrugged, because Momma did always tell me what a special girl I was. But I didn't always feel special. I mostly just felt different. After all, no one else could claim the plantation's mistress as their momma and an unknown field hand as their poppa.

"Come here, Jane." She swept me up into a fierce hug. "You are special, girl."

"How do you know that?" I asked, my words muffled by her generous bosom.

Auntie Aggie laughed, voice husky. "Because I know things. I know that you got a great destiny ahead of you, just like your momma, and that Rose Hill ain't no place for you, not anymore. You need to go out in the big, wide world and find yourself. And the big, wide world needs to find you. There's a whole bunch of folk out there trying to figure out this plague, and ain't nobody done it yet. You ask me, they might be wanting for some fresh ideas."

I stepped out of the hug and frowned at Auntie Aggie. "Being out in the world ain't gonna do me much good if I get gobbled up by shamblers."

She nodded and reached into the pocket of her skirt. "That's why I got you this. Miss Fi-Fi made it for you." Auntie Aggie held out a necklace. It was simple enough, a penny with a hole in it so it could hang on a string. But I knew well enough that if Miss Fi-Fi was involved the necklace was more than what met the eye. Miss Fi-Fi was the woman you went to when you wanted to catch the attention of a handsome fellow, or when your menses were late but you weren't looking to carry a child. Some folks called Miss Fi-Fi a healer. Most weren't so kind.

"Momma don't like hoodoo," I said, but I still held my hand out for that necklace. I ain't never been one to turn down a gift, even if it could be cursed.

"Your momma ain't got to know. Miss Fi-Fi said you should wear this at all times, that it'll warn you when there's danger about. Now hurry, put it on before the truancy man comes and gets you."

I took the necklace and slipped it over my head. The penny settled in the hollow of my chest, its weight warm and comforting.

"Now," Auntie Aggie said, kissing me on each cheek, "go out there and tell that truancy man you're ready to go to school."

The one drawback to attending Miss Preston's is the quiet. It is ever so calm and safe here, with most of us having not a care in the world beyond our studies. . . .

Chapter 9
In Which I Have an Accomplice and We Skulk in the Shadows

I've snuck out of Miss Preston's many times. In the beginning it was because I was homesick, and it was a comfort to be able to lie on the sprawling lawn and know I was under the same big moon as Momma and Auntie Aggie back in Kentucky. I'd lie in the grass in my white hand-me-down nightgown and stare up at the sky, the occasional growls and moans of the shamblers at the barrier fence barely audible over the sound of my crying.

But that didn't last long, and it got so that I was sneaking out less because I was homesick and more because I just enjoyed the freedom. There's something about skulking around while everyone else is fast asleep that you can't put words to. Eventually, after a few months or so, I got bored enough with the sneaking about to jump the barrier fence. After all, Auntie Aggie had sent me away from Rose Hill so that I could see the whole big world, and that meant something besides the grass of Miss Preston's.

This was back when Baltimore County was filthy with shamblers, and sometimes I would hunt them in the dark, just another monster slinking through the deep shadows. Other times I would climb a tree and watch the folks dumb enough to travel at night, their whispers too loud, their reactions too slow. I would try to help out, jumping down from my perch and coming to their aid like some guardian angel. That was how I'd met Red Jack, curse my terrible luck. Most days I think I should've just let him get eaten.

But sometimes I couldn't help the people on the road when the shamblers came. I didn't risk taking a gun for these nocturnal excursions, and my sickles were only so fast. There were too many nights when jumping down to lend my steel would only have ended in my own demise.

Those nights were the worst.

My nightly wanderings more often than not ended well, and I learned a lot from the shamblers I watched. I figured out they preferred to hunt in packs, and that the old ones were slow while the new ones were just as fast as a regular person. I discovered that they couldn't outrun a deer but they could take down a dog if given enough time. I found that their sight isn't as good as it seems, but their hearing is much, much better. I learned that they can't help but gather up in a horde, and the dead are never lonely, that their natural inclination is to have a lot of friends. And I discovered that shamblers are never, ever satisfied. They are always hungry. And just when you think you're safe, when you let your guard down—that's when they get you.

I also learned to tell the look of a man that's been bit and the moment the change starts to take hold, the way he shakes like he's got a chill and the way his eyes begin to yellow. I learned that I can be ruthless when I need to, and I can be merciful when I'm able. I learned that there is nothing to fear in the dark if you're smart. And I had no doubt that I was pretty damn clever.

But no matter how much my nightly travels may have taught me, I am still stupid enough to let Katherine tag along.

A clever girl would've found a way to keep Katherine at the school, frightened her off with tales of evening slaughter on the roads, of shamblers and bandits and men that lurk in the shadows at night, ready to steal a girl's virtue.

A smart girl would've just left her behind and taken the eventual punishment when Katherine told Miss Preston about unauthorized visitors and subsequent midnight departures.

But I am a stupid girl, so midnight finds me leading Katherine out the rarely used side door to the summer kitchen behind the school. The door doesn't make a sound when I open it. It's my usual route, and the hinges are well oiled. That doesn't keep Katherine from squeaking, though.

"What?" I whisper, irritated that we haven't even made it outside and she's already working on getting us caught.

"Something ran across my foot."

"Probably just a mouse. Now pipe down before you wake someone."

I head straight toward an abandoned outbuilding on the far edge of the property. It was once used to house the slaves the men's college owned, but it's empty now that slavery—the kind that ended with the War between the States, anyway—is no more. The building is long and low, with a door on either side. I use the door on the opposite end of the school, just in case anyone happens to glance out her window. The moon is high tonight and casts a pale silver over the landscape, painting it in shadows and light. It's a good night for investigating.

It's also a good night to get caught by a teacher doing her rounds on the perimeter fence. I try not to think about that.

Inside of the old slave cabin, I go to a dusty cabinet and take out my personal sickles, a set Red Jack gave me a long time ago as a gift, and an extra set, since Katherine didn't bring any of hers. Both sets are well made, balanced and sharp, and I take care of them so they stay that way. I set them on a rickety table and take out a pair of trousers, tossing them to Katherine.

"Put these on."

She holds them out in front of her, her horror visible in the moonlight coming in through the empty windowpane. "You want me to wear a pair of men's trousers?" Her voice is just short of hysterical.

"Yes."

She shakes her head. "That is the height of indecency. I am not wearing these."

"We're going to be walking through the woods, up and down hills and through underbrush. Skirts get caught on branches and whatnot. Plus, if we do have to fight off a shambler, skirts are a liability. We're less likely to get killed if we can run. You wear them or you stay here." I take out another pair of trousers for myself before I pause. "You better not be wearing a corset."

She sniffs. "I'm not. I learned my lesson, thank you very much." She casts a bit of side-eye at the trousers once more before sighing. "If you tell anyone about this, Jane McKeene, I will make sure you spend the rest of your time at Miss Preston's on housework."

I snort, because it's an empty threat and we both know it.

But I don't say anything more. Sometimes I am a gracious winner.

I pull on my own set of trousers, tucking my sleep shirt in the waistband. Katherine copies my movements. I show her the loops near the waist for weapons and how to secure the waist ties and extra strings at the ankles. And then, after handing her my spare set of sickles, we secure our weapons and are off into the night.

It takes us nearly two hours to go the scant distance to the Spencers' farm because we have to walk slower than a blind turtle. Katherine is skittish as all get out, and I have to remind myself repeatedly that she ain't used to creeping around in the dark like I am. The woods are dense, with thickets and patches of poison ivy that we have to make our way around. Plus, our part of Maryland is hilly. I don't think there's a single flat patch of land, and huffing and puffing up and down those hills takes a while. By the time we finally make it to the Spencers' farm it's closer to sunrise than I'd like.

The Spencers are one of the most prominent families in the area, and very generous to us Preston girls, so I've been out to their homestead a fair few times. The last was in early spring, when Miss Preston sent the older girls round to the local farms to help with clearing the fields once the thaw came and the dead got a mind to start walking again. Mrs. Spencer was always the kindest, bringing out warm milk and biscuits with jam once the killing was done. She also makes an amazing strawberry-rhubarb pie that won a blue ribbon at the county fair a few years back. The thought of something happening to her makes me a little sad, but I shove the emotion down deep. I need to stay sharp.

Red Jack meets us a little ways from the barrier gate to the homestead proper. He wears a rough-spun shirt and trousers for a change, shedding his flashy attire for something a little more sensible. In the pale moonlight I see Katherine's eyes widen as she takes him in. I understand why. Jackson is just as pretty in rough cotton as he is in fine silk. Plus his sleeves are rolled up, revealing his finely muscled forearms. He used to work on the docks, back before he realized he could make more money taking "odd jobs," as he calls them, on the roads between Baltimore and the outer settlements. It's no wonder poor Katherine is smitten with him.

"You two have any trouble?" Red Jack asks, his voice low.

"No. We didn't see a single shambler," Katherine says, her voice loud and disappointed.

"Not for lack of trying," I mutter, shooting her a dark look. Both she and Jackson ignore me.

Red Jack gestures toward the main house. "I walked up and around the property. There's no one there. All of the windows are still intact, and the front door is latched. It's like they left on an errand and never came back."

There's a slight tremor to his voice, barely noticeable.

I don't say anything, because I understand why he's upset. People—especially those that are well off—are heard to move around, try their luck in a different city or settlement. The Spencers could have done just that and taken Lily with them and somehow forgot to tell anyone they were doing so. But I've learned that the simplest explanation is usually the right one. And that means shamblers. I don't care how "safe" these lands are supposed to be.

Jack said that there was no evidence of a break-in, but he couldn't have gotten a good look inside yet. The dead tend to leave a lot of evidence. Very messy evidence. If the Spencers were attacked, as unlikely as that is, we'll know soon enough.

I sigh loudly, dreading the task at hand. I'm tired of seeing people I care about die. "Come on, I'll check out the perimeter, then we'll let ourselves inside to see what's going on."

We walk down toward the homestead on cat feet, quiet except for the sound of our breathing. Even Katherine, who tromped through the woods like she was flushing rabbits, is silent, her footsteps whisper-soft. Shamblers are attracted to sound, so if we are discreet enough, any dead in the area shouldn't even know we're here.

The Spencers' house is a modest thing. It's newer, built in the years after the dead started to walk. You can always tell by the square windows, which are large enough to allow some light but too small to let a body in. Trip wires with early-warning alarms are scattered throughout the yard, but these are clearly marked by stakes in the ground and we step over them easily. On the small porch, there are a couple of rocking chairs and hooks holding sickles, a scythe, and extra-sharp swords within close reach, in case shamblers get through the barrier fence. These sorts of modest protections and alarms have been adequate for settlements in the county these last few years.

Jackson pulls a set of slim metal pieces from his pocket—a lock-picking set. Katherine's brows draw together in a frown, and her lips purse in displeasure. She opens her mouth to say something, but I catch her eye and shake my head. There are some things she's better off not knowing, and the sordid details surrounding that lock-picking set is one of them.

Red Jack unlocks the door easily, and it swings open on quiet hinges. I grip my sickles, ready to swipe at anything that comes out, but nothing does. I look to Jackson and Katherine, both of whom are looking at me.

"Oh, I take it I'm going in first?"

Katherine sniffs. "You do have the highest marks in close-quarters combat."

I swallow a laugh. She has no idea.

I roll my shoulders a couple of times, trying to loosen up the suddenly tense muscles. Then I walk into the dark.

The windows only let in a tiny bit of the moonlight, so it's hard to see anything. I make out a table, a long cold stove, a few chairs around a nearby fireplace. But there's no one in the room, dead or otherwise.

"There's a lamp on the table," Jackson says, his voice close to my ear. It takes everything I have not to jump.

"Well, light it. I can't see a damn thing in this gloom."

"Jane, language," Katherine calls from somewhere behind me.

Jackson walks over to the table and lights the oil lamp. Once it's turned up it's easy to see that the interior of the house is completely undisturbed. There ain't even a dirty dish in the sink. If their disappearance was the work of shamblers, they were the tidiest shamblers I've ever heard of.

"You sure Lily didn't mention anything about them all heading somewhere?" I ask, even though I already know the answer to my question.

Jackson shakes his head. "Their iron pony is still in the barn, stocked full of coal. And look." He gestures to the wall where a portrait of the family hangs—Mr. and Mrs. Spencer and their two little ones, their pale faces staring out at us. If they'd picked up and left, they most definitely would've taken the family photo.

Katherine drags a finger across the ledge of a china hutch. "They've been gone for a while. Either that or Mrs. Spencer is an inadequate housekeeper," she says, holding up a dusty finger. "Why was your sister staying with them, anyway?"

Jackson's jaw tightens, and I answer for him. "Lily was about to turn twelve."

What Katherine knows—what we all know—is that the Negro and Native Reeducation Act mandates that at twelve years old all Negroes, and any Indians living in a protectorate, must enroll in a combat school "for the betterment of themselves and of society." The argument went that we benefitted from compulsory education, as it provides a livelihood for formerly enslaved, who couldn't find gainful employment after the war. Whites, therefore, were excluded from the law, although some went to the combat schools of their own accord, since it was good to know how to protect one's self in these dangerous times. Still, there's a difference between an education officer showing up with a group of armed men and carrying someone off, and their enrolling in a school on their own.

"Lily is fair," Jackson says. "She's passing, like you, Katherine. I figured if she lived with a white family, the education officers would leave her alone. The Spencers are Egalitarians, and they don't truck with the Survivalists and all their nonsense about Negroes being inferior." Jackson sits heavily in one of the chairs. "I just wanted to keep her safe." There's so much heartache in his voice that I almost go to him, almost offer what little comfort I can. But that ain't my place anymore, and I swallow my concern like a bitter draught.

That's when a chorus of bells sounds from out behind the house, and I quickly extinguish the lantern.

Something tripped an alarm.

Jackson is moving toward the back of the house, and Katherine peers out the window. "There are people approaching." She turns around, her expression indistinguishable in the dark. "They don't look like the dead."

I join her at the window, and she's right. A lantern swings back and forth in the night, revealing at least three people. "Those ain't shamblers, but I'm betting they're trouble nonetheless."

Jackson waves us back toward the bedroom. "The Spencers have a shamblers' hole. This way."

We hurry through the house. In the windowless rear bedroom he flips back the rug, revealing a small door in the floor. He pulls it up and we tumble down into the darkness. I feel around, moving forward until my hands brush against a dirt wall. I half expect to kick something soft and yielding in the dark until Red Jack whispers, "They ain't down here. This is the first place I checked when I couldn't find them."

I'm wondering why Jackson dragged us out here in the middle of the night if he's already checked the house thoroughly. But there's no time to ask him now. He pulls the trapdoor shut, and the small space is loud with the sound of our breathing. A shamblers' hole is a last resort when a homestead gets overrun. Sometimes hiding out away from the dead for an hour or so can mean the difference between life and undeath.

The Spencers' hole was built for a family, so there's more

than enough room to move around. I take deep breaths and force my heart to slow, Jackson and Katherine doing the same. Less than a dozen breaths later the sound of boots on the wooden porch echoes through the house, along with voices.

For a moment, I think maybe this is it. Maybe this is my final moment, the scene that leads to my death. But the penny in the hollow of my throat is warm to the touch, and I know that this ain't the end. When it's time for me to die that penny will be cold, of that I have no doubt.

The realization is calming, and my heart finally settles down. Someone grabs my hand in the dark and squeezes. I ain't sure whose hand it is, but I squeeze back anyway. Not because I'm scared, but because it just seems like the right thing to do.

The boots pause for several long moments before advancing into the house. Once inside, it's a lot easier to decipher what the voices are saying.

"I saw a light on in here. I know I did." The boots sound closer, walking toward us. They pause over our heads.

"I didn't see anything. You sure you aren't imagining things? You've been skittish ever since we left. Even tripped over that warning alarm like a greenie." The voice is hoarse and accompanied by a rasping cough. I recognize the second speaker.

Someone grabs my arm, hard. I swallow a yelp. "That's Miss Anderson," Katherine whispers, her breath warm on my ear.

A feeling, half sick and half rage, blooms in my middle. If Miss Anderson is involved, then I know those folks above can't be up to any good.

"Rupert's got a thing about shamblers," a third voice says, low and even. "Too much time out west in the wide open. He thinks he's safer behind the walls in Baltimore than he is out here." There are footsteps, and the voice sounds again from a new place. "Come on, we need to clean out what's left. The mayor wants everything belonging to the Spencers packed up and out of here by morning."

The voices subside, and I lean back against the dirt wall and let myself think. What did that mean? Did the Spencers leave of their own accord? Or did something happen to them, and these people are trying to cover it up? There's no way to tell, and Jackson looks fit to burst as we listen to the people above move in and out of the house.

"That's it," comes a voice from above after a little while. "We don't need to pack up the bigger furniture. Mayor said just their personal items need to be collected. Now, what are we going to do with the rest of this stuff? Sell it?"

There's a cough, and Miss Anderson says, "Have some respect. These aren't pickaninnies we're talking about. The Spencers are a fine upstanding family."

I clench my hands at the slur rolling off of the lips of one of my instructors. I knew there was a good reason I didn't like that woman. If I could deck her I would, but I'm trapped in a hole in the dark, so all I can do is listen as she keeps talking.

"You and a few of your boys can come back tomorrow and get the rest," she continues. "Load it on their pony in the barn and send it along on the next train."

"I ain't coming back here again!" says Rupert. "Are you out of your mind?"

Rupert and Miss Anderson start arguing, and the other man finally interrupts. "Quiet! Both of you. Rupert, grab the trunk. Miss Anderson, would you be so kind as to assist me in a visit to the Johnson homestead? The mayor believes Mr. Johnson has been organizing demonstrations in opposition to his run for Senate, and I find that mid-night visits elicit the most reliable results."

"Of course, Mr. Redfern."

Their footsteps echo as they leave the house. There are a few moments of swearing and thumping as Rupert takes the trunk out, then silence settles back over the night. The sound of our breathing seems to echo as we wait to make sure the trio is gone.

I ain't sure how long we spent in the shamblers' hole, but by the time Jackson opens the door I'm groggy and sorely in need of sleep. He climbs out and comes back with an all clear. I can't see his face in the gloom, but I can tell that he's holding back some feelings by the lack of spring in his step. Who can blame him?

We're quiet until we clear the barrier gate. Jackson locks

it carefully, even though we all know the Spencers ain't never coming back. Katherine holds herself, cupping her elbows in her palms. Once we're within the shelter of the forest I clear my throat. It's likely dangerous to talk in the woods, but there are some things that need saying and no one seems willing to break the silence.

"Well, I always knew Miss Anderson weren't no good."

Katherine's voice comes through the near dark. "So, do you think the Spencers are . . . ?" She can't finish the thought, and Jackson can't speak, either.

"Dead?" I say finally. "Truthfully, I don't know. It was hard to tell from what they were saying, but . . ." Jackson lifts his eyes to mine. "I don't think so. The way Miss Anderson was talking about taking care of their things, it sounded like they're still alive, somewhere. What we do know is that wherever they've gone, Miss Anderson and those men she was with were ordered by the mayor to cover it up."

"Maybe the Spencers were attacked by a big pack of shamblers but they weren't bitten and even though they survived, the mayor doesn't want anyone to know," Katherine suggests. "He doesn't want people to think Baltimore County is unsafe again. So he packed them up and sent them off somewhere against their will."

I shrug. "Maybe. Or maybe they just picked up and moved to a different city on their own, and the mayor doesn't want anyone to know about that, either, seeing as how popular they were. We've all heard stories of folks leaving without so much as a how-do-you-do, though not as much recently. . . . Still, they could have found somewhere they like better than here. Maybe Philadelphia? Wherever it is, it must be pretty nice if they were fine leaving their things behind."

"They didn't leave." Jackson's voice is almost too quiet to hear. "Not on their own. Lily would have gotten word to me."

"Maybe she didn't have the chance. It's not like she could tell a message runner that she's your—"

"You don't know her like I do, Jane," he snaps. "Even if you always think you do."

I don't say anything to that, because what's the point? He ain't going to listen to reason. Jackson might not like it, but if the Spencers did move on, at least they didn't leave his sister behind like unwanted dishes.

"Well, either way, we need to get on back," I say after a long moment. "The sun's coming up." When I go on my nightly escapades I'm usually back soon enough to get a bit of sleep, but that's not happening tonight. The sun peeks across the horizon, shading the world gray as dawn approaches. If it takes half as long to get back as it took to get here, we're going to be much later than I'm comfortable with. I start walking.

"You can't just leave," Jackson begins behind me. "We have to— Jane?"

I freeze. My penny has gone ice-cold.

"What is it?" Jackson says.

"Trouble."

An unmistakable groan-growl echoes through the trees.

"Is that . . . ?" Katherine starts, her voice trailing off.

I turn around, searching for the sound. Jackson clears his throat. "On your left," he says, voice low.

I turn, and sure enough there stands a shambler, lips pulled back in a hungry snarl. It looks like the little white girl I saw along the side of the road a few days back. Guess the patrols didn't take care of her after all. This close it's easier to see details, like the ragged red ribbons at the ends of her braids and her sickly yellow eyes. She's no more than nine or ten years old. I don't recognize her, and that's a mercy. It's hard having to kill the dead you once knew.

I take out my sickles, ready to end her, when Katherine makes a choked sound. "Bide your time," she says, one of the tenets of defense we've learned at Miss Preston's. I'm ready to snap out something rude when I notice the movement in the trees. Behind the little girl is a whole pack of shamblers, their clothing in tatters, their gray skin hanging loose. There are a few colored folks mixed in with the group, but they mostly look white, scarily nondescript and similar in that way shamblers get when they've been not-dead for a while. From their clothing they're originals, people that got turned during the first dark days back during the war, before the armies realized that they had a bigger threat to fight than each other.

I don't even stop to wonder at a pack this large roaming the woods so close to Baltimore. I just spin my sickles in my hand, relishing their comfortable weight. On my right, Katherine has my spare set of sickles out, and on my left, Red Jack has pulled out a long knife from God knows where.

Around my neck, the penny is now cool against my skin, no longer icy. The small shift lets me know that my time ain't up, at least not today.

We take a step forward, and the shamblers attack. They're slow and ungainly, tripping over their own feet, tangling in the dense underbrush, dragging themselves along the ground when they can't find their footing. Old shamblers are the best. They've lost enough of their humanity that they're dog-dumb, attacking without any sort of organization. Newer shamblers are as fast as regular people, but the long dead are like grandmas, shuffling along. Their danger comes from the large packs they travel in. Killing ten people at once may not be difficult for three people trained in combat, but it's hard for a lone person green as the grass.

I cut down the little girl first. The sickle whistles as it slices through the air, singing in the moments before it separates her head from her body. The gore that gushes out ain't blood but a thick black ooze. The smell, of dead and decaying things, is the worst. But this ain't my first waltz, and I keep moving through the pack, letting my blades do the work.

My sickles ain't like regular blades that you'd use in the field. Instead of a crescent moon curve they're a half-moon, the blades weighted and sharpened on both sides to easily cut in either direction. They're designed to separate a head from a body, since that's the quickest way to put a shambler down. I like to call this harvesting, because you can't really kill the dead, can you? Plus, it soothes my soul to think I'm doing some good when I end a shambler, sending them on to their well-deserved immortal rest.

I cut through a woman in an old-fashioned dress, noticing her long bedraggled hair more than her features. When her body falls to the ground I turn to harvest a large man crawling toward me, his mouth opening and closing without making a sound, his clothing that of a field worker. His dark head separates easily from his body. I spin and let my blades cut through the neck of an old white woman lunging for my throat, her stringy gray hair hanging loose. Her slate strands pick up leaves and twigs as her head rolls away from me across the forest floor. It's such an odd detail to notice in the heat of the fight, but that's just how it is sometimes.

And then, there is no more movement.

I breathe heavily, my sickles and hands covered in the inky mess that is a shambler's blood. Katherine removes the head of a bearded man, shoulders heaving as she searches for any more dead. Jack is bending down and wiping his long knife off on a younger woman's dress. Everyone seems fine.

"No bites?" I ask between heavy breaths as I wipe my hands off on my trouser legs. Both Katherine and Jack shake their heads. "All right." I glance at the sky and the increasingly pink horizon. The world had already gone to shades of gray as dawn approached, but now colors are starting to bloom. It didn't take us long to take down the pack, but it was time we didn't have. "Me and Kate are going to have to run back to make it before classes start. We need to meet up again to figure out how we're going to deal with this."

"What's there to figure out? The Spencers are out there somewhere, and my sister is with them." Red Jack's jaw is set, and there's a ruthless glint to his eyes that makes me think he's got murder on the mind.

"That's great and all, but did you hear one clue in that conversation that could tell us for certain that they're still alive, and if so, where they've gone? There's still a lot of country between here and the closest protected city. We set out half-cocked on a rescue mission, we'll get taken down by shamblers before we're five steps past the county line."

"You say 'we' like you're involved in this, Janey-Jane. Like you get a vote."

My temper flares at his dismissive tone. "Oh, so now you don't need my help? After I snuck out and spent most of the night huddled in a shamblers' hole, you can suddenly handle this all by yourself? You're too good for my blade work?" I'd like to carve my initials into his fool face.

Jackson's voice is even. "This is my problem, and I'll handle it myself. I trust you ladies can find your way back to your school."

And just like that, Jackson, the boy I once kissed in the moonlight, is gone, replaced by Red Jack the ruthless criminal. There ain't no arguing with him once he's got his mind set like this. "We'll be fine," I counter. "Don't you worry none about us."

He gives me a curt nod and bows fluidly to Katherine. "Thank you for accompanying us on our trek this evening. It's nice to know that such a beautiful rose can use her thorns effectively."

Katherine nods and gives a polite smile at the compliment. Without a backward glance in my direction, Jack sets off on his own course through the woods.

Katherine looks at me, and I point my sickle behind her. "Road."

She nods, and we walk. Once our feet hit the hard-packed earth we set off in a run, settling into a pace just light enough for speech.

"These . . . sickles . . . are . . . great. Where did you get them?"

I scowl. Katherine would have to ask the one question I don't feel like answering. "The set you have came from Jackson. Keep them. I like these better."

Both sets came from Red Jack, of course. The set that

Katherine holds were a birthday present. The set I hold? A parting gift. There is probably something to be said about the fact that the gift I got when he put me aside was nicer.

I pick up the pace so that there's no more breath for Katherine's asinine inquiries.

My social calendar is always full at Miss Preston's, and the number of fine folks I meet really is a credit to the education I am receiving here. It's true that being a Negro has its drawbacks, but I couldn't tell you what they are—that's how happy I am being taught my place here at Miss Preston's. I may not ever get to be a debutante, but catering to the fine white women of Baltimore is a far more worthy endeavor.

Chapter 10
In Which I Receive an Unwelcome Invitation and Am Forced to Accept It

Katherine and I manage to get back to school, wash up, and change without being discovered. We miss breakfast, and when Miss Duncan asks where we were, Katherine sheepishly says we both overslept and got to our chores late. The excuse works, mostly because everyone knows that Katherine and I don't really get on well. No one would expect her to lie to protect me.

I sleepwalk through the day. I'm dog-tired, and my body

feels twice as heavy as we do our scythe work. There are no fine ladies to watch us today, so the drills are tolerable. After the midday meal we practice shooting, and even though I'm hitting my target, my aim is off. Miss Folsom, the firearms teacher, scowls at my shot grouping.

"Jane, this is sloppy work. Watch your trigger squeeze, girl. An inch isn't such a big deal at close range, but with a rifle that inch becomes several feet."

"Yes, ma'am," I say, swallowing a yawn.

My only consolation is that Katherine is just as mutton-headed as I am. She drops her sickles during our close-combat class, and Miss Anderson raps her ruler on Katherine's knuckles when she dozes off during our tea-serving lesson. It ain't Christian to revel in the misery of others, but I like to make an exception for Katherine.

After our final class of the day I drop off my weapons at the armory and get ready to head to my bed, using my study time to doze before dinner. If I don't get some sleep, I'm going to pass out in my soup.

I've just lain down and started to snooze when someone shakes me awake. "The building better be on fire," I grumble.

"Miss Preston wants to see us." Katherine sounds as tired as I feel, and I groan as I climb out of bed and follow her down the hall.

We drag ourselves into the headmistress's office. All my exhaustion slips away when I see Miss Anderson and the big

Indian man from the lecture standing there. Miss Preston is nowhere to be found. I straighten, and the man's gaze slips over me. Even with the corners of his mouth pulled down in distaste he's eye-catching. I try to imagine him with feathers in his dark hair and wearing beaded buckskin like in the newspaper serials. I just can't do it. The clothes he wears, homespun shirt and trousers, suit him.

He doesn't look much older than me and Katherine, his brown skin unlined. I wonder if he went to the Indian school up in Pennsylvania, and if he did, how it compares to Miss Preston's. I don't know much about how the Indian schools work, but I've heard they're less focused on teaching folks how to kill the dead than they are civilizing them, whatever that means. It makes me curious about that impassive man's life. Did he come here to Baltimore to seek his fortune? Or is he here against his will?

A wracking cough pulls my attention away from my perusal of the Indian man. Miss Anderson wheezes as she coughs, a handkerchief pressed to her lips.

"Miss Anderson, are you well? You don't sound so good."

She gives one last cough and shoots me an arsenic-laced glare. "My health is of no concern to you, Jane McKeene."

"Well, I just hope it ain't tuberculosis. The nights have been chilly this year, and it wouldn't take much for a cough to become something more if you'd been out in the cold."

I can feel Katherine's glare and the man raises an eyebrow

in my direction, but I keep my expression mild. Auntie Aggie used to say I was like as not to poke Satan with a stick just for fun. Guess not much has changed.

Mostly I'm just thinking about Miss Anderson being in cahoots with the mayor and whatever he's done with Lily and the Spencers, as well as her comment about pickaninnies, and every mean-spirited thing she's done to me. It takes all the self-restraint I have to keep from launching myself at her and beating her senseless. But I'm saved from doing anything untoward by Miss Preston entering the room. She takes in the tableau before her and frowns. "Is something amiss?"

"No, ma'am," Katherine says, a smile breaking out over her face, making her look like an angel from a painting. My anger and disgust grows a little more, fed by a mean streak of envy. I grit my teeth and say nothing. Katherine didn't pick the face she was born with, and it ain't her fault her perfect smile makes me want to break things. My dark feelings are my own problem, and I aim to keep them that way.

Miss Preston sits heavily in her chair with a sigh. "Well, then, I suppose we should get to the reason as to why we're here." She shuffles through a stack of papers on her desk and pulls out a lovely cream-colored vellum envelope. "In recognition of your . . . heroics at the Baltimore University lecture, the mayor's wife has invited you girls to a formal dinner. A few of her close friends have lost their Attendants lately, and she would like you to augment her household staff in order to guarantee her guests' safety."

Katherine gives me a wide-eyed look, but I don't feel any of the excitement I see on her face. The penny under my blouse has gone cold.

Miss Preston continues. "This is an excellent opportunity to present yourself to the finest ladies in all of Maryland. Miss Anderson and Mr. Redfern here will be taking you to be fitted for Attendants' wear. At Mayor Carr's expense, of course. Miss Anderson will also be accompanying you to dinner as your chaperone to ensure that you represent the school with dignity and honor."

My penny is a snowball at the hollow of my neck, and I ain't at all encouraged by Miss Preston glossing over the fact that multiple Baltimore Attendants have been killed, presumably within the city limits. All my anger at whatever Miss Anderson and the mayor have done with Lily and the Spencers disappears, replaced by fear.

I'm shaky and out of sorts as I take a deep breath and let it out. "Miss Preston, I'm honored by the invitation, but I'm afraid I must decline." My words come out too fast, my tongue tripping over syllables. I see my end in this fine invitation, and I ain't a hog to go happily to the slaughter, no matter how pretty the ax.

Miss Preston opens her mouth to speak and I continue, in

an attempt to cover my lack of grace and decorum. "What I mean is, it would be terrible of us to accept such a generous offer without including Miss Duncan. She was instrumental in putting down the restless dead, and I just don't feel right taking advantage of such an invitation without her."

"I'm sure our honorable mayor would be happy to include your teacher as well." Mr. Redfern's voice is a low rumble, and I barely manage to keep myself from jumping in surprise. I'd forgotten he was even standing there in the corner, as intent as I was on not ending up at the mayor's dinner.

Miss Preston smiles. "Well, it's settled then. You girls will be excused from classes tomorrow for your fitting, and next week you will attend dinner at the mayor's residence." Miss Preston levels a withering look at me. "Try to conduct yourselves in a matter befitting a Miss Preston's girl. After all, a contract with a good family is the difference between a future and, well . . ." She trails off, giving us knowing smiles.

"Thank you, Miss Preston! We are doubly blessed, and we will not let you down," Katherine chirps in answer, all but bouncing as we take our leave.

Behind us, Miss Preston asks Mr. Redfern in a low voice, "Have you or the mayor heard anything further on the Edgars' disappearance?"

I whirl around, perhaps too quickly considering that I ain't supposed to know anything about missing families, but

I meet Miss Anderson's eyes. Her smug expression convinces me to keep on walking out of the room and unleashes a barrage of worry that unsettles my stomach.

She's got the look of a cat that just caught a mouse. No wonder I feel like squeaking.

*Momma, I do hope you'll share news of Rose Hill in your next
letter. How is everyone? Did the cabbages and okra do well this year?*

~~*Do you still love me?*~~

~~*Do you still regret having me?*~~

Do you miss me half as much as I miss you?

Chapter II
In Which I Remember Rose Hill and
My Momma's Sworn Enemy

That night, exhausted and preoccupied with the mayor's
untimely invitation, I do the same thing I always do when
I'm fretful: I dream of Rose Hill, and of Rachel, the only
person I ever knew to hate my momma.

My momma is an unusual woman. She didn't much like
the whole concept of slavery no matter how honorable it
was, and there were rumors that she was sore disappointed
with her husband, the major, when he left her to fight for

the Confederacy. But the strangest thing about Momma, the thing that made some of the neighbors smile tightly and alienated all the rest, is Momma's rumored penchant for field hands—the stronger, the darker, the better. They said she took them to bed like some kind of plantation Delilah, stealing their strength in order to keep herself young and strong.

It wasn't true, but that didn't stop tongues from wagging. I discovered later that, even before I was born, Momma had a reputation for going out and buying the worst of the worst at the auctions: the runaways; the dullards; the cheapest, lousiest Negroes you could find. It was how she spent her time, buying up as many folks as she could, and rumor was she damn near bankrupted her and the major doing it. If there was a mother and her children on the block, she would buy the whole lot, cutting a deal with the auctioneers before the family ever went up for bidding. Neighbors would joke, "I'm gonna sell you my girl Bella, she ain't worth a lick," and the next thing you know Bella would be in the kitchen baking bread. Momma never let the slave patrols on the property, even when they were chasing down a neighbor's runaway, and the one time the fellas did trespass she had the kennel master set the dogs on them. It was an all-around curious way of doing business, but Momma was rich enough that the neighbors didn't say much.

Not long after I was born, everyone in the county pretty much suspected Momma had birthed me, the height of scandal in a place like Haller County, Kentucky. During the beginning of the Years of Discord, Momma made it her business to always help a neighbor in need, especially as Rose Hill flourished, so most folks found Momma's peccadilloes less important than her willingness to ride out with a team and help clear a field of dead.

And if folks could overlook the rumors of a white woman birthing a Negro, well, they could forgive just about anything, couldn't they?

It was something I didn't much know about or understand until I was old enough to read, and to learn how to eavesdrop properly. The first time I ever realized that a white woman keeping time with a colored man was cause for scandal, I was six or seven. And the only reason I ever knew of my mother's transgressions was because of Rachel, who hated my momma more than anyone else in the world.

Rachel was mad that day she got to flapping her gums because Auntie Aggie had set her to peeling potatoes, a task that she thought was beneath her. In Rachel's mind, every ill that befell her was the work of someone else. In this case, Momma, who had told Auntie Aggie that she wanted a nice mashed potato with dinner.

"You know the missus weren't no lady afore she married the major, now don't you? She ain't nothing but rabble, she ain't got no class like Missus Hooper, my first mistress, God rest her soul." Rachel had no love for my momma; all her loyalty was for the major. The major had bought Rachel from a plantation down the way before he went off to the war, and she always liked to say how Momma wasn't doing things right. Not enough whippings, not enough discipline, too many Negroes forgetting their place. Rachel had a set way as to how things should've been on Rose Hill, and in Rachel's mind Momma was too soft because she didn't play favorites and she didn't hand out nearly enough beatings.

One of the other aunties, Auntie Eliza, once told me it was because Rachel was the major's favorite before he went to war, and she liked the easy life he gave her. Rachel had adjusted to being owned, to being property, and she didn't like the new situation, where she wasn't nothing but a house servant with wages, a servant that had to work just as hard as everyone else. Slavery had been illegal since the Great Concession, that famous day President Jefferson Davis and the remaining Confederate states surrendered so that President Lincoln would issue the Writ of Concession, sending General Ulysses Grant and the Union troops on their famous march across the South, burning every shambler and abandoned homestead they found and saving Dixie from utter ruin. Slavery had come to an end thanks to President Lincoln and the undead plague, but there were still folks like Rachel that didn't quite know what to do with all that freedom.

At the time, I had no idea why Rachel was so angry, but I figured it was like how Momma always made sure I ate dinner with her and how she taught me how to read in the evenings, while the other kids got to go play or help fix the barrier fences that kept out the shamblers. Rachel had been special when the major was around, and now she wasn't.

But Auntie Aggie said that Rachel couldn't help the way she was, that she'd had a hard life before she came to Rose Hill, and the only way she knew how to act was a vicious kind of way. "Surviving can make people right mean," Auntie Aggie told me. "You stay away from that viper. She don't have nothing but ill will toward you and your momma."

But I couldn't avoid Rachel all the time. The kitchens were where I spent most of my day, since Momma didn't want me out beyond the interior fence, especially after what happened to poor Zeke. So I got to hear more of Rachel's gossiping than I cared to.

"The missus was nothing but trash, singing for coin, before the major lifted her up to being something. And look at how she repays him, rolling around with field darkies like the whore of Babylon. There's an order to things," Rachel said, giving me a hard look where I stood helping Auntie Eliza knead bread. Rachel thought there was a hierarchy that should be followed: field workers, house slaves, mistress, and master. It didn't matter that we were all free, that Momma made sure to pay everyone a small wage each week for their hard work. The bad old ways were still alive and well in Rachel's brain, and anything that flaunted that order was a terrible thing.

Like me.

"That's the reason the dead don't stay down, you know. The whole world is turned upside down. Darkies are free as white folks, don't know their place anymore. If they did, maybe things would go back to normal."

"She uses that word one more time I'm going to throttle her," Auntie Eliza said, giving Rachel a hard look. Auntie Eliza's husband worked out in the fields, and no one talked bad about the field workers when she was around.

"You ain't the only one," muttered Auntie Betsy, who was plucking a chicken.

No one much liked Rachel, but she didn't let that stop her from carrying on. "Mark my words, when the major come home, that woman is gonna be in for a rude awakening. That's all I'm saying. There's gonna be a reckoning when the major comes back." She kept peeling potatoes and tapping her foot, as though she'd like nothing more than to run right out the door.

And maybe, if Rachel had left, things wouldn't have been so bad when the major finally did return, eight years after the end of the War between the States and smack dab in the midst of the Years of Discord, bringing a discord all his own to Rose Hill Plantation.

When I wake in the morning alone in my bedroom at Miss Preston's, groggy and with memories of the treacherous Rachel scratching at my brain, I'm in an even worse mood.

But more than that, I am certain that nothing good can come of this dinner at the mayor's house. Why else would I have dreamed of Rachel, the woman that almost got me and my momma killed?

The curriculum at Miss Preston's stresses loyalty, and I have to say that my dedication to my fellow students is incomparable. Of course, they share my sentiments. I daresay that there is not a thing Miss Preston's girls won't do for one another.

Chapter 12
In Which I Become an Unwilling Co-conspirator

The fittings go without incident. I fidget all the way to the dressmaker's and back, expecting at any moment the driver will pull the iron pony over and Miss Anderson and Mr. Redfern will slaughter us for what we know. But, despite the tension I sensed in Miss Preston's office, they seem completely unconcerned with both the upcoming dinner party and with me and Katherine. That doesn't ease my worry, though. They could just be playing the long game, biding their time, waiting to end me and Katherine until after I've relaxed my guard.

None of that makes any sense—if they somehow suspected we'd been there at the Spencers', we'd likely know already—but that's the way it is with panic. It takes you by the throat and doesn't much listen to reason.

Days go by, and after turning the events of the previous week over in my head, I can't decide how I feel about the mystery of Lily and the Spencers. The longer we go without word from them, the more disconcerting the lack of news; but then, the more days pass without any further panic or shambler sightings, the more likely it seems the Spencers simply did leave for another city, whether by choice or by force. It's an unsettling conundrum, and I don't like it one bit. It sure would set my mind at ease if Lily were to find a way to tell us what happened.

By the afternoon before the mayor's dinner party, Katherine's anxiety seems to have retreated into the background as well, and she is beside herself with excitement. She chatters about it to the other girls, and when they tire of listening to her she finds me and talks my ear off.

"What do you think Mrs. Carr will wear? I wish we could wear a corset, or even a bustle." She flips the pages in her catalog and settles down next to me in the grass. I'm sitting under the big oak out back, what my momma used to call a hanging tree, the branches spread apart and thick and growing parallel to the ground, a tree perfect for climbing or stringing up a man. When I first got to Miss Preston's I used to run off and hide in the branches of this tree, climbing as high as I could and hiding amongst the dense boughs. Eventually Miss Anderson discovered my hiding spot. She waited until I finally came down, taking the strap to me so bad that I couldn't sit for a week. Maybe that's why there ain't no love lost between me and the woman. Even my earliest bad memories of the school are tied to her.

Katherine nudges me. "See, they've modified it so it collapses and you can sit down. Isn't that just marvelous? And look at the silhouette." She thrusts the fashion catalog at me so that I can see the bustle, which juts out of the rear of the woman's hips and makes her look like a demented wasp.

I push the catalog away. "Where'd you get that?"

Katherine gives me a long look before sniffing indignantly. "Really, Jane, as though you're the only one to smuggle in contraband. Everyone has a little something, you're just the only one who gets caught."

I cover my face with my hands and pray to the Lord above for strength. "Kate, has it occurred to you how odd it is that the mayor would invite us to a formal dinner, just like that? It's been over two weeks since the lecture, and he didn't seem to think much of our heroics until a week later. Not to mention the fact that he's embroiled in some scandal involving the Spencers."

She gives me a narrowed-eyed look and sighs, pulling back her catalog and flipping through the pages. "I don't find it odd at all. He's obviously a busy man. And his wife is known for the care and dedication she takes when planning the details of her soirees. Anyway, how do you know the mayor didn't help the Spencers start a new life somewhere fine? All this panic is completely unnecessary. Besides, we'll be there as Attendants, not as real guests. It's not at all the same." Her gaze gets all dreamy and faraway. "I wonder how many courses there will be. My mother went to a dinner once where they had seventeen courses. Seventeen! She said by the end she was so stuffed she could barely even taste the food. Can you imagine?"

I perk up at the mention of Katherine's mom. She's as much a mystery amongst the girls at Miss Preston's as my own mother. "Is that so? Does your mother go to a lot of dinner parties?"

Katherine's expression shutters and she bends back down to her magazine. "A few. What about your mother, Jane?" Her tone is mild, but it's clear she's avoiding my question.

"Oh, my momma's been to a few." None since the last dinner party held at Rose Hill Plantation, though. It was just after the major returned, battle weary and grim, talking about the end of the world and God's judgment. Momma sat me next to her at the table during the dinner as she always did, stroking my hair like a favorite pet. The neighbors were used to this behavior, since they'd been to dinner at Rose Hill a number of times. It seemed normal to all of us, but the major's expression grew stormy throughout the courses. When momma had me grab the Bible after dessert to read a few passages to the neighbors, the major's simmering temper exploded.

"You taught a darkie to read? Have you lost your goddamn mind, Ophelia?" he screamed while the neighbors watched, bug-eyed. Momma sent me off to Auntie Aggie to get tucked into bed before she escorted the neighbors out, making excuses for the major, talking about the stress of war and the horror of watching half of your regiment get slaughtered only to rise up and start eating the other half.

The neighbors nodded and made polite clucking noises as they walked to their iron ponies. They believed my momma, but they hadn't felt the way she tensed when the major yelled, or the way she gripped my arms when he called me a darkie. I was old enough to know that things were about to get bad at Rose Hill. But I wasn't afraid of the major.

No, I'd seen what happened when momma didn't get her way. It never ended well.

Two days later, the major was a shambler with a bullet in his skull and I had my first harvest at ten years old.

"Jane, are you even listening?" Katherine's sigh jolts me from my reverie. There's an ache in my chest from thinking about my momma for too long, and I curse myself for getting lost in the past. Now I'm going to be maudlin for the next few days, remembering times gone by. This is why it's better not to think about Rose Hill at all.

"Jane!"

"What?"

"I do believe that's Jackson waving to you from the tree line."

I glance up, and sure enough there's Red Jack, jumping around on the other side of the barrier fence like he hasn't got a lick of sense. I shake my head and point him toward the back of the school, through the trees to the old slave cabin. We used to meet back there when we were something more than uneasy friends, and I hope he remembers the spot. If anyone from the house sees him, they're going to wonder why a boy is tromping around the school grounds, and I'll be in hot water.

I wait a full minute or so before climbing to my feet and going to the back of the yard. Katherine stays put, flipping pages and muttering to herself about my inability to appreciate good fashion. The sound of fighting comes from the practice grounds as I cut toward the back of the property. The younger girls have their first evaluations coming up at the end of the month. How they rate will determine their rankings, and those rankings will one day make the difference between eking out a living on one of the mayor's cleanup crews or an assignment as a lady's Attendant, offering protection and companionship while living the good life.

I manage to make my way to the barrier fence without discovery, and Red Jack is there, leaning against the tall wrought iron and looking like he hasn't a care in the world. His nonchalance is belied by his split lip, swollen eye, and the blood dotting the front of his waistcoat.

"Uh-oh, did Harvey Parker finally catch you fooling around with his wife?"

Jackson scowls at me. "Very funny. No, this is what happens when you try to sneak into Mayor Carr's estate."

"You went trespassing at the mayor's? Near as I figure, you're lucky to still be breathing."

"That's the same thing his boys told me. Luckily one of them is a fan of the dog races, and he did me a favor in exchange for making sure a few of the well-known puppies never make it to the track to run again." Red Jack winces as he shifts his weight from one foot to the other, hand holding his side.

Katherine gasps, stealing up behind us like a shambler in the night, me near to jumping out of my skin from the surprise. I scowl at her, but she ignores me. "You aren't going to kill a dog are you? That's awful."

Jackson raises a single brow at her. "Of course not, I ain't a monster. There are lots of kids in the city who'd like to claim a stray as their own, that's all. And you'd be surprised how easy it is to switch out a winner for a similar-looking loser."

"You came all the way here, half-broken, just to tell me that the mayor's boys almost stomped you into mush and that you're planning on fixing a few races in the future?" I ask, interrupting. I ain't at all endeared to the friendliness between Jackson and Katherine. It's petty, but I'm okay with that.

Jackson shifts slightly and sighs. "You heard those people at the Spencers'. Mayor Carr has something to do with Lily's disappearance. I need to get into his house and figure out what."

I open my mouth to offer some paltry platitude, when I'm interrupted by Katherine saying, "Maybe we could help. We're going there for dinner."

I shoot Katherine my best *Are you stupid?* glare, but Jackson's already perked up. "Going where for dinner? Mayor Carr's?"

Katherine nods, bouncing up onto the balls of her feet and back down again. "Yes! We got invited to this fancy dinner party on account of saving so many folks at the lecture a couple of weeks ago."

Jackson looks at me and I shake my head. "We're going as Attendants. Fancy servants with sharp weapons. But you didn't want our aid before, and we ain't going to have time to help now with whatever poppycock plan you dream up. Plus, I ain't so sure this whole invite is on the up and up. We'll have our hands full just taking care of ourselves."

Katherine sighs heavily. "You have such a morbid outlook, Jane. That doesn't make any sense. Good Attendant positions aren't getting any easier to land. This is a real opportunity."

"Nothing those Survivalists offer is an 'opportunity,'" I mutter.

"When are you two supposed to go?" Red Jack asks, a familiar twinkle in his eye. He is planning something, and whatever it is ain't going to be good.

"Tomorrow," Katherine says. "We even got new dresses. It is going to be quite the event."

Jackson nods, and just like that I know I'm in for some kind of mischief. I glance at Katherine, hoping maybe I can convince her this is a terrible idea, but she's just giving Red Jack this friendly grin and I bury my face in my hands. Despite my best intentions I'm about to be sucked into some kind of high drama.

I am surrounded by nothing but suicidal muttonheads.

Momma, I do believe that the manners and etiquette taught at Miss Preston's may be some of the best instruction in the whole state of Maryland, if not all of the United States. Honestly, where else do Negro girls get to truly learn their place: serving the fine white folks of the world and keeping them safe?

Chapter 13
In Which I Attend a Rather Eventful Dinner

The mayor's iron pony picks us up at half past four. Dinner is to begin at five thirty with cocktails, and Miss Anderson doesn't want to be late. There's murder in her eyes when she talks about how grand the mayor's dinner is going to be. And the wide smile she gives when Katherine and I climb into the passenger compartment does not help the anxiety clawing its way through my guts. Not one bit.

Katherine is chatty as a magpie on the way to the mayor's

house, and even Miss Duncan looks a bit fatigued from attempting to share in her good humor. Katherine, however, is plain radiant. Her gold-streaked curls are swept into an Attendant's bun high on her head. Escaped ringlets soften the harsh style. Her Attendant's formal dress is a pale pink that compliments her golden skin perfectly and falls to her knees; the undertrousers are a darker pink, and the stockings and boots are cream. Her white gloves, which I refused to wear because they made my hands feel clumsy, are effortlessly elegant. A jab of jealousy hits me every time I look over at her. She looks like some kind of delicious confection. Nobody needs to be that pretty, especially in silly Attendant's garb.

My dark thoughts are misplaced, though. It's only because of Katherine's help that I ain't looking too bad myself. My Attendant's garb is done in shades of green. The dress is an emerald that sets off the deep bronze of my skin in a very nice way, while the undertrousers are a lighter shade, my stockings striped green and white, and my boots brown. I've never had such a lovely dress, the fit snug enough to let me fight yet modest enough not to cause scandal. My sickles—the fancy ones from Red Jack, not the ungainly practice ones from school—are strapped into a fine leather belt tooled to carry such things, the holster on the belt empty, since Mayor Carr doesn't much care for guns in his estate. There are even pockets sewn into the skirt, a request the dressmaker was happy to oblige, and I've hidden *Tom Sawyer* in one just in case I find time to read some later. Katherine helped me do something with my stubborn curls, using a pair of hot tongs to subdue the mess into the required Attendant's bun.

When she'd showed me what she'd done in the mirror, I'd laughed. "Well, look at that. I look right proper."

"Don't worry, Jane, you could never pass for proper," Katherine had said, her tone teasing instead of harsh. Wonder of all wonders, I do believe we are becoming friends.

We arrive at the mayor's estate safe and sound, which is somewhat of a surprise, what with all of Katherine's talking and what I am certain is impending doom in Miss Anderson's treacherous eyes. We get out, and Katherine takes a deep breath. "Jane, look at it. It's breathtaking."

Mayor Carr's house is quite impressive. The barrier fence that surrounds the grounds is made of wrought iron at least ten feet tall, and I wonder how Jackson was able to scale such a high fence. Dogs patrol the grass around the property, sniffing the ground. I've heard of such dogs, they're similar to the dogs the slave patrols used to hunt down runaways in the old days. These dogs are trained to alert on shamblers, barking loudly and getting right vicious when they smell the undead. But right now? They just look like normal floppy-eared dogs.

Still, I make a point not to get too close.

The house itself is monstrously huge. It's equally as big as our school, but tobacco fields, not woodland, surround the back acreage. The mayor's house is newer and made of a white stone that rises up four stories, the roof topped by a plethora of cupolas and gables, looking very fancy and imposing. But there's something else here that catches my eye, something even more impressive than the size of the house.

Electric lights.

I've seen electricity before, of course—word of Mr. Edison's experiments in New Jersey had made their way down the Eastern Seaboard and there had even been a demonstration a year or so back here in Baltimore. I've never heard of them installed in a private home, though, and yet here they are, lighting up the pathway to the entrance. I couldn't help but stare.

This is the house of a man used to being followed and obeyed, a man who has enough people between him and the shambler threat to never feel fear.

Miss Anderson and Miss Duncan lead the way up the front walk. Katherine and I keep a few paces behind, as taught. She walks with the grace and carriage of a true lady; I slouch along, hands resting on the hilts of my sickles, ready to draw them at the first sign of trouble.

Both of our instructors wear sedate, dove-gray dresses, but even the plain attire ain't enough to detract from Miss Duncan's beauty; Mr. Redfern's eyes settle on her as soon as we enter the sitting room where most of the attendees have gathered for drinks. Coming over to greet our party, he's the spitting image of the civilized savage the papers are always discussing: well-cut jacket, fashionable waistcoat, hair pulled back in a queue, well-worn boots, and a Bowie knife strapped to his waist. The perfect combination of gentleman and ruthless killer, just like the main character in some frontier adventure. He wears it like a costume, and I get the feeling Mr. Redfern also likes to use the low expectations of people to his advantage. Either way, it is most definitely a style that works for him, judging from the way Miss Duncan lights up. While Miss Anderson and Mr. Redfern exchange pleasantries, I note that he wears the knife on his right side. Mr. Redfern is left-handed, an interesting fact that I file away for later.

Mr. Redfern's eyes barely even take in the rest of us before he bows deeply to Miss Duncan. "It is a pleasure to have your company for the evening meal, ladies. If you would follow me, I would be happy to make introductions."

Miss Duncan, for her part, smiles widely. "Thank you, sir. I'm afraid I'm at a loss, because I never got the privilege of your name." The two of them make eyes at each other for a minute, sharing a secret.

Mr. Redfern smiles. "My apologies. I am Daniel Redfern."

Miss Duncan gives a quick curtsy. "Pleased to make your acquaintance, Mr. Redfern. Amelia Duncan."

I don't know who they think they're fooling with this act, but I'm convinced utterly that they are already well acquainted. Miss Duncan knows Mr. Redfern, but how? She catches me scowling at her and raises a questioning eyebrow. I smooth my expression and turn my attention back to the introductions.

Miss Duncan gestures at me and Katherine. "I trust you already know the girls."

"Yes, we have met." Mr. Redfern nods politely at Miss Anderson and Katherine before his eyes settle on me, his pleasant expression going hard. "Follow me," he says.

I stand there, baffled, as they all file off to meet the crème de la crème of Baltimore's elite. It might be my imagination, but I do believe this is the third time Mr. Redfern has looked at me as though he'd like nothing more than to use me as shambler bait.

I take my time following for the introductions, getting a feel for the house before making my way through the crowd. The sitting room is large, and off to the side is a massive dining room with seating for forty. The rooms here are lit by regular old gas lamps; I suppose the mayor put the electric ones outside to show off to guests and passersby. I watch as Mr. Redfern introduces Katherine and the Misses Duncan and Anderson to a group of women clustered together like a group of chattering hens, their broad chests puffed out in self-importance. One glance at their faces has me walking in the opposite direction.

Momma always said a healthy serving of scorn before

dinner keeps a girl slim.

I remain posted up near the doorway while Katherine and the instructors circulate through the crowd. From here I can see right into the dining room and the majority of the sitting room while being blissfully ignored.

In the dining room servants are putting out place settings. A pasty-complexioned man barks out orders to the servants, most of them darker than me. They're older, and they have the hangdog look I associate with the folks who came up enslaved, who never knew a taste of freedom until it was too late for them to properly embrace it. But one of the men walks with his head a little too high, as though he knows his worth. He's lighter than the rest, his shoulders thrown back in a proud way, a sparkle of mischief in his too-light eyes.

Red Jack.

He looks out of place in a servant's white shirt and jacket, gloves on his hands. The bruising on his face is barely noticeable, no doubt covered up by cosmetics from one of the working girls he knows. What does he think he's doing, trying to hide in plain sight when the mayor's boys roughed him up not two days ago? He sees me enter and pauses for a moment, raising a single eyebrow in a way that says, *Look at you, all cleaned up.* I give him my best glare, and he just winks at me.

Watching the preparations for dinner causes a lump to rise up in my throat. A wave of homesickness like I've never felt washes over me, and I place a hand on my middle. Sudden tears threaten, and I blink hard to force them away. It's been so long since I've been to Rose Hill that I wonder if the whole memory ain't some kind of fever dream.

Does my momma even miss me? All my memories of Rose Hill are filled with her—her voice, her delicate beauty. But here, so many miles from home, I have to wonder if the place even exists. For all the letters I post to her regularly, Momma hasn't written me in over ten months.

Is she even still alive? I could be writing to a ghost. Or worse, a shambler.

It's a question I've refused to ask myself. I don't want to think about what it would do to my world if Momma is dead. The only thing that's kept me going at Miss Preston's is the way Momma looked at me when the truant officer pulled me away toward the waiting pony. "Be the best. Learn what you need to learn and come back to me," she'd said. So I will.

Now, I'm almost ready to graduate from Miss Preston's, but I have no idea if there even is a Rose Hill to return to anymore. What is my future? This, right here, standing at the edge of a room like a piece of furniture?

The dinner bell rings, jarring me out of my reverie. I slip out of the dining room and into the gathering area, falling back to where the ladies mill about, waiting for their escorts. Katherine looks over as I sidle up, wearing her lemon-eating face.

"Where have you been?" she whisper-yells at me.

"I was right there in the doorway, watching the entrances. Why're you so out of sorts?"

Katherine just gives a quick shake of her head, and I shrug. Whatever's amiss, she ain't sharing.

"Well, Jackson is in the dining room, by the by, all decked out like a servant." I glance over in the direction of the white ladies, who talk to each other behind fans and gloved hands. They cast us curious glances that ain't the least bit friendly. I look around the room and frown. "Where are their girls?"

Katherine glances around as well. "That is an excellent question, Jane. Perhaps you would have heard how most of them were dismissed after their cowardly behavior at the lecture, if you had joined us in the sitting room."

"They dismissed their girls? Just like that?"

Katherine adjusts her gloves and ducks her head in respectful acknowledgment to a young fellow that can't seem to stop staring at her. "Just like that. But get this: apparently there is some sort of scandal with folks going missing. The Edgars never made it home from Miss Preston's two weeks ago. Their pony was overrun and they were consumed by shamblers! All things you would know if you hadn't been off skulking about."

"I was watching the entrance—"

Katherine silences me with a single glare. "There's something going on here. Between the Edgars and the Spencers . . . Keep your head about you, Jane. And in the meantime, don't ruin this opportunity for me."

Folks line up to enter the dining room, the mayor and his wife at the front of the line. Katherine and I stand along the wall at attention, but even though we're doing just what we're supposed to, I can feel Miss Anderson's glare burrowing into me, and I stand a little straighter. I ain't going to afford that woman an excuse to give me any grief. But mostly, I don't want to ruin things for Katherine. The mayor and his Survivalist pals might be as corrupt as the night is long, but this is the life she wants, and even though I'm lukewarm on her, I won't do anything to stand in the way of her future.

Formal dinners require a procession from the sitting rooms into the dining room, a process I find to be the height of silliness. All the men and women pair off and go marching in to eat food that's like as not gotten cold by the time they get there.

A handsome young swank comes to offer his arm to Katherine, and she reddens. "Oh, no, I'm sorry, sir. I'm an Attendant." The man looks like he's about to object to her polite refusal, but then he catches an older woman's eye and moves off to escort a homely girl in a yellow dress instead.

Once everyone has filed into the dining room Katherine and I follow the dinner party in. "Well, that was a whole barrelful of awkward," I say.

"I have no idea what you are talking about," Katherine

says stiffly, her eyes darting around like she's afraid she might be on the dinner menu.

We take up our places along the wall opposite the serving board, a space left vacant for serving girls and Attendants. Someone clears his throat loudly next to me. I look to my left and all but groan.

"Mr. Redfern."

"Indeed, Miss McKeene."

"You here to keep an eye on us? It would be difficult to steal the silver when everyone's using it."

His lip twitches. "You aren't the only one working tonight."

I nod. "Well, then, what exactly are we supposed to do?"

"Wait and watch our betters eat." The man crosses his arms, and there's a recognizable bitterness to his voice that asks for no response.

The first course is served, a cream-based soup the servants ladle out from a large tureen. I sniff the air. Crab bisque. It looks heavenly. Mr. Redfern watches me intently, and I shrug. "What?" I ask.

"You aren't missing anything," he says. "What they're eating is a little past it's prime, carted in days ago from the docks. You girls eat better out at the school."

My stomach growls, and I shift. "Would that we *had* eaten."

Mr. Redfern shrugs. "Lesson learned I suppose."

It's the first time he's been anything but dismissive to me, and I seize the opportunity to pry. "What tribe are you from, Mr. Redfern?"

"Lenape. I doubt you've heard of us, my people don't exactly get featured in the weekly serials."

"Is Redfern a Lenape name?"

His lips tighten. "No, it was the name given to me by a teacher at the school I was sent to when I was six."

I brighten and cling tight to the fact that we have something in common. "Did you go to a combat school?"

He doesn't look at me as he answers. "They called it an industrial school, but yes."

"What was it like?"

"They took me from my family, cut my hair, beat me every time they felt like it, and sent me to work for the mayor when I was eighteen." His expression is still calm.

"Sounds familiar," I say before I consider my words too carefully.

His eyes widen slightly, and he looks straight ahead once more. "You should spend less time conversing and more time listening."

"You don't like me very much, and I ain't sure why. I've done nothing to earn it." His words have opened up an ugly feeling in me, part rage at the unfairness of it all, part anguish, and I don't know what to do with it but throw it back at Mr. Redfern.

"I've seen you skulking on the county roads in the dead of

night, Miss McKeene. Do you know they call you the Angel of the Crossroads, the people you save?"

I get an uncomfortable feeling like I'm sliding backward down a slope into a deep hole that I dug my own self. If people are whispering about me, that isn't good. Stories have power, and how long will it be before Miss Preston hears about my nocturnal exploits?

Mr. Redfern continues. "I don't like you because you're arrogant and self-important. You could be so much better than you are, but you're too selfish to see it."

There ain't much I can say to that. His words sting, and he isn't even looking at me to determine their impact. Next to me, Katherine hasn't said a word during our entire exchange, just kept watch over the white folks eating their meals. Seems like as good a plan as any, so I look straight ahead and wish the time away.

The servants return to clear the plates and set down the next course, a fruit compote with cheese melted on top. Then there's a fish course that smells like something died, yet all those fine gentlemen and ladies gobble it up. All the while, there's a fierce hollowness gnawing at my insides and I try to imagine a life of this, watching fine people eat while I nigh on starve to death. It's the first time I've considered what the life of an Attendant might truly be like. It ain't a comforting thought.

Up to now I've been focused on whatever mischief Jackson

is getting mixed up with, Mr. Redfern's inscrutable glare, and the food everyone has been eating. I've been so preoccupied that I've just now noticed Miss Anderson's companion, a sickly pale man who is draining his third glass of wine. The man sweats, dabbing his brow with his pocket square, his hands shaking as he puts it away. Next to him Miss Anderson is talking, but the man is too far gone to pay her proper attention. Saliva makes a discreet trail down the side of his mouth, and he reaches with clumsy hands for his napkin.

He's turning. Right there, at the table. Any moment now his eyes will start to yellow, and when he does Miss Anderson will be his first course.

I don't have a moment to wonder how on earth this rich man could have become infected. I look around to see if anyone else notices what I do, but Katherine stares into the distance, the disciplined gaze that functions to make our charges feel watched and not watched at the same time; and Mr. Redfern is speaking in low voices with one of the servants, directing the girl to stop serving wine to this guest or that one. Even Miss Anderson is too busy with her own wine glass to see that her neighbor is panting, laboring under the change his body is going through.

I tap my companion's shoulder. "Mr. Redfern."

He gives me an irritated glare before turning back to the conversation with the serving girl on his other side.

I grab his arm, shaking him. "Mr. Redfern!"

His head whips around. "What?" he snarls, all pretense of manners gone.

"Might I borrow your blade for a moment?" I ask sweetly, pointing across the table to the man stumbling to his feet, knocking over glasses as he does so. A low growl comes from his throat and a chorus of answering screams ring through the dining room as everyone realizes that there's a shambler in their midst.

Mr. Redfern seems to be as much in shock as everyone else, so I grab his blade without waiting for permission. I heft the knife in my hand, taking just long enough to get a feel for the weight. Then, as the man lunges for Miss Anderson, I hurl the knife through the air.

It's a good throw, and the blade goes end over end between the heads of the dinner guests before lodging squarely in the temple of the shambler. For a moment the creature continues its grab for Miss Anderson before crashing to the floor in a tangle of limbs.

My instructor backs away in terror, her face gone pale as she stares at me across the table. Everyone's eyes are upon me now, their faces twisted in disgust, as if killing a dinner guest, shambler or no, is a terrible faux pas.

"My word," the mayor's wife says from the far end of the table. The look she gives me makes me feel less human and more like a bear that's managed to stumble into the middle of dinner.

"Yes, it was an amazing throw, wasn't it?" Katherine says, her voice a tad too bright. "Jane was first in our class for knife handling. You should see what she can do at thirty feet!"

No one answers, but the Misses Duncan and Anderson both give me looks that make it clear that I have very much made a mistake.

Feh. I should've let the shambler eat Miss Anderson's face.

I daresay my education here has been more than a little enlightening.
You cannot fathom the benefits I have reaped here in Maryland.
Sometimes riches are bestowed upon me whether I want them or not.

Chapter 14
In Which I Go Snooping

"Yet again, we owe our gratitude to the fine young ladies of Miss Preston's," says Mayor Carr, once everyone at the table has calmed down. "While I do wish they were perhaps a bit more discreet in their work . . . I can't deny that this is twice this month that they've saved us from a rather rare and unfortunate accident." He pulls the napkin from where it's tucked into his collar, folds it, and places it next to his plate. "Well, I think we can officially consider the dinner portion of our evening concluded, no?" At this, he smiles, and his guests give a tentative laugh. "Let's allow my house staff to tidy up in here. Gentlemen, I invite you to join me for cigars and brandy—prewar, of course."

Despite this fine invitation, not everyone remains; a fair few people quietly make their excuses and leave. Maybe it's due to my thrilling knife-throwing skills, but I get the feeling it has more to do with seeing one of their friends turn shambler before their very eyes. He couldn't have been that popular, though. Most of the mayor's cronies and their wives remain, and Katherine and I are informed by Miss Anderson that we are to join the women in the salon while they partake of sherry, fruit, and cheese.

"Are you serious?" I whisper, for the sake of decorum. "A man just turned shambler in the middle of Baltimore County and nobody cares how it happened?"

"What are you suggesting, Miss McKeene?" Miss Anderson smiles tightly to a passing party guest before turning her attention back to me. "That there's a pack of shamblers here in the city? The man was probably bitten on the road coming here and failed to disclose it. A terrible breach of decorum, but nothing more. A rogue shambler slipping through the county line patrols and bothering a pony near the city walls is not unheard of."

"But it's not just one shambler, Miss Anderson," I shoot back. "The Edgars were attacked inside the county line, and the—" I catch myself before letting the Spencers' name slip. "I've heard rumors other families have gone missing as well."

Miss Anderson straightens and adjusts her gloves. When she speaks, her words are straight razors. "I don't know where you have heard this gossip, but I can assure you we're quite well-protected here. Now, unless you two want to find yourselves expelled from Miss Preston's this very evening, I suggest you freshen yourselves up and get into that parlor."

Rather than continue to argue, I nod and curtsy. As Miss Anderson walks away, I ask a servant where the comfort room is and hurry off down the hall. I've heard enough from Baltimore's upper crust, and I aim to find my own answers. But Katherine is hot on my heels.

"Where are you going?" she whispers.

"Anywhere but in there," I say.

"Jane, you threw a Bowie knife at one of the mayor's guests. That man, by the way, was an editor for the *Sun*. His death is going to be all over the front page tomorrow, and the mayor's wife is distraught."

"Katherine, can you hear how ridiculous that sounds? We could've died. Who cares what the newspaper thinks? Half the city can't read it, anyway."

Katherine stops. "I'm not saying you're wrong, Jane McKeene."

"What?"

"I agree with you. Something is very, very rotten here. But you're not going to get what you want from them, especially after throwing a knife into a man's face at the dinner table. All they care about is how it will look in the papers. Now think for a moment. The man could have gotten bit out on the roads, but that's unlikely, don't you think?"

I shift from foot to foot. The fact Katherine is on my side is as much a surprise as her cool logic. The bite takes anywhere from a few minutes to an hour or so to change a person. We were on the last course. How long ago had the man been bitten? Could he have somehow gotten the bite here, at the mayor's estate?

"I don't know, Kate, but I do know that I need to find the comfort room in a hurry or I am going to embarrass myself yet again."

Katherine makes a face. "Look, we need to get to the bottom of all this. If neither of us are in that parlor, they're going to come looking. I'll cover for you as long as I can."

I nod, and hurry down the hall, my brain turning over the possibilities of a shambler being in Mayor Carr's house. The mayor doesn't strike me as a foolish man, so I can't imagine he would tolerate the kind of incompetence that would allow the undead on his property. So does that mean he has them here purposefully? Why would a man like him keep the dead around?

It's such a ridiculous line of thought that I shake my head. There has to be a reasonable explanation, one that doesn't involve Baltimore's mayor keeping shamblers as pets. I just got to figure out what it is.

Despite a head full of questions and suppositions, I still manage to find the latrine, but before I can make use of the mayor's very fancy water closet I see Jackson, waving at me from a doorway at the end of the hall. A quick glance reveals that no one is around to see me, and I sprint down the hallway and duck into the room.

"What are you doing?" I whisper, my eyes adjusting to the low light. There are gas lamps on the walls but they ain't lit, and even though a bit of light filters in through the windows, it is too dark to see anything other than the vague outline of bookshelves and a massive square that I take to be a desk.

"I need your help," Jackson says, striking a match and lighting a kerosene lantern. "I'm supposed to be in the cellar bringing up a couple of bottles of port for the men, but I saw you duck out and figured you were looking for evidence of where Lily is."

"Please. I was trying to use the water closet. Now if you'll excuse me." Even if I am looking for answers, Red Jack is only going to get me caught. I make to leave but he grabs my arm. "Jackson—"

"Jane, you know I wouldn't ask if I didn't have to." I cross my arms and he sighs. "I know things ended badly between us, and you've always been more accommodating than I got any right to expect, but you know I can't read a damn word of the files the mayor's got in here. I don't know what's the household accounting and what might be dastardly. So, I'm asking you, with a whole heap of consideration I don't deserve: Will you please help me?"

The lamplight plays across Jackson's features, but somehow I don't think he's acting. If he's desperate enough to mention our falling-out, then I know he's worried something fierce.

Even so, nowhere in that speech did I hear an apology.

"I just want you to know that I'm doing this for Lily, not you. As far as I'm concerned, you can rot in hell." Relief relaxes his features and he nods. I purse my lips, taking in the desk and accompanying drawers. "Here, hold the light so I can see."

The mayor's desk is well organized, and there are enough cost sheets and file folders that my head spins. I open the drawers beside the desk, but there's nothing unusual, just the normal ledger keeping and invoices you'd expect for a tobacco farm.

I try to pull out the bottom drawer and it refuses to budge. I wave Jackson over and point to the drawer. "Can you get it open?"

He sets the lantern on the desk. "You got a hairpin?"

I touch my hair and pull one out, thankful when the weight and mass of my hair stays put. Jackson starts to work on the lock, glancing up at me, his expression nearly unreadable in the dark. "You look real pretty tonight."

I don't say anything, my heart thumping in my chest. Never once did Jackson ever tell me I was pretty before things went bad. I think he always took me for granted. Even when I was throwing bottles at his head and telling him what a louse he was he still seemed surprised, as though he never thought I'd get mad enough to tell him things between us were over.

"That getup really does something for you, Janey-Jane. I can see why you take your training and all that so serious. You belong to this life. You'll be a brilliant Attendant."

The drawer pops open, saving me from having to answer him. Jackson reaches in and pulls out a thick ledger book.

"Look," I say, tapping the front. SUMMERLAND is written there in gold embossed letters. "What's 'Summerland'?"

"I have no idea."

I open the book, but before I get very far there's the unmistakable sound of a gun cocking. "Summerland is a town in Kansas. Nice place, bit of a work in progress, like most frontier towns. And I get the feeling you're going to get to see it firsthand."

The room brightens, Miss Anderson lighting a gas lamp

on the wall, a macabre grin on her face. The light reveals Mr. Redfern in the doorway, a nice pair of six-shooters leveled at me and Jackson.

"Miss McKeene, Red Jack," he says, drawing room–polite. "I do believe the mayor is expecting you."

I must apologize: this letter has gotten much longer than I expected it to be. Please give the aunties my love, and tell Auntie Eliza that I'm expecting a pecan pie when I return! I love you, Momma, more than anything on earth or in the Lord's heavens above. Please stay safe. I shall be home soon.

Chapter 15
In Which My Fate Is Decided

Miss Anderson strips me of my weapons before she claps me and Red Jack in irons and leads us down a back staircase to a lower part of the house. Jackson's face is impassive, and I try to mimic his calm demeanor. I'm afraid I fail miserably. My stomach is all angry butterflies and nerves, and I feel like I'm going to lose what little control I have at any moment. I also still need to empty my bladder, which is not helping the situation at all.

I've been in trouble before, but somehow the gun pointed at my back and the heavy irons on my wrists make me think that this is much worse than stealing a pie from the kitchens.

The staircase is steep, and just when I wonder if it will ever end we enter a long corridor lit by gas lamps. The flames flicker, making the deep shadows on the stone walls dance drunkenly. From down the hallway comes a long, low howl. The hair along my arms stands on end, and Miss Anderson gives me a wide grin.

"You hear them, don't you?" she says.

"The mayor keeps shamblers?"

"Of course not. Don't be ridiculous. That's his dogs. The kennels are at the end of this corridor. You're even stupider than I thought," she says with a sneer.

I'm beginning to think she truly doesn't care for me.

Miss Anderson stops and knocks on a fancy door carved to depict Adam and Eve fleeing the Garden. The angel casting them out looks a mite bit like the mayor.

That does not help my nervousness one bit.

Someone calls, "Enter!" Miss Anderson opens the door and leads the way in, grinning like a kid on Christmas.

"We got them, sir!" she crows, all but doing a little jig as she presents us like trophy bucks. "They went right for the office like I said they would."

Behind a large desk sits Mayor Carr, puffing away on a cigar, a glass of port in his hand. He leans back in his chair, a massive beast of a man. This close it's easy to see why people stand in awe of him. He radiates power, his dark eyes shrewd and intelligent. The man possesses quite an imposing air, one of barely repressed violence. Not many people stand in the mayor's way and live to tell about it.

He puffs on his cigar, leisurely blowing smoke rings. "I do believe it was Mr. Redfern who said that, given the opportunity to snoop, Miss McKeene and her companion would find themselves hard put to contain themselves. So the kudos must go to Mr. Redfern, not you, Miss Anderson."

Miss Anderson's face goes stormy, and I smile to myself despite the danger we're in. Looks like the mayor ain't so keen on her, either.

"Any way, we caught them, sir. Want us to cut them? They'd make fine shambler bait, and we've quite the issue with a roaming pack out toward the waterfront. Or we could add them to Professor Grooten's experiment. Election season is coming up and no one ever misses a few darkies."

Rage swells in my heart, and my composure breaks. "You vile woman," I yell, unable to contain myself. "I should've let that shambler eat your miserable hide at dinner!"

"SILENCE!" The mayor leans forward, placing his cigar in a crystal ashtray and setting his glass of port down as well before hauling himself from the chair. He walks over to me and Red Jack, a look of careful consideration on his face. "This is your problem, Miss Anderson. You are all passion, no sense. I suppose it's not your fault, being a woman and all."

The mayor grasps my chin, turning my face this way and that like he's inspecting a horse for sale. I jerk away from his clammy touch, and he gives me a grin. "Either way, you need to think about the larger end goal. Both of these Negroes are smart—smarter than they have any right to be. We can't have them here in Baltimore, they're already stirring up too much trouble. And using them for shambler bait is such a waste. We have the criminals in the jails for that. But I think they'd be useful in Summerland. The preacher might be able to curb their baser instincts, and the sheriff has a way about him that is conducive to corralling wayward Negroes. What do you think, Abigail?"

There's movement from a chair to the left, and my mouth opens with shock when Miss Preston walks over to stand next to the mayor. Gone is the kind expression I've come to know. Instead, she gives me a hard glare, and I unwittingly shrink into myself.

"I have no information about this fellow here, but Jane is one of my best girls. Where is her companion?"

"Katherine is still upstairs with Miss Duncan. She doesn't have a thing to do with this," Miss Anderson says, answering too quickly. Katherine has long been her favorite, and whatever this Summerland is, she most likely doesn't want Katherine sent off there.

"I do agree that Katherine likely isn't a part of this." Miss

Preston turns back to the mayor. "But she is too pretty for any respectable woman to hire on as a companion. I've had several possible contracts fall through once the families saw her. She might find better use as an incentive for the men out west. After all, she came to us by way of a house of ill repute. I'm sure she knows a few tricks to keep the men in line."

"I'd like to assign her as a Summerland Attendant, keep the womenfolk happy," the mayor says. "The girls we got from down South didn't pan out, and if Summerland is going to be successful we need investors, that means a better quality of people. In the event that fails, *then* we can set her up as one of the Duchess's girls." He turns to Miss Anderson. "Fetch her down here. Tell her I would like to give her my thanks personally for her valor at the lecture."

Miss Anderson's lips purse, but she does as she's told.

I think about how Attendants never seem to survive much past a couple of years, how girls never come back to visit once they've graduated, not even the girls that don't get contracts with fine families. "How long have you been feeding him girls for whatever this fool scheme is?" I ask, directing my question to Miss Preston.

She gives me a lovely smile and pats my cheek affectionately. "As long as there's been a Miss Preston's School of Combat for Negro Girls, there's been a Summerland. The West is savage, what with the Indians and the shamblers and the wildlife. If one doesn't get you, another surely will.

But my girls have helped to make Summerland a town of the future."

Mayor Carr's expression goes dreamy. "Imagine it, a utopia on the Western plains, safe enough to withstand any shambler attack." He smiles. "America, as it should be, once more. What price can one put on that?"

"You're deranged," Jackson says. It's the first he's spoken since Miss Anderson clapped us in irons, and the expression on his face is murderous, like he'd love nothing more than to gut the mayor and Miss Preston. I reckon my face looks about the same.

The mayor laughs. "Such fire! I do admire the Negro's ability to continue fighting even in the face of overwhelming odds."

A muscle in Jackson's jaw flexes, but he says nothing. The mayor continues. "Summerland is a city on a hill, a place where people can raise their families without worrying about any of this nasty shambler business."

"You mean, what Baltimore County is supposed to be?" I shoot back at him. "I've seen packs of shamblers in the woods. I've killed them. All of that talk about making the county safe, about it being shambler-free . . . It was all a lie."

The mayor shakes his head at this. "It wasn't a lie. Our walls, our patrols, the Native and Negro Reeducation Act, it was all working. For a while. But in the last year, we've come to realize that, no matter how hard we push, those damn shamblers push back even harder. These eastern cities are lost, girl. Finished. We can't rebuild America on a foundation rotted by war and plague. We need to start over again. Summerland is that start."

"You sent the Spencers there, didn't you?" Jackson asks.

Mayor Carr laughs. "The Spencers went willingly once they heard my offer. Safety is a precious commodity in these turbulent times."

Jackson's shoulders fall. "But the Spencers are Egalitarians. They were rallying against your senatorial campaign."

The mayor gives an eloquent shrug. "It's amazing what a few months fighting the undead and struggling to survive can do to change a man's perspective. Some of my best allies were once Egalitarians. People care less about doing the right thing than they do about being safe, especially when they have little ones to look after. Ah, and here is our third musketeer."

The door opens, and Katherine enters, her smile fading quickly when her eyes land on me and Red Jack. "Wait, what is this?" she asks in surprise.

"I am afraid, Miss Deveraux, that this is both hello and good-bye," says the mayor. He nods, and Miss Anderson takes Katherine's weapons and puts a pair of irons on her as well, although judging by Miss Anderson's face it pains her to do so.

The mayor holds his hands out and smiles apologetically.

"Such long faces! Cheer up, friends. Many a scoundrel has made their fortune out west. Of course, that is all assuming you survive."

There's a knock behind us, and a white man with red hair sticks his head into the room. "Sorry to interrupt, Mayor Carr, but we've got another breach. Looks like a good-size pack. George got bit, so Jasper said we needed to let you know we put him down and ain't got no one to handle the dogs now."

The mayor's face flushes, and he points to the man. "Put Evan on the dogs and make sure those damned shamblers don't breach the secondary again! I have guests."

Katherine holds her head high, even though her eyes swim with tears. She's nothing but collateral damage in this whole mess, and it makes me feel some kind of way. Especially when she looks at me and gives me a rueful grin. "Well, Jane, it looks like you were right, after all."

Strange, hearing her say it doesn't give me much satisfaction.

The man hurries out, and the mayor returns to his chair, picking up his cigar once more. "As you can see, I have other, more important matters to attend to. The train leaves in the morning. You'll spend tonight in the cellars, which may be a bit damp but are cool and quite comfortable. I urge you to get as much rest as you can. Life out west is harder than anything you're used to, at least for your kind." The mayor puffs leisurely on his cigar. "And if you prove yourselves useful, as Mr. Redfern has, well, you might just have a future after all."

"One more thing, Mr. Mayor, if you don't mind," I say.

"Yes, Miss McKeene?"

"Might I use your comfort room before we are locked up? I would hate to embarrass myself during my exile."

The mayor smiles and nods. "Of course, Miss McKeene. I'm a politician, not a monster."

Miss Anderson leads the way out, Mr. Redfern gesturing with his revolver for us to follow. We do, our steps slow and dejected.

I have never felt so hopeless in all my life.

PART TWO

The Cruel West

Dearest Jane,

Oh my dear, how good it is to have your words, and to read such lovely penmanship. There is no greater joy for a mother than to know her only child is doing well. I see that Miss Preston's has had quite the positive impact on your life, though I daresay the memory of the day you left still pains me greatly.

Chapter 16
In Which I Have a Revelation

The train leaves promptly at six, and we are dragged through the early-morning dark to meet it. Katherine and I wear our Attendants' uniforms, and Red Jack is still dressed in the white shirt and apron of a house servant. Mr. Redfern walks behind us, gun leveled at our backs just in case we get any fancy ideas. I am sure we make quite a sight to any who witness our parade.

On the train we're guided not to a passenger car but a cargo car. Miss Anderson stands waiting for us, sliding the door open and gesturing for us to climb inside. Jackson catches my eye and winks. "I always told you I'd take you away from all of this," he murmurs, low enough that only I hear him. How he can have such a jovial attitude when the situation is most dire is something I cannot explain.

Miss Anderson locks our chains to steel rings in the floor, tossing the keys to Mr. Redfern, who catches them one-handed. Miss Anderson smiles down at me. "I have waited for this day ever since you first came to Miss Preston's. I hope Sheriff Snyder flays you bloody."

"And I hope a horde of shamblers chews your face off, you miserable wretch," I say. Miss Anderson draws her hand back and slaps me across the face, my head whipping around from the blow. The coppery taste of blood fills my mouth, and I spit, aiming at Miss Anderson's boots. Sadly, I am not even close.

So much for my etiquette instruction.

Miss Anderson turns to go but then hesitates. "One last thing," she says. She reaches into the pocket of her skirt and takes out a thick packet of letters, envelopes of fine lavender vellum. "These are from your mother, Jane. The postmaster is a friend of mine and was happy to help me make sure you didn't continue to violate school rules. And I believe at this point your mother probably takes you for dead, since she hasn't received one of your letters in ever so long, either."

Miss Anderson tosses the packet of letters just out of reach, partway between me and Katherine. One look reveals the writing as my momma's, and something breaks in me.

"I will kill you, you conniving bitch!" I scream, straining against my chains and lurching forward as far as they will allow. Miss Anderson just laughs as Mr. Redfern helps her down from the train car, the door slamming closed. I scream, a sound of pure animalistic rage, and before I know it tears are running down my cheeks, my pain and frustration a living thing. All this time I despaired over my momma: whether she was alive, whether she'd be happy to see me when I returned, whether I'd imagined her tenderness and her love. All this time I waited for answers and got not a one, my slavish devotion answered with silence from her. Or so I'd thought.

"Jane, you have to calm down. It's going to get hot in here, and they didn't leave us with any water. Jane." Katherine's voice is tremulous, and I realize that I ain't the only one being sent off into the unknown. Red Jack and Katherine are here with me, and I owe it to them to try to retain some of my sanity.

"I'm going to kill her," I say, my voice low. I use the fine material of my skirt to scrub my face of the snot and tears, the chains around my wrists digging into the soft skin. I take a deep, shuddering breath. "I'm going to kill her, and Miss Preston and the mayor. All of them. I'm going to gut them like fish and use them as shambler bait, then I'm going to burn both the school and the mayor's house to the ground and dance upon the ashes."

"That's good, Jane, that's good. It's good to have goals," Katherine says, her voice trembling. She hiccups and begins to cry. I should offer her some soothing words, but I am a knot of rage and violence, and I ain't got anything like her platitudes.

Outside, the train whistle blows, and I settle in for the long haul, planning my bloody revenge. On one side of me Katherine cries quiet tears and on the other Jackson says nothing, the sound of his heavy breaths the only indication that he is even there.

*Life at Rose Hill is much the same as when you were here, although
I must admit that we all sorely miss your sunny disposition. . . .*

Chapter 17
In Which I Am Welcomed to Summerland

The next few days are a lesson in slow torture. The train car
is an oven, and the vibration of the wheels rattles our bones
until I'm positive we will arrive out west little more than a
bowl of jelly. Every so often the train jerks to a stop, throwing
us violently to the side, the door opening up to reveal Mr.
Redfern. He gives us water and hard bread before taking us
out to relieve ourselves along the track. We have no weapons, so it's nerve-racking to squat amongst the tall weeds and

do our business. The movement and the fresh air are a brief respite before we are loaded back onto the train and we begin our journey once more.

I lose all track of time, although I do eventually pick up the packet of letters. It's too dark in the gloom to read them, but there's no mistaking my name scrawled across the front in my mother's handwriting. I hide them in my skirt pocket next to *Tom Sawyer*. I ain't sure when the last letter arrived, but just looking at them is enough to ignite my rage all over again.

One day I will return to Baltimore, and when I do, there will be hell to pay.

We don't talk much on the trip. I suppose we're all stuck in our own dark thoughts. At night, when the train car cools enough for us to sleep a little, I hear Katherine crying softly, trying to hide the sound of her tears by burying her face in her knees. I feel bad for her. She really did get the worst kind of deal. Here she is, following the rules for years, working toward nothing more than being some lady's Attendant, and the powers that be decide she's too pretty for such drudgery and ship her out west. It's the worst kind of betrayal.

The third night that I wake to her crying, my guilt gets the better of me. "I'm sorry you got caught up in this. I'm sorry you won't be an Attendant," I say. Katherine laughs in the dark, the sound flat.

"Oh, Jane, I never much cared about being an Attendant.

All I ever wanted was to be free."

Her words give me too much to think about.

"Why do you think the Survivalists lied about Baltimore being safe?" she continues.

"Power," Jackson says, bitterness lacing his voice. "It's the only thing that men like them want."

"People wanted to believe them," I mutter, thinking about poor Othello from the lecture and his willingness to die for Professor Ghering's delusions. "They wanted everything to go back to the way it was before the war. Before the killing, the shamblers, the walls, all of it. That's how men like the mayor maintained control. You believe strongly enough in an idea, nothing else much matters."

"If everything the Survivalists have been saying is a lie, then no one is safe," Katherine says.

"We never were," I say. The memory of Miss Preston's betrayal stings anew.

There ain't much to say after that.

After what seems like months, but in reality is only about five days, the train stops once again. This time when the door opens wide, and my eyes finally adjust to the too-bright light, there are three rough-looking fellows holding shotguns.

"Welcome to the great state of Kansas. Wonder how long you'll survive," one says, his voice high and squeaky. He gives us a gap-toothed grin.

It's all I can do not to roll my eyes. After nearly a week of being cooked alive and shaken out of my skin I'm irritable and in no mood to deal with a bunch of toothless bullies. I hold my chained hands up. "One of you gonna unlock these, or are you just going to stand there wasting daylight?"

Squeaky takes a step back, his grin fading to a look of surprise. I reckon most folks show up scared as a mouse in a trap after such a brutal trip, but Miss Anderson's revelation and the long, slow ride to mull it over has just given me a mean feeling. Right now, I don't care about much else but the two tasks before me.

First, find my momma. My mother is alive and probably thinks I am dead. I have to find her and tell her the truth. That means I have to find a way back to Rose Hill, and quick-like.

But I have to bring Katherine and Jackson along as well. I can't leave them stranded on the prairie. Plus, I'm going to need their help to survive the trip.

Before I can do any of that, though, I have to survive. By any means necessary. And from the stories I've read of the Western frontier, that ain't going to be easy.

The three dimwits staring at us don't move, so I shake my chains at them. "Yo! You want us to get out or not?"

"Gentlemen." Mr. Redfern's low voice causes the louts to step aside uncertainly, and he leaps into the railcar with an easy grace. He unlocks our chains, and for a moment I think about hitting him upside the head and making a run for it. But just like before, like the many stops along the way, I don't. I have no idea where I am and how to get back to civilization. No weapons, no food, no nothing. I will plan my escape, but now is not the time or place.

Unfortunately Jackson is not possessed of such calm and reasoned logic. Once his hands are free, he hauls back and punches Mr. Redfern in the face. The man ain't expecting it, and he goes down like a sack of rocks.

"Let's go!" Jackson yells before launching himself from the train car and running off. Katherine is still chained to the floor, and our eyes meet in surprise and disbelief.

Mr. Redfern climbs to his feet, fists clenched and jaw locked. I hold my hands up. "That boy is all impulse. I ain't running nowhere." He gives me a short nod and jumps down from the train car. "Hey, at least leave the keys so I can unlock Kate!"

The keys fly backward over his shoulder and I snatch them out of the air. I unlock Katherine's chains and help her to her feet. "Ugh, you smell," she says, holding the back of her hand delicately to her face.

"You ain't a bed of roses yourself." I jerk my head toward the opening. "Come on. I wanna see what they do to old muttonhead."

We jump down from the railcar, unsteady after so many days locked up. Katherine and I are just in time to see Jackson tackled by the three men a little ways down the street that leads away from the rail yard. Mr. Redfern runs down to help, and I cross my arms and watch as the scene unfolds. Katherine frowns.

"Well, that wasn't wise."

"Nope."

Jackson struggles against the men, finally slumping in their arms after Mr. Redfern gives him a little payback by way of a fist to the chin.

"What was that boy thinking?" Katherine murmurs, shaking her head. I wonder as well. Jackson's had run-ins with the mayor's men before, what does he expect in a place like this? The West is lawless as all get-out from what the papers say. I doubt a town founded by Baltimore's no-good mayor and his Survivalist pals is going to be much better.

"Do you think they'll kill him?"

"Naw, not yet." At least, I hope not. I am not proud to say it gives me a perverse kind of joy to see Jackson take a few licks. After all, it's mostly his fault I'm here in the first place. Him and those damned blue-green eyes. "They went through a lot of trouble to bring us all this way. We're needed for something, so I don't think they're going to be so quick to kill us right yet."

The men pick Jackson up and haul him toward a wooden front building with bars on the windows. I ain't sure if the bars are meant to keep the shamblers out or people in. My accommodations didn't exactly give me the bird's-eye view of the town, and what I'm seeing now is just mystifying.

Everything here is new. The buildings ain't anything like I'd imagined in a frontier town. Everything is whitewashed and a boardwalk runs along the front of the buildings, raising the foot traffic above the dusty main street. I spy a saloon, bank, dry-goods store, and a hotel. The road is flat and well maintained, and beyond the town is the flattest land I've ever seen. There's a cluster of houses off in the distance, but there's no telling how big they are or if they're even occupied. The plains are golden yellow, fading into a sky so pale it's like a sun-bleached version of the sky back in Maryland. It's hotter than Hades, and the sun beats down mercilessly. Far off there's a strange ridge, even and uniform, and I can't make out what it is even as I squint against the sun.

Katherine shades her eyes and looks around. "Oh my. Is that a barrier wall?"

She points in the same direction as the ridge, and I shake my head. "It can't be. A wall that large . . . how could they maintain it?"

Mr. Redfern returns to where Katherine and I stand, and he gives us a quick bow. "My apologies, ladies."

I snort. "You kidnapped us and dragged us to the middle of nothing, and you're apologizing for putting a hurting on Jackson? You're a strange man, Mr. Redfern."

He gives me what I've come to think of as his death glare

and turns to Katherine. "If you would please follow me, Sheriff Snyder is waiting to meet you," he says, completely ignoring me.

We make our way down the street, our passage kicking up dust that coats my skin and clogs my nostrils. If I didn't feel like a mess before, the short walk to the sheriff's office from the rail station definitely does the trick. In Baltimore the roads are all cobblestone, civilized and clean. Even the country roads around Miss Preston's are a dirt so hard-packed that they might as well be stone. But even though the street here looks lovely from far off, close up the pockmarks reveal themselves. Large piles of something that looks suspiciously like feces dots the lane. I point it out to Katherine, raising my eyebrows. She shrugs.

"It's horse manure," Mr. Redfern answers out of nowhere, and both Katherine and I look at him in disbelief.

"Horses?" Katherine asks.

"You have horses?" I squeak. I've never seen a horse, apart from paintings of them. Great beasts that people once rode, before the shamblers made them a ready food source. The iron ponies replaced horses as transportation, and I'd love nothing more than to see a horse up close.

Momma used to talk about her favorite horse, Cassandra, named after some doomed woman from ancient myth. Apparently the name was prophetic: the first time Rose Hill was hit with a wave of shamblers they went after the horses, tearing into the poor beasts before Momma and Josiah, the big dark man who led the field work, could put them down. It was a small group, and we were lucky. It gave us enough warning to prepare for future attacks. Most of Rose Hill's neighbors weren't so fortunate.

Next to me Katherine sighs. "I'd love to see a horse."

I nod. "Me too."

Mr. Redfern gives us a bit of side-eye. "Well, you'll get your wish. They ride horses along the perimeter fence. I don't know what the sheriff has planned for you, but it will probably include some patrols. There aren't nearly enough bodies to fill them properly." There's something behind his expression that tells me there is more to his words than he's letting on, but I leave it alone for now.

We stop short outside of a building with a large, fancy hand-lettered glass window proclaiming "Sheriff" and a flag of red and white stripes. Survivalists.

Mr. Redfern holds the door open for us, and Katherine and I file into a plain-looking office. "Good luck," he says under his voice before falling in behind us. What he means by that, I can't know, but his tone is earnest.

Even with the large front window, the room is gloomy. It takes a few moments for my eyes to adjust, and when they do the vague shapes form into a desk, some chairs, and a cell along the back wall that is currently occupied by Jackson. The whole place carries the smell of unwashed bodies and tobacco smoke with a faint air of decay.

The walls are bare wood, with notices breaking up the empty space: a large sign proclaiming "No Drinking After Eight"; a weekly prayer-meeting schedule; two sets of town laws, one for coloreds and another for whites; and, most curious of all, a long document labeled "The Summerland Bill of Rights" posted right next to the door.

"These the girls the mayor wired me about?"

Katherine and I halt at the deep voice, and a loud thump follows, the sound of boots hitting the wide plank floor. I'm half wondering where they got all of this wood from. I ain't seen a single tree around here, just that golden grass and flat landscape. Did the mayor bring all this building material west on the train? No wonder he was carrying on about investors.

Behind us Mr. Redfern clears his throat. "Yes, Sheriff. Jane McKeene and Katherine Deveraux, both recent graduates of Miss Preston's School of Combat for Negro Girls."

"That'll be all, redskin. Tell Bob and William they need to come back to escort these two after I'm done talking with them."

"Of course." Mr. Redfern's voice is tight, but a glance over my shoulder reveals nothing, his face impassive. I know he has to be hot over being called "redskin" like that, which is an insult in the highest degree. After all, his skin isn't even red. But, his expression is mild. I sure wouldn't want to play poker with Mr. Redfern.

The door opens and closes as Mr. Redfern departs, and I turn my attention to the sheriff. The white man who stands before us has the reddened skin of someone who has spent many long days in the shadeless sun of these plains. He wears a wide brim hat even though we're indoors, and I figure that a place as lawless as this probably ain't got much use for manners. His sandy mustache droops on either side of his mouth, and despite his relative youth, his movements as he sits are slow and deliberate. I suppose he would be considered attractive, yet there's something I don't like about him. There's a spark in his blue eyes that makes me think the man is more dangerous than he looks, the way they say gators in the swamps down South pretend to be logs before taking a bite out of a man. This is a man who likes to be underestimated.

"Jane McKeene. Your reputation precedes you."

"Well, sir, I don't see how that could be. I'm nobody."

"A nobody who makes the front page of the *Sun*." The man reaches back on his desk and grabs a newssheet. It's the paper from nearly a month ago. The date puts it the day after the lecture and the headline reads MAYOR AND THE MISSUS SAVED BY NEGRO GIRL'S DERRING-DO. The illustration that accompanies the story is a crudely drawn version of me, my hair sticking up in twenty different directions, my lips thick and my eyes wild as I gun down no fewer than ten shamblers.

"Sheriff Snyder, I must confess, this is the first time I've seen such a headline. Might I borrow your newssheet to peruse the story at my leisure?"

An expression I can't identify crosses his face. "You read?"

There's a sudden tension in the room, and I hunch my shoulders and shuffle a bit, letting a slow drawl enter my voice. I prefer to be misjudged as well. "No, suh," I say, my words slow and deliberate. "I jes like to look at the pictures, if'n that's okay."

The sheriff hands me the newspaper with a grunt before leaning back against the desk and crossing his arms, and I tuck the paper into the top of my boot while the man talks. "So, the ground rules. Curfew at eight each night unless you're assigned to a patrol. You will be responsible for the protection of this town. Scythe, sickle, knife, club, you want it, you got it. But no guns. We don't let the darkies carry 'em, only my boys. I used to run patrols back in Georgia before the war, and I know how crafty you people can be." The sheriff's voice goes hard, and I swallow.

He takes out a pouch of tobacco and begins to roll a cig-arette as he continues. "You ain't slaves, because as far as I know that's still illegal, more's the pity, so you'll be paid two dollars a week plus your room and board. You also get a bath once a week, should you choose to use it. I know your kind have an aversion to water."

Katherine and I exchange a look. Who is this man? And just how many Negroes does he know?

"Also, no drinking and no fornication. Summerland is a

town of high morals, so none of that will be tolerated. Breaking my rules results in swift penalties. Do you understand?"

For a moment the world falls away and I can see the future as it opens up before me: toiling away, working in the fields or on patrols, killing the dead while people like the sheriff live a life of safety and leisure. On the surface it seems to be equal to my potential future in Baltimore, but there I still had a choice. Well, at least the pretense of one. It always seemed I could strike out on my own should I choose to leave Miss Preston's. It would've been an ill-advised choice, but an option nonetheless.

Here, there's not even the subterfuge of such a possibility. The trap is sprung well and tight. I know what things were like before the War between the States, and even though the years after were chaotic, at least colored folks like me were free. But this place is the brainchild of a bunch of Survivalists, built on a dream of prewar America, which is how I know that my next words will change everything.

"Suh," I say, "I ain't sure why you're making Miss Katherine listen to all this. She ain't a Negro."

The sheriff turns to me as Katherine's eyes go wide. Behind me, his men shift; I've gotten their attention.

"Jane," Katherine says, fists clenched, color riding high in her cheeks. "What are you—?"

"It ain't your fault the mayor put you to the side, Miss

Katherine, ain't your fault at all. And I know you's about to be cross with me, but you can't toil in the field. You're better than that."

Katherine buries her face in her hands. I ain't sure whether she's laughing or crying, but I use the moment to finish my plan before she can ruin it. I step closer to the desk. "I graduated from Miss Preston's, that's the Lord's own truth, Sheriff, but Miss Katherine here is a lady, my charge. The mayor took a fancy to Miss Katherine and his old windbag of a wife conspired to have her sent here. That's why she's dressed like an Attendant. She was tricked."

Katherine is now staring daggers at me as the sheriff turns to her, a glint of interest in his eye.

"That true?" he asks.

Katherine turns her head, refusing to meet the sheriff's eyes, her lips clamped shut. Even after five days of rough treatment, she's still beautiful, which is how I know this is going to work.

The sheriff turns to Jackson, who's sat up enough to watch the goings-on in the office. "You there, boy, this woman white or is she a darkie?"

Jackson's jaw clenches, he looks the sheriff in the eye, and slow as winter molasses drawls out, "She definitely ain't a darkie."

The door opens behind me. The sheriff looks over my

shoulder and says, "Go fetch the professor, tell him I need him to bring his tools." I look over my shoulder as one of the men that waited for the railcar nods and ducks back out of the door. The other man leers at me, and I just give him a flat stare in return. I'm tense from the ride, and I'd like an opportunity to knock some sense into one of these boys.

The sheriff sighs. "We got ways of figuring out whether or not someone's colored, never you fear. We'll table that discussion until the professor gets here. So, as I was saying: Summerland is a town of high morals. Church every Sunday, a dance the last Saturday of every month, providing there's been no infractions. Bible study on Wednesdays and Fridays. The pastor seems to think the word of the Lord will keep your kind in line, but I ain't so sure," he mutters as he licks the rolling paper, sealing his cigarette closed. He lights the thing, and blue-gray smoke fills the room.

I say nothing, but Katherine looks like she's about to cry. The sheriff has taken every opportunity to insult us and remind us of the circumstance of our dark skin, and I'd like nothing more than to tell him what I think. I can take down a pack of shamblers like nobody's business. I am clever and can work my way out of any bad situation. I know I am more than my skin color. But there's nothing to be gained by an outburst right now. I need to get the lay of the land and figure out how to get myself a few hundred miles east in one piece.

"Oh, and one last thing," the sheriff says as the door opens behind us. "You step out of line and you'll find yourself swiftly reminded of your place."

A tall white boy wearing a bowler, a blue waistcoat, and a white shirt with the sleeves rolled up to his forearms pushes past me and Katherine. The sheriff looks at him and puffs on his cigarette. "'Bout time. This one says she ain't colored. I need you to measure her up. And you can use the other one as a test subject for your new experiment."

"Sheriff, how many times do I have to ask that you send them down to the lab? I can't do anything here, and it takes a while to distill the vaccine." The boy turns around and I realize he's older than I first thought, maybe early twenties, with stubble darkening his cheeks. He ain't handsome, but there's something indescribably appealing about his face. He's pale—not sickly, but like he doesn't get out in the sun much. His dark brows are pulled together in a scowl, and his muddy hazel eyes dart around the room like he's calculating . . . something. There's an intelligence there that draws me in. I don't much mind looking at him, even though he's probably a rat bastard, since he's working with the sheriff.

The sheriff, for his part, just continues to puff on his cigarette. "Fine, take them to that hole of yours. I don't need your back talk."

"Of course." The boy's words are clipped. He might still be

a bastard, but I'd wager he doesn't like the lawman too much, which maybe counts for something.

The sheriff doesn't seem to detect the tone, though. He kicks his feet up onto the desk, leaning back in his chair with a smile. "Welcome to Summerland, girls. Try not to die before I can replace ya."

Jane, I hope that while you are away you are keeping in mind all the things that I have taught you. We live in very troubling times, but that is still no excuse not to be a lady. Always mind your manners!

Chapter 18
In Which My Reputation Is Slandered

As the nameless boy turns to me and Katherine, his expression softens. "Would you ladies please follow me? I'll need to take you to my lab."

Before I can exit, the fellow behind me gives me a none-too-gentle shove with the barrel of his gun, and I turn and give him my best side-eye. "Sir, please refrain from the liberal use of your rifle. Otherwise, I will show you some creative places to put it."

The man just gives me a gap-toothed grin full of malice, and we make our way out of the sheriff's office and back onto the boardwalk, the pale, dark-haired boy leading the way. As he walks, his left foot drags a little. I wonder how he got such a limp, if he was born with it or if something bad happened to him when he was young. I reckon we all have our childhood scars, whether we wear them on the outside or not.

The man behind me shoves me with the rifle barrel again, this time causing me to stumble. I catch myself against the front of the general store as he chuckles.

"What are you gonna do? Nothing, that's what, you uppity darkie. You ain't in no position to be giving me any lip."

I smile sweetly at him as a black temper sweeps over me, all of the indignities of the past few days coalescing into a dark cloud that erases all thought. Then I center myself and, quick as you please, drop into a crouch and whip around to sweep his legs out from under him. Once he's on the ground I kick him in the side before placing my knee on his throat. All of this happens in less than a rabbit's heartbeat.

As he gurgles and flails I lean in close. "Right now, sir, with my knee on your throat, I am in the perfect position to counsel you on your bad manners. A lesson to be learned: Lady Fortune is as fickle as they come. And in a land full of shamblers you'd best not test my good nature, you hear me? You never know when you'll end up with the bite."

The sound of a revolver cocking is deafening next to my

ear. "Miss, would you please get off of Bill? I'm afraid he's the sheriff's cousin, and the sheriff would be quite upset if anything happened to him."

I glance back to see the pale boy above us, the lovely Colt in his hand pointed straight at my head. I give him my sweetest smile and climb to my feet. "Of course." I even bob a little curtsy.

The boy puts his revolver away, tucking it back into the holster that hangs low on his hips. "And, Bill, please show some restraint. These ladies are trained in the art of killing the dead. I know you haven't heard of Miss Preston's, but the girls from that school are well respected. They are a far cry from the Negroes we get from the Southern enclaves. It would be a small matter for them to turn that talent on you."

Bill picks up his hat off the ground and spits. "I don't take orders from you, boy."

"No, you don't. But you do need someone to treat that malady of yours, so I would caution you to check your baser impulses, sir. It is a delicate procedure, and Doc has been known to have shaky hands when he doesn't get his whiskey. And like I tell the good doctor often, you never know when the town might suddenly go dry."

Bill goes whiter than a sheet, and I can't help but wonder what kind of treatment he needs, and what might make a man so fearful of a pair of shaky hands.

The boardwalk ends and we step into the dusty street and

keep walking. Bill falls back a little, probably worried that I'll feed him my foot again. No chance of that, not in these shoes. My feet hurt, and I think longingly of my boots back at Miss Preston's, worn in and so very comfortable. Me and Katherine still wear our finery from the night we were shanghaied, and these things I'm wearing are for looking pretty, not strolling through a frontier town.

"Hey there, Gideon, you bringing me some new girls?"

A woman hangs out of a doorway across the street. It takes everything I have to keep my mouth from dropping open in shock. The woman is generously appointed, her white bosom spilling out over the top of her low-cut gray gown, her hand on one of her wide hips. Her hair is red as cherries and piled messily on top of her head. Behind her a few other women peek out into the street, everyone trying to get an eyeful.

The pale boy, who I am supposing is named Mr. Gideon, stops and tips his bowler. "Good day to you, Duchess. I'm afraid at least one of these girls is headed to the patrols, and neither are intended for employment in your fine establishment."

The women in the doorway all titter at Mr. Gideon's pretty words, and as we continue walking, Katherine leans in close to my ear. "I do believe that is a house of ill repute."

I nod solemnly. "Yes, Kate, I do believe you are correct."

Katherine sniffs. "I cannot believe she thinks we're meant to work there."

I stare at Katherine, trying to figure out if she's serious or having a go at me. Her expression is that of someone who has suffered a grievous insult, and I have to fight to swallow a hysterical laugh.

Her mouth drops open. "Jane, tell me you aren't insulted."

I lean in close so that the men don't hear me. "*Insulted?* Kate, we have been put in chains and sent halfway across the continent. We are currently at the mercy of a man who believes that Negroes are put here on this earth to fight shamblers at the white man's behest, and is going to send us out to do it without guns. Jackson sits in a jail cell awaiting some unknown fate. This town is a dirt spot in the middle of nowhere. There are no trees and the land is disconcertingly flat. My virtue is honestly the last thing I'm worried about. I'm hungry, tired, a little afraid, and a whole bunch angry, but a few hurt feelings are the furthest thing from my mind right now."

My voice rises as I talk, and by the time I get to the end Mr. Gideon has turned around.

"Don't worry, Miss Deveraux. The Duchess just likes to have some sport with all the girls that come through. Her sense of humor tends a bit mean. Members of the patrol may spend their sleep shifts under the roof of her saloon, but no one in this town will believe they are doing anything but resting there. I've taken steps to ensure that past mistakes are not repeated."

I force him a tight-lipped smile, but his words only serve to agitate me further. Every minute in this place reveals a new, terrible fact. "Past mistakes?"

He doesn't elaborate, and we finally reach his hole, as the sheriff called it. It's a small building, not much bigger than the privies we passed a little ways back, and Gideon turns to Bill when we arrive.

"You can stay here. I'll be back in a few minutes."

Bill says nothing, jaw tight, but takes up a guard position, while Katherine and I follow Mr. Gideon down into the gloom.

The most distressing change here at Rose Hill is that, due to the undead plague, most of the people in the valley have abandoned their farms for easier living out west. I daresay that if it weren't for the aunties, even our happy community would be torn asunder. But Auntie Aggie and her sisters have proven to be as wise as ever, and we are living still in relative comfort.

Chapter 19
In Which I Am Vaccinated and Become a Beacon of Hope

The narrow staircase is dark, but a yellow glow from up ahead provides a bit of illumination. I walk behind Katherine, my fingers brushing hard-packed earth on either side.

The staircase ends and deposits us in a sizable room. The walls and floors are buttressed like a basement, and the entire space is much larger than the small building we entered. Katherine is looking around the room, her expression filled with wonder, and it's no surprise.

We are in a genuine laboratory.

One of the weeklies a few months ago had been about a scientist who went mad, turning himself into a terrible creature that ravished women. The scientist eventually kills himself after he sees the horror he hath wrought, and I think that, had the story been real, this is the kind of place that might have been his lair. Small lights are embedded into the ceiling, but I find it hard to believe there might be gas lines in this hellscape. Beakers and bits of metalwork are strewn across a wooden workbench, and there are a number of strange, shiny steel things that I reckon are weapons along one wall.

"What kind of place is this?" Katherine breathes. She's just as awed as I am. I ain't never seen something so amazing, and I'm half afraid that this ain't real, just a fever dream from being locked up in that railcar.

"It's my lab. I'm responsible for a lot of the technology you'll see around Summerland. Electric lights," he says, pointing to the ceiling. "Some of the farming equipment we use. I designed a lot of the weaponry. It's my job here. You heard the sheriff up there—everyone in Summerland has their place, and it's important to remember what it is." There's a tone in his voice, and I wonder if Mr. Gideon ain't here by choice any more than me and Katherine.

He sighs and waves us over to a workbench along the back wall. A dozen different pieces lie across the surface, and he holds up a sharp needle attached to a glass vial.

"Every Negro who comes to Summerland gets vaccinated. The purpose is simple: the vaccination keeps you from turning if you get bit while on patrol."

I roll my eyes. "Right."

His eyebrows raise. "You don't believe me?"

"While in Baltimore, I had the benefit of attending a lecture given by a professor named Ghering. You heard of him?"

Mr. Gideon puts down the syringe and crosses his arms. "I have."

"Well," I say, bending down to take the sheriff's newspaper from the top of my boot. "I happened to kill the man the professor turned after his vaccine failed. Professor Ghering was no Louis Pasteur, I can tell you that. You can ask my Miss Katherine, she was there, too." I slip back into the faithful servant act I put on for the Sheriff for just a moment. I don't know this man, and I have to question the sanity of anyone who thinks sticking a needle in my neck is a good idea.

Mr. Gideon turns to Katherine, and she gives him a tight smile. "What Jane says is true. His vaccine didn't work."

Mr. Gideon gives me an appreciative smile. "Well, that doesn't surprise me at all. But this is my vaccine, not his, and I happen to know for certain that this is the genuine article."

"Oh. You test it out on Negroes as well?" I ask, the black feeling growing just a smidge. Despite his kindness, this man is just like the rest of his kind: polite until you tell them no.

"You'll be the first. I tested it out on myself and a few

unwilling cats. Now, please let me finish vaccinating you. I assure you that it's perfectly safe. If you decide to put up any resistance, Bill back there would be happy to assist. I'm sure a lady of your bearing would much rather face adversity with her head held high than in physical restraint." He takes a deep breath and lets it out. "Please. I know what the sheriff has planned for you. It really is for your own good."

I purse my lips to keep from telling him what I think of his assumption as to the nature of my character and inherent needs. I don't like the idea of that needle punching holes in me. But I ain't in any position to put up a real fight right now. I'm even more tired and hungry than when I got off the train, and I've no desire to get pummeled like poor Jackson. An uncertain future is still better than no future at all.

Besides, I have yet to find a jam I can't get myself out of. One day this whole Summerland fiasco will just be an interesting footnote in the story of my life.

I step forward, pulling down my collar so Mr. Gideon can stick the needle in the hollow of my neck. He pulls up the leather string with my lucky penny on it, a single eyebrow raised. "Are you superstitious, Miss McKeene?"

"It's only superstition if you don't believe, Mr. Gideon." This close his eyes are more green than brown, and they dance with humor as a smile quirks his lips.

"Quite so, Miss McKeene, quite so." His hands are gentle, and the metal is cool as it pierces my skin. "Thank you," he says, his voice low. It causes an odd shiver to go running down my spine, and I step backward a little too quickly, anxious to put some space between the two of us.

"Now, Miss Deveraux, it seems the sheriff believes you to be a white woman. Why is that?" Mr. Gideon takes off his spectacles and wipes them with his pocket square.

Katherine shoots me a glare. "Because someone told him I was."

Mr. Gideon nods. "Well, phrenologists claim we can identify someone's character and racial derivation by measuring the skull." He goes to a drawer and pulls out a set of calipers.

I cough to cover my laughter. I'd been thinking Mr. Gideon was a fair sight smarter than the typical fellow in this place, but if he believes that he can tell anything by the size of someone's head, he's just as daft as the rest of them.

Katherine doesn't say anything, but Mr. Gideon is gentle as he takes several measurements and jots them in a notebook.

"It looks like you're telling the truth, according to my calculations," Mr. Gideon says with a frown.

"Hooray for science," I say.

He shakes his head. "I don't believe in phrenology at all. It's easily disproven, the pet hobby of bigots."

I cross my arms. "Kate is white."

Mr. Gideon gives me a tight-lipped smile. "Well, it doesn't matter what I think. Pastor Snyder is the Sheriff's father, and the real power in town. The preacher makes the final decision on all matters. These numbers are for him."

"So this town is a family business, then? Good to know." What a degenerate group of kinfolk. No wonder they found themselves exiled to the middle of the continent.

Katherine gives me another dirty look while Mr. Gideon packs away his implements and I shrug and give her an apologetic grin. I feel mighty bad about getting her shipped out west with me and Jackson. If I can make sure she can live here as a white lady, that should go a long way toward squaring us. I don't much care about Katherine, but I hate owing anyone anything. Most especially someone as put together as her.

Mr. Gideon sighs, dragging my attention back to him. "I'm sorry you find yourselves here, ladies. Truly, I am. Now, if you'll follow me, we'll get you some clothing better suited to frontier life and some food. I expect you're both hungry and tired after your long trip."

We both nod and follow Mr. Gideon up the stairs. Halfway out of his laboratory Katherine grabs my wrist and gives me a proper glare.

"I hope this thing about me being white is part of some grand scheme you have to get us out of this," she whispers. Emotion is heavy in her voice, and I worry that she's about to break on me.

I give her a saucy wink. No, I don't have any idea how

we're going to get out of Summerland. But I'm a patient girl, and all I need is time.

Stepping back out into the sun after the cool shadows of Mr. Gideon's lab is like a punishment all its own. Bill leans against the side of the small building that shelters the staircase, hat forward to keep the sun off of his face.

"Ladies," Mr. Gideon, says, tilting his bowler as he shows us out. Bill startles awake, loosing a thick stream of tobacco juice in my direction. I manage to jump aside before it hits my fancy boots.

"I bet you're a big hit with the ladies," I say.

He says nothing but just glares in my direction before yanking his head to the side. "Come on so we can get you outfitted. The sooner we get your black ass out to the border, the sooner you'll lose some of that sass."

I smile sweetly in Bill's direction as we follow him back to the general store. Bill is not the kind to open a door for a lady, so Katherine and I let ourselves in while he posts up next to the entryway, tilting his hat low again.

The man behind the counter of the general store, a Mr. Washington, is kind and helpful, and gives me two sets of loose-fitting trousers, two shirts of a rough material, a pair of sturdy boots that appear used, and a single set of underthings.

"This is all you get for free. Anything else you have to buy. Shopping day for Negroes is Tuesday. Don't try to come round any other day than that, the sheriff will just have you thrown out. Also, you'll need to buy winter gear early. Last year I was clean out of coats come November, and I don't know where you're from, but January here is no joking matter."

"You got anything nicer for Miss Kate?" I say, raising my head defiantly.

Mr. Washington narrows his eyes at me. "That's all I got for clothing."

Katherine gives Mr. Washington a kind smile. "I apologize, sir. Jane is a good girl but a bit protective, as an Attendant should be. She meant to ask, do you have any clothes suitable for a lady?"

Mr. Washington's expression softens and he shakes his head, looking truly saddened. "No, miss. I'm afraid you'll have to see Mrs. Allen for that."

He moves away, and I lean in to Katherine. "At least it ain't striped," I say. She scowls at me and I grin wide. "And hey! You stopped arguing about being white."

"You'd better be right about this. I dislike lying."

"It gets easier the more you do it."

Mr. Washington comes back with a ledger and asks us to make our mark. I put an *X* where he indicates while Katherine signs with a flourish.

We thank Mr. Washington and carry our bundles out of the store. Bill stands when he sees us and gestures down the street.

"You'll share a room with the rest of your kind above the Duchess's place. Sheriff won't send you out to the line today, he's a good Christian and the pastor thinks even animals deserve a day off after the trip out here. You'll eat with the rest of the girls, patrol with them, what have you. For now you'll use the weapons out on the line." Bill spits again. "Try not to get yourselves killed too quickly. I bet Pete you girls would last to All Saints' Day at least."

The door to the sheriff's office opens, and another of his flunkies walks toward us. "Pastor says the blond one is white. Test checks out. We gotta walk her to the church. Other one can go on patrol, though."

Katherine stands up straighter. "I require my Attendant by my side. It isn't proper to be walking around unprotected."

"Don't worry, we'll keep an eye on you," the man says, giving Katherine a grin that makes me feel like I ate something foul.

"Not likely," I say, putting myself between Katherine and the man. "It ain't proper and I'm here to make sure Miss Katherine is cared for like the lady she is." I spread my feet in a defensive position. Attendants get training in hand-to-hand combat because the dead ain't the only threat to young ladies of good breeding. Besides, I'd like nothing more than to have a reason to break one of these fella's faces.

"Let the girl walk Miss Deveraux to the church. You know how the pastor feels about his ladies," Bill says, voice low. He leers at Katherine for a moment before he leans in close to me. "I look forward to straightening out that sideways attitude of yours."

He and his friend walk off back toward the sheriff's office, leaving me and Katherine alone for the first time since we arrived in Summerland. She turns toward me, her expression impassive. "Jane, I fear we have landed ourselves in a certifiably terrible place."

A bubble of hysterical laughter threatens to well up, and I have to swallow it back down. "What was your first clue?"

"As I said earlier, I trust your devious brain is working through a way out of this pickle. This town is terrifying."

I set off toward the church, Katherine yapping all the while. I ain't sure what to expect in Summerland's house of the Lord. Nothing good, though. Even under the best of circumstances me and preachers don't mix so well. And these circumstances ain't anywhere near the neighborhood of good. Katherine and I both stink to high heaven, and I can't expect that a man of God will want to tolerate our stench any more than we do.

As we walk, Katherine's voice is getting more and more hysterical. "There's a separate shopping day for Negroes, I have been called a darkie at least four times today, and I'm pretty sure that Bob called us animals."

"Bill."

"What?"

I sigh. "That fella's name was Bill. Bob was the other one. And you're a white woman now, so don't get your knickers in a twist whenever someone says something about Negroes. You're supposed to enjoy talking down to colored folks."

Katherine stops and puts her hands on her hips. I pause as well, half turning toward her. Her lips are pursed with displeasure. "How on earth am I supposed to live a lie, one that will surely end up with me dead if anyone discovers the truth?"

I don't say anything, because she's right. A couple of years ago a Baltimore shopkeeper named Rusty Barnes was discovered to be a Negro who'd been passing as a white man. A mob looted his shop and burned it to the ground. They would've killed Rusty as well if Jackson and I hadn't managed to sneak him out of the county. There's nothing white folks hate more than realizing they accidentally treated a Negro like a person.

"Well," I say after a long pause, "you let me worry about that. We're in this together, whether you like it or not." Katherine rolls her eyes, but she keeps up with me when I start walking again. Time to change the subject. "I ever tell you about the garden back at Rose Hill?"

Katherine shades her eyes as she looks at me. "Jane, what are you going on about?"

I pull Katherine up into the shade of the boardwalk. The church is just across the street, a white picket fence setting it off from the rest of the town. "Back at Rose Hill, Auntie

Aggie—that was the woman that mostly raised me—would plant a huge garden full of okra and carrots and cabbage, green beans, and black-eye peas, everything you needed to feed a plantation full of hungry people. Everyone had to work the garden at least a couple of times a week if they wanted to eat good, and even my momma would put on her big sun hat and go out and pull weeds. It was a necessity in a place where a trip beyond the barrier fence to the market could mean death.

"One summer, the garden was plagued by a rabbit. This wasn't no ordinary rabbit, this was a hare of unnatural ability. It would always find a way inside of the fencing, filling itself up on the fruits of our labor. It was, as Momma said, a bastard of a rabbit."

Katherine gasps and looks around. "Jane! Such language."

"Let me finish my story. Anyway, Auntie Aggie and a few of the boys put out snares and traps galore, everything from crates baited with carrots and bits of lettuce to complicated tie snares I found in an old frontiersman's book Momma had from her dead daddy. Nothing worked. Every morning we'd go out and see the parsley munched down to nubs, or nibbles in the cabbage. The frustration was enough to put one off of gardening altogether, truth be told.

"But Auntie Aggie never let it faze her. Every night she would set out the same kind of snare, a simple loop knot that someone had taught her long ago. And every morning, when the rabbit wasn't caught, she'd retie that snare, same as she did the day before. I asked her once if she was scared the hare was going to eat the whole garden clean before that trap of hers caught him.

"'Jane,' she said, 'look at this garden. Look at the lettuces and those beans! And those tomatoes? They are especially fine this year, don't you agree? Trust me on this: it's just nature for creatures like him to get greedy.' That was all she said to me."

Katherine's listening now, her eyes narrowed. "So what happened?"

I grin. "She was right. After nearly two weeks of trying to catch the hare, Aunt Aggie made us a nice rabbit stew from that fat bunny. See, while the rabbit was skinny and hungry, that snare couldn't catch him, and he was cautious enough to avoid it. But once he got fat, he couldn't fit through the same holes he used to. I ain't lying when I say he was big enough to feed darn near all of Rose Hill that night. And tasty? Well, all of his good eating meant even better eating for us.

"The point is, sometimes when the rabbit gets too fat, too comfortable, he makes mistakes. But the gardener, she ain't got nothing but time. Because even the hungriest rabbit can't eat the entire garden. At some point the good sheriff will make a mistake, some gross miscalculation, reveal some weakness, and that's when we'll find our freedom."

Katherine is nodding now, her expression thoughtful. "We will be patient gardeners."

"Yes. We will be the most patient gardeners, and we will fatten up that bunny like nobody's business. And when that rabbit is nice and plump, we shall set the snare, and let him run right on through it."

Katherine nods. "Thank you, Jane."

I smile, because I'm relieved that she didn't ask the question I've been dreading since we got here.

What if we're not the gardeners, but the rabbits?

One of the biggest challenges here at Rose Hill is boredom, and making sure that the people here don't fall into vice.

Chapter 20
In Which I Meet a Questionable Man of God and a Kind Madam

Summerland's church is bigger than I expect. I've only seen a handful of folks walking around the town, but the church is easily the size of the First Baptist, the second largest church in Baltimore. While the rest of the town looks ragged and tired, the lone house of worship is fresh and clean: the building's walls are crisp with whitewash and a real stained glass window is set high in the front of the building. The only similarity between the rest of the town and the church is the small windows covered with iron bars, but the shambler proofing is barely noticeable on such an impressive building.

We walk up the path in silence, and before we can reach for the door it swings open. The whitest white man I ever saw beckons us, his blue-veined hands shaky, his false teeth overly large in his mouth. "Miss Deveraux. Please, join me inside. The sun is frightful fierce today."

Katherine gives the man a beatific smile. "Sir, your kindness is greatly appreciated. Oh, I fear what this sun is going to do to my complexion. I can already feel a powerful flush coming upon me."

She sweeps inside the church and the cool darkness beyond the threshold. I make to follow her but the old man stops me with a hard look. "I'm sorry, but it's our way here that those bearing the Curse of Ham don't enter the church."

I scowl. "The Curse of Ham?" I ain't ever heard of such a thing, and I have a feeling it's got nothing to do with supper.

Katherine sighs softly from behind the old man. "It's a euphemism for the curse Noah put upon Canaan, Ham's son. It's the reason the Negro was enslaved," she says. There's a tightness in her voice that reveals she doesn't agree with this particular line of thinking, but the old white man doesn't notice. He nods in agreement with Katherine's explanation.

"In these days of His castigation upon the earth, we must reaffirm the hierarchy of His creation and His will. Your soul will be cleansed in Heaven; in the meantime, your kind are made to serve His image through toil and labor, girl."

"What part of the Scripture is that from?" I mutter. The old man either doesn't hear me or chooses to ignore me.

"Your mistress won't have use of you any longer. Here in Summerland we take care of our blossoms the way the Lord has always intended. We have no need for Attendant companions to live alongside our fair blossoms, no matter what Mayor Carr has instituted in those heathen cities of the east. Here, we have worked to reestablish the Lord's natural order, and peace and safety has been our reward. You'll serve the patrols. Take yourself to the house of soiled doves. The Duchess will take care of you."

With a vacant smile, he closes the door in my face.

I stand there for a few moments, sweating, arms piled high with boots and clothing. I consider kicking in the door, but then what? I don't know how anything works around here, and I have nowhere to go.

So I turn around and go back the way I came, toward the house of ill repute.

When I reach the end of the boardwalk, I keep walking past the saloon and back toward the rail yard where we entered town. For a moment I think that maybe I could just keep walking, out toward the mystery of the wall, past that to the open prairie, continue moving until I've left this whole mess behind. Running away has never been my style, but it doesn't seem so bad, now.

The road past the rail yard is lined with poles, and beyond it are houses, which I can get a better look at now. Beautiful houses, whitewashed and large, the kind of house where you could raise a nice family. Screams filter up the road from the houses, and I tense until I see a pack of kids come running around the side of one of them, playing some game of chase and laughing in between their proclamations of mock terror.

The sight stops me in my tracks. When was the last time I saw kids running and playing, not a care in the world? Even back on Rose Hill we tended to be cautious in our play, the memory of Zeke casting a long shadow for years to follow.

If kids can run and play and scream in delight, then maybe Summerland ain't all bad.

I turn back the way I came and head to the saloon.

As I walk, I think of what Miss Preston said, that Katherine came from a brothel, and wonder if that's why she has such pretty manners. Even now, in the midst of a full-fledged crisis, Katherine has managed to retain her deportment. I grew up in the big house on Rose Hill, and even I didn't have manners as pretty as Katherine's when I got to Miss Preston's. I figured she'd grown up someplace where appearances would be important, but not a cathouse.

Of course, everything I know about brothels I know about from books. I read a novel, *The Captain's Forbidden Woman*, that was all about a poor girl named Annabel who ended up as a working girl after her father's rival ruined her family; she was eventually rescued by a dashing ship's captain. I think Jackson got it to scandalize me, since the red velvet cover was decidedly lurid, but it ended up being a very good story. Annabel spent many paragraphs relating the extravagant furnishings and decorum of the brothel. It all sounded very glamorous, although the idea of tossing up my skirts for pay struck me as being even more laborious than killing the dead. Especially if being a working girl meant a lot of swooning. Annabel swooned at least once every chapter, sometimes twice.

Thinking of Jackson and the things he used to smuggle me makes me think of my mother—the silence from the postmaster every time Jackson came calling, or so I thought. I touch the small packet of letters tucked in the pocket of my dress. I've been gone from Rose Hill going on three years, but it's only been a year since the last letter I got from my momma. The packet seems too small to hold a year's worth of correspondence. What if she gave up on me? What if she is dead?

I need answers about my momma and the fate of Rose Hill, now more than ever. That is enough of a reason to find a way out of Summerland, fine town or not.

I draw even with the brothel and find the doorway empty. There's no door, and the room beyond is so dark that I ain't sure there's even anyone inside.

"Hello?" I call. "Is anyone there?"

"Come on in, sugar," says a voice from inside, dark and smoky like whiskey. My penny hasn't gone cold, and this seems like the place where I'm supposed to be, so I walk on in.

The room beyond the doorway comes into focus, the haze from a trio of half-dressed ladies sitting around a table smoking cigarillos and playing cards. Along the one wall is a bar, a half-dressed Negro girl perched at the end talking to a rough-looking fellow. Behind the bar, a white man, bald and shiny, leans against the polished wood counter, eagle eye on the coarse fellow and the girl.

I suspect that every kind of vice an enterprising sort could imagine can be found under this roof. And I am determined that I will not let this place cow me.

I zero in on the redhead I saw earlier and head straight to her. She sits next to an empty hearth in a big tapestried chair, the kind you'd find in a ladies' sitting room.

"Ma'am," I say, bobbing a curtsy. "I reckon you might be the Duchess?"

She puts down the book she holds, *Gulliver's Travels*, and fans herself with a ragged peacock feather fan. Up close, it's easy to see the layers of face paint she wears. "I am. And who might you be?"

"My name is Jane McKeene. I'm begging your pardon for disturbing your afternoon repose, ma'am, but I was directed to see you about lodgings, a bath, and the possibility of some sustenance." The last two are my own additions. I ain't sure what the standard protocol is, if there is one, but I might as well ask for the sun, moon, and stars while I'm at it.

The woman laughs, showing a gap in the back of her mouth where she's lost a few of her teeth. "Look at you, with those pretty manners. Wherever did they find you?"

"At the junction of hard luck and bad times," I answer. It's something that my momma says.

Used to say?

Best to just not think about it.

The Duchess's expression softens, and she hauls herself to her feet. "I reckon I've passed through there a few times myself. Well, follow me, I'll show you where you can draw your bath and where you can sleep. As for food, you've got a couple of hours until we eat, but you're welcome to join me and my girls if you'd like. Everyone on this side of town eats down at the meeting hall. Only the respectable folks get the luxury of preparing their own food." There is a tone to her voice, and I wonder what it is that I'm missing.

She leads the way up a narrow set of stairs and past a room with curtains hung as partitions. The sounds of someone visiting with one of the girls filters out of the room, and I'm very careful to keep my eyes forward lest I see something I ain't expecting.

The Duchess stops at a door at the end of the hall. The room beyond is small, with a shelf along one wall. About half the spaces are taken up with extra sets of clothing, and the Duchess points to the shelves.

"You girls stow your stuff there. You got anything worth a damn, you're going to want to keep it with you. There's a bunch of thieving bastards in this place." She eyes the gown I wear greedily, and I get the sense that she's including herself in that group. Makes no matter to me, she can have the dress. The only things I want are my lucky penny and the packet of letters secured in my pocket.

And *Tom Sawyer*, of course. I've taken a liking to the little urchin, and I'd like to see where he ends up. It seems the boy is always running afoul of a pack of shamblers in the midst of his Missouri adventures, and the boy's derring-do reminds me of my own exploits.

I put my extra set of clothing on one of the far shelves, then follow the Duchess down a back staircase. "These are the stairs you'll use. Don't come down those front stairs, those are strictly for my girls and their clients. Negroes ain't allowed to drink in the saloon, anyway—or anywhere in Summerland, strictly speaking." She leans back and whispers, "You want whiskey, you'll get your spirits from the kitchen entrance. Woman named Maybelle. Don't let anyone catch you, though. They're free with the strap around here. The preacher sees to that."

"The preacher?" I ask. She can't possibly mean the old man

I saw just a few moments ago. He was too frail to wield any-thing.

The Duchess nods. "Don't let that old man fool you, he's got a vicious streak. The sheriff is his son, and nothing in this town happens without one of them saying so. The preacher thinks it up, but the sheriff makes it happen. Watch yourself around the two of them."

"Good to know. Anything else of note regarding the sher-iff and the preacher?"

The Duchess purses her lips for a moment before telling me in a low voice, "Sheriff lost his wife to the plague going on three years ago, right before the wall was completed. She was a pretty blond thing, as sweet as he is sour. Went out to gather berries by a nearby creek and got surprised, turned right in front of his eyes. Anyway, you want to make your life easy? Don't question his authority when it comes to the dead. He's never reasonable when the question of the undead plague is involved."

I nod and file the information away for later.

The stairs are impossibly narrow and cramped, and we have to walk single file. They empty out into a laundry room, with a glorious copper tub in the middle.

"This is where you'll wash your clothes. Some of my girls take in laundry, so if you want them to wash your things you can ask. That tub is yours to rent for a nickel, but I'll let you use it today for free since you . . . just been through an ordeal. You want hot water you have to pump it into the big cistern in the corner, then light that stove right next to it. After that, turn this fancy spigot here. After you're done, pull that plug in the bottom, and the water will run right out back to the trough I keep for the garden. Understood?"

I nod, and walk over to the contraption. I look at the copper pipes, the hand pump that brings water up out of the ground, the water heater that looks to be pressurized. "You got a way of handling the silt?" I ask, gesturing to the hand pump.

The Duchess shrugs one pale shoulder. "I don't rightly know. You'd have to ask the professor, he's the one that rigged up the contraption."

"The professor?"

"The tinkerer. Gideon. Most of the fancy gadgets you see around town are his creation." She pulls a pocket watch out of her skirt and sighs. "Dinner is in an hour or so, I need to get the girls fed before fellas start arriving."

I incline my head. "Thank you, ma'am, for the fine tour of your establishment," I say before bobbing another curtsy.

She gives me a bemused smile in return and just shakes her head as she slips through a door, off to see about her business.

There's a shelf of glasses along a wall and I grab one,

twisting the handle above the spigot. Water flows out, clean and clear. I fill the glass and drink deeply. The water tastes strange, as strange as anything else in this town, but not lethal.

At least, not yet.

The Bible has been a comfort, and one of the younger girls has even started a school for the little ones. It is such a miracle to listen to them read the Scripture, although I must admit it does make me heartsick for you, darling Jane.

Chapter 21
In Which I Attend Church

After a bath, I head out to find dinner. The town ain't all that big, and it's easy to see what the Duchess meant when she said that all the girls ate together. Everyone spills out of a plain, whitewashed building with a cross hammered onto the door. The meeting hall is next to the church but separated from the grander building by a garden of white crosses, memorials to the deceased. In the old days it would've been a graveyard, but most sensible folks have taken to burning their dead and mounting a cross in a field or yard, like these. It's just safer that way.

The meeting house smells of good things, so I push aside my worry that God will strike me down when I walk through the doors. I'm too hungry to worry about my tainted soul.

As I enter, every pair of eyes lands on me. Toward the back of the building are two large tables of boys and girls, all Negroes, hungrily shoveling food off tin plates. The Duchess and her girls sit at their own table near the door, plenty of room around them, some of the girls making lewd gestures to a few rough and ready white fellas sitting at a nearby table. I don't see Jackson. More important, I don't see Lily or the Spencers, and I wonder if we made a mistake, if we got ourselves sent out here for nothing.

I get a plate of a thick, hearty stew and a slice of bread from the woman at the window. My serving is about half that of the white man in front of me, my plate hammered tin instead of the stoneware. I open my mouth to complain, but I ain't given the chance.

"Keep it moving," says a high voice. Bill stands over me, shotgun propped on his shoulder. Why's he need a shotgun at dinner? No one else is armed.

The old man from the church glides up to me. He smiles, but there ain't nothing friendly about it. "Jane, Miss Deveraux will be so happy to hear you're settling in nicely."

"I got this, sir," Bill says, a quaver in his voice. There's an air of fear about him, and after I spot the large gold cross around the old man's neck I figure this must be the preacher the Duchess warned me about.

"No, Bill, you have other matters to attend to. It's Bible study night. Go watch the door. I won't have the whores sneaking out again." Bill walks off. The old man still smiles, thin red lips stretched garishly over large front teeth. His eyes are watery, the brown washed out to the color of a penny, his hair completely snow white and thinning. He looks like a walking skeleton, sun bleached and pale, and I involuntarily shrink back from him when he reaches a hand out to guide me toward the back of the building.

"Allow me to formally introduce myself; I am Pastor Snyder. You've no doubt already met my son, Sheriff Snyder. While my son enforces the laws here, my purpose is to give Summerland both spiritual and moral direction. It's a task I do not take lightly, as you will see."

There's a feverish gleam to his eyes, and his wide grin hasn't left his face. I didn't even know it was possible to smile and lecture someone at the same time, but here I am.

"Miss Deveraux told me that you're a bit impulsive and she was worried for your welfare. Told me your services were a gift from her now deceased father, and how valuable she finds your companionship." As we walk, the preacher keeps my right arm in a bruising grip, but I can't shake him off without dropping my dinner.

"In any case, believe me when I tell you that I understand how to deal with headstrong Negroes. In my youth, I was an overseer in what was formerly South Carolina. Tobacco fields, sometimes cotton. It was there that I came to understand the divine order that the Lord saw fit to bestow upon we men. I also learned many of your kind fail to understand this order, and I know that you can deal with obstinate Negroes as long as you remember they are, at their heart, children. 'Spare the rod and spoil the child,' as the Scripture tells us."

My penny has gone icy under my shirt, and I stop walking as the preacher stops. His eyes haven't left my face, not once, and I get the feeling I'm being cataloged, like a butterfly in a collection.

"I'm sure you will find that your place is a comfortable one if you make it so, Jane. God can be merciful and kind, as long as you follow His laws. But how you find your life here in Summerland is entirely up to you. Do not disappoint Him and do not disappoint me, and you will prosper. Enjoy your meal."

Preacher Snyder finally releases my arm as we pull up alongside the tables full of Negro boys and girls. Most of them are about my age, but none of them look familiar, and I wonder where they're from. I'm glad there ain't any other girls from Miss Preston's, as I ain't in the mood for any kind of heartfelt reunion. Still, I wonder where the girls Miss Preston has been feeding to Mayor Carr have gone off to. Is there more than one town like Summerland?

A dark-skinned girl with tight rows of braids looks up and gives me a guarded smile. "Hi. You want to sit here?" she asks, gesturing to the empty chair next to her.

I sink gratefully into the chair, my hands shaking as I set my tray down. "Pleased to meet you. I'm Jane."

"Likewise. I'm Ida." Her voice is whispery and low with the deep-throated accent of the Lost States, those places in the Deep South where shamblers outnumber people. Ida keeps casting furtive glances in the vicinity of Bill and his shotgun. "So, I see you met the preacher."

"I did. Charming fellow."

"About as charming as the serpent in the garden. Watch yourself around him."

I nod. Bill is now looking at us a little too intently and I decide to change the subject. "How long have you been here?"

Ida's expression hardens. "Too long. Most of us came at the same time, shipped up on a train from the Jackson compound."

"Compound?"

"Yes'm. Ain't you never heard of the compounds?"

"Once, briefly. It wasn't exactly an enlightening conversation. Mind telling me more?" Not much is known about life in the Lost States. It's generally thought of as a place even more desperate than the Western frontier.

Ida talks while I scoop up my food with my fingers, since

no one saw fit to give us forks. "Well, at ten you start your initial combat training. We have a test every year. If you fail it, they put you in the fields. But there are a lot of shamblers out there and chances are you'll get eaten, so that's no good. At thirteen, you join the patrols. But if you mess up—like if you don't listen or they think you're uppity—then they'll move you to another compound. Or, in our case, they put you on a train."

"Not in the fields with the others?"

"Only the little ones work in the fields, since they need all the grown folks they can get to keep the dead out. And if they can't use you, they sell you to someone who can."

"Slavery is illegal," I say.

"Not necessarily. They got loopholes in that there Thirteenth Amendment. If you've been bitten by a shambler, the amendment says you're no longer human, even if you haven't turned yet, which means you don't have rights as a person anymore. And there's a reward for capturing bit Negroes, since everyone is convinced we're immune. I've seen folks testify Negroes have been bit and then those Negroes get sold off by the compound. Same if you're a criminal—and you can guess how that goes, when white folk are the ones who write the laws." She catches herself, then looks around and lowers her voice. "Lots of different ways to pretty up the same old evils." Ida looks down at her hands, wringing them something fierce. I can't tell whether she's angry or upset. "If I would've known they were going to send me here, I would've run off a long time ago."

"Is it worse here?" I ask, not really wanting an answer.

Ida just shrugs, and a girl on the other side of her leans forward. "It ain't so bad now that they got the whores to take care of the drovers. It was worse before they had something to keep them occupied."

My stomach turns, unsettling my supper so that I have to swallow hard to keep it down. "Who lives in those houses on the other side of Summerland?" I ask, since she's being so chatty.

"The good white folks do. They don't eat with us. Most of the good people in the town are put over there on the southern boundary. It's safer, and it's mostly families and such. The only folks here in the town are the Negroes and the trash. The nice white folks don't even attend church with us, because we might soil their souls."

I nod. "So I heard."

There is a loud banging. I look toward the noise to see the preacher standing at a podium that's been set up next to the serving window. He looks out across the room, smiles his ghastly smile, and says, "Gather round, gather round, children. No need to be shy. There are some new faces in the flock today, and that is a boon. God has blessed us, because a growing flock is a lucky flock. As Summerland grows, as we welcome more souls into our humble town, so does the dream of a new Jerusalem, of our own righteous city on the hill."

There's some noise as chairs are moved closer to the podium. No one bothers moving where I sit. The tables full of colored folks are farthest away from the podium, and it feels intentional.

The preacher continues. "Tonight, I want to tell you the story of John, one of the first farmers to settle here in Summerland. John was a flawed man. See, when he came here to our fine town it was the beginning of the war, before the dead walked, and John had strange notions about justice and equality and God's will. He'd come to us from South Carolina, my own home state, and he came west a man who was missing something, some vital part of the self.

"His father had been an overseer, and rather than follow in that man's footsteps, he fled. Because John had lost his faith, you see. He couldn't understand how God could let so many live in suffering and bondage while others profited off that misery. Like the abolitionists who unleashed this Sinner's Plague of the Dead upon us, John doubted God's will."

It takes everything I have to keep my mouth shut, my thoughts to myself.

People in the crowd, mostly the white men at the tables full of roughnecks, are nodding and murmuring in assent. The Negroes just sit there. This ain't the first time they've heard this sort of story.

The preacher closes his eyes and puts his hand over his heart. "And because he questioned, the Sinner's Plague found him one day as he plowed his field. The problem with John—the problem with all nonbelievers—is they think they understand God's plan. They think God sent His son to earth to die for our sins because, down past the roots, we are all sprung from the same seed. But that isn't so! The Lord God Himself desires, above all things, order. An understanding of where we all fit in His church, this earth. The senseless tragedy that was the War between the States disrupted the order God had given to us, by His grace. For failing to understand this law, fundamental to His love, He has unleashed His wrath upon us. It was hubris to think we are all equal in His eyes, friends. Not in this world. But perhaps, later, in the Lord's kingdom." At that last bit he turns and gestures at us sitting in the back, as though the meaning in his words wasn't clear enough. A few of the white folks, both the whores and the drovers, turn to look at us. I sink down a little lower in my chair, feeling very, very exposed.

The preacher smiles, as though he knows exactly the effect of his words, and continues. "But there is hope. You can cast off the sins of your past, and you can cleanse yourself of the Curse of Ham. You can toil and labor for the good of those God has made in His image, and thereby find peace and contentment. Because that is the dream of America, and it is God's will; to work hard in the role God has provided for us, to be deserving of good fortune, and to prosper."

Most of the white folks in the room are nodding and giving praise. I glance around the Negro tables and realize a few of those folks are as well. That makes me sad and scared.

The preacher clears his throat, and shakes himself a little, as though casting aside the somber feeling in the room. He smiles widely at us, his eyes shining in the low light. The penny around my neck is frigid. That man, that false prophet, might just be the most dangerous man in town.

"Now," the preacher says, his smile unfaltering, "Let us pray."

We've lost quite a few of our folks over the past few weeks, not just to shambler attacks but also to a group of men calling themselves Survivalists. They've been riding through the countryside stirring up no end of trouble. Too many of them are of the rough sort that used to run in the old slave patrols, riding down escapees for a few coins. If you should find yourself in the path of any of these men, run in the opposite direction. There is nothing to be gained from their acquaintance, and I fear for the Negro should these men ever come to any real power.

Chapter 22
In Which I Learn a Tune I Don't Care For

The next morning, we are woken early, shaken awake by someone's meaty fist. "Time to go," the big girl says before walking away.

"Well, good morning to you, too," I mutter, climbing out of my nest of blankets. I scratch at my arm as I stand. I'm pretty sure that my makeshift bed has fleas, if the creepy-crawly sensation over my skin is any indication. Ida gets up and looks at me as I scratch my arm.

"You're going to need to launder them blankets," she says, pointing to my arm.

"Yeah, maybe I can get one of the Duchess's girls to do it?" I hate doing laundry, and a few pennies seems like a fair price for dealing with flea-infested blankets.

Last night, after nearly two hours of listening to the preacher, I walked back to the sleeping spot with Ida. She helped me find blankets in the pile in the corner, telling me that "when a girl passes we just throw her blankets here for the next one," before showing me where to sleep. There are no beds, just blankets on the floor, everyone squished in tight as sardines. I thought Miss Preston's was bad, but now I long for the days of hard cots and meals served with cutlery.

The rest of the girls are pulling on their boots and heading out the door, so I hurriedly do the same. I barely have time to spare a thought for Katherine. Did she wake up in a feather bed, toast and coffee served on a silver service? Wherever she got to, it has to be better than this.

The sound of many boots on the back stairs rolls like thunder, and as we exit the saloon a couple of bleary-eyed cowpokes leaning against the back of the building raise their heads and curse us out. No one I'm with says anything, so I stay silent, too.

Once we're out on the street we fall into two lines. The boys are pouring around the back of the general store. They must have a room up above it, like we girls do at the Duchess's. No one in our group looks to be much older than twenty, and I wonder if everyone here is like Ida, someone rounded up from one of the patrol schools and sent out here.

I crane my neck to see if Jackson is amongst the boys, but I don't find his ocher skin anywhere. A midnight-skinned boy, tall and rangy, catches my eye and gives me a wink, but I look away before he can get the wrong idea.

The sheriff comes down the street atop a large, ill-tempered-looking beast. I elbow the person next to me, a small girl from Georgia who Ida introduced as Sofi.

"Is that a . . . ?"

Sofi looks at me from the corner of her eye. "A horse? You for real? Ain't you never seen a horse before?"

I shake my head, and I wonder what kinds of places in the Lost States have horses amongst so many shamblers. The animal is big and the color of cinnamon, with a long nose and a tail of straight hair. There's more hair along the thing's elongated neck, and its hoofed feet make a hollow *clip-clopping* sound in the packed dirt as it walks down the road toward us.

"We ready?" Sheriff Snyder calls, and I crane my neck around. Behind me are Bob and Bill, each on a horse of his own, their shotguns slung across their saddles. They give a curt nod, and the sheriff turns his horse around and starts off toward the edge of town, the thing walking pretty fast with its long, spindly legs.

The columns on each side follow at a trot, and I glance over at Sofi as I realize that we're supposed to run wherever we're going. Her face is impassive, as is everyone else's, as we're herded forward.

Old Professor Ghering called Negroes livestock the night of the fateful lecture. I can't help but think of him as we scurry along.

The pace ain't too fast, nothing like the wind sprints we had to do at Miss Preston's, but my boots are new and I haven't had much to eat over the past couple of days, so even a little bit of a run feels like too much. By the time we've cleared the rickety buildings of the town and get into the outskirts of the settlement I know that this trip is going to be brutal. The horse in front of us kicks up too much dust, and I'm still weak from the train ride, but I get the feeling that not keeping up would be much worse than a few blisters and a side cramp.

We've gone about a mile at our shuffle run when one of the boys calls, "Sheriff, sir!"

The sheriff, who is rolling a cigarette, glances back over his shoulder. "Mm-hmm?"

"Might we sing, sir?"

The sheriff strikes a match and lights his cigarette, then gives a curt nod.

I have no idea what the whole conversation pertains to until the same boy closes his eyes and sings out, "You get a line and I'll get a pole!"

Around me everyone responds with a chorus of "Honey! Honey!"

"You get a line and I'll get a pole," the boy calls out again, his voice strong and even. This time everyone responds with "Babe! Babe!"

And then everyone sings together "You get a line and I'll get a pole, and we'll go down to that fishing hole, honey, oh baby mine!"

The sound of that many voices raised in song brings goose bumps to my arms. It reminds me of home, the way the field hands would sing during the worst of the work, the hard things like hoeing or tilling. It was a way to make the work go faster, to take their minds off the difficult task at hand. They'd sing about far-off places and about days gone by, about silly things like peach cobbler and the devil trying to steal their soul. It was something I always felt outside of back on Rose Hill, since Momma wouldn't let me go into the fields. She always said it was too dangerous, but I wondered if maybe it was something else, like she was afraid that she could lose me to a song.

I ain't sure how I feel about the need for work songs in a place like this.

We sing as we shuffle along for the next few miles. Eventually I get the hang of it, and I join in, grateful for something to take my mind off the blisters forming on my feet.

When those shamblers gather round,
Honey! Honey!
When those shamblers gather round,
Babe! Babe!
When those shamblers gather round, swing your scythe and bring
them down,
Honey, oh baby mine!

Ain't no use in looking sad,
Honey! Honey!
Ain't no use in looking sad,
Babe! Babe!
Ain't no use in looking sad, shambler's bite ain't all that bad,
Honey, oh baby mine!

When my eyes go shambler yellow,
Honey! Honey!
When my eyes go shambler yellow,
Babe! Babe!
When my eyes go shambler yellow, then it's time to end your fellow,
Honey, oh baby mine!

Swing your scythe and take me down,
Honey! Honey!
Swing your scythe and take me down,
Babe! Babe!
Swing your scythe and take me down, before I turn the whole damn town,
Honey, oh baby mine!

By the time we get to the end of the song I ain't enjoying it so much.

"Halt!"

We all stumble to a stop. There's a cook wagon in the middle of the field, something I've only seen from drawings about Western life. A grizzled old colored man stirs a big pot of something over a fire, and a couple of small, dark-skinned boys run to and fro as the old man barks out orders.

"All right," the sheriff calls, turning his horse around so he can look down on us. "You got ten minutes to eat. Now git."

Everyone rushes to the cook fire, pushing and shoving to get next to the little boys, who hold wooden bowls that the old man ladles some kind of porridge into. I stand back, not bothering to shove my way into the throng. Once the melee has cleared I walk up to the front.

The old man looks at me with rheumy eyes. "Ain't nothing

left," he says, scraping the pot. He manages to produce a bit of burned mush from the bottom and puts it in a bowl for the little boys to share. To me he hands an empty bowl.

"What am I supposed to do with this?"

"Don't you sass me, missy. I gave you the bowl because you'll need it for lunch. Now clear on out."

I blow out an angry breath and go to stand next to Ida, who is poking at her burned porridge piece in dismay.

The big girl, Cora, looks at me, shoveling her porridge into her mouth with her hand. "You'd better learn, Negro. Them fancy manners ain't gonna keep you alive for long out here."

I watch Cora eat, and feel a little ill. There are no utensils to eat the porridge, so the options are use your hands or starve. The rest of our group stampeded to the trough like hogs because they knew there wouldn't be enough food for everyone. And this is all after we were herded out to the work site.

Ida sidles up to me, her expression worried. "Watch out for Cora. She's one of his favorites," she says, eyes hooded as she watches the big girl reach into a boy's bowl and scoop out a mouthful of porridge. "You want a little?" she asks, and I shake my head.

"No, you eat it. I ain't all that hungry, anyway." It's a lie. I'm starving, but Ida is tiny, and she looks like she needs the food more than I do.

"Let's go!" the sheriff yells from his horse, cracking a whip over our heads. Everyone shoves the rest of their porridge into their mouths and forms back up into their lines, bowls clutched in their hands.

Once again, we start running, our destination unclear. This time when everyone starts singing, I don't join in.

We stop a short while later, our second run of the morning much shorter than our first. The ground is flat, the sun is already hot, and the grass is high, but I barely notice any of it on account of my aching feet. My boots are laced tight, and each step is painful, blisters already forming. I don't even want to imagine what my feet look like under the leather.

The sheriff turns around and gives us all a steely gaze. "Fence menders, get to your business." About half the boys and girls run off and each pick up a spool of bobbed wire, slinging it over their shoulder before they head off to a fence line a few hundred feet in the distance, the waist-high grass parting as they move through it. Cora is one of the fence menders. So fence mending must be easier than patrolling, if what Ida said about her being one of the sheriff's favorites is true.

Beyond the fence, much closer now, is the imposing exterior wall. I'm guessing that's where I'm bound.

"Patrol, go get your weapons." The sheriff points to a ramshackle-looking shed, and this time I run out ahead of the group, ignoring my throbbing feet. I am not going to fight shamblers with a bowl.

I'm one of the first to the shed, Ida right behind me. When the girl next to me, Iris I think her name is, opens the door, my heart falls.

These ain't weapons. They're garden implements. There are several sets of sickles and quite a few scythes, but none of them have been cared for. The blades are rusty, the edges dull, and the pair of sickles I pick up ain't even weighted properly. No wonder the girls on patrol don't last long.

I grab the sickles and march over to Sheriff Snyder. I've had enough of this. I spent three years at Miss Preston's honing my combat skills, refining my manners, getting an education. I ain't no flunky to be prancing around the countryside just waiting to get bit. If I'm going out against shamblers, I need to be properly equipped.

"Sheriff, might I trouble you for a moment?"

The man looks down his nose at me, and his horse snorts and paws at the ground. "Why aren't you lining up with your people?"

"Sir, I do believe you should know that these weapons are highly inadequate for any kind of patrol." I hold up one of the sickles and point to the curved blade. "These haven't been sharpened in ages, they are rusted, and I doubt they could cut through grass, much less a shambler's neck."

"Jane McKeene, I realize that you are new here, so I'm going to let you go back and have one of the girls explain how things work to you."

"Sir, I ain't going to need to know how things work when I'm dead from a shambler's bite. Would you please look at this sickle?" I hold it up higher so that he can see what a disgrace his "weapons" are.

Quick as a snake, the sheriff's boot lashes out, hitting me in the shoulder. I stumble backward, and something hits me in the back of the head. I drop the sickles, and as I fall to my knees someone kicks me again in the back, the boot digging deep between my ribs.

"Hold there, now Bill. She's still gotta work."

I climb shakily to my feet, rage coursing through my veins. The pain is a distant throb to my desire to do a little sickle work across Bill's face.

Ida runs to my side. "Don't worry, Sheriff, it won't happen again. We'll school her up right."

The sheriff says nothing, just nods and spits, missing me by only a few inches. What is with these men and all their spitting?

Ida grabs my arms and whispers into my ear, "That right there is suicide. The sheriff is a whole lot of mean and not a lot of smart. You might as well poke a rattlesnake. Your death'd be easier."

I say nothing, steeling my expression to blankness. I just pick up my sickles and storm over to where the rest of the girls gather.

I'm getting out of here. But before I do, I'm going to get a little payback of my own.

I trust you aren't getting into too much mischief, Jane. You were always such an impetuous child, and I genuinely hope you aren't letting your temper get the better of you.

Chapter 23
In Which I Taunt the Devil

The attack leaves me in a black mood for the rest of the day. I talk to no one, only opening my mouth to answer questions when asked. My job is to walk the top of the exterior wall.

I'd thought the walls around Baltimore had been a sight, but Summerland's wall puts it to shame. It stands at least the height of three men and looks to be made of stacked mud bricks. There are bits of grass mixed in with the mud bricks to hold it together, and the wall is at least half as wide as it is tall. I ask one of the girls standing next to me, "How did they build such a thing?"

She glances at Bob and Bill before answering in a low voice. "You know the story of the Pharaoh and the Israelites?"

The holy book is not my favorite tome, but I know it well enough. I nod and she continues, "Let's just say this wall was built like the pyramids: most of the builders didn't live to tell about it, and ain't no Moses come to liberate them."

After that we are split into teams and assigned sections to patrol.

On the way out here, we had picked our way through an inner, double-strung bobbed wire fence and the interior fence, which boasts five lines of wire. It's a crime that a place with such excellent defenses would have such terrible weaponry available to the patrols.

Behind me Bill's smug satisfaction radiates off him in waves, and the spot on my back that met his boot aches. More than once I imagine sinking my rusty sickles into his skull.

But I don't. Instead, I shove my anger down, burying it deep, letting it temper my soul. Auntie Aggie always said the hard times make us stronger. If things continue like this, I will be nigh on invincible by the time I take my leave of Summerland.

I am teamed up for patrol with the dark-skinned boy that winked at me earlier in the day. His name is Alfonse, and he seems to be a nice enough fellow, if maybe a little too chatty. After twenty minutes of him relating to me his life story, I finally tell him, "I ain't interested in anything you have to say unless it's how to get out of here." He clams up after that, shooting me a few black looks when he thinks I ain't looking.

The wall we walk gets more disgusting the more of it I see. On the far side, in the space between us and the rest of the world, are some dead. Actual shamblers, walking around, moaning for a bite to eat, all grouped up like they're going to share a secret. There ain't a lot of them, but there's enough. The wall is too high for them to climb, but it's got some footholds in it so a person could climb down if needed, and I'm about to do so and end them when Alfonse says, "We ain't supposed to kill them, just make sure they don't try to climb the wall."

"What's the point of that?" I asked, the sound of their wailing making me feel more than a bit stabby.

Alfonse shrugged. "The sheriff has this idea that killing one just attracts more of them. If you do it, you'll get in trouble, and the sheriff is quick with the whip." The sickly sweet stink of rotting corpses hangs heavy in the air, and every time the wind shifts, I gag.

Me and Alfonse are walking our stretch of wall for what must be the tenth time when I hear the most god-awful, bloodcurdling scream.

A little ways down the wall behind us, a girl has slipped

into the no-man's-land of the prairie. Another girl is climbing down the wall, to save the girl who fell, it appears.

And a knot of shamblers is already running toward the both of them, hell-bent on dinner.

I turn to run to their assistance, but Alfonse grabs my arm. "We ain't supposed to leave our posts."

"Alfonse, you any good at math?" He shakes his head, and I sigh. "Well, I am. Two people with glorified butter knives ain't going to be able to take on that many shamblers, especially when a few of them look to be new turns." It comes out in a lightning-fast bit of speech, and then I'm running full tilt along the wall.

I forget my blisters, my hunger, my thirst. Everything fades into the background as I count the shamblers, note their gait. You have to kill the freshies first. They're the fastest, the smartest. The ones that have been running for a while are always slower, like a clockwork toy that just won't wind. From my observations there looks to be three that are moving well, the rest of the group kind of straggling behind.

By the time I get to the girls I have a stitch in my side and my feet are screaming, but I push it all aside. I pick my way down the wall, jumping too early and dropping a sickle, nearly losing my balance when I hit the bottom. I grab my fallen weapon and pick my first target, a Negro girl wearing clothing that looks eerily like mine, and leap, sickle swinging to take the thing down.

Here's the thing. If these were *my* sickles, my beloved, sharp, well-weighted combat sickles, they would've gone through the shambler's neck like a hot knife through lard. But these are not my sickles. So the blade gets stuck halfway, the beast snapping its teeth at me and clawing at my arms as it tries to get free.

I place my foot behind the shambler's and use my sickle to push it backward. Once it's down I use a mule kick against the curved edge to force the blade through. The head goes rolling off down into the culvert and the body goes still.

But my kill has taken time. The other two patrol girls, whom I don't know, are grappling with the remaining two freshies in close quarters, shoving them and swinging their scythes ineffectively. The rest of the pack is still fifty yards away and moving like elderly folks, hunched over and slow. If I can take down the other two, then we might have a fighting chance.

I switch my grip on my weapons as I run up behind the one closest to me. I cross my arms and use a blade on each side of the neck and pull the metal through. But as I'm trying to yank the sickles through the shambler's neck I get a good look at its face, and my heart stutters to a stop.

The dead girl reaching for my throat is Maisie Carpenter.

Maisie was in her last year when I got to Miss Preston's. The last time I saw her was the night of Professor Ghering's lecture, when she stood along the wall, nodding in agreement as I protested using that poor man in that professor's ill-conceived experiment. And now, here she is.

My penny goes cold, and the sensation is enough to snap me out of my poorly timed ruminations. I grunt and yank the blades the rest of the way through Maisie's neck. It's not as efficient as a swing, but with the rusty blades it's the best I can do. Still, it takes entirely too much effort. In the time I've taken down two shamblers, I could normally have taken down five or six.

One of the other girls finally gets her scythe up and swings it at a shambler's neck. The thing goes to the ground; it's another girl dressed like an Attendant. I recognize this one as well. It's the girl that ran off, leaving Mayor Carr's wife to her fate.

Looks like I found the answer to what happened to the girls assigned to the fine ladies of Baltimore. I file the fact away for later, another piece of a puzzle I ain't sure I understand or even want to parse.

I rest my hands on my knees and breathe deeply as the antique shamblers amble close enough to be a threat. I have to take care of them quickly, before any others show up to see what's going on. After all, we still have a wall to climb. The other two girls stand a few feet behind me, their expressions dazed and more than a little shocked.

"Go on, get back up. I'll take care of these." I don't have to tell them twice. They run toward the wall, trying to find the handholds that'll allow them to climb to the top. That's the problem with walls: they don't just keep the enemy out.

The remaining shamblers are practically ancient, wearing uniforms from the war, and it takes very little effort to separate their heads from their bodies. They're all extremely decayed, a few of them missing arms. One has a cavalry sword hanging from his belt, and after I put him down I unsheathe the sword and test its weight. It's a real sword, not a decoration like the major used back at Rose Hill. I ain't partial to swords—the time on the reverse is too long if you miscalculate your swing—but it's better than a couple of rusty gardening blades.

I use the sword to put down the rest of the decrepit pack. The euphoria, that light-headed feeling I get after every battle, is stronger than ever, most likely because this is the first time in a very, very long time where I could have died. Another few seconds removing poor Maisie's head, another couple of shamblers, and I could be lumbering and dragging along just like them.

After the last of the old dead has been dispatched, I wipe the sword off on the nearest body. I toss the sword onto the top of the wall and locate a couple of possible handholds before backing up a few steps to get a running start. I run and jump, my hand digging into the uneven spots in the wall. I haul myself up to the top, groaning from the effort, kicking and scrabbling in a downright ungainly manner. But I've managed to clear the wall, and that's a feat in and of itself.

A crawling sensation tickles across my skin as I stand. That's when I see Bill, below me on the inside of the wall, his rifle trained on me. Next to me, the girls have their hands up in the air. "Put 'em up!" Bill says.

I raise my arms over my head, sword at my feet. To the right of me the other two girls raise their arms a little higher, hands shaking. Their eyes are wide, and they're clearly terrified.

Bill stares at us for a long time. He's sweaty and unsettled, like maybe lunch didn't agree with him. "Sir, what seems to be the problem?" I ask, keeping my voice calm.

"You got bit," he says, moving the rifle from one of us to the next.

I look at the other girls, one of whom has started crying quietly. Bill didn't even bother to climb the wall, there's no way he can know what went on right below it. I turn back to Bill. "No sir, none of us got bit. Sure, took us a bit longer to put down the shamblers than it should've on account of the poor quality of weapons we're given, but we are all safe and sound."

Bill turns the gun on me, then the girl next to me, then finally the one on the end. "No, you ain't. Them shamblers bit you. Ain't no way you're coming off that wall!"

By this point Bill is yelling and gesturing, spittle flying, and I'm a little shocked at how he's gone from spiteful bully to raving lunatic. I glance at the girls, to see if either of them was in fact bit, when thunder splits the humid air, warm fluid spattering my face. I turn to Bill, whose eyes are wide and surprised, and then back to the girls. The one closest to me is flat on her back, most of her jaw missing, eyes wide and staring.

A deep sadness rips through me, followed quickly by anger. I didn't even know her name.

I whip back to Bill, who is now frantically chambering his next bullet. My anger loosens my tongue, and I drop my arms and bend down to grab my sword, gesturing at Bill with it. "What the hell is the matter with you? All you had to do was look at her arm! What kind of bastard just goes around shooting people?"

But Bill can't or doesn't hear me. He lets out a frightened squeal as his eyes go wide, staring at the girl on the end. She's dropped her head and she's starting to shake, the full body shudder of someone turning. A low growl comes from her throat, and Bill hastily raises his rifle. The shot goes wide, but it gets the girl's attention, and her head snaps down, yellow eyes locked on Bill.

I bring the sword up and through her throat, hard and fast. The blade does the job, her body falling on the shambler side of the wall, her head tumbling the other way.

Bill is frozen, and so I climb down the wall, grabbing what handholds I can but mostly sliding. It takes a good while, and my temper is hot as I make my way, sword in hand. The dark cloud has settled over my thoughts once again, and I'm only half-aware of what I do.

I march up to Bill where he stands, wide-eyed. His joints finally loose and he tries to point the rifle at me, barrel shaking. I knock it to the side in one motion. He's all out of shots, anyway.

I point the sword at him, the rusty tip only a few inches away from his nose, the blade dripping the poor girl's life-blood in the space between us. I'm sad and angry and a whole host of other feelings, but mostly I'm fighting very hard not to kill Bill.

"You just murdered an innocent girl, you cowardly bastard. All you had to do was check their arms! How hard is that?"

Bill just stares at me.

"Say something, you sad sack of manure! Give me a reason not to take your head off."

Bill says nothing. He looks away, shaking. I want so much to end him here, to vent my anger and frustration and fear in a single swing of a rusty cavalry sword.

But I don't.

I take a deep breath and wipe the blood off on Bill's shoulder before I prop it on my own. If I kill him, I have no doubt that the sheriff will execute me while that no good pastor and most of the town looks on in judgment, and I ain't fixing to die just yet.

"If you point a gun at me, you'd better use it, because next time I might not remember that a lady doesn't go around lopping the heads off of random folks, you goddamn yellow-bellied jackass."

I turn and walk back to the wall, climbing it easily this time. A few feet away Alfonse stands, openmouthed, waiting for me. I give him a long look. "Don't. Say. A. Word."

He nods and we pick back up where we left off, walking up and down our portion of the wall. The moans of the shamblers seem farther away now, like they've lost interest now that fresh meat isn't in the immediate vicinity. Inside, my thoughts churn. This can't be the first time Bill has shot an innocent person out of fear. Do we truly mean so little around here? I laugh mirthlessly at the obviousness of the answer. Maisie, and the other girl, the one I didn't know . . . it wasn't an accident that she ended up in a field full of shamblers. Maisie was always top-notch when I knew her; there's no way she got bit during a routine patrol. So how did she turn?

I ain't sure I want to know.

As I walk the wall for the remainder of the day, one thing becomes clear. There is no such thing as the good life in Summerland for Negroes. The only thing here for us is death.

Whatever form that might take.

I'm sending along some money for a new dress. The tobacco this year did very well, as did the tomatoes. Of course the tobacco fetched a far better price. It's amazing that even in the twilight of the Apocalypse people are willing to pay a premium for their vices. I'm thinking of buying the Parkers' old homestead and using the fields for additional corn for the whiskey, since our small distillery has become quite popular. One of the field hands, a big man named Kingston, says he knows a thing or two about running a still, and I think he might be able to take on the additional work, since our own still is so very small. I feel this would be an excellent way to ensure Rose Hill's financial stability. I will not have you return to a hovel.

Chapter 24
In Which Some Time Passes and I Grow Restless

Every day is just like that first day. We run out to some place along the wall, grab breakfast, run some more, the rotations decided upon by the sheriff and his men. Once there, the fence team checks out the interior fences, while the patrols walk the wall, watching the shamblers boil and froth beneath us. I get the feeling there are other groups of boys and girls doing this same task at different times of the day, but the sheriff is careful to keep us separated, and I only see the twenty or so girls and boys who make up my group. I ain't paired with Alphonse for every patrol, and the ever-changing roster of partners is mind-numbing.

Sometimes I walk the wall with Ida, who tries her damnedest to draw me into conversation, to no avail. Sometimes I walk with one of the other girls or one of the boys. Our job is simple: walk along the wall, make sure the shamblers don't get too intrepid and climb over. The rotting remains of dozens of shamblers line the lee side of the wall, including the ones I put down my first day, and no matter how much time I spend on the berm I never get used to the smell. It is a foul task the sheriff has set us to, and I ain't sure why we ain't allowed to harvest the whole lot of them.

The only possible joy in my life now is putting down shamblers, but I am denied even that bit of relief except in the rare case where a shambler decides to test out the wall. It quickly becomes clear that the idea of a single shambler climbing the spare handholds and making it to the top is a ridiculous one, but we're still permitted to swing down and harvest any that tries, for which I'm thankful.

I keep my sword, and Alfonse must say something to the rest of the patrol team about what happened on the first day, because no one makes a move to snatch it from the shed where we put our tools at the end of the day. No matter how long I take to get into the weapons shed, the sword is always right there where I left it. I manage to make it passable-sharp as I walk the wall, using a decent rock and a lot of spit. It still needs oil, and it's nowhere as good as my sickles back home, but it's better than anything else, and I'm glad for it.

In the evening we run back, eat dinner, go to church whether we care to or not—the sermons are all about as inspiring as that first one—and go to bed. On Tuesday, nearly a week since we got to Summerland, we collect our meager pay. Most folks immediately take to the general store, a line of dark faces lining up out front waiting to spend their money. The colored folks ain't all that different from the white working-class folks, since Tuesday is payday for the cowpokes as well and they're all up in the saloon spending what little they got. The only change is Bob and Bill standing near the line of colored shoppers, only too happy to use their rifles if anyone should get out of hand. After what I saw my first day at the wall I have no doubt they would.

I watch the line, noting a few unfamiliar faces, older folks I don't recognize. They most likely work and live in the nicer side of town with the fancy houses. That must be where they're keeping Lily and the Spencers, and Katherine. I'm sure Katherine is fine—she's too contrary to be anything else—but I'm desperate to get to Lily and see if she's okay. I can't leave town without the two of them in tow, so until I can find them I'm trapped here.

I'm also anxious about Jackson. I haven't seen him since the day we arrived, and after witnessing Bill's itchy trigger finger, I fear the worst. But I've heard no news of him being killed, so I nurse the tiny ember of hope the same way I nurture my rage.

I don't go to the general store, even though I'm hungry and could do for some extra chow. I take my money to the Duchess for a bath, clean clothes, and to see if one of her girls can braid up my hair. The light-skinned Negro girl I saw perched up the bar on the first day, Nessie, comes into the bathing room while I sit in the rapidly cooling bath, weaving my hair into rows so tight it makes my eyes water.

"Why didn't you go and spend your money at the general store like everyone else?"

I shrug. "I will at some point. I'd rather have clean blankets and clothes for now."

Nessie laughs, the sound high and lilting. "You the only one. You're smart to stay away from the general store, though. You go there, your pockets empty real fast. They got the prices so high, even a penny whistle costs two bits!"

After Nessie finishes braiding my hair, my head throbbing because of her braiding skill, I finally ask the question that's been plaguing me all week. "How'd you end up in the cathouse? All the other girls are white."

She ducks her head and shakes it. "Ah well, the sheriff, he took a liking to me back when I first got here. If you haven't noticed, he's kind of a sucker for a pretty face. Offered for me to work for the Duchess, instead of marching out among the dead." She looks embarrassed, tugging at the low front of her dress, trying without success to pull it up. "It don't matter much anyway now, but I was never any good at taking down shamblers. I always got stuck wondering who they'd been before. And after the last big massacre before the wall was finished, well, I didn't have the stomach for it. I would've just gotten someone killed out on the line." She goes quiet for a while, the sound of her breathing the only clue she's still behind me. "Whoring ain't so bad once you get used to it, just ask the other girls. Most of the men are okay . . . the sheriff's boys can get rough, though."

I nod, feeling like a lout for asking such a personal question. She offers me a hand mirror to check her work. I turn my head from side to side before pointing to my hair. "Thank you."

She smiles wide, the shadows of shame fleeing her face. "Not a problem. Let me know if you'd like me to do it for you again. I'll have the Duchess give you a discount. You got good hair, not as thick as some of these other girls."

My lips quirk. Auntie Aggie used to always say that about my hair as well. It makes me homesick for Rose Hill, the ache so bad that I nearly cry.

Later I lie on my blankets, still damp from being laundered, and reread my letters from my momma for the millionth time. The night sky out here in Kansas is somehow plenty bright to read, and as always, a kind of pain blooms in my chest, part homesick and part grief. The last letter is from nearly a year ago, and in it Momma plaintively wonders why I haven't written. I think of all my letters, all those memories and clever anecdotes, gone into the ether. I know Red Jack posted them for me. But if the postmaster never forwarded them, then they never went. What happened to those letters, anyway? Did Miss Anderson read them and laugh at my girl-ish sentiment? Or did she snatch them up and burn them? I imagine Miss Anderson tossing the letters into the fireplace, her hatchet face smiling evilly, and a white-hot rage seizes me so firmly that I'm half afraid I might murder someone just to watch them die.

I take deep breaths, pushing the rage aside, plotting instead of giving way. I've been in Summerland for a week, and I still got no idea how to get myself back east to Bal-timore and Rose Hill. It seems like an overwhelming task, a mountain of adversity, separated from what few friends I have and a plain full of shamblers between me and where I want to be.

I doze in fits and starts, my near-empty belly and discon-tent stronger than my fatigue. Eventually I wake. I need to move, to go somewhere of my own free will, otherwise I'm going to explode in an ugly way. The feeling roiling around in my chest reminds me of the night the major tried to kill me, his hand tight around my throat, fear and hopelessness and rage warring deep within my being.

That was the third time a person tried to murder me.

It was the night before the major turned shambler. He'd come in to visit Momma. It was late, and his footfalls were heavy as he climbed the stairs in a whiskey-fueled haze. He slammed the door open loud enough that even the aunties sleeping in the kitchen had heard the crash.

Momma, for her part, was unperturbed. She was busy reciting a bit of Shakespeare, *The Tempest* to be exact, when he walked in. I hadn't been able to figure out why she wanted to read at such a late hour, but one glance at the major's bleary-eyed glare and I had an inkling.

"Pet and I are reading, Jonas." Momma never called me Jane in front of the major. Her own grandmother's name had been Jane, and perhaps she feared that the coincidence would be enough to make the major peer more closely at my features, to compare my stubborn chin and narrow nose to Momma's own features.

"Yer my wife," he slurred. "I demand you fulfill your duties."

"Your belly is full, your estate is safe and prosperous, and you're drunk on whiskey from my own still. I'd say I've done more than enough to fulfill my duties."

For a moment the air was heavy with tension, and I huddled closer to Momma, fearful of what was about to happen.

The major laughed, a bitter sound, before crossing the room and snatching me up by the back of my head and dragging me across the bed so that he could grab me by the throat. He lifted me up effortlessly, his large fingers wrapped around my neck.

"I am the master here, you ungrateful bitch. I'll tell you when enough is enough."

He then squeezed, slowly choking me, pressing so hard that I saw spots. I clawed at his hand, but I was little, and nothing I did seemed to make much difference.

That was when Momma stood up and slammed the complete works of William Shakespeare into the side of the major's head. His grip immediately went slack, and I crashed to the ground, sobbing as I was finally able to breathe again.

"Jane, go down to the kitchens and tell Auntie Aggie that you need to stay out of sight for a few days, okay?"

I'd nodded, hot tears running down my face, and I ran down the stairs as quickly as I could. Auntie Aggie was waiting for me, and she hurried me back to her room, tucking me into bed next to her and whispering kind words as I cried myself to sleep.

The next night the major turned shambler and that was the end of him.

Now, I climb out of bed in the dark, grabbing my boots, carrying them so I can put them on once I'm outside. I can't stay here, suffocated by my thoughts, choking on my dark memories. I need a moment of freedom, no matter how fleeting it may be.

From below come the sounds of merriment, men shouting and women laughing. Payday has been the loudest night yet, no surprise there. I ain't sure what time it is, but apparently the party never ends, despite Sheriff Snyder's alleged curfew.

"Where you going?" someone whispers at me from the dark. I don't know anyone's voice well enough to be certain whose it is, but I'm guessing it's Ida.

"Out."

"You can't. There's curfew. You leave and the sheriff and his boys will make an example of you."

I shrug, then realize that whoever it is can't see me in the dark. "Don't worry about me, I can deal with the consequences."

"Let the chickenhead figure it out herself," someone else snaps. "And be quiet. The rest of this town may not care about getting a full night's rest, but I do."

The room settles down amid grumbling and I go to the door to slip out. Only, when I go to turn the knob, it doesn't move.

At some point in the night they locked us in.

I don't even blink, just step carefully through the room trying to get to the open window, making all attempts to keep my feet away from sleeping forms. I've almost made it out when a hand grabs my ankle.

"You should go back to bed," the deep voice mumbles blearily. The big girl on the team that mends the interior fences and the one that woke us up the first day. Cora. She always seems to be watching me, and I don't need a spotlight to know a snitch when I see one.

"I appreciate the concern, but I've had enough sleep."

The hand ratchets down tighter.

"We don't cause trouble here, girlie. As long as we follow the rules things are fine. So that means you go back to bed, or I'll put you there."

I cross my arms and consider my options. I could go back to the pile of blankets that passes for my bed and wait for morning to come, which by my estimation would be another few hours or so. But that means backing down from Cora, and I've seen her kind. She'll do everything the people in charge tell her to, even if that means she ends up broken and bloody. She's one of those people that never learned to breathe, never understood the true meaning of freedom. She's a dog, happy even with a cruel master. She eats her three squares and takes her bit of pocket change and happily wears the collar around her throat, because that's enough for her.

But it ain't for me.

So instead of meekly going along with her commands, I ready myself, and say, "If you don't let me go, I'm going to break that arm of yours, and I'm afraid that would be a most unfortunate turn of events."

The grip on my ankle tightens painfully, and Cora pulls my foot, unbalancing me and sending me crashing to the floor.

It's exactly what I expected her to do. I swing my legs around, a whirlwind of motion, catching her in the face as she goes to stand and using my momentum to climb to my feet.

I stand over her as she holds her face. "You kicked me in my mouf," she says, the words garbled.

"I think you'll find it's better to just let me do as I please."

She's smart enough to say nothing in response.

I make my way to the window again, which has been left open to let in some semblance of a breeze. The night is dark and looming, heavy and warm. For a moment I consider going back to my spot, lying down, and trying to get along with the status quo. But I ain't never listened to that little voice before, and I ain't about to start now.

A quick jump, and I'm out on the roof. Before I can even look for a way down, a bright light a few hundred yards away catches my eye. At first, I think it's the sun coming up, but it's way too early for that. It's only then that I understand what I'm seeing.

Electric lights. Dozens of them, lining the streets and dotting the houses on that luxury section on the southern side of Summerland. The lights shine soft but bright in the night fog, and it's more lovely and peaceful than anything I've seen in a long time. Maybe in my whole life. I know now why I've been able to read by what I thought was moonlight each night.

But those lights ain't for me. I'm two stories up, and there doesn't appear to be any way down from here. Below me a couple of cowpokes stumble out of the saloon singing some song, the words too slurred to make much sense. An ugly feeling of hopelessness wells up in me, and I have to fight tears.

I ain't giving up. No way, no how.

Pulling on my boots, I walk to the edge of the roof. The next building is only a few feet away. It looks to be abandoned, the second-floor windows covered in a thick layer of dirt. I try to remember what's on the first floor, but I come up blank. With a running start, I jump to the adjacent roof. The window is open a bit, so I jimmy it wider and climb in.

I stop just inside of the window. Through the darkness comes the sound of someone breathing. I wait, letting my eyes adjust to the gloom. Lying in a bed, arms hanging over the side, is the tinkerer I met on the first day, Mr. Gideon. His pale skin glows in the little bit of moonlight, and I'm a bit scandalized to see that he's naked from the waist up. He's too tall for the bed he's in, and his feet hang off the side. He looks like a broken baby doll, half-dressed and tossed where he lies.

There hasn't been much time for social visits and I ain't seen him since I got here. I ain't sure if he's friendly or not. I remember the way he pointed that revolver at my head, and decide that he's probably not someone I want to risk waking.

I take a step backward to climb out the window, and my

foot catches a squeaky board. The movement from the bed is explosive. Mr. Gideon sits up, and a pistol gleams in the low light, the business end pointed right at me.

My heart pounds in my throat, and for the first time in my life I wonder why I always leap before looking. But there ain't ever much time for regrets, so I swallow down my heart and raise my hands in surrender. "You sure do like to point that thing at my head."

"Miss McKeene?"

"None other."

"What are you doing in my sleeping chamber?"

I take a deep breath and let it out. I feel like I'm about to jump right out of my skin, but I'm in no immediate danger. The penny under my shirt is warm.

The view, what I can see of it with the moonlight coming in the window, is the nicest thing I've seen all week. Gideon is all slim muscles and interesting boy angles, and it's hard to formulate an answer.

"I suppose . . . the proper answer is that I don't rightly know. The honest answer is that life in this place is untenable, and if I don't get out of here soon something bad is going to happen."

I think of my momma's warning about my temper, the temper I inherited from her. "Do not let things get to you, Jane. Do not give in to your rage," she'd always say, her voice full of warning and a knowledge I was afraid to plumb. But now, that anger is building up, making me feel like I'm going to lose my mind. In here with this boy I don't know, this is the calmest I've felt all week.

The tinkerer puts his revolver away and gives me a wry smile. "Miss McKeene, this is a place where terrible things happen more often than you know. Go back to bed before Sheriff Snyder discovers that you've gotten out."

I should leave, should turn and go back to my crowded room, but I don't. Instead, I lean against the wall, bold as can be. "You mind answering a few questions before I go?"

He crosses his arms, and I feel his regard more than see it. "You barge into a man's room in the wee hours of the night, where he pulls a gun on you and tells you to leave, and now you wonder if you might ask some questions?"

"You did put the gun away."

His chuckle echoes through the room. "Well then, how could I say no?"

"Why ain't we trying to thin out the dead that surround the settlement? Whole plain is full of them, and all we do is keep them off the wall. Sooner or later they're going to be more than we can hold back. I figured the point of settling in a place like this would be that it was far away from the eastern cities, largely empty of people to turn shambler?"

The tinkerer sighs, running his hand through his hair, and I see the telltale glint of a bracelet on his wrist. I wonder if it was a gift from someone important. I ain't known many men to wear jewelry that wasn't a gift. That makes me wonder if he has a wife, and if he does, why ain't she here?

"You're right," he says, not really answering my question. "You met the drovers? Mean as a shambler and about as bright?"

"Yeah, I've seen them."

"There aren't any cattle here in Summerland. The only thing they're driving are the undead. At the pastor's and sheriff's orders."

The revelation leaves my mouth dry, and my hands itch for my sickles. "Why?"

"I can't tell you that. I've told you too much already." I just stare at him, and a soft sigh comes from the bed, a creak as his weight shifts. "The last person I told ended up turned. And I'm not about to endanger another Miss Preston's girl."

I think of Maisie Carpenter, mouth gaping, hands grasping. "You talking about Maisie?" He starts, and that's all the answer I need. "How'd she end up out there on the plain?"

"She asked questions, too," he says, his voice heavy with unsaid things.

I cross my arms, chilled despite the warm night. "What's up with the other side of Summerland? Those nice houses?"

"Where the well-to-do folks live? They have their own stores, paved roads . . . You've probably seen the path that leads to the side of town, lined with electric street lamps?"

I remember the sounds of children playing my first day

here, and the sight of those lights, and nod. The professor has just confirmed what Ida told me; now I need to hie myself over to that side of town and find Katherine and Lily.

I scratch at my braids and ask, "Why are people coming out here in the first place?"

"Money. Land. Empty promises. A lot of the folks out here were facing prison sentences if they didn't go west, people like the Duchess and most of the roughnecks. The Survivalists think if they can make a go of it out here in the middle of nowhere then they'll win more people to their cause."

"I'd say they were pretty popular already."

"Looks can be deceiving. The Survivalists have had trouble getting a foothold in the Northern states. People up there are more solitary, and still believe in the legacy of Lincoln."

I snort. "And what exactly was that?"

"'A house divided against itself cannot stand.'"

I shake my head, because it's the silliest thing I've ever heard. Colored folks working *with* white folks, not just *for* them? Not in this lifetime.

"Anyway," Mr. Gideon continues, yawning widely, "the idea is to make Summerland the city of the future. Electric lights. Running water. A wall that will keep the undead out. They provide safety, real safety, then people will make their way here, and we can start to rebuild something solid."

"You don't seem to believe that."

"The Survivalists are going about it all wrong. You can't

force the Negro to bend to your whims. You have to convince him that you can offer him a better life. Slavery is finished. Trying to live in the past will get us nowhere but undead. That wall we built may seem fine, but it won't last forever. The dead are adaptable. It's just a matter of time before that barrier comes down."

I watch him for a long time, trying to decide what to think about him. I decide I mostly like him, despite him pointing a gun at me. Twice. And I swear that ain't just the fluttering feelings I'm getting from seeing him lying in a bed half naked, either.

"You don't seem like you belong out here, Mr. Gideon."

"I doubt that I do."

I grin. "I know why I'm here, but who'd you tick off to get sent out here?"

"My father."

It's not a response I'm expecting, and any type of rejoinder dies on my tongue. "I'm sorry."

"Don't be. It's been a learning experience, one I never could've gotten at Harvard."

I tap out a rhythm on the wood behind me as I think. I nod, and swallow before I ask my final question. I haven't seen Jackson all week, and his disappearance has been preying on my mind in a way I don't like. It's not that I have feelings for him, because I don't, it's that I'm worried about what it means that I haven't seen him in so long. I remember the girl and her wide staring eyes, how easily Bill shot her, and I have the feeling that something equally bad happened to Jackson.

"There was a boy . . . He was thrown in a cell in the sheriff's headquarters after we arrived together last week. I don't suppose you know where he got to?"

Mr. Gideon shakes his head. "No. I didn't see him when I was last there, and I can tell you that the jail only has a couple of cells for a reason. No need for them, when we have a sheriff with a short temper and a penchant for watching folks turn."

The implications of his words hit me like a punch. I've heard of such folks, deviants who believe that some kind of enlightenment exists in watching the moment a man becomes a monster. It doesn't surprise me that the sheriff would have such predilections, and I wonder if there ain't some more sinister truth to the story about the loss of the sheriff's sweet-tempered wife.

But Jackson . . .

Mr. Gideon seems to realize that the boy in question was more to me than just someone on the same train I'd taken here. "I'm . . . sorry," he says.

Tears spring to my eyes, and a great big wave of ugly feelings wells up. "Okay, then. Thank you."

"You're welcome, Miss McKeene. I'm afraid that we're all prisoners here of one kind or another, for better or worse."

"Oh, it's for worse, all right. Most definitely for worse."

I slip back out of his window without saying good night, making my way back to the room by the light of Summerland, and with a heavy heart. It's much easier to get back into bed than it was to get out, and when I find my blankets I roll onto my side and cry silent, angry tears, clutching my lucky penny.

They killed Jackson. There's no doubt in my mind that he's dead. Just like Maisie Carpenter. He's probably somewhere out there on the plain, hungry and yellow-eyed, a shell of the boy I once knew.

I curl up into a ball, biting my fist to hide the sound of my sobs. I barely feel my teeth sink into my hand. I'm too focused on the agony of being torn in half, like something inside of me is being savagely ripped out. The one boy I was stupid enough to love is dead. I'd thought my heart broke when he'd told me he didn't love me, that we were better off alone than together. In a world where people are always being ripped away by the undead plague, I'd thought his words had destroyed my heart.

I was wrong. This is what a broken heart feels like.

Jane, I caution you to prudence. I hope you are reading your Bible and using the Scripture to temper your emotions, to always keep a cool head about you. But if you do not find solace there, perhaps you should take up embroidery.

I suppose it is obvious that I worry about you, a little girl all alone in the world. I worry too much.

Chapter 25
In Which I Embrace My Recklessness

After Mr. Gideon tells me of Jackson's demise something in me breaks. Jackson might not have been mine, and it might be his fault that I'm stuck in Summerland in the first place, but I still loved him. I didn't want him dead, and knowing the sheriff and his boys could murder someone without so much as a how-do-you-do makes me despair at the chance I have to outsmart a bloodthirsty man like that. I should be coming up with a way out of Summerland, plotting and scheming. But I ain't. Instead, I'm just surviving.

And barely at that. I'm weak. Moments after eating, my belly growls for more, demanding sustenance that ain't coming. It ain't that I'm working any more than I did when I was at Miss Preston's; it's that the sheriff don't feed us enough. The portions at breakfast keep getting smaller and smaller, and even dinner—the only normal-size meal we get—is getting leaner by the day.

"It's all the new families in town. The more white folks arrive, the less food we get. They're quality, and they can't miss a meal," Ida says, running her finger across the surface of her empty plate before licking it.

"What do you mean?" I ask. I've just finished my own stew and am barely restraining myself from licking the plate. Even the roughnecks are looking hungry and perturbed. Their rations have been cut as well, meaning that there really is a problem with the food. This ain't just another of the preacher's initiatives to reform the Negro.

"Ain't you been paying attention? There's been two trains of families in the past week. Fancy folks, all bedecked in finery. Before that we used to get maybe one train a month, and never anyone wearing silk. Something's happening back east, but who knows what," Ida says. "You'd better just hope they don't think about expanding the brothel, otherwise you're going to be out of a place to sleep." She casts a dark look across the room where the Duchess's girls are calling out to the table of roustabouts. I don't know why they bother. It's Thursday. Those fellas are already broke. They spend their money as fast as we do.

There's more folks moving into the nice part of town, but we haven't gotten any new Negroes for the patrols. Something just doesn't add up.

Maybe it's time to take a little trip.

I think about it all that night and the next. I think about the other side of town as I push aside a girl to get my break-fast, a dark feeling welling up in my middle when she starts crying, just as hungry and desperate as the rest of us. I think about it as I watch a small pod of decrepit shamblers attempt to climb the wall, their hands digging uselessly into the dirt, my blade flashing in the sun as I slide down the exterior of the wall to take off their heads.

I keep thinking about the other side of town until I can't stand it no more, kicking off my covers in the warm heat of the night. No more wallowing. It's high time I find my friends and get an idea of what's going on in this other side of town. There's an itch in my brain, a thought that needs to be scratched. But more than that, I need food. My stomach growls so loudly that I cannot stand it, and next to me Ida is no better off, just as awake and miserable as me.

"I'm going to find some grub," I whisper to her over the soft snores of the girls around us.

Ida props herself up on her elbow. "It isn't safe, Jane."

"We're slowly starving to death, Ida. We won't survive long on what we're getting. We can either die peacefully or survive by any means necessary."

Ida purses her lips in the near dark before nodding. "Be careful," she warns.

I climb to my feet and grab my boots. Food and some answers—one or the other would be fine, but I'm greedy, so I'm hoping for both.

I walk out on the roof and look for a legitimate way down this time. There's a small overhang off the western edge covering the boardwalk, and I'm thinking that if I can land on it then I can ease myself to the ground from there and make my way to the other side of town. The only problem is that the overhang is almost directly across from the sheriff's office, so there's a chance I'll be seen if they're looking. It's not a risk I would take lightly.

I debate going back to bed, or trying something different once I've been able to make a proper plan. But then my stomach growls, so loud that I'm sure they heard it all the way back in Baltimore.

I ain't waiting for an opportunity. I'm making one.

I walk to the edge of the roof, dangling my feet off it and easing forward until I can jump. My landing is too loud, and I throw myself flat on the overhang, breath held, waiting for someone to yell up at me. After a span of frantic heartbeats and slow breaths I realize no one is coming for me, so I lower myself the rest of the way off of the overhang and take off at a sprint away from the buildings.

It's dark, and I trip often. There ain't much light to see by, but the rich side of town glitters like a jewel in dung. It doesn't take me long to get there, in my haste; once I get close to the circle of light cast by the bright lamps that line the road I can maneuver more quickly, using the shadows as my cover. That's when I realize there's a strange buzzing, like cicadas. At first I wonder why the bugs would be active this late at night, but then I realize it ain't cicadas. The sound is coming from the streetlamps themselves. Must be the electricity coursing through them.

I have no idea where the Spencers might live, but of the thirty or so houses in this part of town, not many of them appear to be filled at this point; there are only a few on the street with lights on.

Peeping in windows ain't ladylike, but it helps me to quickly assess who lives in what houses. The preacher sits in the study of one, reading some book, and I quickly duck away.

I've soon looked in all the windows of the houses with lights on, and none of the folks I see are the Spencers or Katherine. But like Ida said, they're definitely quality. I recognize a couple of the folks from Mayor Carr's dinner party. It looks like his diabolical scheme is proceeding according to plan.

If Katherine and Lily ain't to be seen, that leaves the

houses that ain't lit up. So, like any desperate type, I start breaking into them.

The first house is completely empty, still waiting for a family to move in; the second contains furniture, but no sign of people. The third, though, has pictures on the walls, ones I recognize from the night Jackson, Katherine, and I snuck into the Spencers' homestead. I'm in the right house.

The click of a gun's hammer cocking back ain't good news, though.

I put my hands up. "Mr. Spencer, we've never met, but my name is Jane McKeene." I turn around slowly. Only the rifle ain't held by Mr. Spencer.

It's Lily pointing the rifle at my face.

"Jane McKeene," she says, the barrel wavering just a little. The electric lamps from outside cast enough light that I can see her clearly. She wears a sleep shirt and her hair is piled on top of her head. She's skinnier than I remember, but other than that she looks fine. "You better tell me why you're here and my brother ain't."

I smile despite myself. Now, here's the thing about Lily. She's a good girl. Sweet as can be. But there's only one thing she cares about, and that's Jackson. You ain't never seen a brother and sister dote upon each other the way Lily and Jackson do. But that's where I have a problem. Even though I had nothing but love for Lily while Jackson and I went together, she had nothing but an abiding rage for me.

There's not a lot of love for the girl who steals your brother away in a world where family is so fragile, where people lose each other daily. I understood it, even if I didn't much care for her attitude.

After Jackson and I had parted ways, I think she'd developed a bit of a grudging respect for me. But that ain't going to matter if she thinks Jackson is in trouble and I had something to do with it. Which is why there is no way in any of the seven hells that I'm going to tell her that her brother's likely turned shambler, especially not when she's pointing a rifle right at my face.

"They got him with the work detail," I say. It's the hardest fib I ever told. "Mind putting the rifle down?"

She does, her reluctance visible. "My brother know they got us living with shamblers over here?"

"What are you talking about?" I shake my head. "Wait— start at the beginning. How did you and the Spencers end up here?"

Lily props the rifle on her shoulder and sighs, a sound that is far too grown-up for her small frame. "The Spencers' crops didn't do so good last year, so Mr. Spencer was having trouble paying the mortgage in Baltimore County. He went to Mayor Carr to ask the man for a loan, and you know what Jackson says about borrowing money from rich people."

"'Borrow a dollar, pay with your soul,'" I say. It was how Jackson got locals to trust him instead of the banks, even though his rates were straight usury as well.

Lily nods. "It so happened that Mr. Spencer couldn't pay when the mayor's men came to collect. So the mayor gave him a choice: he and his family could leave the county on their own, or go west to this new settlement. You can guess which one Mr. Spencer picked. Before I could even get a note to my brother, we was on the train here."

"So, the Spencers brought you here voluntarily. That must have been tough for you."

Lily shrugs. "It's been mostly okay. A few of the families came here because they ain't got a lot of sense. They talk a lot about how the Negro should be serving white folks, that we needed to reinstate that 'natural order' the pastor is always going on about. That's why everyone is mad right now. The drovers they brought here to oversee the Negro patrols and fortify the border think the Negroes in your part of town should be taking all the risk to herd the dead, not them. Of course, Miss Katherine says everyone is right to be concerned, that this place ain't safe, no matter what kind of precautions we take."

"Kate is here?"

"Yeah, she lives next door. She's the one that's got people to talking about safety and such. She's so pretty and smart! She's brilliant at smiling and saying a few words that gets everyone to thinking the way she does without them even knowing it. I want to be like her when I grow up."

I scowl. "Figures, I'm starving and she's over here having tea parties and pontificating."

"Anyway, Pastor Snyder says that the Lord will deliver us from hardship, but Miss Katherine says it's all a lie, and after what I seen . . . I'm scared, Jane. I don't know what's going to happen next."

"Well, I've been out on the walls for a week now, and I don't want to make you feel any worse, but I've seen one too many fresh shamblers to feel like these folks have the protections of Summerland figured out."

"It ain't the walls or border patrols that concern me."

I blink. "What are you scared of, then?"

She sighs heavily. "Right. Okay. Let me get my boots, and I'll show you."

She disappears and comes back carrying the rifle awkwardly and a pair of boots. She hands me the gun. "Just for a minute. That's mine."

"Where'd you get it from?"

She pulls the boots on. "I won it fair and square from the Elkton boys up the street. I got a pair of boots out of it as well. You never seen a couple of stupider boys."

I grin. I always did like Lily.

"But it's how I won it that caused this whole problem I've got," she continues. "Come on."

We make our way outside, Lily leading the way. We've walked a little ways before it occurs to me to ask, "Ain't you scared to be out this late by yourself? What will the Spencers say?"

Lily snorts. "Nothing. Things've gone straight to hell since we got here." She gives me a quick look. "Don't you dare tell my brother I swore."

"Wouldn't think of it."

"Anyway, soon after we arrived, things kind of fell apart. Mr. Spencer's been hitting the whiskey pretty hard and meeting in secret with folks who want to get rid of the sheriff; Mrs. Spencer's fallen into the laudanum."

"What about the little ones?"

"The baby got the colic and passed right after we got here. It's just me and Thomas right now. We're getting by, barely."

Her voice is heavy with emotion, and I realize that I ain't the only one who's had a hell of a time here in Summerland. "But . . . what about the other families? Are they happy with the electric lights, and the gourmet meals, these big houses?"

"Some of them are, sure. But if people feel a bit safer here than they did in Baltimore, it's only because they don't know what I know. This whole town's got a rotten soul, Jane. Everything is built up on a house of cards that's gonna come crashing down sooner or later."

"What are you on about, Lily?"

"That's what I'm about to show you."

We stop in front of an unmarked building that looks rather

like the tinkerer's lab. A sign on the door reads "DANGER: ELECTRIC—Keep Out!" There's a picture of a lightning bolt through the sign. I frown. "We're going in here?"

"I ain't," Lily says, a tremor in her voice. "The Elkton boys told me this place was haunted, that they heard strange noises coming from it at night. That's how I won my rifle—I went in on a double-dog dare. I ain't never going down there again if I can help it. But if you want answers, that's where they are."

Before I can tell Lily thank you she's heading back toward her house, head down, gait determined. For the first time in my life I have a real regret. I should've told her about Jackson.

Well, there'll be time enough for sorrys later. I hope.

Auntie Aggie worries about you, too. It's a cruel world, with cruel people. I hope you haven't run afoul of too many of them. This world is a place that can eat a girl alive, even smart ones like you.

Chapter 26
In Which I Make a Terrible Mistake

The building isn't locked, and the door swings out on silent hinges. My heart pounds in my chest, and there is a part of me, the cowardly, yellow part, that urges me to turn around and scamper on back to bed. But there was too much nonsense in Lily's words, and my brain hates a mystery the way dogs hate cats, so before I can talk myself out of it I'm descending the stairs.

There ain't enough light to see properly, but I make my

way, hands grazing the walls on either side of me to keep steady. The stairs ain't dirt like in Mr. Gideon's laboratory, they're wood, but everything else reminds me of my first day here. There ain't no electric lights, just good old kerosene lanterns set into a nook here and there, and I grab one to make my passage easier. At this point my fear of getting caught is a faraway thing, I'm more keen on solving the mystery of the angry townsfolk than anything else.

The stairs empty into a narrow hallway, and the scent of something powerful rotten hits me. I bury my face in the crook of my arm, the stink of me preferable to the stink of whatever's down here. I'm dog-tired and still too hungry to think straight, so it takes me a long moment before I realize exactly what it is I'm smelling, and the moment I do, that's when I hear the noises.

Shamblers.

I follow the scent of the dead, the sounds of the moans getting louder, and move cautiously down the tunnel. It ends in a large antechamber, nearly the size of a concert hall. I ain't sure who or what dug out such a large space, but it must've been a pretty impressive undertaking. The ceiling extends far above my head, the light cast down by a cluster of those same electric lamps, conspicuous in their constant glow. But I ain't nearly half as distracted by the lights as I am the sight that meets my eyes.

Before me is a giant, rolling shambler cage. And in the

cage: at least fifty shamblers, running toward an old Negro man sitting in a chair, dozing, the shamblers turning the cage like a giant, metal wheel.

I ain't even got time for my normal fear response to rise up. I just watch the shamblers turning the entire mess in a circle, my brain trying to make sense of it all. I've heard lots of people suppose that shamblers could be useful for labor and such. I read the story of a man who hitched his plow to a team of shamblers and tried to use them to till his field. The problem was that they took off after his boy, catching the kid and eating him and a good part of the rest of his family, before the entire clan set out for the local municipality and turned most of them as well. This was the problem with shamblers: one little slip and everyone you knew was a ravenous monster. It didn't make much sense to do anything but put them down.

"Isn't it terrifying?"

I startle at the voice, the fear I couldn't feel at the sight of the shamblers finally making my heart jump painfully. Mr. Gideon walks out of the shadows, wiping his spectacles on a corner of his untucked shirt. He's unshaven, and the scruff of beard shadowing his cheeks makes him look tired and just a bit dangerous. It's an appealing look in a man. But I squash those soft feelings like bugs. I still ain't got the full measure of him, and if he thinks he's going to try something I need to be ready for it.

"Relax, Miss McKeene. I'm not the one you need to fear."

"Funny how the ones that turn on you always say something like that."

A smile ghosts across his lips before disappearing. "True enough. Here, let me show you how this works."

"What makes you think I care?"

He laughs a little. "You're smart. Your brain has been putting facts together since you got here, whether you realize it or not. And since you're here, you might as well learn every single last one of this town's terrible secrets."

He's right. A strong curiosity has always been one of my flaws. I nod, and my stomach chooses that moment to rumble loudly. My face heats and Mr. Gideon's eyes soften. "I do believe I may have some canned peaches somewhere down here as well. Follow me."

He walks toward the back of the room, past the giant shambler wheel. The dead in the cage stop walking for a moment, their yellow eyes fixating on us instead. But the cage has enough momentum that the few who are distracted lose their balance and fall down, their compatriots trampling them as the whole contraption keeps turning. One of the shamblers gets caught underfoot the wrong way, and its head is crushed by the others. It doesn't move after that, the body flopping at the bottom of the wheel while the whole thing keeps turning. I'm sure it's all some kind of metaphor, but I'm too tired and hungry to figure out what for. The rest of the fallen shamblers eventually regain their footing, and they all turn their attention back to the old man sleeping in the chair.

I follow Mr. Gideon down another hallway for quite some time, the sound of our breathing loud in the enclosed space. This hallway is lit by electric lights, and I take the time to watch Mr. Gideon. He walks stiffly, but his limp is gone.

"What happened to your limp? Was it an affectation, or the real thing?"

Mr. Gideon laughs. "You don't mince words much, do you?"

"I find that my lot in life has less to do with what I say than who I am," I answer.

He nods and looses a long sigh. "I can see how that would be true. Well, I have a mechanical brace for my leg. It helps me walk, but it's tiresome, so I don't wear it all of the time. Plus, the limp makes the sheriff think I'm weak, and to speak truthfully, I prefer him underestimating me."

"You don't like him much, either, huh?"

"The man is a monster. And that apple didn't tumble far from the tree." I'm surprised by the vehemence in his voice. We fall silent after that.

The hallway eventually ends, and I'm surprised to find us back in Mr. Gideon's lab. "These tunnels are one giant rabbit warren," I murmur.

"Yes, they are. I use that tunnel to get back and forth from town. It's actually a more direct route than the road. It also helps me hide my movements from the sheriff." There's a metal gate separating the hallway from the lab, and Mr. Gideon unlocks it with a key around his neck. He holds the gate open until I pass through, and then secures it behind me. It's the gentlemanly thing to do, and I suddenly feel very nervous being alone with him. It ain't just that it's improper, which it is, but the last time I was alone with a boy was Jackson back in the day, and despite my fearsome predicament a wave of loneliness overwhelms me.

I miss my momma and Auntie Aggie, and Big Sue back in Baltimore. I miss Jackson and his stupid plans and little Ruthie and her nothing-but-fluff braids. I miss Miss Duncan and her make-your-arms-mush scythe drills. I even miss Katherine, which I never thought I'd be saying.

Mostly, I miss being hopeful. There ain't a lick of hope in Summerland from what I can see, despite the advertising, and the drudgery of it all is enough to make a girl just lay down and die.

I collapse on a long bench before a table a good distance away from the lab equipment. Mr. Gideon goes to a cabinet and removes a jar, returning to the table and sitting on the matching bench on the other side.

"Here. I'm afraid I don't have a fork, but at least they're tasty. My mother sends them along, since we haven't gotten around to planting trees yet out here." Mr. Gideon slides a jar of peaches across the table at me, and I pick up the Ball jar and twist off the two-piece lid. The scent of the peaches hits me, and I dig in with my fingers, pulling out a peach slice and shoving it in my mouth. It's sweet and juicy, and I've eaten half the jar before I remember my manners enough to offer Mr. Gideon some.

He waves me away with a smile. "I'm good, thank you. Our rations haven't been cut like yours have."

I think about Ida, back up in the bedroom, and I refasten the lid, saving the other half of the jar for her. She's been kinder to me than anyone else here, mostly keeping me out of trouble, and it's the least I can do for her.

"So," I say, once I've wiped my fingers on the front of my raggedy shirt, "tell me about them shamblers you're keeping in that cage."

Mr. Gideon sighs heavily and sits down. "Well, first of all, this wasn't of my making. I had an idea, and the result is a gross perversion of it."

"So what was your idea, then?"

"Technology! Innovation! A modernized state in which all Americans—Negroes, whites, Indians—could live together." He jumps to his feet and begins pacing. "Summerland was supposed to be a shining beacon of hope, a noble Egalitarian vision for the future, a place to carve out a new idea of what our country could become, risen from the ashes of oppression and death." He waves his hands around before running them through his hair, and there's something about watching a man talk with that much passion that makes me sit up and take notice.

"Electricity was at the heart of my vision," he continued. "It would keep the town safe, and perform labor. Electrified fences. Electrical appliances to wash clothing, to cook food. The war ended slavery; electricity could lay the foundation for an automated settlement where we could continue the march toward a fair and equal society. I worked for a time with Mr. Edison in his compound in Menlo Park; when I returned home to Baltimore, I told my father about my ideas and he got the notion of me going west to improve some of the frontier towns. He convinced me to discuss the plan with a small group of his political allies. I needed financing, and it was my hope that they might see the potential in the idea. They did, and my father took steps to put it in action. But when I arrived here, it was nothing like what I had laid out." He finally stopped pacing and sat down. "My idea was to locate a town near a natural resource to run the generators: a river, a stream, coal veins. This area has no viable power source, but they had already established the foundations of the settlement, with dozens of people living here."

I think back to the night of Mayor Carr's dinner party— the electric lights on his house, the newspaperman who was mysteriously bitten. "Hence, that contraption I just saw back there."

Mr. Gideon sits next to me on the bench and pulls a piece

of paper and some charcoal toward him. He sketches out a drawing. "It's a simple Faraday machine. The wheel turns, making the magnets shift, and causes power to flow down the wires. In an effort to keep the town from collapsing, I retrofit the generator to run on physical labor. The undead never tire; they don't need much in the way of sustenance to maintain locomotion, they need only be replaced every once in a while . . ." He grimaces as I give him a look. "I'll admit it's not one of my best ideas. It runs the lights, and that's about all, to be honest. The idea was to have the electricity power a barrier fence, much more deadly and effective than bobbed wire or even the brick wall. Something that would last much longer, and keep undead out of a large area. But the single generator could never power a viable perimeter fence, if we even had the manpower to finish building one. So, there are electric lights, and a wall to keep the deathless out. The town looks pretty, but in the meantime, we have the same society we did back east, one that subjugates and kills more than half its population to guard the smaller portion. What is the point of that? How is this progress?"

I know why the tinkerer is frustrated, but I don't have an answer to his question, and just shake my head.

He continues. "So, here we are. Shamblers—I mean, the undead—are generating the electricity in the town, such as it is. We might be able to create more power if we could build more generators and improve the electrical infrastructure, but the Negroes and roughnecks have their hands full maintaining the barrier, and the Snyders refuse to make the whites within town work on the fence. They just waste their time having tea and drinking."

I frown. "Mr. Gideon, I beg your pardon, but this all makes absolutely no sense. Shamblers, here, within the walls?"

He leans forward, a shine in his eyes that I'm pretty sure ain't entirely from the electric lights. "With my help, they've turned this place into a Survivalist nightmare. They believe the undead, like the Negro, were put here to serve whites, and that it's our place to guide, but not to labor. Meanwhile, the Survivalist drovers and laborers are tired of being forced to tend the fields. They believe it should be their turn to enjoy the good life. But the interior fence isn't even finished, and it's only the patrols that are keeping us from being overrun."

"And all the people over there in the town? The fancy ones? They're Survivalists, too?"

Mr. Gideon leans back suddenly, his expression shuttering. "Not all of them. But that's all I'm going to say about that, Miss McKeene. The hour is getting late, and while I worry for the future of Summerland, it isn't going to fall tomorrow. You should get back to your bed before the sheriff and his boys finish sleeping off last night's revelry."

I climb to my feet, clutching the jar of peaches. "Thank you for the food."

"Don't mention it. The town is headed for a reckoning,

and I have a feeling things are going to get worse before they get better."

I hesitate a moment before I reach into my waistband. *Tom Sawyer* was the last gift Jackson ever gave me, and I haven't finished the book just yet. But I hate owing anyone a debt. And who knows, maybe if everything works out, I can find myself another copy. "Here. For the peaches."

Mr. Gideon takes the book uncertainly, turning it over in his hands. "I . . . thank you."

"Sweet dreams, Mr. Gideon," I say over my shoulder as I climb the stairs.

"Sweet dreams, Jane," he says, his voice far away.

I let myself out of the lab and slip past the outhouses and the abandoned hotel. The sun is just starting to hint at its rise over the horizon to the east, but it's still mostly dark, and I'm almost to the saloon when I hear the unmistakable sound of a gun cocking.

"Well, hello there, Jane," Sheriff Snyder drawls. He stands just a few feet behind me, grinning, and I'm once again reminded of the stories I've heard of alligators. "I do believe you are breaking curfew."

I open my mouth to come up with some story to excuse myself, but the sheriff has a hell of a left hook, and I go down before I can utter a word.

It's sad news that our neighbor to the east, Mr. Berringer, has been overrun. We've taken in twenty of the Negroes who lived on his land and a nasty old overseer named Duncan. I have a feeling that Duncan is not going to last here in Rose Hill. I must say that it is curious that so many of these men who subscribed wholeheartedly to the peculiar institution are turning shambler.

Chapter 27
In Which I Have Had Enough

When I come to, Sheriff Snyder and Bill have me by either arm and are dragging me through the dirt of the street. I try fighting, but that punch from the sheriff has me seeing stars and I'm no match for two grown men.

I'm tied to the whipping post in front of the sheriff's office.

I try to climb to my feet, struggling against the ropes, alarm and a powerful headache both clanging in my head, but there's no getting free. I'm dizzy, but whether it's from taking a hit or the combination of exhaustion and hunger there's no telling, but I fully recognize that I am not in a very good place.

Next to me comes a low chuckle. Bill is leaning against the pole, whittling and whistling, looking like he ain't got a care in the world.

"You think you're smart, doncha? Told ya you were going to learn some manners here. And it looks like the sheriff is just about ready to dispatch that lesson."

"Bill." The voice behind me is raspy. "Go round up the flock. They've slept enough, and this sermon requires sinners."

"Yessir," Bill says. He moves off, and the preacher shuffles nearer.

"Now, I know what you're thinking, Jane. You're scared, and that's natural. You're wondering how you ended up here, if there wasn't some kind of thing you could've done differently to avoid this whole mess."

My heart pounds, loud enough that I'm sure he can hear it. I can't see him, so when his breath tickles my ear, the scent of him filling my nose, I flinch.

"The reality is that you couldn't do anything. This is all as God wills it to be. In the wake of the punishment laid down by the Lord are His laws laid bare. All His creations are not equal, but we are all His children, all with our place. The rapture, such as it is, is here, on earth. The white man ascends;

his dark counterparts are His servants, laying the stones in the pathway to Heaven. That we ever thought otherwise, that we once entertained the notion of equality for all of God's children on earth, that we fought and killed one another over it . . . well, we know how that turned out."

He rests a hand on my shoulder, patting it affectionately, and his touch nauseates me. "This punishment will be brutal, my dear, but your mortal flesh will bear it, because it must. Take comfort that in reaffirming His order we give Him thanks."

He backs away and coughs, the sound wet and phlegmy. "Trust in the Lord and He will guide you through this hardship."

From behind me comes the sound of footsteps and murmurs. I try to twist and see who it is, but I cannot turn that far around.

Under my shirt, my penny has gone to ice.

"Oh, don't worry, girly. You're gonna have quite the audience," Bill says, back from rousing the patrols. "The sheriff is a fair man, but he knows an instigator when he sees one. No different than dogs, really. And every now and then you just get a bad dog. Maybe it's poor breeding, maybe it's poor training. Only thing you can do is punish him and hope he learns who his master is. And if not, well . . . sometimes you've just got to put a bad dog down."

His footsteps echo on the wooden boards of the walkway

as they move away from me, and I test my bonds to see if there's any way to wriggle free. Panic digs its broken fingernails into my soul.

I remember the day I'd asked Auntie Aggie what it was like back before the shamblers walked, back before the war. "It was bad then, Janie. A different kind of bad, but bad all the same. I once saw a man whipped to death for stealing a loaf of bread from the mistress's kitchen. Not your momma, mind you, but the missus that came before her. Overseer took the skin clean off of him till there wasn't nothing but meat left. So don't let nobody tell you any different about the old days. Life is hard now, nothing but suffering, but some kinds of suffering is easier to bear than others."

I'd never asked her again about the bad old days, but now, with my hands secured to the whipping post, I wish I had.

Behind me the sounds of footfalls and murmuring rises, and this time when I crane my neck around I get a glimpse of the crowd, gathering in the first bit of sunlight. Right now it's mostly Negroes, a few drovers mixed in here and there. I don't recognize many of the faces and I figure it must be the night crews. I stop straining against the bonds securing my hands, since there ain't no use to it and all I'm doing is giving myself a fine rope burn.

After what feels like hours but is actually only a few minutes someone exclaims, "Jane, what are you doing?" I twist as far as I can. Behind me Ida stares with wide eyes. "I told you not to get caught!" Her voice carries all the fear and panic eating at my middle, and I squeeze my eyes shut like I can somehow hide from what comes next.

But I can't.

I've never been scared of death. Everyone dies, and I don't like wasting energy fretting about certitudes, but Aunt Aggie's words keep echoing through my brain: *whipped to death, took the skin clean off.* The fear is so powerful that I can't do anything but stare straight ahead, gaze locked on the wooden post in front of me.

Behind me someone clears his throat. "Listen up, y'all. The sheriff has a few words to say."

Boots echo on the boardwalk in front of me, stopping just a little off to the side. I look up, and the sheriff squints down at me. His expression is blank, but there's a glint of something in his eye. Satisfaction? I turn my gaze back to the wood post in front of me.

"Summerland is a place of laws and order, and I am the long arm of that law. Our goal here is not the glorification of the individual but to create a harmonious community that can serve as a model to the chaos of those cities in the east. Just as the Israelites left Egypt for the promise of a better life, so have all of you. But for that harmony to be achieved, each of us must know his place. You don't let a dog pretend to be a horse, and the same it must be with our dark cousins. There is a natural order to things, as the pastor tells us, and when that order is not obeyed, disaster rides hard on its heels."

There's no comment from the crowd, no murmur of dissent, no valiant objections on my behalf. The only sound is of someone coughing far off. I know that if I'm going to say anything, this might be my last chance. People deserve to know about the danger festering underground. "You have to listen to me! Back in town, these men have built a—"

A crack comes across my jaw, hard enough to shake my brain something terrible, and Bill steps back, shaking his hand and cursing. Blood fills my mouth, and I fall silent. It's no use. The sheriff continues.

"This darkie broke curfew. That transgression calls for a minimum of twenty lashes. It gives me no pleasure to hand down this punishment, but hand it down I will."

I half expect him to start praying, but thankfully I am spared that blasphemy. Someone, likely Bill again, steps close to me, and I jerk in surprise as the back of my shirt is grabbed. There's a tearing sound, and then a gasp as my garment is torn in half. I roll my shoulders forward, suddenly modest. The air is warm on my bare back, and my breath comes in short pants, my embarrassment almost overriding my fear.

"What's this?" Bill asks, leaning close. He reaches down the front of my shirt, and I jerk away from him, fearful that he's reaching for my bosoms. Instead his hand comes up with my penny. He yanks the cord hard enough to break the leather thong. "Don't think you'll be needing this," he says, his breath hot and rank on my cheek.

The sheriff steps down from the boardwalk into the hard-packed dirt of the street, standing behind me. I can almost see him slowly uncoiling the whip at his side, relishing the drama and anxiety of the crowd.

"Bill, would you be so kind as to keep the count?"

"Of course, Sheriff." The satisfaction in his voice makes me long to put a bullet in him.

The whip whistles through the air before it carves agony across my back. I inhale sharply and arch away from the pain, my chest slamming into the post.

"One."

The second lash comes too quickly, stealing my air and making my muscles tighten.

"Two."

The whip comes round again, and I'm trying to think of something else, trying to be anywhere else, but I am bound to my cursed flesh, and tears make their way down my cheeks as the whip tears into my back again, and again, and again.

"Three."

"Four."

"Five."

"Five."

My heart nearly stutters to a stop when Bill counts five twice in a row. My back is a fiery mess of agony, and when the whip comes across again a sob tears out of me.

"Six."

I'm shaking from the pain, delirious with it. With each crack of the whip I make a new promise to the Lord Almighty. "I will never lie again if this stops." *Crack.* "I will dedicate my life to your good works." *Crack.* Either the good Lord is unimpressed with my offerings, or he thinks I deserve this, just as the preacher told me.

Bill has just counted off the eleventh lash when the crowd behind me begins murmuring. I can't think, the pain robbing me of whatever wit I possess. I'm crying and muttering, half-mad with the pain. Nine more lashes, and that's if Bill keeps the count correctly. Somehow, I know he won't. He's enjoying this as much as the sheriff.

"Stop, please, stop!"

Katherine's voice is unmistakable, and at first I think my ears are deceiving me. But the sheriff pauses and says, "Miss Deveraux, this is no place for you. You should go back to your home. What brings you here?"

"I did," comes another voice. "You're killing her Attendant, and she has a right to know that since the girl has been in her employ."

"Gideon, you are not the law in this town." There's tightness to the sheriff's voice, but I'm too relieved that the whip has ceased its torment for the moment to analyze why he would even listen to Mr. Gideon in the first place.

"Sheriff, it is said that the man who exercises compassion

is the wisest of all. I'm urging you to be a wise man. It's obvious that the girl won't survive much more. And neither will this town. You've done enough."

"Gideon—"

"Please, Sheriff," Katherine pleads, a tremor in her voice. "Jane is a bit headstrong, but she is also an excellent companion. I've become fond of her, and I would be heartbroken if she were to come to any more harm. Please let her go. Show her mercy."

Behind me the sheriff sighs. "Miss Deveraux, you are a kind girl, but law and order must be upheld."

"'And if a man smite his servant, or his maid, with a rod, and he die under his hand; he shall be surely punished.' That's Exodus, chapter twenty-one, verse twenty. I'm certain this isn't what the good pastor meant to happen. There is no doubt that Jane broke the rules, as she is known to do from time to time. But she is suffering greatly, and as she's my servant, my soul would bear the burden of her misfortune. Please, Sheriff," Katherine says, her voice choked with emotion. I know without even looking at her that her face is probably streaked with tears, her light eyes too bright. "Have mercy."

There's a pause, and the sound of my labored breath fills my ears, heartbeat keeping time to the seconds ticking by.

After too long the sheriff says, "You are right, of course. Compassion is critical in a leader."

"Yes, Sheriff. No one doubts your word is law."

My hands are suddenly released, and when I try to stand I stumble. Katherine is there to help me, and when she turns me around two things strike me at once.

The first is the sadness and anger warring on Mr. Gideon's face as he watches me. His jaw is tight and his fists are clenched. Whether these emotions are about me being whipped or because he just don't like the sheriff, I don't know.

The second thing that strikes me is the way the sheriff is looking in my direction. It's a soft kind of look, the way one would watch a baby or a bunny, full of wonder and interest. At first I can't figure why the man would look at me in such an indulgent way, but then I realize that he ain't looking at me. He's looking at Katherine.

And just like that, the plan I've been struggling to come up with for weeks explodes in my brain like a stick of dynamite with a too-short fuse.

Katherine half carries, half drags me past the assembled crowd. I lift my head just long enough to see Cora give me a smug look, and I know at that moment she's the reason the sheriff caught me in the first place. The Duchess comes over, worry on her face.

"You bring her to my room, I'll help you get her cleaned up."

"Jane doesn't belong in a whorehouse," Katherine says, as muttonheaded as ever.

"Her bosoms are hanging out for the world to see and she

won't make it to the proper side of town," the Duchess snaps back.

"She's right," Mr. Gideon says. "I'll bring by some salve. Let the Duchess take her. You're going to have to contend with Pastor Snyder."

Katherine sighs. "Fine. Take good care of her. I'll be by later."

Then it's just me and the Duchess and the endless walk to the whorehouse. Every movement sends agony singing across my back. My skin is hot and aching, and I fight to keep from sobbing. I ain't successful, though.

We enter the house of ill repute, heading straight for the Duchess's room, which is on the first floor. She helps me sit on the edge of the bed, and I lean forward, resting my elbows on my knees, and groan.

"Until Mr. Gideon comes by with his concoction, there ain't much I can do for your . . ." She trails off.

"Thank you."

"There's no need for thanks. This is wrong. Everything about this place is wrong." A slight brogue has appeared in the Duchess's voice and when I glance up at her, tears stream freely down her cheeks.

"Are you okay?" I ask.

A bark of laughter escapes from her. "Here you are flayed within an inch of your life and you're asking after me."

I sigh. "Sometimes it's easier to think about other folks'

small hurts than your big ones."

She sits next to me on the bed, sniffling. "I was married before I came here. Leopold. He was the most beautiful man I'd ever seen, skin like it had been kissed by the night. We thought we'd be safe if we could just get far enough away." Her gaze goes distant, her face twisted with the memory of some distant horror. "You can never get far enough away from people like the preacher."

I half laugh. "I suppose so. And the sheriff."

"The two of them are peas in a pod, but the sheriff is only following his daddy's lead. He's mean, but he isn't smart enough to run this town on his own."

The uneven sound of boots on the wooden floor makes me raise my head, and Mr. Gideon stands in the doorway with a small pot of something and his eyes averted in deference to my modesty. Not that it much matters now. I reckon nearly all of Summerland had a chance to spy my bosoms had they cared to.

"I shall take care of this," the Duchess says, rising and plucking the jar of salve out of Mr. Gideon's hand. Behind him stands Nessie, the colored girl who braided my hair, with a steaming bowl of water and a cloth.

"Thought you might need this," she says in a low voice. She sets the water on a nearby table.

The small kindness warms. "Thank you," I say. "Could I trouble you for a glass of water?"

"Of course," Nessie says before disappearing from the room, Mr. Gideon stepping aside to let her go.

He clears his throat. "Jane, the sheriff has agreed to allow you a day of rest from your patrol. Katherine has asked him to give you back over to her supervision, but I'm not sure she'll get her wish. It's doubtful the preacher will allow it." He hovers in the doorway uncertainly, and a glance at his face reveals a worried expression.

"What's wrong, tinkerer?" I ask, my voice rough from the pain of my back.

"This isn't right," he says, as though he ain't quite sure what else to say.

The Duchess pushes the edges of my shirt aside and begins to clean my wounds. I can't help but cry out in pain, eyes watering from the agony.

"No, this ain't right," the Duchess finally says after a few heartbeats. I'm too befuddled from the whipping to think proper, my entire existence narrowing to the screaming of my back. "The question, Professor, is what exactly you plan to do about it?"

From the doorway comes a heavy sigh. "I told you that patience is required for things like this."

"I'm running out of patience, Gideon. So is most everyone else. We're starving. The Negroes are ill-treated, and there are undead within the boundaries. I know that pretty little lass of yours has been working on the men, but even a face as pretty as hers isn't going to end all this suffering."

"I know this, Maeve. What can I do about it? What is there to do? What can be done that we haven't tried before?"

"The preacher is an unassailable mountain," I mutter. "He relies on the sheriff to enforce his will. We need to get someone on our side in with him; someone who can control him. Someone who can help put the sheriff in a compromising position, one that he doesn't anticipate, so we can use that opportunity to take him down."

The Duchess pauses in her ministrations. "We've tried that before. He beat the poor girl something fierce, nearly killed her," she says, low enough that the tinkerer doesn't hear.

"Not sex—love," I say, panting as the Duchess goes back to cleaning my wounds. "The sheriff is not a man laid low by something as banal as carnal pleasures. But the sheriff is a man who knew love once, who fell for a good woman. That hole in his heart is the doorway to our freedom."

"So what exactly are you saying?" Mr. Gideon removes his glasses and wipes them clean.

"You heard the sheriff out there with that nonsense about the Israelites. He really did come here for a better life, just like everyone else who got on a train by choice. The promise of something more. And what did he get in return? To watch the woman he loved get eaten. If we want to take down the sheriff, we need to dangle bait that he cannot resist. A woman who can give what he once had with his wife and who can help him elevate his social status. A girl of good breeding—*that's* what the sheriff will fall for. He's a man that pretends to greatness and at the same time aches for love. He would crumple under the attention of a true lady. And once he does, we get rid of him."

"You talking about murder?" the Duchess asks.

"It ain't murder if a man gets turned."

She snorts, dropping the rag into the bowl of water with a wet plop. "And I suppose you plan on dangling your companion on that hook."

"I saw how he was looking at her. He's already half in love," I say.

"It's not a bad idea," Mr. Gideon says. I look up just long enough to take in his expression, his eyes sparking with intelligence, his lips pursed in thought. My heart flops like a trout on a riverbank.

Here's a thing about me: I have always been a complete and utter muttonhead for a clever boy, even when I'm half delirious with pain.

"Yes," I say, closing my eyes and sucking in a sharp breath as the Duchess uses a light touch to spread the salve over my back. "Just imagine if the sheriff knew all about Miss Deveraux's tragic past."

"What tragic past?" Mr. Gideon asks.

I swallow drily, and Nessie appears just then. She hands me the glass of water and I drink it down before I tell my tale.

I'm counting on knowing Katherine. If I'm right, she hasn't told anyone about where she came from, but rather distracted them with small talk. It's been her modus operandi since I met her, and old habits die hard.

"Did you know she is actually one of the Chesters, of Chester County, Virginia? She ended up in Baltimore nearly destitute because her stepmother is a dastardly woman." The lie darn near spins itself. "Her father passed quite unexpectedly, and Miss Deveraux's stepmother sent her up north to live with cousins. Only, her cousins were quite savagely attacked and murdered by the undead. Family by the name of Edgar. The mayor of Baltimore took pity on her and invited her to stay in his own house until she could contact her relatives. But, well, Old Blunderbuss took a shine to her, and the missus wasn't about to have that. So here she is, the proverbial Moses in the basket." The burning in my back settles into a steady throb, the salve the tinkerer brought actually helping.

A strange look has come over Gideon's face and his lips twitch as though he's fighting back a smile. "That is quite a tale, Miss McKeene," he says.

"Weren't no tale. It's the God's honest truth. Miss Deveraux is as tragic as poor Ophelia."

"Ophelia?" he asks.

"Yes, from *Hamlet*. Ain't you never read Shakespeare?"

"Oh, I have. I'm just surprised you have."

"You shouldn't jump to conclusions about people, Mr.

Gideon. I contain multitudes."

Nessie slips out of the room as quietly as she appeared, and from the look on her face I know that the story of Katherine Deveraux will be on every drover's lips by nightfall.

The Duchess stands and shoos Gideon away. "You need to get going, so I can help Miss McKeene get presentable."

There's a discreet cough from next to the door. "Of course, of course. Well, thank you for the information, Miss McKeene. I'm willing to bet that the sheriff would be horrified to discover how shoddily the world has treated a lady of Miss Deveraux's caliber. He'll want to see to her comfort personally, I'd wager."

Gideon's uneven gait echoes down the hall, and after the door closes the Duchess stands over me. "Remind me never to play poker with you."

I allow myself a small smile before standing. The Duchess helps me to pull on a clean shirt. I ain't sure that I can trust her, but there ain't been much kindness since I got to Summerland, and I've yet to see the Duchess on the dispensing end of any cruelty. "Why you helping me, anyway? It can't just be because of your long-lost love."

The small smile she wears is wiped from her face. "Let's just say that I got some stains on my soul that I wouldn't mind getting scrubbed clean."

"And you think helping a Negro girl is going to do that?"

"I think being the kindest person I have the wherewithal

to be is going to do that."

I nod and think of Lily. I hope she's safe this morning. "Think you can get your hands on some laudanum?"

The Duchess smirks. "Do shamblers have yellow eyes?"

"We're going to need some, the stronger the better. And a bottle of wine, the finest available in this place."

"How soon?" she asks as I finish getting dressed. I lie face-down on her bed, pillowing my head on my arms, completely drained in the aftermath of a hellish morning.

"If everything goes as planned, soon. But let's aim for the end of the month. Two weeks," I say, before finally giving in to my exhaustion.

Jane, please write back as soon as possible. I ache to hear about the escapades you are having in Maryland. Is it as refined as all of the papers would have us believe?

Chapter 28
In Which I Beg for Forgiveness

I wake to Katherine yelling.

"Jane McKeene, did you tell Mr. Gideon that I have been sent here because of a man's jealous wife?"

"Shh, there's no need to yell." I groan and attempt to get up, forgetting the trauma to my back until agony explodes across my skin. Firm hands push me back down.

"Just lie there, there's no need to move right now," Katherine says, her words gentle but her tone still sharp. I settle back onto my stomach and Katherine climbs onto the bed next to me. She smells of lavender water, and it reminds me of my mother so much that I nearly hug her.

"Jane," Katherine says after a moment. She measures her words, trying not to lose her temper with me. "Why did you tell Mr. Gideon my secret? After I expressly forbade you to tell anyone?" Her words are still too loud, and I worry that someone might overhear.

I open my mouth to explain and then pause. "What?"

Katherine leans in close. "Jane McKeene, we have been acquainted long enough for me to know one of your plots when it comes knocking. There are about four of the Duchess's girls pressed up against the door right now, listening in. Even now they're memorizing all this to tell their customers later tonight. And no one gossips like men."

I grit my teeth. "You're a lady, Miss Katherine. You shouldn't even be here," I say loud enough to be heard.

"Feh. The sheriff is out of town on some business, and the preacher is giving his nightly sermon to the sinners of Summerland." Her lips twist when she mentions Pastor Snyder, and she lowers her voice. "Anyway, I figured sneaking in here was worth the risk. What's your plan?"

"What makes you think I have a plan?" I ask.

She gives me a bit of side-eye and I sigh. I shift and sit up, even though it hurts something fierce. "I don't know what's beyond the walls of Summerland, but it can't be worse than what's inside them. If we're going to get out of here, we need to get rid of the sheriff. He has eyes everywhere, and not just his men, but folks on the patrol like Cora, too, and who knows who else—there's no way we're getting free while he's in charge. Which means we have to get close to him, compromise him. And he's much too careful for anyone else to do it, so . . . it's up to you. We need him to fall in love with you."

"Absolutely not! I will not compromise myself for that man."

Under the indignant anger, I can tell Katherine is close to tears. These last few weeks must have been just as hard on her as they were on me. It's clear from her voice what she thought I was asking of her, and I swallow hard. Katherine ain't got no reason to believe that I wouldn't ask such a thing of her, and it makes me feel ugly to know that she thinks I would. I haven't always been the best to Katherine, and being trapped in this awful place reminds me of that. I reach out and take her hand, squeezing it. "I ain't asking you to give yourself to him, Kate. I might be coarse, but I ain't a monster."

Katherine says nothing for a long time, and when she finally does speak her words are choked with emotion. "Good. Because I won't barter my body for your freedom, Jane, nor mine."

"No, and you won't have to. You just need to get close to him, drug him, and leave the rest to me. Then we'll liberate ourselves and hightail it out of here."

"What about everyone else?"

"What about them?"

"We cannot just hightail it out of here and leave everyone to that man's nonexistent mercy, Jane!" Katherine is whispering much too loud, and I shush her. This is most definitely not part of her act. I could tell her there won't be a sheriff left when I'm done, but I doubt she'd go along with the plan if she thought it was predicated on unsavory business.

"Keep your voice down! Like you said, walls have ears and all. I already figured we'd take whoever wanted to go with us. That's the best I can offer."

"That's not good enough," Katherine says, her voice low. "What about Lily and the Spencers? What about Jackson?"

"Jackson is dead," I say, my voice flat.

Katherine jerks as though she's been slapped. "Well, when were you going to share that little revelation?" Her voice is hollow, and I hate her for feeling anything for Jackson at all. Even with him gone, I still think of him as mine. What a stupid, selfish girl I am.

"I just didn't think to share it. I'm sorry. I know you fancied him."

"I did not fancy him," she says. "I don't fancy anyone. But he was a good person, and his passing is unfortunate. In the future you need to tell me these things instead of suffering the truth in silence." Katherine's tone is haughty, even as she whispers. "And if I'm meant to get close to the sheriff and get his guard down, I ain't doing it alone." She jumps off the bed, and I notice she's wearing a lovely blue silk day dress, akin to what the ladies of Baltimore used to wear. "I appreciate your dedication, Jane, but I'll not have you injured so badly again," she says, loud enough for anyone to hear. Her tone is polished, befitting a lady of her supposed station. "As soon as you've mended enough to be useful you will return to your Attendant's duties. Understood?"

"Of course, Miss Katherine," I say, slipping into the characteristic speech patterns of an uneducated serving girl. "I'll try to get better lickety-split. Don't you worry none about me. I'm a real fast healer."

Katherine shoots me one of her too-familiar dirty looks, an expression I haven't seen in a while, and I smile as she slips out the door.

I feel better than I have in weeks, even with my mangled back. I'm confident that I will be en route to Rose Hill and my momma soon. If it means playing lady's maid to Katherine in the meantime, so be it.

How bad can it be?

Auntie Aggie sends her love, by the way. She wants me to remind you to keep out of trouble, and to always wear your lucky penny. She also wants me to tell you that the beets just haven't grown right since you left. It seems even the garden misses your presence.

Chapter 29
In Which I Struggle to Keep from Committing Homicide

I discover even before joining Katherine in the rich end of town that she has taken to her role of displaced lady like a duck to water. A very arrogant, snobbish duck.

After a week of rest I'm mostly healed up. The cuts and raw spots have crusted over enough that I can mostly move around, and even though my back twinges when I move too quickly, it's nothing I can't ignore.

When the Duchess brings me clothes to put on they are

nothing like the trousers and rough-spun shirt I was given before. I stare at the lovely calico dress in awe, fingers grazing the fine blue-patterned weave. Blue is my second favorite color, and I'm almost afraid to contemplate that the lovely dress might actually be for me.

"What's going on?" I ask.

"Since the story of Miss Deveraux's dire straits have made the rounds, Sheriff Snyder has been bending over backward to see to her comfort. Katherine asked that you be given a new dress, since it is unseemly that her Attendant should be seen in the garb of a field hand." The Duchess says this last bit in Katherine's accent, and I snort to keep from laughing out loud.

"Yes, that sounds like my Miss Katherine, all right," I say, going along with the act just in case anyone might be listening. For the sheriff to believe that Katherine is a lady, he needs to believe that I'm her faithful companion. A month ago, it would've been a hard sell. But my time in Summerland has most definitely changed that, and I am willing to pretend to be just about anything in order to win my freedom from this place.

Luckily, Katherine has already laid most of the groundwork for me.

I dress quickly, the movement tugging the scabs in an uncomfortable, but not painful, way. The dress fits perfectly, as though it were made for me. The hem is a little shorter than could be considered modest, hitting me just above the tops of my knees, right where I like it to be. What I like to think of as fighting length. There are a pair of loose trousers to go underneath for modesty's sake, and although I don't have all of the weaponry, I'm wearing a very close approximation of an Attendant's garb.

I pull on my boots and stand, feeling pretty good even though I've been abed the past week. The Duchess purses her lips and hands me the Confederate sword I'd been using. Someone found a scabbard for it, which raises all kinds of questions. "They sent this on over for you as well. The Lady Katherine is waiting for you in the sheriff's office."

I nod and take the sword, belting the scabbard around my waist. I feel better having a real weapon, but I still ache for my sickles. Swords are nice and all, but they don't much compare to a pair of well-made short blades.

"You have any luck with that medicine I was asking about?"

The Duchess shakes her head. "The girls' been suffering through their menses, even though I been asking. Guess your Miss Katherine is going to have to suffer as well." The meaning behind her words is clear: no laudanum.

"I don't suppose there are any opium joints in town?" It's a stretch, but I'm thinking that maybe I can lace one of the sheriff's cigarettes with the drug, make him compliant, and then just finish the job.

The Duchess purses her lips and shakes her head. "We

don't allow any Chinese folks in town, the preacher's made that clear."

I sigh. "Well, thank you for your help anyway, Duchess."

She nods. "You can repay me by convincing the tinkerer to fix my bath, since you seem to have his ear."

I raise my eyebrows in surprise but say nothing.

I leave the saloon through the side entrance my patrol used every morning, brain working through the possibilities. I need to find a way to get out of town once the sheriff is put down, and fast. I get the feeling that the sheriff's men will quickly be able to ascertain what transpired and who the likely culprit is. I have my concerns about making it back to Rose Hill in one piece anyway, but I ain't getting out of town at all if I'm lynched.

So outright murdering the sheriff in broad daylight is off the table, more's the pity. But there's a hundred ways a man can end up dead without any kind of real knowing who did it.

I'm working through a couple of scenarios, one of them involving rat poison and soup, even though poison is a cowardly way to murder a man, when I stop short. A few feet away, decked out like the belle of the ball, is Katherine, surrounded by a few of the drovers. That ain't at all unusual, since from what I've seen there ain't many unattached ladies in Summerland, and those that ain't spoken for make a living on their backs.

But what ain't normal is the look of sheer panic on Katherine's face.

I duck my head and make a beeline to the group. "All right, fellas, move it along." I make a shooing motion with my hands, falling right back into my Attendant training.

A couple turn to look back at me, but no one steps away from Katherine. They're like bees on a particularly sweet flower, stubborn and focused. Good thing I know how to handle bees.

I draw my sword and smack the nearest suitor across the back of his head with the flat of my blade. "Hey, what's the big—" His eyes go wide when he realizes my blade is now only a few inches from his eye.

"Move. Now."

He scampers off, along with a few other fellows, the lot of them muttering curses but too cowardly to do anything more than that. Their departure clears enough of a path that I can grab Katherine's arm and wrench her away from the rest of her suitors without any further violence. The men say nothing, not even a single swear, and I take that to be because they're still trying to put their best foot forward with the mysterious Katherine Deveraux, fine lady from the east.

"Thank goodness you got here when you did. I was about to wield my parasol," Katherine says, scowling.

"I would think a Miss Preston's girl would know better than to let herself get so hopelessly outnumbered."

"I'm a lady, Jane. I would never turn my hand to violence; that is what my Attendant is for. Besides, as long as I am trapped in this godforsaken place I will have to do all my dealings in the currency of besotted idiots. What would you have me do, alienate the entire town? It is not as though I have a fortune at my disposal. I must be charming no matter the predicament." She snaps open her parasol and gives me a haughty look over her shoulder. I can't decide if she's brilliant or utterly insane. She's playing the role of debutante so well that I'm wondering if maybe Katherine ain't really the daughter of some long-lost princess. It would explain quite a bit.

She sniffs, and gestures toward the boardwalk. "Now, let us go call upon the sheriff. I believe he might have something for us. Try to look contrite, would you?"

I give Katherine my best puppy-dog look, but she only rolls her eyes heavenward before marching out smartly across the dusty lane.

I have to run to open the door for Katherine, she's set such a frightful pace. She sails into the sheriff's office unannounced, like she owns the place. The bastard sheriff and his boys are guffawing at something, and an ugly emotion rises up in my chest—part rage, part indignation, mostly bloodlust. What he did to me, what he's most likely done to others before me . . . My vision goes dark as I imagine taking my fists to the sheriff's face, pounding away until it loses shape and resembles nothing more than a mound of meat. I blink quickly, clearing the savage vision, a sick feeling settling in my middle.

There is nothing I want more right now than to kill Sheriff Snyder. Not my freedom, not to return to Rose Hill, nothing. Just the sheriff, on the ground, his lifeblood seeping into the boards.

The strength of my rage is terrifying. It's all I can do to swallow my fear and anger as the men jump to their feet at Katherine's presence, as if they have some sense of civility.

"Miss Deveraux," the sheriff says, tipping his hat. His gaze barely flickers over me, and I keep my eyes downcast so he won't see how much I'd like to stab him in the heart with my rusty cavalry sword.

"Sheriff, I have a request to make of you."

"Well now, I reckon you been doing a lot of that lately." There's bemusement and affection in the sheriff's voice but no anger, and I'm relieved to know that I didn't misread his fondness for Katherine. It's a sad thing, but there are few men that can't be softened by a pretty face. For the first time I can remember I'm thankful that Katherine is fetching enough for two girls.

"My girl needs a better weapon than this woeful sword, something more befitting an Attendant. I was hoping we could have your leave to procure some proper weapons for her."

The sheriff strokes his yellow mustache as he thinks, and I fight to keep the excitement from my face. A genuine weapon would be more than I've been hoping for. Not that I couldn't kill the sheriff properly with my cavalry sword, or my bare hands if it came to it.

"You want me to give your darkie a gun?" the sheriff says with a smirk. His gaze is heavy on me, waiting for a reaction, a flash of indignation or anger. But I am playing the role of a faithful Attendant, so I school my expression to blankness. Luckily his eyes are on me, so he misses the anger that flashes across Katherine's face before she smiles politely.

"Of course not, Sheriff. Jane is terrible with a rifle. I was thinking more along the lines of the sickle, a weapon designed specifically for the close-combat techniques of an Attendant."

Sheriff Snyder's smile fades and he nods. "Hold on a moment, I think I got something." He disappears into a room off the side and returns with a pair of sickles.

My sickles. My much-loved and much-used sickles.

"That man Redfern left these behind. If you think they'd be useful, your girl can have them."

Katherine inclines her head regally. "Thank you, Sheriff. And as soon as I am able to reach my uncle by telegram, I am sure he will tell me how happy he would be to repay your generosity."

"Not necessary." The sheriff approaches Katherine,

reaching around her to offer me the sickles. He's closer than would be considered decent by any standard, but Katherine doesn't step backward. "Would you privilege me with a moment of your time?"

"Of course, it would be a pleasure." Katherine's smile reveals none of the discomfort that emanates from her. Maybe the sheriff doesn't notice how she's shifted her weight back, putting a few more inches of space between the two of them, but I do. I've known Katherine for a long time, and the last thing she wants to do is spend another moment in the sheriff's presence.

But this is the role that I've asked her to play, and Katherine is not one to back down from what's required of her. She's a much better person than I am.

I take my sickles from the sheriff, then open the door. Katherine exits, the sheriff close behind. I'm about to follow when from behind me one of the men calls out.

"How's that back of yours?"

It takes every bit of discipline I have to keep walking, to not look back. Mocking laughter follows me as I leave the building, hurrying after the sheriff and Katherine.

They're deep in conversation, him leaning in, her using her parasol as an effective barrier against him getting too close. My boots echo on the boardwalk as I approach, and he glances over his shoulder and grunts. "I daresay you're safer with me than anywhere else in Summerland. Why don't you send your girl to see to your house and I'll drop you off after we enjoy a short stroll?"

Katherine gives the sheriff an indulgent smile. "A lady's Attendant is not there just to protect her from the restless dead. She also protects my virtue and my reputation, Sheriff."

"Miss Deveraux, do you think that I am a threat to your virtue or reputation?"

"I would say that you are the only one who knows the answer to that question, sir."

The laugh that booms out of the sheriff is genuine, and an ugly feeling rises up in me. He's looking down at Katherine like he's a starving man and she's a steak that just landed upon his plate. It's an expression I don't care for one bit. I could kill the man without a single shred of remorse, and I'm near about to do just that when the sound of hoofbeats stays my hand.

"Sheriff! Sheriff!" A man I don't recognize rides up in a cloud of dust, and both Katherine and I shrink back into the shade of the boardwalk while the sheriff strides out into the middle of the street to meet the rider.

"What is it, Bean?"

"Bob, Bill, and now Bean," Katherine mutters. "Is it a requirement your name has to start with the letter *B* to work for the man?"

I only catch snippets of the conversation, but I do hear the words *breach*, *eastern fence*, and *townsfolk*. Whatever is happening, it's enough to turn the sheriff's expression stormy, as he sends the rider off with low-voiced instructions.

Sheriff Snyder comes back, giving Katherine a deep bow. "I'm sorry to cut our conversation short, Miss Deveraux, but there is an urgent matter I must attend to."

Katherine actually manages to look disappointed. "What seems to be the issue?"

"Nothing that me and the boys shouldn't be able to take care of, but I'd caution you to get inside of your house and stay there. Keep your girl close. There might be some trouble afoot, and I wouldn't want you to get caught up in it."

"Thank you, Sheriff."

He gives Katherine one last tip of his hat before striding out smartly back toward his office, yelling for Bob and Bill. They come running, rifles in their hands. All three of the men jump on their horses and ride off, kicking up a generous cloud of dust as they go.

"Well, that is interesting," Katherine says, eyes narrowed.

I grab her by her elbow and pull her a little. "Come on, this is our chance."

"Chance for what?"

"To snoop around the sheriff's office. If you haven't noticed, there's still too much about this land that we don't know. They might have a map and compass so we can navigate once we hightail it out of here."

I leave Katherine sputtering on the boardwalk and make a

beeline back to the sheriff's office. It's nearly midday and the streets are deserted. The morning patrols would be out and the evening patrols getting what sleep they can, so this is the perfect time to get in a bit of uninterrupted sneaking.

I dash down the boardwalk, skidding to a stop in front of the office. Katherine is close on my heels, huffing and puffing even though it was only a couple hundred feet. I glance at her over my shoulder. "Are you wearing a corset?"

"Yes, Jane, I am. Because a lady wouldn't go about without one."

I shake my head and walk inside, pulling Katherine in as well. She leans back against the wall next to the door, fighting to catch her breath.

"What is it you said you're looking for?"

I shrug. "A map, a compass . . . Anything that seems like it could be useful."

Katherine's eyes skim around the room. "Well, that's vague enough."

I roll my eyes. "Why don't you search that room over there? I'll go poke through his desk."

Katherine heads over to the room off the main office and I hurry over to the desk, opening drawers and peering at their contents. I have a flashback to the last time I went snooping where I didn't belong, and for a heartbeat I wonder if maybe I should've learned my lesson. If we get caught our situation will be dire, but I have no idea what the next closest town might be, or even how far. A map and some kind of direction finding will be vital for our escape.

I also want to see if prying through the sheriff's belongings reveals anything about him. The sheriff has weaknesses. I already know Katherine's pretty face is one of them, so what others does the man possess? The more I know about the sheriff, the easier it will be to get quit of him.

Well, at least that's what I'm hoping.

The drawers I open reveal nothing remarkable: rolling papers, some loose tobacco, a few bullets. There's an apple and a nice hunk of wax-wrapped cheese in a bottom drawer, and I have to fight from snatching it up. Even after days of doing nothing and eating decently in the Duchess's care, I'm still as hungry as I've ever been; but if I take it, the sheriff will know that someone has been in his desk, and him being suspicious ain't in the plan.

It doesn't take long to figure that there's a whole lot of nothing in the sheriff's desk. I close the last drawer and stand with a sigh, moving to check on Katherine. I'm halfway there when boot steps echo outside on the boardwalk.

I freeze, every muscle in my body tensing. My back tingles with phantom pains as I remember the kiss of the whip along it, and I know that this time there's no way there will be mercy. Not for me, or Katherine, either.

"Kate!" I whisper-yell, as loud as I dare. The boot steps are getting closer, deliberate in their plodding pace. In just a few seconds someone is going to walk in on us, catch us red-handed in our snooping.

Katherine comes out of the room, irritation on her face. "Jane, I found the most interesting map—" She stops talking. "Someone's coming."

"Yep. Now stand there and look out of sorts. Shouldn't be too hard for you." I pluck a pearl hairpin from her hair and fall to my knees, crawling around the floor.

Behind me the door opens, and the person stops short in the doorway. My heart pounds in my chest, loud enough that I'm sure our unexpected guest can hear it. Katherine inhales sharply, and my stomach just about falls out, every last drop of dread and fear settling right where it used to be.

"Well, if that ain't a sight for sore eyes I don't know what is."

I close my eyes and start to pray, because there is no way I am hearing what I think I hear.

Either Red Jack is behind me scandalously taking stock of my derriere, or I have finally lost my mind.

Some nights I lie in my bed and wonder if it was all a dream, if I really ever had a beloved baby girl. But then I remember your smile, and I know that the good parts truly happened, and that one day we shall read Shakespeare together again.

Chapter 30
In Which I Get a Visit from the Dead

The voice cuts through my burgeoning terror and sends me springing to my feet. I turn around, heart beating out a staccato rhythm against my ribs—not from fright, but from a wild kind of hope that I ain't never felt before. There, standing in the doorway, grinning like the cat that got into the cream, is Jackson.

Before my good sense can get a word in edgewise I'm running across the room, throwing my arms around him in an embrace to beat all embraces. He laughs and picks me up, swinging me in a circle. When he sets me down he leans in and steals a quick kiss, and I'm just as quick to slap him.

"Just because I'm happy you ain't dead doesn't mean you get to kiss me."

"Ah, Janey-Jane. When have I ever passed up the opportunity to steal a little sugar?"

Jackson moves over to Katherine and bows over her hand like a true swain, murmuring pleasantries. I close the door to make sure we don't have any more guests, then I turn to Jackson, arms crossed.

"So you ain't dead."

He grins, a full on Red Jack smile. "Nope. Your friend made me an offer I couldn't refuse."

"Oh?"

Jackson nods, propping up a hip on the corner of the desk. "Seems that Daniel Redfern ain't the loyal follower of the mayor that he pretends to be. After you two went off, the sheriff told Daniel to take me out back and put me down like a rabid dog. Lucky for me, Daniel handed me a knife and a canteen, led me to a side of the town's boundary that is a bit lighter on shamblers, and told me to walk north for two days. I did and ended up in Nicodemus, a town founded by a bunch of Egalitarians."

"Wait, hold on a minute now. Mr. Redfern helped you? And there are Egalitarians here?" I'm trying to put Jackson's words into the context of what I've learned over the past few weeks and I'm failing miserably.

Jackson nods and shifts his weight. "Yep. Daniel ain't a murderer like the rest of these folks, he's just a man trying to play the hand that life dealt him."

Katherine's eyes go wide. "Well, there you go! We just have to get them to help us get rid of the sheriff and his father."

Jackson shakes his head. "The Egalitarians got no interest in interfering with Summerland. They're happy to give any of us refuge, but don't expect them to take part in any sort of fight. They're pacifists."

I shake my head sadly. "Well, so much for that idea. So, if you're all cozy in the next town over, what are you doing here?"

"Stealing some bullets. Pacifists apparently don't own guns and are terrifyingly light on ammunition. And searching for Lily. I didn't want to risk being seen again for fear of dooming both me and Daniel, and I was only barely able to climb over the wall between patrols and keep my head down as I made my way to town, terrified I'd be recognized. But if she's here, I need to find her."

He stands up and stretches, and I watch him greedily. I feel like I can't get enough of looking at him, of knowing that he's alive and still out there, up to no good. I turn as I feel Katherine's gaze land on me. She's giving me a look like she's seeing something for the first time, and I school my expression to blankness, worried that I somehow gave too much away.

"She's safe," I say finally. "Lily. She's over in the fancy part of town. I talked to her the other night, before things went south."

Jackson grins. "Lily's alive? Ha, I knew it!" He pauses and the smile melts into a frown. "Wait, what do you mean 'went south'?"

I quickly outline what's happened to me and Katherine since we arrived in Summerland. Jackson's expression darkens.

"That bastard deserves to die."

I shrug. "No doubt. The question is: How?"

Red Jack shrugs. "Not sure. My plan after finding Lily was to make a run for the Mississippi River before it freezes, head south to New Orleans. Ain't no way I'm going back east, and I've heard rumors that city has been fortified. Strong walls, with its back against the water. But there's no way we can get there without supplies, and those Nicodemus folks ration everything carefully."

"Same here," Katherine says.

He nods, opening his mouth to answer when the sound of footsteps outside interrupt him.

"Look, I'll talk to Daniel and Amelia and get back to you two," Jackson says.

"Amelia? You mean Miss Duncan is here?"

"Yes, she and a bunch of the girls from your school. They came to Nicodemus when Baltimore County was overrun."

His words send a cold shock through me, and I tense. "Overrun? By shamblers? When did that happen? Did everyone get out? How come you're just now mentioning this?" I think of little Ruthie and Big Sue, and dread is a cold hard lump in my middle.

"Not now, Jane!" Katherine admonishes. "We need to get out and waylay whoever is heading this way so Jackson can get what he needs."

Jackson gives Katherine a smile of thanks and an ugly feeling rises up in me, part jealousy and part shame and part anger at myself for getting just a tad bit hysterical. But what do they expect? I swallow my aggravation and open the door for Katherine while Jackson ducks into the small room.

Katherine sweeps out of the office like a queen leaving court. I follow behind her, carefully closing the door as she exclaims, "Oh, my apologies! Pastor, I did not see you!"

The preacher stands there, his rheumy brown eyes locked on Katherine's bosom and a smile that borders on indecent on his thin, pink lips.

"Oh, Miss Deveraux, what a pleasant surprise."

Katherine gives the man a small smile and takes a mincing step back, putting a few additional inches between her and the holy man. "It is lovely to see you as well. Why, I was just telling my girl that she missed a very moving discussion on moral responsibility at our last Bible study."

The man gives me a condescending look, the smile on his lips not reflected in his eyes.

"Yes, she could use the message of the Lord more than most here. Well, I won't hold you up, I just came by to drop off some information for Sheriff Snyder."

"Oh, he isn't there. He was called off on some urgent business."

"Well, if the sheriff isn't there, then what exactly were you doing in the office?" The preacher gives Katherine a long look, and for a moment I think that she's done it, going and running her mouth when she should've just bid the man good day and carried on about her business.

"Oh, I had sent my girl in to find my pearl hairpin, and was just fetching her. I'm afraid sometimes even the smallest task is beyond poor Jane." She lowers her voice conspiratorially. "You know how easily they're distracted."

The suspicious look disappears from the man's eyes and he gives Katherine a warm smile. "My dear, the penitent show understanding to all those beneath them, no matter their flaws. Was she able to find your hairpin?"

From inside of the office comes the faint sound of footsteps, and Katherine tenses. But the preacher doesn't hear them, most likely thanks to his advanced age and his single-minded focus on the stretch of material covering her bosoms.

She flashes the man a brilliant smile. "Yes, thank goodness.

I have so few nice things, and if it wasn't for the message of the Lord I'm certain my strength would have fled me long ago. Just to keep living every day . . ." Katherine closes her eyes for a moment, as though the struggle causes her physical pain. When she opens her eyes they shine with emotion. "I know this is just the Lord testing me, and I know that I will survive it with his grace and love. But, Pastor, it has been a very difficult journey, and I am afraid that I have doubted my place in the Lord's heart at times." She sniffs, not too much, just like she's fighting back tears. "I was beginning to lose my faith, but your words last Sunday and the charity of this magnificent town have restored my belief that the Lord has a plan for me, and it is majestic."

I fight to keep my mouth from falling open. She's good. Katherine's ability to play the farce rivals my own. The preacher is rapt with attention as Katherine begins spinning out a tale of woe and misery so pitiful that it belongs in a weekly serial.

By the time Katherine finishes detailing the viciousness of her nonexistent stepmother and the death of her father, the preacher is near to tears himself. It sickens me to think that such an evil man can feel pity.

"Oh, you poor child. The Lord has blessed you with so many charms that you must believe that He loves you, and has a plan, and a fine husband, in store for you."

"Oh, I do, Pastor, I do." Katherine shakes herself, and she

forces a polite smile. "Well, I'm afraid I must be going. Now that I have my Negro back, she needs to get everything put to rights." We've been stalling on the boardwalk for nearly a quarter of an hour. If Jackson is still poking around for whatever he needs from the sheriff's office, he's on his own.

"Indeed, Miss Deveraux. Enjoy the rest of your afternoon."

Katherine gives him a small curtsy before setting off across the dusty road. I scurry along behind her, and once we're clear of the preacher Katherine mutters, "What an odious man."

"That was quite impressive," I murmur.

Katherine snorts in a way that is not at all ladylike. "What did you expect, Jane? I grew up in a whorehouse. If there's anyone who knows how to put on an act, it is a woman dependent upon the appetites of men for her living." There's a sharp tone to her voice, a reminder that she's playing this role because I asked it of her, not because she wanted to.

I consider Katherine's words the rest of the way to the better side of town.

Perhaps I don't know her as well as I think I do.

Jane, I am glad to hear that you have ever so many companions with whom to while away the hours. There is no greater gift than the gift of friendship. Just make sure that those you give it to are deserving of such a fine thing.

Chapter 31
In Which I Have a Heartfelt Conversation

After a silent walk down the dirt road to the proper side of town, Katherine and I end up in front of the house where she's been staying since she arrived in Summerland, right next door to Lily and the Spencers. Lily and a small boy play in their front yard, and even though our eyes meet neither of us acknowledges the other. Lily knows how to play the long con; her brother's made sure of that.

Katherine's house is downright luxurious, particularly

when compared to the squalor I've gotten used to. The door opens onto a nicely appointed sitting room, the small windows opened to catch any bit of a breeze. Oriental rugs cover the wood plank floors. In the bedroom to the rear there is a sumptuous feather bed for Katherine and a relatively clean cot has been brought in for me. The bowl and pitcher on the dressing table are real china, nicer than most anything else in Summerland, and there are several lovely dresses hanging in a wardrobe for Katherine, as well as a lady's dressing gown.

The kitchen has no stove but it does have a large sink with a pump, just like the tub and cistern the Duchess showed me back at the cathouse. The sitting room has a hearth and a modest stack of something that looks to be dried dung. I decide that I'm glad for the warm weather. On the end table is a jar of peaches and a simple note from Mr. Gideon: "Please enjoy this modest gift."

The sight of those peaches causes a warm feeling to spread through my middle. I ain't seen the tinkerer since the day of my whipping, and I owe him a hearty thanks. Without his salve my back would still be a ruined mess, and I don't think it's a great leap of reasoning to think that I owe him my life.

As soon as we close the door Katherine sighs and her shoulders slump. "Would you please help me get out of this thing?" she asks, all traces of haughtiness gone.

I walk over and begin to unfasten the row of tiny buttons along the back, slipping it over her head once it's loose enough. I follow her into the back bedroom, hanging the dress up on one of the wooden hangers in the wardrobe as Katherine pulls the lacing to remove her corset, donning the dressing gown, a bright silk garment that features embroidered dragons along the front.

I bend down and pick up the corset, a smile finding its way to my lips. "Did you get that robe from one of the Duchess's girls?"

Katherine gives me a glare that would stop my heart if looks could kill. "No. The sheriff gave it to me as a gift. Said he got this from a Chinese man that used to live here."

My stomach drops as I remember the Duchess's comment about the lack of Chinese in Summerland. What happened to the man who had originally owned that robe? Nothing good. I read an article entitled "The Great Yellow Menace" in which the author went to great lengths to malign the Chinese immigrants out west in California, who apparently charge very steep rates to protect folks from shamblers. I'd only read the article because I'd thought it was about shamblers, not immigration. It seems strange that in these very fraught times folks would be more concerned about hardworking people trying to find a better life than the monsters that actually want to eat them.

Katherine heaves a sigh and doesn't speak again, and I perch next to her on the bed. "What's wrong?"

She shakes her head and looks down at her lap, not saying

a word. I wait, and after a moment she begins crying—soft, ladylike tears that make her eyes pretty and bright. Somehow I envy her and pity her at the same time.

"Katherine—" I begin, but I don't get much more than her name out before she cuts me off.

"Do you know what it's like to have every man in this miserable town panting after you like a rabid dog? Do you know what it's like to have to spend weeks pretending to be like the rest of them, to say such despicable things about yourself, to laugh at jokes that cut like rusty knives?" She keeps her voice low but the emotion is still clear.

I shake my head, as Katherine ain't really looking for a conversation.

"I hate this. I hate pretending to be white, to be like most of the folks in this town. I hate the way they think. And I hate knowing that my face is worth more than all the rest of me."

"Well, maybe not all of the rest of you," I mutter, but Katherine doesn't hear me.

"Do you know what Miss Anderson told me before we got in the train car to come here? 'I wish you weren't so pretty, Katherine. Maybe then someone would've taken you on and you would've had a chance at a future.' I had a chance, Jane, but because of my damned face, no one would take me on as an Attendant. I was first in our class."

"Well, only because I'm terrible with a rifle. Besides, we

still had final evaluations to go through, and my rifle work has greatly improved—"

"Jane, please, shut up. Don't you get it? No white woman would have taken me on as Attendant because of my stupid face, and colored girls don't like me because I'm too light by half. My future, if we ever get out of this miserable patch of dirt, is to belong to some man, just like my momma did. I left Virginia to escape that fate, yet it seems to have found me anyway."

I laugh softly, and shake my head. "Haven't you figured it out yet?" She looks at me and I smile. "You're passing fair, Kate. No one in this town doubts that you're white. That's your future. Your manners are pretty enough that everyone believes you're from a fine family, without a moment's hesitation. You could make your way to a nice place, marry some fine man and become respectable, set up housekeeping and have fancy dinner parties that would put the mayor's to shame."

Katherine sniffs. "But don't you see, Jane? That's exactly what I don't want. I don't want to live the rest of my life as a liar. To turn my back on my own people. And I definitely don't want to be someone's wife. I don't want a man."

I shift uncomfortably next to her. "Is this your way of telling me you fancy women?" Not that I mind that. I've been distracted by a pretty face every now and again myself. But trying to imagine Katherine pledging herself to a life as a spinster doesn't quite fit.

Katherine jumps to her feet and begins to pace. "No! I don't fancy anyone. I've seen the way you look at Mr. Gideon and I've seen the way you look at Jackson. I've even seen the way you used to look at Merry Alfred when she was at Miss Preston's."

My face heats. "Well, Merry was very pretty and she had that amazing right hook." Merry was also a very good kisser, taught me everything I know, but Katherine doesn't need to hear about that.

She keeps talking like I haven't said a word. "But I don't feel that way about anyone, Jane. I never have and I'm not sure I ever will."

"Oh, well, there's nothing wrong with that."

"But that's what makes it so hard. I don't want to get married. I don't want to chase after some man or set up housekeeping with another woman. I'm just not interested. I want to see the world! I want to write my own future, like Hattie McCrea."

I laugh. "Well, everyone wants to be Hattie." Hattie McCrea's story is the dream of every Attendant-in-training. She was the first real Attendant, assigned to Martha Johnson, President Johnson's daughter. They say she single-handedly killed a horde that tried to swarm the White House back in '69. Whether the story is true or not, it made Hattie famous. She traveled the world after that, her name made, teaching girls how to defend themselves against shamblers, and finally marrying a handsome French duke. Well, at least that's how the story goes. She could've just as easily been killed by some random shambler in a swamp down south in the Lost States, for all we really know.

Either way, Hattie was the example we all strove for—Hattie and her selflessness, or Hattie and her fame, or even Hattie and her ability to make her own decisions about her life, free from the restraints the rest of us labor under. All of us Negro girls wanted to be like Hattie, respected and admired.

Even Katherine, who could've passed as a fine white lady if she wanted.

"If you want to see the world like Hattie, you can. I ain't never met someone half as determined as you are." I put my arm around her shoulders and squeeze. "We just need to get out of here, first. I am truly sorry I've put you through this, but you do understand that your pretty face is just as much a weapon as your rifle, right?"

Katherine wipes her eyes and gives me a strange look, like I just sprouted an extra nose. I lean back a little. "What? What did I say?"

"Jane, I've never thought of it that way, that beauty could be a weapon."

I laugh. "That's because you've never met my momma. She used to say the only thing more lethal than a bullet was a woman with a pretty face."

"Strangely enough, that actually makes me feel better."

"Good. But let's not forget that isn't the only weapon in your arsenal now. You've still got the promise of your virtue." I give Katherine a wry smile. "The thing is, what are we going to do with all of this admiration you're getting? More important, what are we supposed to do once we get clear of this place?"

Katherine purses her lips in thought, the storm of her earlier emotions subsiding. "Well, that is a question. I'd figured we'd go back to Baltimore, but since Miss Preston's is no more, there isn't much there for us."

I shake my head, because I'd never planned on going back there except to kill Miss Anderson, but now that's not going to happen. I'm a little disappointed, but the gnawing worry in my gut is stronger. How many survived that devastation? Are my friends out there in the wild somewhere now, or are they still in Maryland, yellow-eyed shamblers all?

I take a deep breath and push my worry to the side. One crisis at a time, thank you very much. First, freedom. Then, everything else.

"Well, I think for now there ain't much we can do besides find our rest. A fine lady like yourself, well, this heat would just be entirely too much for you. You should get some sleep."

"What are you going to do?"

"For now, the same. Tomorrow I'm going to implore the

good doctor for some laudanum." Katherine arches a brow at me. "You know, for your lady problems."

"Jane . . ."

"Look, I've got plans, and it isn't just stealing some supplies and hoping I can make it to the Mississippi River and hitch a ride south, like Jackson. I told you before, that boy is all impulse."

"And what plan is this?"

Quickly I fill Katherine in on how I'd planned on dosing the sheriff.

"Jane, that's thoroughly dishonorable!"

"I ain't planning on killing the man, just turning him shambler." Of course, I'm going to kill him after. Nuance is important, that's what I always say.

Katherine disagrees. "You turning him into a monster is just the same as murdering him, Jane."

"Not if he's already a monster."

Katherine sighs. "I want to be rid of him as much as you, but—"

"Yeah, you tell me that after he's taken the lash to your back," I snap, the fear and pain and humiliation of the memory rising up quick and sharp. Katherine falls silent, her expression troubled. I sigh. "I'd have no problem putting a bullet in the man in a duel, Katherine. But there's no way we'd make it beyond the berm if I do that. He ain't a good person, and I ain't pretending like he deserves to live. Think about the way he's starving most of the Negroes and drovers in town while he and his boys and all the good white folks stay fat. Summerland was supposed to be about a better life for all, but it's worse here than it was in Baltimore. Do you think that's the word of a good person?"

"But that's the point, Jane. If you kill him, that makes you no better than he is."

"I'm okay with that."

Footsteps outside on the porch silence whatever else Katherine was going to say. She gives me a wide-eyed look of alarm. "I don't think I can handle any more company today."

"Well then, it's a fine thing that you have an Attendant to handle it for you, ain't it?" I jump up from the bed, closing the door to the bedroom behind me. I don't bother stopping, just go straight to the door and yank it open.

Mr. Gideon is on the other side, hand poised to knock. He startles as he looks at me, adjusting his spectacles before doffing his hat in a lovely display of manners that I've seen men lavish on white ladies, but I sure ain't used to. The movement draws my attention to his fetching eyes and the fullness of his lips, and a flutter starts up somewhere low in my belly. Katherine's words about the way I look at him ring like a fire bell in my head.

Lordy, I hope this foolishness is due to my having missed lunch. Ain't nothing good going to come from losing my head over the tinkerer.

"Miss McKeene," he says.

"Mr. Gideon. I'm sorry, but Miss Katherine is indisposed." I put a bit of a drawl in my voice, stressing the natural cadence of my words. Hopefully he won't hear the lie in them. For some mysterious reason I find it difficult to lie to the tinkerer. Perhaps because I get the distinct feeling that he sees through each and every one.

His brows draw together slightly. "Oh, I do hope she's okay?"

"Oh, yes, she's just feeling a mite dizzy because of the heat. Was there something I could help you with?"

"Well, perhaps, but I'd rather wait to discuss it when both of you are present. I know I'm being terribly forward, but would you and Miss Deveraux consider joining me for the noon meal tomorrow?"

"That's a fine idea," I answer before I've properly thought through why I'm so eager for the tinkerer's company.

His expression brightens, and he dons his hat once more, settling the bowler into place. "Fantastic. I'll come by tomorrow at noon to escort Miss Deveraux to the lab. Sheriff Snyder said that he is in the process of refortifying the town's defenses in the wake of an unanticipated shambler pack pressing against the eastern wall, and it's all for the better that Miss Deveraux remains in her rooms until the problem has been rectified."

"Of course, Mr. Gideon. I wouldn't want Miss Katherine

to come to any harm." There's a hidden warning in his voice, and I sense that he knows more about the current dangers in Summerland than he's letting on.

He strolls off and I watch him go, his limp more pronounced than usual.

As I close the door, I worry that he's pressing himself too hard, and just that little bit of concern is enough to make me realize that I'm in a heap of trouble.

My heart ain't never going to be safe.

I will not tell you that I am not worried about you. That would be an outright lie. These are dark times we live in, and it is only by keeping our wits about ourselves that we can truly survive.

Chapter 32
In Which I Am Invited to a Battle

Word of Katherine not feeling well gets around quicker than a brush fire in August. A few minutes after I speak with Mr. Gideon, a few roughnecks come by with a basket of blackberries that they found out along the creek, like some fruit is going to cure whatever ails her. I smile and thank them before closing the door, firmly refusing them entry. They're followed by another group of men, this time with a handful of wild onions and another with a rabbit, cleaned and ready to be cooked. By the time all of the shifts have returned, Katherine and I have the makings of a rather fine meal, and even though it's far too hot to stoke a fire in the hearth, I do it anyway, roasting the rabbit along with the onions over patties that thankfully smell more like grass than anything else.

Once the entire mess is ready, Katherine and I eat it greedily, the past week of good eating not quite able to make up for the weeks of starvation. Around mouthfuls of rabbit and blackberries she confesses that even the rations for the white folks have become smaller and smaller since so many families have arrived in the past couple of weeks. It makes me feel a little soft toward the drovers for bringing Katherine their food. Most likely they were counting on it to round out their own dinner, and it says something that they were willing to give it up for Katherine.

She is less impressed.

"Those men are just another part of the problem, and willing enablers. Where do you think Mr. Gideon gets shamblers for that machine you told me about? There's danger right below our feet, and they're the ones keeping the cycle going. Not everyone is a prisoner here, Jane. Some of them deeply want Summerland to succeed, no matter what the cost."

Katherine has removed her hairpins so that the mass of her honeyed curls hang down her back. She looks younger with her hair down, the shadows around her eyes more pronounced. Now that I know what it costs her emotionally to go along with my ruse I'm even more anxious to put our plan into action. It's only been a few weeks since Katherine went from being just another colored girl at Miss Preston's to a white lady, and the change in her is obvious as we eat. She is careful in her movements, and the sound of footfalls past our door causes her to look up with a fearful expression. The guilt that rises up in me is near to crippling.

I miss the old Katherine, the one I knew back in Baltimore, even as that girl was sorely vexing. I don't like this quiet girl with the haunted eyes, and I'm starting to think that maybe I didn't do her a favor after all. But I can't change the past; I can only push headlong into an uncertain future.

"Kate," I say after we've eaten our fill as a sudden thought occurs to me. "I came poking around on this side of town the night before I took that whipping. I recognized a couple of the families that just arrived. They were at Mayor Carr's dinner."

Katherine purses her lips and leans back on the settee. "Oh, I met them. You don't have to worry about them, Jane. The funny thing about rich folks is they never remember the hired help. I assure you, my secret is safe."

When a knock sounds at the door, loud and forceful, Katherine turns apologetic eyes to me. "Jane, I'm sorry, but would you get that?"

"Of course. Why don't you go ahead and retire for the evening while I make your apologies. It's near curfew, anyway."

The fire in the grate has burned low, and the air coming in through the open window in the front room bears a chill, the land getting cool as the sun sets.

Katherine gives me a grateful look and I get up and trudge once more to the door. It's too late for respectable callers, but there ain't a whole lot of respectable folks in Summerland. So it's with some surprise that I pull the door open to find the last man I ever want to see. Every muscle in my body tenses.

"Sheriff."

"Jane. Where's Miss Deveraux?"

"She's retired for the evening, sir." It kills me a little to have to give the sheriff even the barest semblance of respect when all I want to do is test the edge of my sickles against his neck.

"I need to speak with her."

"It will have to wait until the morning."

"It can't wait," he snaps. He attempts to glance past me into the depths of the rooms and I move to block his view.

"Is there something I can help you with, sir?" I ask, all icy politeness. There's something a little off about the sheriff; I don't think he's been drinking, but his insistence has an undercurrent that puts me on alert. There's no way I'm going to let him into our rooms.

"Sheriff Snyder, is there something amiss?" Katherine appears in the doorway to the sleeping chamber, clutching her wrap tightly. I scowl at her. I had the situation under control. She ignores me.

The man removes his hat and bows. "Miss Deveraux, I apologize for the intrusion, but I need to borrow your girl." I bristle at being referred to as an object, but say nothing.

"What's going on?"

"There's been a breach on the eastern edge that is more serious than I initially suspected. I need everyone who can handle a weapon with me to take down a pack of shamblers heading toward town."

"How many?" I ask, forgetting my place.

"About thirty, maybe forty. They've already ripped through half my patrol. They're about two miles away, heading straight toward us." The sheriff shivers in a way I've not seen from him since I arrived.

Katherine and I exchange a glance, and I give her a slight nod. She turns to the sheriff. "Please, take Jane. She'll be able to help you."

The man plops his hat back on his head. "Much obliged, Miss Deveraux." To me he says, "You got one minute to prepare yourself." He stomps off without another word, off to rustle up whoever else he needs to help.

I hurry back into the rooms, pushing past Katherine and grabbing the cavalry sword and my sickles. I'm about half a dozen weapons short of what I'd like to have to take on a horde, but it'll have to do.

Katherine runs to the wardrobe. "Jane, help me get into

this thing." She pulls out a modest dress of calico, similar to mine but the full length that real ladies wear.

"No."

Katherine freezes and turns to me. "You can't—"

"No, you ain't going," I say. "You're a lady, Katherine. This is too dangerous for you." I move closer to her and whisper, "Someone has to be here for Lily, especially if Jackson sees this breach as an opportunity to come looking for her. The girl's right next door. Please."

"Okay, Jane. I'll look out for Lily."

"There's something powerful frightening about this, Kate. I've seen the wall. There's no way a shambler can get over it. If it's been breached . . ." I trail off, the idea of all those shamblers on the prairie making their way into Summerland stunning me into silence.

There's yelling out in the street as the sheriff continues to round up folks, and I turn toward the door. "Make sure you bar this, and don't let anyone in. Certain death can make a man act in unusual ways, forgetting right and wrong."

Katherine nods. "Jane, be safe."

I grin. "Ain't no shambler going to put me down, Kate. You should know that by now."

She glares at me and closes the door as I leave. I pause on the porch until I hear the bar slide into place, then I jog out to join the knot of men gathering in the street. A few of the girls from the day patrol are there as well, including Ida. Her eyes go wide when she sees me.

"I thought you was dead."

I shake my head. "Not yet."

"How'd you end up over here in the fancy part of town?"

I just wink at her. Let her come up with a good rumor by herself.

"Do you know how the wall was breached?" I ask Ida.

She shakes her head. "No. It seems strange. It ain't like shamblers can destroy the wall, they can't even figure out how to get over it."

None of the Negroes milling around have weapons, which is hardly a surprise, but if what the sheriff says is true, everyone needs to be armed. I'm about to open my mouth to say so when I remember how my concerns were addressed last time.

Mr. Gideon rides up on a fine horse, the beast dancing sideways in agitation. I move over to him, even though the last place I want to be is anywhere near the monster he rides. "Mr. Gideon."

His expression softens as he looks down at me. "Miss McKeene."

"How exactly did that grand wall come to be compromised?" I ask him.

The corners of his mouth turn down. "That is a question I would also like answered," he says, his tone grim. It troubles me that the smartest man in town doesn't have the answer to what should be a simple question. But I have more pressing issues to fret about.

"I can't help but notice that none of the Negroes are armed," I murmur. "It would be a terrible tactical error to go into battle against the dead without the proper weapons."

The tinkerer quickly assesses the situation before nodding. "I'll have a word with the sheriff." He rides off, and Ida walks up as he leaves.

"What did you say to him?"

"That we need proper weapons."

"That would be a nice change." She eyes my sword enviously, and for a moment I catch a glimpse of a girl that is maybe more than she seems. But then she sees me watching her, and the glint disappears, her usual dull expression taking its place.

"Ida."

"Hmm?"

"Would you like my sword?"

She startles. "You serious?"

"Yes."

"But what would you use?"

"My sickles."

"Those are weapons?" she says, looking askance at the blades tucked in the ties at my waist.

"Yes, they are. Besides, you don't honestly think all those drovers are going to last long out there, do you? I'll grab one of their guns when they fall." It's a bluff, but I got a feeling about Ida, and if I'm right then I want her feeling indebted to me in a way that assures that she won't be likely to betray me.

I hold out the sword and she takes it reverently. "It's beautiful."

"I'll get you a whetstone and oil for it if you make it through this."

Her expression goes hard, fierce and determined. "Oh, I will."

I smile. "Good to know." Momma used to say there were lots of ways to survive. *Don't be afraid to pretend to be something you aren't, Jane. Sometimes a little subterfuge and chicanery is in order and the quickest way to achieve one's goal.* It ain't hard to imagine Ida pretending to be just another dumb colored girl in order to make it out here. Survival by any means necessary.

The sheriff rides up on his big horse. He exchanges a few words with Mr. Gideon, who gives me a nod as he rides back to the rear of the group.

"My boys are opening up the armory next to the generator shack for everyone to equip themselves. Even the colored folks," he says, giving me a pointed look. To one of his boys the sheriff says, "No guns for the darkies. The last thing we want is one of them shooting us in the back."

The man runs off and the sheriff turns back to the group. "You colored folks can avail yourselves of the bladed weapons.

I see you even touch a rifle I'm going to have you put down."

It's nice to know that even Summerland's impending doom doesn't make the sheriff change his mind about giving Negroes a fighting chance. Still, something is better than nothing.

"The dead are about a mile or so to the east. The majority of them haven't crossed the inner fence yet, and the patrols have been mopping up the stragglers all evening. We've lit the line so there's some visibility. We're going to ride out there and see if we can't finish off the rest of the pack. The plan is to let them come to you. You cross that interior fence, you're on your own. Is everyone clear?"

There are silent nods of assent, and then everyone breaks off and files into the nearby armory. The drovers are allowed in first, and they come out holding rifles that look as near to new as anything I've ever seen.

Finally it's our turn, and I'm one of the first into the armory; the sight of it is enough to make me swear and cry happy tears all at the same time. Row upon row of bright, edged weapons are held in proper holders, their blades gleaming even in the low lamplight. A collective gasp goes up from the Negroes around me as they take in all of the fine implements before us. For the first time they are seeing just what the sheriff has done to us, day in and day out, sending us out to die on the front line with nothing but garden tools for defense when real weapons were waiting all the while behind lock and key. We could've cleaned out the plains with this arsenal.

"I'd like to kill that man," mutters the stocky boy next to me, his skin dark as pitch.

"Get in line," I say. He gives me a small smile, and stands next to me as the crowd clears out. I'm angry, and I want a moment to compose myself before I go back outside.

The boy watches me, his gaze weighty. "What're you looking for?"

"Nothing. I got my sickles."

"Difficult weapon to wield."

"Only if you don't know how."

"True, that." He walks to the far shelf where the heavy weapons are kept and picks up the porcupine, a weighted wooden club with fierce metal spikes embedded in the rounded end. It doesn't require a lot of skill to wield but does require a good bit of arm strength. "Maybe you should try one of these."

"Porcupine ain't for me. I got chicken arms."

He laughs, the sound low. "Well, try not to get turned, Chicken Arms."

"You, too. And be patient, that lawman will get his just desserts."

His lips twist, filled with malice. "I ain't yet seen the man who can do that."

"Maybe that's your problem. You been waiting for a man."

He hefts the porcupine, propping it on his shoulder,

expression thoughtful. "All right, then. My name's Lucas. You need any help with anything, you let me know."

He leaves without waiting for my answer. I grab a small throwing knife, slipping it into my boot before I exit. I pass Bill on my way. I give him my best smile and he stops.

"What're you grinning about?"

"I want my penny back, Bill."

He chuckles mirthlessly. "You ain't getting it. Besides, you got bigger things to fret about. I'd bet you won't last till morning."

"I will. And when I do, I'm going to march right back here and take what's mine. You got my promise on that."

Bill gives me a hard look. "Keep walking, you crazy-ass coon."

I don't let the slur move me, because I feel more confident than I have in a long while. Instead, I just level a flat look at Bill.

"You have no idea."

Jane, as this is my last letter, I suppose I should finally confess the news that I've been afraid to share these long few months, wondering if you were ever going to return home: I have decided to take a husband. A fine man, to be sure. I am most assured you will find him every bit as enchanting as I do.

Chapter 33
In Which I Demonstrate My Worth

The sheriff sets a grueling pace out to the rendezvous point. Halfway through the run I understand why he picked the people he did to accompany him. Because it's all Summerland has to offer. There are only about thirty of us in all, mostly Negroes, with a few of the younger roughnecks to round out the ranks. It ain't nearly enough people to defend a town of this size.

We keep pace with the horses' canter, following the

lanterns the riders carry. A few of my wounds pull open during the run, the blood dampening the back of my dress, but it's nothing compared to the exhaustion I read on the drovers' faces. There ain't enough horses to go around, and a few of the younger men have to run with the colored folks. I end up keeping pace with a sandy-haired youth with a sparse beard. He looks to be around my age, and he gasps like a fish on a riverbank as we run.

"Take deeper breaths," I say, trying to help him out.

"Don't need yer help," he snaps, his accent thick and rich like good gravy.

"Well, you keep panting like a dog and you're like as not to pass out, and you don't want that, do you? You're much easier to kill flat on your back." From his new boots and sad beard I surmise he's a boy trying to be a man, and the last thing he's going to want is to have a fainting spell like some fine corseted lady.

He stops gasping and begins to breathe deeper, and I swallow a smile. "What's your name?"

"Cary. Cary MacAfee."

"You a Scotsman, Cary?"

"My daddy was a Scotsman. I'm a Georgian."

"That explains the accent. What brings you out here to the middle of the frontier?"

"Damn, girl, you sure are chatty for someone about to die," he says.

"Oh, I ain't about to die. This is a normal night's work for me." Already his breathing is easing up, and the wide-eyed panic in his face is receding. He's forgotten that he's running and started letting his body do what it was built to do, and now everything is a little easier. That's good. He needs to save his energy for the shamblers.

The people ahead of us stop suddenly, and there are screams as a horse rears, whinnying in surprise.

"It's the dead!" someone yells.

"Get on line!" yells the sheriff, terror in his voice.

We form up, moving with all haste. It's an old Army tactic, marching in a row and mowing the enemy down as you move forward. The problem is we ain't soldiers. We're a few untried roughnecks with rifles and a bunch of Negroes with reasonably sharp knives. So instead of orderly precision, it's chaos as everyone begins moving around in the dark, the moonlight too dim to see much.

"We need light!" I yell. "Turn up the lanterns!"

Someone heeds my call, and one by one the lanterns are turned up as high as they will go. From behind me, the tinkerer calls out. "Hold a moment, I've got something that can help." There's a hollow pop and then what looks like a shooting star flares suddenly to life over our heads, turning the night day-bright. I glance at the scene before us and gasp. I'd been expecting forty shamblers, nothing that a group our size couldn't take care of. But there are easily a couple hundred undead moving toward us, many newly turned and moving so quickly that for a moment a dark wave of fear threatens to drown me. The nearest ones are about a hundred yards away, swarming over what I'm reasonably sure was once a horse and rider.

"Mother Mary," Cary says, and I get a glimpse of his face, wide-eyed with panic.

"Listen to me," I say. "You are not going to panic. You're going to stay calm, and you're going to survive this. You panic, you're dead. You got that?" He whimpers assent, and I pat him on the back. "Good. Now listen. They ain't going to try to fool you; all you got to do is let them come to you. Wait for them to get close, and kill them for good this time. That ain't so hard."

The shamblers' growls grow louder. The lamps the riders carry illuminate the silhouettes of the dead, magicking them into lumbering caricatures of humanity. The closest members of the pack shift their attention to us.

"Get on line!" the sheriff calls again, alarm clear in the timbre of his voice. The fear amongst the drovers is thick now, and I ain't surprised when one of the men bolts, high-tailing it back to town. One of the riders curses and chases after him, and the indecision of the other white men is clear as they weigh their own lives against . . .

What? Why exactly are these men here? Wealth and fortune? A country like the one they had before the war, one that some of them only know from stories? When are these damn fools going to realize that world is gone, and they ain't never getting it back? The tall tales they've been told ain't worth their lives, either way.

But these drovers are here now, and without them fighting alongside us Negroes, I don't see how any of us are going to survive the night.

I twirl my sickles. I've learned a lot in the past few years. Including that a group of panicked people ain't that different from a herd of sheep. Nip at their heels a little and they'll go wherever you tell them to.

"All right, get on line." The words come out louder than I intend, and while I have the attention of my companions, ain't no one moving their feet. Yet. "That wasn't an invitation. Get moving, unless you want to be shambler bait. Line up, double arm interval. Mind your neighbor, make some friends. You ain't got time for indecision."

My voice carries over the moans of the approaching shamblers, steady and assured. Surprisingly enough people start moving, quick shadows in the dark.

"You there, with the lanterns. Hand them down, make a line." The riders are hesitant to give up their light, and I snap my fingers in irritation, like Momma would've done. "You ain't helping anyone shining it down in our eyes like that. Hand them down, and let's get them lined up every few feet."

The sheriff rides over, horse dancing in agitation, the

beast's temperament a mirror of its rider's. "What do you think you're doing?"

"Saving your damn town. You might feel like a big man when you have your boys at your side and you're pushing a bunch of Negroes around, but shamblers don't care about your badge, or your guns, or the fact that you're the preacher's son. You're just as scared as everyone else here, and so someone's got to save our skins. Now you can stand here and try to stop me, or you can ride back and start preparing folks for the hell that's going to rain down upon them if we fail."

The sheriff is quiet for a moment, giving me the darkest of looks, before riding off without a word. I know that I'll have some misery to sort through later, but for right now I'm more interested in surviving.

"All right, let's take a big step back. You're going to keep the lanterns between you and the dead. Keep talking, keep chattering. Remember, the dead don't talk. Let your pals know you ain't a shambler." I turn out into the abyss before us, still lit softly by the tinkerer's firework. The riders have fallen back behind the line of fighters on the ground, and the shamblers are quickening their pace as they move toward us. "Mr. Gideon!"

"Yes, Miss McKeene?"

"How long does that illumination of yours last?"

"A couple of minutes. But I have more flares here with me. Shall I fire them at regular intervals?"

"That'll do well. Please give us a cue before every launch."

"Yes, ma'am." There's a teasing tone in his voice, and it's enough to draw a smile from me.

The line is shoddy, but secure. The Negroes crouch in the ready position, while the drovers don't look like they know what to do with themselves. You can always tell a combat school-educated fighter. Mr. Gideon's flare has nearly gone out, darkness encroaching on the plain once more.

"Do not cross the line! Let the shamblers come to you!" I shout.

"Kill the fresh ones first," someone says.

"Take one down, move on to the next—there's always another!" someone else shouts helpfully.

Bits and pieces of basic combat advice continues to echo through the line. "Up and across, never down," "Maintain your balance; lose your footing, lose your life," and so on and so forth, until the night is filled with the shouts of roughnecks and Negroes, all of us ready to fight for our lives.

I wait, one heartbeat, another, straining my ears for the telltale sounds of the shamblers until my pulse pounds in my ears. The dead weren't all that far off when the light faded, and the fact that we've yet to have one stumble into the light of our lanterns is more than a little strange.

I don't much care for things I can't explain.

"Flare's up!" the tinkerer calls, and the night is lit once more. My blood goes cold despite the warm air, and the calls of encouragement on the line die a vicious death as we take in the sight before us.

The shamblers are there, a few feet outside of the glow cast by the lanterns, motionless. In the sudden absence of our shouts it's easy to hear their growls, muted to the point that they're less a moan and more a whisper of sound. They just stand there, weaving in place like drovers on payday, drunk and barely coherent. Waiting. Almost as if it were they who were hunting us.

Fear floods my mind, tries to make me believe I've lost before I've even begun. I adjust my grip on my sickles and roll my shoulders.

"Ain't no one but the dead dying today!" I scream as the flare's light softens. Defiance, rage, and terror lace my voice. I refuse to quit, and I won't let my companions fail, either. "Only the dead die today!"

Up and down the line others take up the call. Impossibly, the shamblers answer our defiant roar with one of their own.

And then they're upon us.

They come fast and hard, the freshies leading the pack. I detach a woman's head from her body and move on to the man behind her. As I harvest, I shout out to my fellow combatants.

"Stay behind the line!"

"Make them come to you!"

"The newly dead die first!"

I continue to yell, swallowing hard when my voice starts to go. I mark time by the flares the tinkerer fires, and the third one has just gone up when to my left one of the roughnecks goes down, screaming as the dead begin to devour him.

The wet sound of the dead feeding and the man's fading cries cuts through my heavy breathing and the growls of other approaching shamblers. I fall back enough to end the dead that surround the drover, kicking their heads to the side so I don't trip over them, grabbing the knife that the roughneck still clutches in his hand and driving it through his eye. I ain't got time to mourn the fallen, but I need to make sure there ain't any enemies at my back. There are more dead to kill.

Even though I continue to yell encouragement, the drovers are being overwhelmed. We're outnumbered nearly four to one, and it's easy to see that the roughnecks ain't soldiers. They fire blindly into the dark, and most of them grabbed guns but no bladed weapons. They're quickly out of bullets. We lose a few drovers, and one girl from the patrol as well. When I see Cary bash a shambler's skull in with the butt of his pistol I realize it's time for another tactic.

"Riflemen, to the rear! Everyone else, close up those holes." The drovers fall back, and the rest of us cover down to take up their slack. "Shoot until you're out of ammo, then fall back." I look behind me, but I can't tell if anyone is listening anymore. The air is thick with the putrid scent of the dead, and my hands are slick with shambler goo. Still, the dead keep on coming, and I can't do anything but continue to swing my sickles.

Time ceases to exist for me. There is only the constant moan of shamblers, the swing of my sickles as I harvest, the inevitable double thump when the creatures fall to the ground, head rolling one way, body the other. I'm amassing quite a pile of dead before me, and I take a few steps back, giving myself a bigger space to work. From down on the line someone calls out, "'Ain't no pain in heaven, but there ain't no you, either.'"

Someone sings the next line, "'Ain't no shamblers in heaven, but there ain't no you, either.'"

"'Ain't no killing in heaven, but since there ain't no you, I'm gonna fight to stay here.'"

I don't know the song and I've got a terrible singing voice, so I just listen, letting my arms move to the rhythm of the words as the voices continue to sing, lifting my spirits and making the fighting easier.

I've killed ten, fifteen, maybe twenty shamblers when the sky lights up again, revealing the vacant prairie. I drop my arms to my side, heaving as I gasp for air. My arms burn from swinging them, and even though I'm an absolute mess I feel particularly light.

"I'm clear," I yell. "Tell us where you are and that you're still out there."

Voices echo up and down the line, more than I could've imagined would survive.

"Check for bites, and give your companions a gentle end." It's the typical refrain for the end of a shambler battle, a way of giving people permission to kill anyone who has been bitten. I think of Mr. Gideon's vaccine for a moment, but there's no way that thing works. I could fill a train car with the number of shamblers we've seen who used to be part of the Summerland patrols.

"Jane." I startle at the light touch on my shoulder, spinning around. Bloodlust still sings in my veins, and it's no easy thing to shut it off so quickly. Mr. Gideon jumps back, hands up in surrender. "You did it. They're all dead. Again."

I wipe the back of my sleeve across my forehead, smearing viscera across my face. A quick glance down reveals that my sickles are covered in shambler's blood, and I give them a quick spin to clear some of it off before scrubbing my face clean with my sleeve. "We got a casualty count?"

"Not yet. A colored boy and a drover are walking the line and counting how many of those bodies used to be folks we know. Are you okay?"

I grimace, even though he can't see it in the low light. "Mostly. This could've gone better. I saw at least four people go down myself."

"It also could've gone a lot worse."

"Tell that to those who died."

A growl comes from over my shoulder. I spin around to remove the shambler's head but its skull explodes, the monster falling back to the ground. I turn back to the tinkerer, who is very calmly reholstering his pistol.

"So, you can use that thing after all." My ears ring from the gunshot, but it's preferable to being dead.

Mr. Gideon's lips twist into a hint of a smile, the low light casting interesting shadows across his pale face. "So it seems."

"You know your serum don't work, right? Just in case you were still wondering." I gesture toward the shambler with a fresh hole in its head, thanks to Mr. Gideon. It's poor Cary, the Georgian. "That's one of our boys. He started the battle human."

Mr. Gideon says nothing for a long moment, his lips pressing together in a thin line. After a long moment he finally speaks. "The sheriff isn't going to let you forget that you took over his little battle."

I shrug, taking the change of subject in stride. "No, he ain't. But I'll worry about that after I've cleaned up and had a good night's rest. Right now I'm more concerned with making sure no one turns."

"And if they do?"

"What do you think?'

"My vaccine works," he says, taking off his spectacles and

wiping them with a handkerchief.

I laugh. The man is more stubborn than a shambler. "Then consider me insurance."

He nods. "I do not envy you, Miss McKeene."

"Not many people do, Mr. Gideon. Not many do."

I hope you will understand my giving my heart to another. Someday, if not today, you will see that this life is nothing without people to love.

Chapter 34
In Which I Am Overcome by Dread

When I was five, my momma tried to drown me.

She thinks I don't remember, that I was too young to recall the way she told the girls to draw her a bath, and how she put me in my best dress, the white one she'd used for my christening. By that point in my life it was too short to be decent, hitting me somewhere around my knees. But those were in the early days of the undead plague, when a trip into town could mean death by shambler, and we had to make do with what was at hand. That christening gown was the finest clothing I had.

After the big, deep, claw-foot tub was filled—too full for a little girl, almost too full for a grown woman—Momma sent the girls away. Then she called me over.

"Janey, sweetness, can you get in the tub, please?" I'd wondered why her voice sounded so strange, hoarse and broken, more like a bullfrog than my sainted Momma. I'd climbed into the tub without hesitation, standing in the water uncertainly. The christening gown rose up and swirled around my hips, the warm water hitting me at my belly button.

"Janey, I need you to sit down." Momma's voice was stern, but still there was a quaver of uncertainty there.

"But Momma, it's too deep."

"Nonsense. It's just the right amount of water. Go ahead and sit down, sweetling."

I hesitated, sinking down into a crouch. Momma had done the rest, lunging toward me and pushing me down, water sloshing all over the fine floor as I went under.

This is where my memory gets hazy. I remember holding my breath, my lungs screaming for air, Momma's hands on my chest. But more than anything I remember the feeling that I had done something wrong, that this was my fault.

It was my fault that I'd barged in on Momma and her fine lady friends who were visiting from Frankfort, even though I'd been told to stay out of the sitting room.

It was my fault that I'd beamed when Miss Davenport, Momma's loathsome cousin by marriage, had mentioned what a precocious child I was and how familiar my features seemed.

Most important, it was my fault that my skin was brown and Momma's wasn't and that she had the terrible misfortune to love me anyway.

I don't remember much after that. Auntie Aggie came in and pushed Momma to the side, lifting me up and thumping me on the back as I coughed up the water I'd swallowed. Momma had sobbed and Auntie Aggie had scolded her, wrapping me in a blanket and taking me down to the kitchens where she made me a cup of warm milk sweetened with honey. But it didn't matter.

For the next few months I lived in fear of my momma, and I never let her give me another bath. I loved her, even after that, but I knew better than to trust her the way I had before. She was like a dog that had bitten me, and you only need to be bitten once.

I get the same uneasy feeling when I see Sheriff Snyder the next morning, after telling him off in front of the drovers the night before. I know I should be safe from him for the moment since Katherine walks with me, but I still can't shake the sense that something bad is going to happen.

We're on our way to lunch with Mr. Gideon, who sent us a note stating he would meet us at the door to his lab. I follow behind Katherine, who looks absolutely stunning in a day dress bedecked with appliqué roses along the hem. It's a cheap dress and several years out of style, yet she makes it look like the newest fashion plate from Paris.

"Good morning, Miss Deveraux," the sheriff says when he sees Katherine, tipping his hat. He looks toward me and I avert my eyes, attempting to look remorseful. My back is mostly healed from the last whipping, but most of the scabs pulled open last night and I'm of no mind to take another beating.

Here's a thing about me: I regret most of my actions five minutes after the fact. I'm rash in my decisions and I spend half my time trying to extricate myself from situations of my own making. But I don't regret taking charge last night. Without me, we would have died and the town would have been overrun. So whatever the sheriff has planned for me, I have to believe that everyone's survival was worth it.

"Sheriff," Katherine says, dipping into a slight curtsy. "How does this fine morning find you?"

"Well, considering. We've refortified the breach in the outer wall and the patrols are back on the job. Did your girl fill you in on the details of our engagement last night?"

"I'm afraid she did. We were on our way to see you so that she could offer you a formal apology for forgetting her place." Katherine and I had decided this was the best course of action, a preemptive strike on whatever the sheriff had planned in retaliation. I also wanted to examine the shamblers in the daylight after speaking with Mr. Gideon, to see if there was anything different about them than the ones we'd faced back east. When I told Katherine about their strange behavior before the fighting started, she blanched.

"Jane, can you just imagine the trouble we'd all be in if shamblers started reasoning the same way we do? It would be a catastrophe," she said. I agreed. Shamblers are dangerous because of their numbers. A group of the dead can easily overwhelm even a competent fighter if there are enough of them. But shamblers ain't smart; they can be tricked by hiding, or by climbing a tree. If the dead have gained the ability to reason like normal men, well, that is a problem.

"I'm afraid Jane's intervention was warranted, Miss Katherine." The sheriff's words cut through my reverie and draw my gaze up in surprise. "I know I may seem like a . . . stubborn man at times, but I truly only want what is best for this town, and everyone here. Last night, that was letting Jane take charge of the line. We only lost three men and a handful of Negroes to the pack, and Jane's instincts are to thank for that."

I fight to keep my surprise from my face, but I ain't very successful. Katherine makes a small sound in the back of her throat before saying, "Well, Sheriff, thank you for that. I'd planned on disciplining Jane, but this will save me some effort."

"Of course, Miss Deveraux. Now, I must be off. Good

day." He tips his hat again. We watch him leave, his path taking him to the saloon, and after he's entered the building I pinch Katherine's arm.

"Ow, Jane, what was that for?"

"Something's happening. There ain't no way the sheriff is going to let a colored girl like me show him up in battle. You didn't see him last night, the look he gave me when I called him out in front of the makeshift army. We need to figure out what's going on here before it's too late."

Katherine sighs. "Fine, Jane. What do you suggest?"

"We need to put our plan in action sooner rather than later. Let's go see the Duchess. If we can get our hands on some laudanum, we can slip it into his tobacco. While the sheriff is sleeping it off we hightail it out of town. Then, we won't have to worry about whatever big bad is coming down the pike."

"I thought we agreed that we need to liberate everyone in Summerland, not just ourselves? Besides, I want to keep our lunch appointment with Mr. Gideon. His note indicated that whatever he wanted to share was of the utmost importance."

I swallow a sigh of exasperation. "Katherine, we ain't got time for that. Something's afoot, and we need to discover what it is."

"Exactly. And Mr. Gideon is our best hope for enlightenment." Katherine sets off, heading toward the entrance to the lab, parasol propped on her shoulder.

Mr. Gideon waits for us there, shifting his weight from one foot to the other, looking a bit fidgety. He sees us and his face twists into a welcoming smile, his gaze lingering on Katherine perhaps a moment too long.

The ugly jealous feeling lifts its head and roars, and I beat it back.

"Miss Deveraux, so pleasant to see you. Miss Mc-Keene . . ." Mr. Gideon tips his hat to us, and I force a tight smile out of politeness.

"Mr. Gideon, so lovely of you to invite us to share the midday meal with you."

"Yes, and thank you for coming. I'd worried that after last night's incident my overture came too late, but it looks like we still have a little time."

I grimace. "Mr. Gideon, no offense, but I ain't really in the mood for riddles," I say, even though I'm just supposed to be Katherine's Attendant, a dark-skinned girl of no consequence.

He smiles and inclines his head. "Of course, Miss McKeene. I think it might be easier to explain if I could show you the data I've collected." Mr. Gideon offers Katherine his arm. "If you don't mind, Miss Katherine. All of my research is down in my lab."

"Of course." She takes the tinkerer's arm and after a brief hesitation I stomp along behind them, fervently wishing I'd been born with golden skin and flaxen-streaked curls instead of hair like sheep's wool and skin the color of dirt. It's a completely irrational thought, but it's hard knowing that my life could be much better had I only been born looking a bit more like my momma.

We descend into the bowels of Mr. Gideon's lab, and I am once again enthralled by the magical appearance of the place. The electric lights, the various mechanical pieces spread across the worktable, the shelf of neatly labeled solvents—the tinkerer's laboratory is a completely different world than the one I was used to.

Mr. Gideon walks over to a map marked with colored pins, removing his hat and hanging it on a nearby hook. He looks younger without it, and the weariness in the lines around his eyes is more pronounced.

"I apologize that all I have to offer for the noon meal is some cheese and bread, but it looks like now even I am subject to the current rationing within the town."

"Is the rationing really because of the extra families or because the supply line from Baltimore is gone?" I ask, settling into a very comfortable looking brocade wing chair that is completely out of place in the otherwise functional lab. The chair is just as sumptuous as it looks, and I ignore the assessing look from Mr. Gideon and Katherine's openmouthed surprise as I settle my backside into the cushions.

"Jane, perhaps we could approach the manner a little more diplomatically?" Katherine murmurs, her expression somewhere between anger and fear. She looks at Gideon, and I realize that she doesn't entirely trust him. I file that information away for later.

"Look, Jackson hasn't come back yet and we need answers. Last night I faced down a pack of shamblers that possessed intelligence I ain't never seen before, the sheriff is probably even now plotting my death, and there is apparently nothing left of Baltimore County. I'm tired and I want answers, and it appears that Mr. Gideon has them, for better or worse." I turn to the tinkerer. "Mr. Gideon?"

He grins at me, a genuine smile that lights up his entire face. "In the interest of time, tell me what you know."

I very quickly fill Mr. Gideon in on the bits and pieces of information we gleaned from our brief reunion with Jackson. He nods as I speak, pulling out a small chair for Katherine and propping his hip on an empty workbench. When I've finished, he sighs. "It seems like you know quite a bit."

"So, is it true? Is Baltimore County really gone? Had we ever gotten an edge on the shambler plague, or was that all just some Survivalist nonsense?" Katherine asks.

"A bit of both, I'm afraid. It's more about politics. See, the war never really ended. When the dead began to walk at Gettysburg, both the Federal troops and the Confederates decided it was for the best to stop fighting each other and to fight the undead. And now, with life slowly returning to normal, there are plenty of folks with feelings about what the shambler plague means for the future of the country.

"I am an Egalitarian, and my father was a Survivalist. Both the Egalitarians and the Survivalists have run on platforms that involve recapturing the cities of the East and making them safe. Baltimore, New York, Philadelphia—these places represent American civilization, and many figured that the only way to keep the country together would be to rebuild it."

I shake my head. "But people living that close to one another . . . all you need is for one person to go feral and the whole place is a shambler's paradise."

Mr. Gideon nods. "Yes, and that's what I've told my father for years. But he's convinced that if you can sell people on a dream of security and prosperity, then the facts are irrelevant. And, he's right. The Survivalists provided jobs—building the walls, manning the patrols, all of it in the name of the appearance of safety, of normalcy . . ." Mr. Gideon trails off and scrubs his hand across his face. "But holding onto the cities was never sustainable. There are too many factors we cannot account for, and soon even the Survivalist leaders— the mayors, the congressmen—realized that it wasn't a long-term plan."

Katherine frowns prettily. "So, then, what was?"

"Something like the compounds that have risen from the ashes of the lost Southern states. Georgia, Alabama, Mississippi, they were all nearly destroyed by millions upon millions of shamblers, and what little pockets of humanity remained eventually pulled together under something like military law to survive. The compounds are nothing more than a reinstitution of the plantation system."

"So we're really just talking about prosperity built on the back of slavery once more," I say.

"Yes, a fresh coat of paint on the same old problems. My father is very good at that sort of thing."

"Who's your father?" I ask, curiosity digging its claws into me.

"Abraham Carr."

I jump to my feet. "What?"

Katherine closes her eyes and reopens them. "You father is the mayor of Baltimore?"

The tinkerer's mouth twists with distaste. "*Was* the mayor of Baltimore, since the city is no more." His voice is rueful, but there's no sadness on his face.

"Why didn't you tell us?" Katherine asks.

"Would you have trusted me if I had?"

It's a good question. I wonder for a moment if he had any other motives, but his words have a ring of truth to them, and I begin to pace. I think better when my feet are moving.

"So Gideon ain't your last name?"

"No, it's my first name. Gideon Carr."

I stop pacing. "All this time we've been using your first

name as your surname and you never enlightened us. I guess because then we would've known who your daddy is?"

"Yes. I suppose that was cowardly of me."

"Damn straight. So you'll be okay with us just calling you Gideon now."

One side of his mouth quirks. "I suspect that conspiring to overthrow this town should put us on a first-name basis."

A thought occurs to me, and embarrassment flushes my face. "Wait, so when I was telling you all that mess about Kate being a lady and being taken in by the mayor and being booted by his wife—"

"I knew it was a lie. I still exchange letters with my mother regularly. But you were so enamored of your story that it seemed a shame to tell you." He grins, and I groan.

"Let's change the subject. Data, big news, and so forth?"

Gideon adjusts his spectacles and stands once again. "Yes, of course." He moves across the room to the map with the colored pins, his limp more pronounced than usual. "So, for the past two years I've been cataloging the makeup of the undead beyond the outer wall. Last night isn't the first time a large group has been able to breach it. The sheriff's wife was killed in a similar attack. Hence my extreme dissatisfaction with the sheriff, the pastor, and the inability of this blasted town to electrify the fences."

Katherine shoots me a questioning look and I shake my

head. I can catch her up later.

Gideon continues. "The attacks are increasing. The number of undead in this part of the prairie? Also increasing. The type of attire the undead wear can sometimes lend clues as to their origin, and I've seen undead that wear the furs of the northern trappers, the uniforms of Mississippi militia . . . Somehow, the dead are coming from all over the continent and congregating in places like this."

I stare at Gideon, a warm feeling suffusing my chest. He's so smart that it's downright distracting. "How do you think they're doing it?"

"I'm not completely sure. An entomologist in France, Jean-Henri Fabre, has written about how male insects are attracted to females. He believes there's some kind of undetectable scent or signaling compound that insects use to talk to one another, like the way bees know to swarm to protect a nest. I think the dead can communicate in a similar way, that's undetectable to us."

"So, you think they're signaling to all of their friends, even ones miles away, that there's food here?"

Gideon nods. "It would also explain the behavior we saw last night. And their tendency, more and more common, to join up into a horde, as they clearly have in Baltimore County. It's instinct."

"Have you told the sheriff?" Katherine asks, her voice

filled with the same despair I feel. "What does he think?"

Gideon runs his hand through his dark hair, mussing it. "Oh, I've told him. I don't believe he understands the danger. He thinks the undead are just wandering aimlessly, that the patrols will be able to handle any limited attempts to break through the defenses, even after last night. He simply cannot fathom a pack of the size that I'm predicting. The group last night was just a warning; the packs beyond the walls will number in the thousands soon, and it's only a matter of time before they try to breach again. I've been working on some advanced munitions for the patrols to use, but the sheriff still refuses to arm the Negroes in town. We're going to need every man, woman, and child carrying if we're going to defend ourselves from the undead."

"Even that isn't going to save the town," I say. "Unless you can build a shambler-destroying machine, it's just a matter of time before Summerland is overrun. We need to evacuate before another horde comes through."

Katherine lets out a shocked sound. "And go where?"

I shrug. "I don't know. But we're sitting ducks in the middle of the prairie here, waiting for all the shamblers in the Midwest to hear the call."

"I think Jane's right," Gideon says. "The problem is that the sheriff and the preacher see Summerland as a safe haven, as do many of the other families. It won't be easy to convince them to leave."

My eyes meet Katherine's, and I know that she's thinking the same thing I am.

The only way we're going to get anyone out of here, including ourselves, is if the sheriff is taken care of.

I'm not certain what else to say. Your silence these past few months has convinced me that either you are deceased, or I have earned your vexation. Just know that no matter how long it takes until you return to Rose Hill, you will always have a place here.

Chapter 35
In Which Trouble Comes to Call

After a sad lunch of stale bread, cheese, and a few berries grown in the lab by Gideon, Katherine and I set out toward her home. Just a couple miles past Katherine's house is the site of last night's battle. The sheriff claims the breach in the defenses has been repaired, but with the horde that Gideon described on the way, I want to see for myself. Katherine and I can use the time to lay our plans for the sheriff.

We've only gone a little ways when I glance over at

Katherine and see that she looks a bit peaked. It's hot out and the sun is making its presence known in a significant way. I'm sweating under my dress, which is still a mess from last night, and I know that Katherine must be suffering as well, especially since she's wearing at least three petticoats.

"You going to be able to walk the whole way?"

We've cleared the last of the town proper and have reached the dusty road that leads to the barrier fences. Katherine glares at me but says nothing, a thin sheen of perspiration shining on her skin.

"Are you wearing a corset?"

"Dammit, Jane, what is your obsession with me and my undergarments? I'm fine, all right?"

I clamp my mouth shut, because I've never heard Katherine swear before, so I know her temper is short. The sound of a wagon trundling along comes from behind us, and I look back to see a drover sitting at the reins. He sees us and stops.

"You want a ride, Miss Deveraux?" he says, a smile on his lips.

"Miss Deveraux would love a ride, you are too generous," I say before Katherine can answer. She sighs but, with a helping hand, climbs onto the seat next to the man.

I start to climb aboard as well and he shoots me a dirty look. "I think it would be best if'n you walked. The sheriff doesn't like coloreds in the wagon."

"Nice to see no good deed goes unpunished," I mutter. I

walk alongside, the big old horse setting a plodding pace that is easy to keep up with.

"I'm Alan, by the way. I brought you a rabbit yesterday for your supper."

"Oh, yes, thank you, Mr. Alan; it made for quite a lovely meal," Katherine says, a polite smile on her face.

"It's just Alan," he says, face red as a boiled beet. I can barely keep my eyes from rolling out of my head the way he's fawning over her.

"What are you doing out this far, Miss Deveraux?" Alan asks.

"Jane was telling me all about the battle last night, and I wanted to see the repair of the wall for myself. She said there were at least two hundred shamblers, and that you faced them down all by yourselves! The thought alone is terrifying, and I will not rest well until I see that Summerland's defenses have been rejoined."

Alan's jaw tightens and he looks straight ahead. "It was mostly the colored folks that fought the shamblers. No surprise there. Government pays to send them to those fancy schools while real men like me are left to fend for ourselves."

Katherine and I exchange a look, but Alan keeps talking.

"If it wasn't for all that money going to educate darkies, we'd have better weapons to fight the undead, and better training for real men, too. This is why that horde is taking out the East. Like the preacher says, 'You reap what you sow,' and the buffoons in Washington have sown this country's ruin in their experiments with Negro enfranchisement."

Katherine coughs delicately. "Taking out the East? You mean Baltimore, yes?"

He glances at Katherine in alarm. "I'm sorry, Miss Deveraux. I should have known it would be a bit of a shock since it's where your people are from, but it's not just Baltimore County. We received word that all of Maryland and Delaware have now been overrun by undead."

"My goodness," Katherine breathes, and Alan leans in just a bit, seeing her distress as an opening.

"Yes, ma'am. They say Pennsylvania is next; heard the rich folks there set out for sea instead of trying to save the city. Haven't heard word on Washington yet, but the way the horde was heading it shouldn't be long until it's overwhelmed as well, despite its strong defenses."

"Horde? You mean to tell me that there's a single pack taking out the Eastern Seaboard?" I ask. It's the stuff of nightmares—and precisely what Gideon had said was happening.

Alan looks down at me. "What, they didn't teach you about hordes at your fancy government school?"

"No suh, dey only taught me how to keep hapless white folks alive," I say.

Alan scowls at me, not sure if I'm being sincere or goading him. Katherine pats his arm to get his attention again.

"So what will happen to our little town now? I suppose we'll all end up at the mercy of these hostile lands. Is there no winning this battle with the undead, even after all these years of resistance?"

Alan shrugs. "Don't rightly know. Me and a few of the other drovers have been talking about leaving, maybe heading out over the hill to a settlement called Nicodemus. Word is they've got plenty of work and food, and even though they're friendly with the Kansa and Pawnee I've heard tell they've got a stronger wall to keep the dead out. After last night? Shoot, that seems like paradise." At this, we've nearly reached the inner fence, and Alan sighs and stops the wagon. I raise a hand to help Katherine down and he watches her wistfully.

"Thank you for the ride," she says, gifting him with a radiant smile. He simply tips his hat in acknowledgment.

"Maybe you should give that boy back his heart before we start poking around at the undead," I whisper to Katherine.

"Quiet, it's your fault he's all twitterpated. I could've walked."

I snort as we cross through a gate in the fence. "That corset will be the death of you."

The battle site looks much less frightening in the daylight. My memory of the place is painted in flickering shadows and lumbering figures, a chorus of shamblers' moans ringing out in accompaniment. But now, in the bright sunlight of midday, the place looks like just another worthless patch of prairie.

Well, excepting for the bodies hidden in the tall grass.

"Something's amiss," I say to Katherine.

Sheriff Snyder is here, overseeing the removal of the bodies, him and his boys sitting easy in their saddles, joking like they ain't got a care in the world. He spots Katherine and his face relaxes into a pleasant smile as he rides over.

"Miss Deveraux. Fancy seeing you here." The sheriff doesn't bother to get down from his horse, just leans forward and looks down at Katherine.

"Yes, Sheriff. I know it's highly indecent of me, but I couldn't help but wonder about the breach in the wall. I just wanted to see for myself that the town was safe once more."

The sheriff gestures toward a patch of wall in the distance with a group of Negroes and drovers patrolling it. It's easy to see where it collapsed, a valley betwixt two hills. Nothing about the exterior wall looks repaired, and a chill of apprehension runs down my spine.

Sheriff Snyder lied to us earlier. Who else did he deceive?

The lawman takes out a pinch of tobacco and begins rolling a cigarette. "Looks like my secret's out. We had more than one breach last night, and it's going to be a while before Summerland's defenses are secure once more. You and your girl should really head back to town, seek shelter in your quarters. After all, most ladies like to hide behind closed doors with their Attendants nearby."

"Perhaps, but I find that I am interested in understanding more about the pitiful creature that is the shambler. How could such a mindless ghoul wreak such havoc? What is the nature of this menace the Lord created to test us?"

"It matters not, my dear. It is God's wrath for our sins." The sheriff lights his cigarette and looks out at the horizon. "The dead never walked until brother fought brother. Until we penitent folk betrayed one another."

Katherine makes a choked sound, but when the sheriff turns back to her she is all smiles. "Yes, sir, thank you for explaining."

He just nods. "Well, then, enjoy indulging your curiosity. Why don't you and your girl join me for supper? I know you haven't gotten your rations yet today, and I'd hate to see a lady such as yourself go hungry."

"Thank you, Sheriff. I look forward to the company." There's not a hint of fear or doubt in Katherine's words and the sheriff rides off.

I step nearer to Katherine. "Do you think that was wise?"

"I don't think I have a choice. And besides, we're looking for an opportunity to take him out, aren't we? You have your sickles now—"

"Ain't much use against guns," I hiss. "Surely, he'll be armed and probably have a few of his boys in attendance if he knows I'm going to be there."

"Well, I suppose you'd better think of something else, then!"

I open my mouth to argue and quickly snap it closed. The set of Katherine's jaw warns that she's sorely vexed, and I ain't one to tempt a tiger. I once saw Katherine thrash a girl soundly who had the bad fortune to slander her name. I have no intention of getting on her bad side, especially not now when I'm going to need her help. She might be highly unreasonable, but she's still my friend and we are in this together.

So I say nothing as we walk through the bodies of the dead toward the outer wall. I move off to examine a pile of them. From what I can tell most of them were recently turned. There's little of the decomposition you see on most long-dead shamblers, none of the older clothing or loose hanging skin. But I don't recognize any of the faces, either. Where'd all these folks come from? Gideon's theory is looking more likely every minute.

"Jane," Katherine calls for my attention, kneeling next to one of the dead. "Did you know this one? She's wearing the same clothing as you had from working the patrols."

I move over to see what she's looking at, a surprising bubble of sadness welling up. "Well, that ain't no good. Yeah, I know her. Knew her."

Lying on the ground, her head a few feet away from her body, is Cora. I didn't like the big girl, I ain't never been a fan of snitches, but turning shambler is not a fate I'd wish on anyone, not even the girl who got me whipped.

I look around at this group, and gesture with my hand. "It's half the fence team, as well as a few folks from the patrols."

"Oh God, Jane. That's Mr. Spencer."

I look over to where Katherine points and swear loudly. Katherine doesn't reprimand me, just purses her lips.

We keep walking, our hearts growing heavier with every person we recognize. There are a few more white folks in finer clothing, and I'm starting to wonder why they ain't storming the sheriff's office, asking where their loved ones are. Sure, no one is going to miss the Negroes from the fence team, but Mr. Spencer and these other white folks? They have families here.

"Kate."

"Hmm?"

"The fence team was turned and they work out on the fringes. How did townspeople from the good part of town end up out where the fence-mending team usually works? No one would leave the inner safety of the town willingly."

Katherine's brows draw together. "What are you thinking? That the sheriff dragged them out to the edge?"

I nod. "Maybe you're right. Maybe the white folks in the nice side of town were getting restless. Alan said the drovers are looking for greener pastures . . . What if the sheriff had his boys drag a few malcontents out there to the fringe to teach them a lesson and something went wrong?"

"You think they got overrun?"

"If the sheriff's boys had taken a large group of people to the wall to show them why Summerland was their only hope, it might've been enough to make the dead swarm. Like bees detecting a threat, but in this case food. When we patrolled the wall we worked in groups of two, but there are at least twenty well-dressed folks out here."

"So?"

"That many folks loitering about may have put the dead into a frenzy. What if there's more on their way as we speak? The prairie looks clear now, but Gideon said the attacks would get more frequent and larger, and we have two unrepaired breaks in the exterior wall."

Katherine stumbles to a stop. "Jane, this is bad."

"I know."

"We need to go and speak to the sheriff, convince him to barricade the town before it's overrun. Consolidate everyone into a few defensible buildings. We're too vulnerable, waiting for the next attack."

"Kate, that's suicide. Besides, you know there's no way that he's going to listen to us."

She sighs and purses her lips. "Maybe, but we have to try."

Katherine stalks off back toward town, and I look to the pale blue sky for strength before following after her.

Return to me, Jane. Please. As soon as you are able, come back to Rose Hill. We need you.

Chapter 36
In Which All Hell Breaks Loose Once More

Once we're back within the city limits, Katherine heads straight for the sheriff's office. But before we get there we're intercepted by Ida, her eyes wild as she runs full tilt toward us.

"Did you hear? Did you hear?"

When she reaches us she's panting, her chest heaving. I shake my head. "No, we didn't hear anything, what's happening?"

"A pack, bigger than last night's, was spotted a few miles

off the eastern border once more. The sheriff is sending everyone out to meet them, but the drovers refuse to fight this time, and the sheriff can't do anything about it. He's sending just the patrols. We've woken the night teams, but there just aren't enough of us to take on a horde." Ida looks from me to Katherine. "We're not going to survive this time, Jane."

I exchange a look with Katherine. "We're too late."

Ida looks from me to Katherine and back again. "Is there something you're not telling me?"

We quickly fill her in on what Gideon told us, her warm bronze skin going gray. "We can't win against that many shamblers. That man is a monster. He and his boys are going to send us all to die."

I nod. "Yep, but we intend to stop that from happening."

Katherine puts her hands on her hips. "Right, I'll go speak with the sheriff, you go ask the Duchess if she'll spread the word that everyone needs to fight if we're going to beat back the approaching horde."

"Have you lost all the sense in that pretty head of yours? Fighting is suicide. We need to run."

"Jane, where are we supposed to go? We're in the middle of the prairie. It's better to shelter in place here than take our chances on the open range, where they can just run us down." Katherine flounces off toward the sheriff's office, and I turn to Ida.

"Don't listen to her. Tell the patrols to grab whatever weapons they have and any rations they can find and leave. Pretend like you're going out to face down the dead if anyone asks you. I'm going to take care of the sheriff while you all get out. Half the folks should head north and half should head east. We need to get clear of the wall before the shamblers get into town." Walls didn't just keep things out, after all. They also kept folks in. I worry that everyone will try to flee the same direction and the wall will end up a grand choke point, serving up panicked folks to the dead.

Ida gives me a lopsided grin. "Got it. Good luck."

I give her a wink and run inside of the saloon. I pause just past the threshold, waiting for my eyes to adjust. Once they do I realize that the saloon is empty excepting for the bartender, polishing glasses.

"Where's the Duchess?" I call.

"In her room back down the hall."

"She got company?"

"Nope."

"There's a horde headed this way, you need to grab what you can and get out of town."

The bartender looks at me all wide-eyed. "What about the wall?"

"That damn wall ain't helping anyone now. Only running can save us."

I dash full tilt down the narrow hallway. When I get to

the Duchess's room the door is closed, and I knock.

"Duchess, it's Jane. We need to get out of town."

There's rustling on the other side of the door, and then it opens a few inches. I walk in.

"Shut the door behind you." The room's got a sick, coppery scent to it, and I do as the Duchess asks. It's pitch-dark, the curtains drawn, and hotter than the dickens.

"You okay?"

"I'm going to cut right to it, my dear. The sheriff knows that Katherine ain't a real lady." There's a choked sound to her voice, and I swallow the lump of dread in my throat.

"How you know that?"

"He came by this morning for his weekly appointment and told me." The curtain draws back, flooding the room momentarily with light, and I get the glimpse of the Duchess's face, her lips swollen, eye blackened, before the curtain falls back into place.

My heart nearly stops. "I don't understand. How'd he find out?"

"That father of his. He apparently followed up with a couple of the newer families in town once the sheriff took a shine to Katherine, and after some conversation it seems they remembered a pretty blond Attendant who was light enough to pass from a couple months back. Sheriff Snyder threatened me, told me he'd kill me if I didn't tell him the truth. She's dead, Jane. Both of you are."

I can scarcely believe this is all happening, right now. "All right. I need to go get her. But we've got even more pressing issues to tend to."

"I tell you the sheriff is out for blood and you say there's something more important than that?"

"There's a horde on its way. Big enough to wipe us off the map. We don't get the town evacuated, we're all dead."

The Duchess doesn't move for a long time. "We can just hole up here. The wall—"

"The wall is wrecked, it ain't going to do naught for us but trap us in." What is it with people and their fixation on this damn town? "We need to run, you need to gather up your girls and make a break for it."

The Duchess doesn't answer for a long moment, and I take a deep breath. "Please. You've been kind to me, and if it wasn't for you I'd most likely be dead of infection of some sort. You have to grab what you can and run. I know it feels hasty, but trust me when I say Summerland ain't safe. It never was."

And with that, I run out of the room, hightailing it to Katherine, hoping I ain't too late.

Oh Jane, I was a fool. So, very, very naive. I'm afraid it's all gone wrong, and the only person I have to blame is myself. I knew one day my secret would be out—Auntie Aggie told me as much—but I never thought it would ruin everything we'd built.

Chapter 37
In Which I Sin Yet Again

I dash across the street, dodging the folks gathering in the road. The drovers are bunched up in front of the sheriff's office shouting and waving guns. From snippets of conversation I gather that they want the sheriff to open the door, tell them what's happening. They still can't see that it's time to cut bait and hotfoot it out of town.

"Move," I yell, pushing through the drovers, throwing my sharp elbow into soft bits when a few of the men refuse to budge. A particularly large man looms before me, an impassable wall, so I change my trajectory, moving parallel to the boardwalk until I find an opening. All the while a little voice in my head is urging me to hurry to the sheriff's office. How long does it take for a man to strangle a woman? My brain runs through a million violent tableaus, and still I haven't made it to Katherine's side.

"That's it," I mutter. I grab the man in front of me, boosting myself up onto his shoulders. He's barely had time to react before I've hopped to the next man, using the drovers as stepping-stones. I lose my balance before the sheriff's door, tumbling against it. It bangs open and I half fall into the office.

"Now, Jane, that's what I call an entrance," the sheriff drawls. "We were just coming to find you." He gestures with his pistol, the business end pointed right at me, and I crawl the rest of the way in, the door closing behind me. I try to climb to my feet, but before I can, a boot lodges itself in my side, digging into the soft spot just below my ribs. I instinctively curl into a ball.

"Boys. Boys! There will be plenty of time for that later. Get her on her feet."

"Elias, this is highly unnecessary. Kill them and be done with it." The pastor's voice is ice water on my soul, and the wave of fear I've been fighting to hold back threatens to drown me.

"Not now, Pop. Let me deal with this in my own way."

I'm hauled up by hands on my upper arms, my breath still a bit ragged from getting kicked.

"Kate, you okay?" I ask. I can barely see her in the gloom of the office. The window was boarded up sometime between last night and today, and the furniture is all pushed around, almost like the sheriff is planning on hunkering down in his office rather than facing the nightmare that's about to greet the town.

"Oh, I'm fine, Jane. But I do believe the good sheriff has lost his mind." Her voice is just as matter of fact as ever, and my relief bubbles up in ill-advised laughter, which I swallow back down.

"Well, good to know." I shift my weight, and address the sheriff. "You do realize there's a horde on the way."

"Gideon may have mentioned it."

I keep my voice even. "There's no way a place like Summerland will survive a pack of that magnitude. Your big pretty wall didn't save your sorry hide, what do you think a few boards on the window will do?"

"The Lord will see us through this trial the same way he saw the Israelites through the desert. I've sent the patrols out to put down the approaching pack, after which those men out there will repair the wall, and things will be as they were."

"The Lord helps those who help themselves, Sheriff. We

need to hightail it out of here. Get that father of yours to pray for us along the way. Otherwise none of us are going to see the sunset."

There's a long pause and then a wheezing sound, like someone is choking on a hard candy.

"What the hell is that?"

"Language, Jane," Katherine says. "And I do believe that sound is the sheriff laughing."

"I am indeed having a good chuckle. I figure that the only way this is actually happening is if someone is having a go at me. Because there is no way that some random darkie girl is telling me how to run my town." The sheriff grabs Katherine, Bob and Bill taking that as a cue to raise their guns as well. I can feel the weight of their regard, but I stand my ground.

From his chair, the pastor sighs. "It's about time."

Outside, the clamor grows as people begin to pound the door. The number of folks in the streets must be increasing as word of the approaching horde begins to make its way through the town. At this rate we'll have mass hysteria before too long, and when that happens we're all goners.

"Sheriff, the horde on its way is of remarkable size. We need to leave, not try to save this godforsaken place. Why can't you see that?"

"Summerland is a city on the hill," the pastor says, raising his hands in supplication, as though he's appealing to a higher power.

I ignore the man and direct my words to the sheriff. "This town was built by Mayor Carr and his politician cronies. You willing to give your life for some rich man's delusions?"

"Delusions? Summerland ain't no delusion. This place is the foundation of a new America, one that embraces the promise of greatness our founding fathers once made. Don't you see? Darkies, they got their place, and it ain't brushing elbows with respectable folk!" He yells this last bit at Katherine. Spittle flies from the sheriff's lips as he speaks, and as she fights to maintain her sense of calm she still flinches away from the sheriff's crazed words.

Even in the low light, I can see an unholy gleam in the sheriff's eyes. Plenty of folks share his attitude, but something fundamental has snapped in him. I wonder what pushed him over the edge, what made a man so coldly reasonable sink into what very much looks like madness.

Maybe he truly did fall in love with Katherine. And maybe the knowledge that she was playing him broke his heart as well as his mind.

My heart pounds, and mentally I'm counting the seconds as they tick past. How much closer is the approaching horde? Have they breached the wall? Have they reached the interior fence? I turn to Bill, who sweats, his shotgun shaking visibly. "You look like a man who wants to live. Please tell the sheriff that ain't no amount of proselytizing is going to keep that undead horde from overrunning us."

Bill points the rifle at me. "What's that mean?" He turns to Bob, who is just as agitated as the sheriff. "What does that even mean?"

"To proselytize means to preach a certain way of thinking, in this case the cause of the Survivalists," I answer, mentally calculating distance and time. Each moment talking with these fools means we're a moment closer to death. "Even Daniel Boone couldn't have survived a horde of shamblers, there ain't no way we're going to."

While I'm talking, I edge closer to Bill. He's distracted, terrified at the thought of a horde descending on the town, and even Bob looks a mite bit unsure. If I work quickly, I could grab Bob's rifle and take him out of the equation.

I catch Katherine's eye, and something about the jut of her chin makes me think that she's thinking the same thing I am, that maybe she's also planning a bit of heroics. It's dark, though, and only a small bit of light filters through the window, so I could be wrong. I raise an eyebrow in Bob's direction and she twitches her head.

Anyone else, and I would question this reckless act. But this is Katherine. She's a Miss Preston's girl, and I trust her with my life.

I grab the barrel of Bob's gun, spinning around and using my momentum to wrest it from his grip. He falls forward, unbalanced, and I put him in front of me as a shield just as Bill pulls the trigger. Bob falls and I quickly level the shotgun at Bill. This close, the buckshot rips through his chest, sending him to the ground, his rifle clattering to the floor. Two down, one to go.

I rack the shotgun and turn it on the sheriff, who now points his revolver at Katherine's temple. Her defiant look changes to one of naked fear, and I swear to myself. I'd thought she was planning her own maneuver, but since she still has a gun pointed at her head, maybe not.

"Looks like we got ourselves a bit of a Confederate stand-off," I say, ignoring the voice inside that urges me to hurry.

The sheriff gives me an evil smile. "If you don't want me to paint the wall with her brains, you'll put the shotgun down right now."

"Just shoot the pickaninny!" the pastor yells, lurching to his feet. Spittle flies from his mouth, and the distraction is just what I need to end this whole mess.

Katherine must think so as well. She goes limp in the sheriff's arms, dragging him off-balance. Sheriff Snyder stumbles forward so I pull the trigger.

As does the sheriff.

The sheriff flies back, but I am frozen in time and space. All of the ruckus outside disappears, and there is only a rushing sound in my ears. I am certain that my recklessness has just killed Katherine.

But then she quickly scrambles to her feet, scooping up Bill's fallen rifle as she crosses the room to stand next to me.

A heavy relief nearly weighs me down; the sheriff's shot went wide.

Katherine turns around and looks behind her. Blood spatters the side of her dress. "You shot the sheriff."

"That I did."

"You tore apart his throat," she says, voice flat, and I think she might actually be in a bit of a battle haze.

"Well, if it makes you feel any better I was aiming for his face," I say. I'm still reeling from thinking I'd murdered Katherine and the overwhelming joy I now feel. The last time I felt this way was when Jackson came traipsing through the door. "Miss Folsom was right. An inch really does make a heap of a difference."

"She was talking about long range with a rifle, Jane."

I shrug. "Whatever."

Katherine stares at me, and I give her a small smile. "You just killed a man, and you're smiling?" she says.

"Well, he wasn't a very good person. I'm glad he's dead."

Katherine looks back at the sheriff's dead body, lifting one of her fair hands to her cheek, which is dotted with bits of the dead man. "I worry about your immortal soul, Jane."

I flash her a toothsome grin. "Ain't you got enough real world problems to keep you busy?"

She starts to laugh, the sound quickly turning into a broken sob. I wrap her up in my arms and squeeze her tight.

"Hey. Hey! It's okay. You're okay, and we're okay. Well, at

least until that pack of shamblers gets here."

Her arms wrap around my middle, returning the embrace. "I know, I just, for a minute, I thought he was going to kill me. I'm not ready to die, Jane."

"Well, then, I reckon we should get out of here."

"Negress Jezebel," comes a wheezing voice from the side of the office. We turn. In my joy at seeing Katherine unharmed I'd completely forgotten about the pastor. He lies on the ground, a hole in his shoulder and blood soaking his jacket. I have my answer as to where the sheriff's wild shot got to.

"Harlot," the preacher says, bloody foam flecking his lips. He struggles into a sitting position.

Katherine takes a step forward but I put her to the side, handing her the shotgun I hold. "Why don't you go see what else the armory has in your size? We still got a whole bunch of dead to face."

"What about him?" she says, her voice uncertain.

"Oh, I'll take care of him."

"But . . ." She drifts off, pushing her lips into a thin line.

I bend down to pick up the sheriff's revolver. It's a nice piece, and the heft and weight of it feels just right in my hand. The sheriff's hat, with its wide brim, is a few feet away and mostly free of blood. I pick it up and put it on, adjusting it so that it sits at a jaunty angle.

Katherine scowls at me. "Jane."

"What? He's dead, he ain't going to need it anymore.

Besides, this is a quality bit of haberdashery." Katherine says nothing, and finally makes her way to the armory. "See if they got a belt to hold my sickles," I call. Her response is silence.

The preacher's breath is coming in pants and whistles now, and his front is pretty well soaked through with blood. He won't last much longer. I grab a chair and swing it over near where he reclines on the floor. His breaths come faster as I sit down, and I give him a wide smile.

"Now, now, no need to panic, I ain't going to kill you. I reckon that leak in your chest is going to do that." I cross my legs and lean back in the chair, the revolver heavy in my lap. "Since you're a man of God, I'm going to tell you a story, confess some sins."

The pastor doesn't respond, so I continue.

"You recall the Years of Discord? I was only a child, but I remember them. The constant fear of someone turning, the packs of dead prowling the countryside, the news that another person had died, only to return and eat half the household. It was unbearable. I still picture the fear on my momma's face whenever we got word another person went missing. But we endured. We came to be self-sufficient, we built strong fences. And we learned to work together to survive.

"But my momma's husband? Well, he was a man like you. Enamored of the past. Stubborn. He returned home after things had settled, as the Years of Discord came to an end, as something like that *order* you speak of was restored. And he brought with him all the fear and turmoil of that time.

"He had the idea that he was still the master of the plantation, that the old ways should hold sway. He beat anyone who stepped out of line. He sent children out on patrols. People died needlessly, and he counted it the price of progress. He had it in his head to build something like your Summerland right there on Rose Hill, and damned if anyone was going to stand in his way.

"So one night, after he had gotten a bit drunk and more than a bit violent, I snuck down to my momma's study and stole her gun. And the next morning, while he was still abed, I shot him twice in the head, the way my momma had taught me to put down a shambler."

The pastor's eyes go wide with terror and I shrug. "See, the problem in this world ain't sinners, or even the dead. It is men who will step on anyone who stands in the way of their pursuit of power. Luckily there will always be people like me to stop them."

I stand and resettle the sheriff's hat, now my hat. "That horde will be coming through town soon enough, and if you ain't already dead by then, the shamblers will surely oblige. As for me, I've got quite enough stains on my soul, so I hope you meet your end quickly.

"Either way, when you get to hell, give the man who fathered me, Major McKeene, my regards."

I head into the armory. Katherine stands there, open-mouthed. I don't know how much she heard, but it seems to have been enough. I can't meet her gaze.

"My momma is passing light, just like you," I say, because she deserves to know. "She was a slave. When her mistress died on the road to meet her fiancé, my momma pretended to be her, and that's how she came to be the mistress of Rose Hill. It near drove her mad, all the lying and subterfuge, but she did it to save her family. To save everyone. When I was born, it was only a matter of time before her secret was compromised. She should've killed me, and one time she tried, but I survived."

"Jane," Katherine begins, but I hold up my hand.

"I know what I asked of you, and I'm eternally grateful. You helped to save my life," I say. "Now, we might not survive what comes next, and I just wanted you to know that I appreciate you."

Katherine grabs me up into a hug, her tears hot against my face. I pat her awkwardly.

"Not now, we got a horde bearing down on us. I reckon we've dawdled long enough."

She gives a hollow laugh and releases me, then steps forward and grabs a pair of Mollies, twin swords as long as a woman's forearm and wickedly sharp on either side. Of course, Katherine would naturally grab the flashiest weapons available.

Our moment of confession is over, and now there is only work. Katherine catches me watching her as she straps the swords across her back. "These are quality blades, Jane."

"How can you even tell? I can barely even see anything in here."

She crosses her arms and taps her foot. "That is not something I want to hear after you just shot a man who had been standing right behind me."

"I suppose you're right. Now, let's see if we can't generate a few more miracles between the two of us and save some of these miserable people."

Katherine nods, and we head to the door. I pause on the threshold, my hand on the knob. "Kate?"

"Yes?"

"Take off that damned corset. We're going out to face down a horde, not to a ball."

"It's isn't a full corset; it's a half corset. It's the newest style. Besides Jane, the day I cannot take down a few shamblers wearing something fashionable is the day I turn in my rifle."

I grin at her and say nothing, just tip my hat in acknowledgment.

I'm almost out the door when I look down and pause. A

few inches from the toe of my boot is my penny, looking just the way it did the day Bill took it from me. I lean and pick it up. It's clean of blood, and the leather thong looks new. In my hand it's warm, and a sense of rightness heats me from the inside out as I drape it over my head.

"What's that?" Katherine asks.

"Just a bit of luck."

She purses her lips. "Good. We're going to need it."

Hopefully this letter finds you, although none of my other letters have been answered. I love you, my darling daughter, and the news I share is grim. Rose Hill is gone, Jane. I have been betrayed by a pretty face, my secret writ large for the world. Those of us who are left have fled. We travel west, to California, and the promise of a new life.

Find me, Jane.

Chapter 38
In Which We Reach the End of Our Tale

Katherine and I stand in front of the entrance to the sheriff's office and survey the chaos. People yell at us, a hundred questions at once, spittle flying as they work themselves into a fine fit.

"We should probably tell them something," Katherine says.

A scream pierces the air, so loud and fraught with fear that it gives me a chill despite the heat of the day. And like an angel on high delivering a message from the Lord Almighty, comes the shout, "SHAMBLERS! THERE'S SHAMBLERS IN TOWN!"

I glance at Katherine and grin. "Sometimes a problem solves itself."

People go running past, men and women, and I grab Katherine by the arm and drag her off the boardwalk in the direction of the church as the men start to scatter. A few have the presence of mind to run into the sheriff's office to hide, but I ain't got time to pay them any mind now.

"Jane—"

"We've got to get to the other side of town and fetch Lily and the Spencers. Mrs. Spencer and her boy won't be any good at fighting the dead, and Lily is just a little girl."

Katherine purses her lips and nods. "Lead the way."

It is utter chaos. Men and women run here and there, seemingly aimless, while shamblers walk the street leisurely, grasping for whoever gets close. Most of these shamblers are old and barely holding together: men in wool uniforms missing limbs, women in full dresses that are decades out of fashion, Negroes wearing the wretched uniforms of the old plantations, boys and girls who drag themselves along, tiny nightmares in their own right. Here and there is someone unexpected, a man dressed in the heavy garb of a fur trapper, an Indian woman with long dark hair wearing the rough homespun of white settlers, men wearing uniforms I don't recognize, the red and dark blue very different from the Union and Confederate uniforms that most shamblers wear.

And there are so many of them. A tidal wave of the dead breaking over the town. I'm frozen for a few precious moments, taking in this horrible scene, watching the inexorable march of the shamblers, when a strong grip on my arm jolts me out of my shock.

"Let's move!" Katherine demands, as bossy as ever.

"Jane, which way?" The Duchess and a couple of her girls run up to me. I'm happy to see one of them is Nessie, the colored girl who braided my hair and brought me water the day I was whipped. I don't recognize the other girl, a white girl with brown hair and freckles who gives me a shy smile. "Everything is chaos."

Just like that, the uncertainty disappears and I know what we have to do. "Follow me. We can cut through town using Gideon's tunnel."

We hurry through the street toward the lab. But when we get there the door is locked.

"Gideon never locks his door," the Duchess says, worry making her bruised face look even more tragic.

"These are extraordinary times." A tendril of worry tries to rise up, but I smash it flat. I glance toward the street. The shamblers are getting more numerous, flooding into town. Pretty soon they'll be too thick to maneuver and that's when the real trouble starts. "I think we're going to have to run to the other side of town."

And so we do.

All of the Duchess's ladies are wearing corsets, and our passage is slower than I'd like. I herd them before me like a dog nipping at the heels of livestock. People rush past us, fleeing the dead, and we're about halfway to the better side of town when I realize there ain't no way we're going to make it. The dead are slow, but so are ladies who can't breathe.

I grab the Duchess and pull her to the side. "What's the problem, Jane?" she pants.

"We need to cut those lacings. If we don't, we're never to going to make it to the other side of town. We're moving too slow. Eventually people will get bit and turn, and they're going to move faster than those raggedy old shamblers. The fresh ones always do."

"I am not cutting this corset," Katherine announces. Only Katherine would have a tantrum in the midst of fleeing for her life. I give her a hard look and she rolls her eyes and stomps her foot. "Fine."

I pull a knife from my boot, unfasten the back of her dress, cut the top few lacings, and fasten her back up. I do this with the Duchess and her girls, then tuck my knife away.

"All right, ladies," I say. "Pick up those skirts and run."

We make better time, and when we get to the rows of houses there's no sign of the dead yet. It's just the better families, packing up to leave. People are running between the houses, grabbing what they can, piling it in wagons. No one is even going to try to save the town. They're just running for their lives.

Bitterness twists my lips and a hard feeling settles over me. These folks were more than happy to send us out there, day after day, but when it's their turn to fight they ain't got the stomach for it.

I lead us to Lily's house, one of the few without the front door open. I pound on the wood. "Lily, it's me! Open up."

There's a scraping on the other side of the door, and then "How do I know you ain't a shambler?"

"Shamblers don't talk. Stop being a muttonhead and let me in."

The door opens and Lily flies into my arms. I hug her tightly more out of surprise than anything else. "Someone came through, yelling about the town been overrun. I didn't know what to do."

"Get Mrs. Spencer and the little ones, we need to get out of here," I say, pushing past Lily into the house.

"Mrs. Spencer is gone. She left yesterday afternoon and never came back. It's just me and Thomas." A toddler plays on the floor with a wooden horse, and he beams at me.

I think about Mr. Spencer's body, missing its head. Was Mrs. Spencer out there as well? I didn't see her, but I also didn't peep at every decapitated shambler.

Katherine, the Duchess, and her girls come into the house.

The Duchess's expression goes soft when she sees Thomas. "Well, hello there, precious," she says, picking him up. He offers her his horse before snuggling against the Duchess's unfettered bosom.

I turn to Lily. "The Spencers got a pony? There's a town a couple days' ride north of here called Nicodemus. That's our best bet."

"No one has a pony out here. We've got an old horse and a wagon. But I don't know how to hook him up."

"I do, and Sallie here can help me," Nessie says with an uncertain smile, gesturing to the white girl with the freckles.

We follow them out to the small stable behind the house. The door hangs open and there's a group of three drovers there, fighting with the horse, trying to hook it up to the wagon.

"Hey, that's our wagon!" Lily exclaims.

One of the men turns around, drawing down on us. The revolver catches the sunlight as he points it at Lily. "Sorry, little girl. That horde is picking up speed. And we ain't about to be turned."

"At least take the children with you," the Duchess says. There's resignation in her voice.

The man looks behind him to where the two drovers have almost hooked the horse up. "No deadweight."

I reach for my sidearm, but before I can clear the holster there's a gunshot. The drover is on the ground with a bullet right between his eyes.

"Chivalry is apparently dead." Behind us stands Jackson, and the scream of joy that Lily lets loose as she throws herself into her brother's arms damn near shatters my eardrums.

I point my drawn gun at the remaining drovers, who have gone still.

"Nessie, Sallie, make sure those fools have the horse hooked up right and then take those straps."

"They're called reins," Jackson says, an amused drawl in his voice.

"I don't care if they're called shoestrings," I snap. "That dead fellow was right. The horde is picking up speed."

"What's gotten into you?" Red Jack asks, and I sigh.

"Leave it to you to pick the last possible moment to show up and save the day," I grumble.

The women move quickly, fastening things and saying soft words to calm the horse. After a few seconds Nessie nods at me.

"It's good. Want me to drive?"

"Yes," I say. I point my pistol at the remaining men, waving them away from the wagon. "Clear on out now before you end up like your friend here." I move to the body and pick up the man's pistol, handing it up to Sallie who sits next to Nessie. "You know how to use that?"

"Yep," Sallie says, taking the gun with a gap-toothed smile.

"Take us with you," one of the men says as Lily climbs into

the wagon, the Duchess handing up Thomas before doing the same. I realize the man pleading for his life is Alan, the boy who gave us a ride in the wagon only a few hours earlier.

I give him a sneer of disgust. "I don't take kindly to child killers or their friends."

"But, you're leaving us here without any weapons! We'll be overrun."

The click of a hammer being pulled back echoes loudly in the barn. The men turn to look at Jackson, who wears a half smile. "As long as your feet work you can run. I suggest you go before that option is lost."

I tilt my head, feeling a calm that cannot be ascribed to the situation. Later, I will look back and wonder at myself, my lack of compassion. I know this from experience. But for right now there is only survival. "I believe the phrase is deadweight? Sorry, no deadweight."

Nessie slaps the reins along the horse's back and the beast takes off, carrying the working girls and the children. She steers the wagon out of the yard and down a road along the back of the houses. Once they're clear I tip my hat to the worthless drovers. Red Jack and Katherine take off after the wagon in a jog, and I follow not far behind.

We leave town quickly, passing other people running for their lives as well. I stop briefly by the entrance to the shambler wheel chamber, but the door is locked. The armory next to it hangs open, the room beyond, empty. Dread rises up in my middle, but I put it to the side. I'm hoping that Gideon got out alive; perhaps there was another chamber down in that rabbit warren of his.

Nessie sets a good pace out of town, and we pass other families in their wagons as well as a few folks running. The dead are behind us, too far to see, too close to get comfortable. I get a side stitch and walk for a while, but not too long because I don't want to lose sight of the wagon.

Once we clear the breach in the northern wall, I pause and look back. The wagon trundles down the road that Jackson tells me leads to Nicodemus but I'm in no hurry to follow it.

"Ain't you afraid you're going to turn into a pillar of salt?" Jackson says from next to me. Katherine has stopped as well.

"Naw. My soul is too sullied for the Lord to bother much with me." I remember pulling the trigger and watching Bob go down, the sheriff's face as the buckshot hit him in the throat, the look of surprise and then nothing. How easy it was, little more than a muscle spasm, yet world-ending for those men.

But more than that, I remember the rage on the major's face back at Rose Hill the night before I shot him. And I remember the soft repose of his face as he slept, as I pulled the trigger, knowing that Rose Hill would never be safe as long as his will was law.

After everyone came running it was easier to say that he'd

turned shambler than to tell the truth, how I was trying to protect Momma from him and his rage, how I'd gotten the pearl-handled revolver from her desk one night while everyone was asleep just because I was afraid of what a man like that could do.

Like I've said, the truth and I are uneasy companions at best. The fib was an easy one to tell.

No one much asked, anyway. No one much wanted to know, I suppose. Who wants to think a child can murder a man? Especially a man everyone knows to secretly be her father. Either way, I am many things, a murderess just happens to be one of them. It's not something I think about all that much, and now I have two more dead men on my soul. I'll be fine.

I'm an excellent liar. Even to myself.

An arm wraps around my shoulders, and I look up in surprise as Jackson smiles down at me. "I have something for you, Janey-Jane. You remember that girl you used to run with, Sue?"

"Big Sue?" I say. "She's alive?"

He nods. "She and some of the other girls made it to Nicodemus. She found something as they were evacuating Miss Preston's and I thought I should bring it to you."

Jackson digs into the space between his vest and his shirt, pulls forth a letter, and pushes it into my hand. Then, he kisses me lightly on the lips. "I'm glad you made it, Jane," he says, before turning and striding toward the wagon.

I look down and sure enough it's from my momma, my name scrawled across the front. I grip it too tightly, the fine vellum crumpling.

"Jane, do you want some space?" Katherine asks, and I shake my head.

"Can you wait with me while I read it?"

She nods, and I tear the letter open.

The letter is dated nearly two months ago, only a few days before Katherine and I were sent here to Summerland. My hands shake, and as I read, the world narrows to a pinprick of light, all sound fading away until only the roar of my heartbeat fills my ears.

Rose Hill is no more.
Overrun by the dead.
Betrayed by my new husband.
We have gone on the run.
A safe place, run by Survivalists.

And then a name that I read over and over again.

Haven, California.
Haven.
California.

I stare at the letter for a long time, breathing in and out, my world coming apart one piece at a time.

Rose Hill, my dream and my future, is no more. Betrayed by her new husband after he discovered she was a Negro pretending to be white, my mother has gone to California to start a new life.

To a town settled and run by Survivalists.

I turn behind me to look at the wagon heading to Nicodemus, another frontier town just like Summerland. It strikes me that all of us everywhere are running. From the dead, from the uncertainty of the future, from ourselves. We are just always on the move. Is there really such a thing as home when it's so easily destroyed?

No matter what we do, each town is just the same as the last. Another chance to be overrun, to watch as everything and everyone we love is put in danger time and time again. Doesn't matter the name of the place, it's only a matter of time until it's swept away in a wave of the dead.

That doesn't seem like any kind of future to me.

I look back at the letter I hold, *California* scrawled in my mother's hand, hastily, desperately.

Find me, Jane.

"Jane McKeene, what is it?" Katherine asks, her eyes wide with worry. I get the feeling it isn't the first time she's asked me.

I laugh, loud and long. "Oh, I am Fortune's fool," I say,

knowing Katherine won't get the reference. But the quote is too apropos.

I hold the letter up, feeling calmer and more focused than I have in weeks. I told the preacher that there would always be men like him, and people like me to stop them. And I meant it. After the trials and tribulations of Summerland, I know my life's path: Stop the Survivalists and all those like them. I'm done running away from trouble. Why not meet it head-on?

Stopping the Survivalists. It's a lofty goal, but I ain't ever been one for half measures.

"Kate, we're going to California."

She gives me an incredulous look, but before she can ask any questions I'm striding toward Nicodemus, quickly enough that she has to scurry to keep up with me. My sickles are heavy at my side and my penny is a warm, comforting weight around my neck. For once I'm happy and I can't help but smile.

It's a good day to be alive.

Author's Note

I felt I would be remiss to end this story without telling readers that the events in this book are based on actual historical occurrences. While zombies did not stalk the battlefields of Gettysburg, the United States did have a system in which Native American children were sent to boarding schools where they could learn to be "civilized."

Beginning as early as 1860, whites would remove Native children from their homes and send them to boarding or industrial schools. The point of these schools was to destroy Native culture and force Natives to assimilate into white or European cultural norms. The most famous is the Carlisle Indian Industrial School, established in 1879 in Carlisle, Pennsylvania. I moved the timeline up a bit to account for Mr. Redfern's education there, but its existence is real.

It is now Carlisle Barracks, a US Army post, and I first visited the base in 1999 and was amazed at the murals in the gym that depict Olympian Jim Thorpe, a Native American from the Sac and Fox Nation who attended the school at the turn of the century. I'd never heard of Native American boarding schools before then, and in the abstract it seemed like a pretty cool thing.

However, when I attended a master's program at a nearby university some years later I was able to visit the Carlisle Historical Society and learn the truth about Indian schools and the Carlisle Indian Industrial School in particular: how they broke up families, erased Native culture, victimized vulnerable children, and hired out students for backbreaking labor to nearby farms and households in a system that was eerily reminiscent of chattel slavery.

This exploitative school system became the basis for the fictional combat school system in the alternate historical timeline of *Dread Nation*. Because if well-meaning Americans could do such a thing to an already wholly subjugated community in a time of peace, what would they do in a time of desperation?

I encourage everyone to read further on the Carlisle Indian Industrial School and the American Indian boarding school system as a whole. I'm including a list of books I found helpful and that I have seen recommended by Native scholars, who most certainly know better than I:

Archuleta, Margaret L., Brenda J. Child, and K. Tsianina Lomawaima. *Away from Home: American Indian Boarding School Experiences*. Phoenix: Heard Museum, 2000.

Child, Brenda. *Boarding School Seasons: American Indian Families, 1900–1940*. Lincoln, NE: Bison Books, 2000.

Ellis, Clyde. *To Change Them Forever: Indian Education at the Rainy Mountain Boarding School, 1893–1920*. Norman: University of Oklahoma Press, 1996.

Hyer, Sally. *One House, One Voice, One Heart: Native American Education at the Santa Fe Indian School*. Albuquerque: Museum of New Mexico Press, 1990.

Happy reading.

Always,

Justina Ireland, 2018